TRUTH
BE TOLD

Books by Carol Cox

Love in Disguise
Trouble in Store
Truth Be Told

TRUTH
BE TOLD

CAROL COX

BETHANYHOUSE

a division of Baker Publishing Group
Minneapolis, Minnesota

Published by Bethany House Publishers
11400 Hampshire Avenue South
Bloomington, Minnesota 55438
www.bethanyhouse.com

Bethany House Publishers is a division of
Baker Publishing Group, Grand Rapids, Michigan

Printed in the United States of America

Library of Congress Cataloging-in-Publication Data
Cox, Carol.
    Truth be told / Carol Cox.
        p. cm.
      Summary: "1890s Arizona newspaper reporter Amelia Wagner means to expose the truth about the Great Western Investment Company, no matter what—or who—they send to stop her" —Provided by publisher.
      ISBN 978-0-7642-0957-4 (pbk.)
      1. Women journalists—Fiction. 2. Corporations—Corrupt practices—Fiction.
I. Title.
PS3553.O9148T88 2014
813'.54—dc23   2014003416

Scripture quotations are from the King James Version of the Bible.

Epigraph Scripture quotation is from the New American Standard Bible®, copyright © 1960, 1962, 1963, 1968, 1971, 1972, 1973, 1975, 1977, 1995 by The Lockman Foundation. Used by permission.

Cover design by LOOK Design Studio

Author represented by Books & Such Literary Agency

14 15 16 17 18 19 20   7 6 5 4 3 2 1

To Dave and Katie:
Your unceasing inspiration and encouragement
keep me going.
Without you, this writing adventure would
never have been possible.

To Kevin and Samantha,
Emmalee, Madilyn, Wyatt, and Benjamin:
as you begin a new adventure of your own.

"If you continue in My word, then you are truly disciples of Mine; and you will know the truth, and the truth will make you free."

John 8:31b-32 (NASB)

CHAPTER I

GRANITE SPRINGS, ARIZONA TERRITORY
MAY 1893

Amelia Wagner stepped down onto the platform of the Granite Springs train depot and drew in a deep breath of clean mountain air. She closed her eyes to sort out the different scents tingling her nostrils—the sharp tang of pine trees growing on the nearby slopes, the pungent odors of fresh-cut lumber wafting from Martin Gilbreth's sawmill, and the fragrance of the creosote bushes that dotted the hillsides of Arizona's high desert. The scents mingled together to form a fragrance more pleasing than the costliest perfume any Denver emporium had to offer.

Amelia took in another deep breath, savoring the fragrance of home.

"Welcome back!"

Amelia's eyes flew open, and she spotted Thomas Rafferty, station agent for the Prescott–Phoenix Railroad. Prior to that, he had served as the stagecoach depot agent for the local line and had been a fixture in Granite Springs for as long as Amelia could remember. He nodded a cheery greeting as he rolled a hand truck laden with wooden crates into the depot.

She grinned back at him. "Where are my peppermints?"

Mr. Rafferty set the hand truck upright and patted his pockets. A slight flush tinted his weathered cheeks. "I'm afraid you caught me unprepared. I didn't realize you were arriving today, or I'd have stocked up." He tilted his head and chuckled. "Besides, I expected you outgrew that sweet tooth of yours."

Amelia brushed his apology aside with a laugh. "No need to worry. Standing here on the platform just brought back a host of memories. Getting a peppermint drop from you whenever I came home is one of my favorites."

The flush on the station agent's cheeks deepened as he tipped the hand truck back and wheeled it toward the doors. "It was always a special day when you arrived. It's good to have you here again, and I know your dad will be glad to see you, too."

As Amelia watched Mr. Rafferty disappear inside the depot, out of the corner of her eye she saw someone approaching on her right. She swiveled around to see a lanky cowboy striding along the platform.

He swaggered up to her and tipped his hat. "Afternoon, Miss. I've always thought Granite Springs was a right pretty place, but the scenery got a whole lot nicer the moment you stepped off the train."

Amelia straightened her shoulders and looked the brash young rider straight in the eye. "Thank you for the compliment, but you seem to be under a misapprehension. I'm not a stranger here—I was raised in Granite Springs. I'm not some Eastern debutante ready to swoon at the sight of her first cowboy."

A dark red flush rose from the man's shirt collar to his

hairline. "Beg your pardon," he mumbled. "I didn't mean any offense." Ducking his head, he trotted down the steps to the street below and hurried on his way.

From her position on the station platform, Amelia turned her attention back to the bustle surrounding her. A smile curved her lips. Though small compared to Denver, the town had grown since her last visit.

An incredulous gasp from the street caught her attention. Two matrons stood engrossed in conversation just below where Amelia stood. The taller one drew back and pressed her fingers to her lips. "You can't mean it! The bank is going to foreclose?"

Her companion nodded vigorously, setting the long black feathers on her hat into a bobbing dance. "I heard it straight from Bart McCaffrey's wife. My husband says it's due to poor business management, but . . ." Her voice trailed off when her eyes strayed up to the platform and focused on Amelia. Nudging her friend with her elbow, she gave a sniff, and the two women moved several yards away, out of earshot.

Foreclosure? On McCaffrey's property? Amelia forgot her embarrassment at being caught eavesdropping in her eagerness to make a note of what she'd heard.

Why, oh why, had she packed her notebook in her trunk? She scrambled in her reticule and pulled out a scrap of paper and a pencil. One of the first things her father ever taught her about journalism was the need to jot down details while they were still fresh in her memory. With the information she provided, he or Homer Crenshaw, his able helper, would be able to track down the rest of the story.

Or . . . She caught her breath. Maybe she could persuade her father to let her chase down the facts and write the story herself. What a wonderful way to begin this summer's visit to Granite Springs! Her heart quickened at the thought.

She scribbled a quick note, then looked up to see a towheaded boy about six years old rolling a hoop along the street in front of the platform. The hoop suddenly appeared to take on a will of its own and veered from its path straight toward the spot where the two matrons stood.

Neither woman seemed to notice the hoop until it struck the taller one from the rear. She let out an indignant yelp and turned to locate her assailant. Her face tightened when her eyes lit on the boy.

"Come here, you young scalawag!" She reached out as though to snag him by the ear, but the youngster evaded her fingers with ease.

Snatching up his hoop, he called out a quick apology and scampered off. Seeing the impish grin on his face, Amelia doubted that the incident was entirely accidental.

She pressed her lips together to hold back a smile at his antics and scanned the street, hoping to catch sight of her father. It wasn't like him to miss her arrival. Where could he be?

There had to be a good reason. Being the editor and publisher of the *Granite Springs Gazette*—as well as its chief reporter—filled nearly all his waking hours. Perhaps he'd gotten wind of a good story and lost track of the time.

The office of the *Gazette* was only a few blocks away. Amelia glanced over at her luggage. Her trunk would be safe under Mr. Rafferty's watchful eye. Her valise was heavy, but she could manage to carry it that short distance.

Hefting the small bag, she made her way down the steps and walked briskly up First Street, studying the false-fronted buildings along the way. The land agent's office sported a fresh coat of creamy yellow paint instead of the graying wood she'd seen on her last visit. A steady stream of people flowed in and out of Kingston's General Store, and a neatly painted sign reading *Bon-Ton Café* hung over the building where the Coffeepot Café used to be. Amelia felt her stomach rumble at the thought of food.

She scanned the street again, and her lips curved in a broad smile when she saw Homer Crenshaw making a beeline for the depot. That confirmed her earlier supposition—her father must be on the trail of an important story if he had to send his right-hand man to meet her.

She watched Homer's lanky form as he walked along with a purposeful stride, obviously a man on a mission. His bowler hat didn't completely hide the wisps of white hair sticking out in wild disarray atop a frame so spare that it seemed as though a mere puff of air might blow him into the next county. Anyone seeing that scarecrow-like form for the first time would never guess that Homer was not only a whiz at operating a printing press but a competent reporter in his own right. If her father was the captain of the *Gazette*, he couldn't have asked for a better first mate.

"Miss Wagner? Amelia!"

She looked over to see Emmett Kingston hailing her from the front steps of the general store, just beyond the café. She stopped and waited while he loped across the street.

His path and Homer's converged on her at the same instant. Homer came to a halt when he spotted her on the boardwalk in front of him.

Amelia bounced on her toes, scarcely able to contain herself as she waited for him to break into the glad smile of welcome that always lit his face when she arrived. To her surprise, his expression remained solemn.

Emmett Kingston stepped up onto the walk beside them. "I thought that was you." The merchant wiped his hand on the front of his storekeeper's apron before extending it to her. "I'm sure glad to see you here. Tell your father I'll be by to visit in the next day or so. It's a shame . . . " Kingston's voice trailed off as he focused on a point over Amelia's shoulder. She turned in time to see Homer finishing a shake of his head.

"We'd best be on our way," Homer said. "Good to see you, Emmett." He reached for Amelia's valise and set off at a rapid pace.

"We have a new eatery in town." Homer pointed to the Bon-Ton on the other side of the street.

"I noticed that," she panted, trotting to keep up with his long-legged stride.

"The food there is quite tasty," he continued. "'Blithe souls and lightsome hearts have we, feasting at the Cherry Tree!'"

Amelia laughed out loud. She had grown up hearing Homer quote snippets of poetry at odd moments. The lines from Wordsworth made her feel even more at home.

Homer's mouth curved in a shadow of its usual smile, but the expression in his eyes remained bleak.

Something was wrong. Amelia felt sure of it, but she had no idea what the problem might be. Trying to keep her voice light, she asked, "Where's Papa? Out chasing down a story?"

Homer's lean face tightened even more, and his eyes took on a shuttered expression. "He wasn't feeling up to it today. Didn't he write to you about that?"

"He mentioned not feeling well, but that was last month. You mean he's still ailing?"

Homer kept his eyes focused on the street ahead and drew a ragged breath. "He's worse."

He pulled off his hat and ran the fingers of one hand through his hair. White strands stood out in a billowy cloud around his head. "But he's looking forward to seeing you. Let's keep moving."

Two blocks later, they reached the two-story, whitewashed board-and-batten building. A sense of belonging swept over Amelia at the sight of the sign hanging above the door, proudly emblazoned with the name *Granite Springs Gazette, A. J. Wagner, Proprietor,* and directly underneath it, a line that read *Job Printing.*

Homer swung the door open with his free hand, and she stepped inside. At first glance, nothing had changed since the last time she'd set foot in the newspaper office. The smells of ink and paper permeated the large room dominated by the sturdy Washington Press, her father's pride and joy. On the far side of the type cabinets, she could see the smaller Peerless jobbing press. To the right of the stairs in the rear, the door to her father's office stood open. From where she stood, Amelia could see one corner of his oak rolltop desk. At any other time, she would have headed straight to it to flesh out the notes she had taken at the station, but today concern for her father overshadowed her urge to get to work.

She walked to the back of the printing office, intending to climb the stairs that led to the second-floor living quarters, but Homer's voice stopped her.

"No need for you to go up just yet. I'll carry your valise to your room." He skirted past her and started up the steps.

Amelia followed on his heels. "I don't mind waiting to

unpack until after my trunk arrives, but I want to go up and see Papa first thing."

Homer half turned to face her, but his gaze didn't quite meet her eyes. "He's been staying down here since he took sick. We fixed up that little storeroom near the back door when going up and down the stairs got to be too much for him." He turned and went on up, leaving Amelia standing with one foot on the bottom step.

A wisp of apprehension wound its way up her spine and coiled around her heart. Until that moment, Homer's words hadn't fully struck home. Her father's recent letters had mentioned not feeling well, but they'd given no hint that anything serious might be going on.

Now she wondered whether he had been completely open with her. *If Papa can't manage the stairs, how sick is he?*

CHAPTER 2

Setting her reticule on a stool next to the nearest type cabinet, Amelia walked toward the storeroom. When she reached the closed door, she paused a moment to brace herself, then pushed it open and stepped inside.

In the dim light she could see that the shelves used for holding bundles of paper were gone, and a set of file cabinets had been pushed up against one wall. A bed took up the opposite side of the room, where smooth, white sheets and a matching pillowcase framed her father's tired face.

Amelia's breath caught in her throat at the sight. His hair, once as thick and dark brown as her own, was now gray and wispy. He looked so small beneath the bedclothes, almost shrunken—a mere shadow of the man she'd said farewell to at the end of her last visit. His eyes were closed, but his chest moved up and down in a steady, reassuring rhythm. Amelia crept closer to the bed. "Papa?"

His eyelids flickered open, and his thin lips parted in a smile of welcome. "You made it. How was your trip?"

Relief washed over Amelia when she heard his voice. Though his body appeared worn, the deep baritone still sounded like her father. She closed the distance between them and reached out to brush a strand of hair back from his forehead. "The trip was very pleasant, especially the last part. The new road-bed they put in last year made the final stretch from Ash Fork much smoother. There isn't much they can do to straighten out all those twists and turns, though. No wonder they call it the Peavine." She smiled as she reached for his hand, and his fingers twined around hers.

"I'm glad you're here, honey."

"So am I. Spending time with you is always the high point of my year."

"Mine too." He patted her arm with his free hand. "We've had some grand times together, haven't we?"

Amelia felt her throat constrict at the wistfulness in his tone, and she sought for some way to lighten the mood. "We'll have more of them this summer, just as soon as you're back on your feet again."

"That would be nice." He gave her hand a gentle squeeze. "But if not, we can look forward to some great adventures when I meet you at the Eastern Gate."

A flutter of panic rippled through her at his often-used reference to a reunion in heaven. "It will be a long time before that happens."

His expression softened. "For you, certainly. But I—"

Homer bustled into the room, carrying a green glass bottle and a spoon. "Time for some of that medicine Doc Harwood left for you." He poured out a spoonful as he spoke and held it out.

Her father swallowed the dose, then grimaced as he settled back against the pillow. "If a bad taste is any indication of curative properties, that concoction ought to work miracles."

The bell to the outer door jangled, and a voice called, "Anyone here?"

Homer set the bottle and spoon on the small table beside the bed and hurried out to the printing office. "I'll take care of it. You two enjoy your visit."

Her father watched him leave, then turned back to Amelia. "This illness of mine has put a heavy burden on Homer. He's an expert at keeping the presses running, and he has a way with words. But having to set the type, print the paper, and do all the writing, too—not to mention nursemaiding me on top of it all—is more load than any one man should have to shoulder."

He scooted up higher on the bed, and Amelia hurried to arrange the pillows so he would be more comfortable. He gave her an appreciative smile. "Now that you're here, you can take over most of the writing. If Homer only has to deal with the machinery, that will ease his burden considerably, especially since the Peerless has been a bit cranky lately." A dry chuckle rattled in his chest. "It's getting old and on its last legs—like me."

As Amelia opened her mouth to protest, Homer darted back into the room. "That was Martin Gilbreth. He wanted to talk about his next advertisement, and he said to tell you—" He broke off when the outer door opened again and footsteps sounded on the pine plank floor.

He stepped toward the sickroom door and stiffened when he caught sight of their visitor. "It's one of those fellows from Great Western. What can he want?" He walked back to the printing office, closing the door behind him this time.

Amelia heard the murmur of voices when Homer greeted

the new arrival. As she turned back to her father, Homer's voice grew louder. She couldn't make out the words through the closed door, but his agitation was evident.

The sight of her father's taut expression and the way his fingers picked at the bedcovers sent her hurrying out into the newspaper office, where she found Homer squaring off with a man she didn't recognize. She laid her hand on Homer's arm. "I'll tend to this. Why don't you go see if Papa needs anything?"

Homer's mouth worked as though he wanted to say more, but he settled for a dismissive shrug before stalking off toward the makeshift bedroom. "Nothing much to tend to," he muttered. "He was just leaving."

Amelia turned to the stranger, a tall man a few years older than her own twenty-three years. He stared after Homer, turning his hat in his hands. Amelia took advantage of the moment to study him more closely. Wavy, russet hair topped off a pleasant face and an athletic build. To her mind, he didn't appear threatening in the least, but Homer's obvious dislike and her father's reaction were enough to set warning bells clanging in her mind.

She addressed him in a cool tone. "Was there something you needed?"

He turned back to her, a puzzled look in his hazel eyes. "I'd like to speak with Mr. Wagner, please."

Amelia arched one eyebrow. "Are you a friend?"

He shook his head. "My name is Benjamin Stone. I'm on business for my company."

"And that would be . . . ?"

"The Great Western Investment Company."

The note of pride in his voice only served to set Amelia's

teeth on edge. Was that name supposed to mean something to her? "Did you wish to place an advertisement in the *Gazette*?"

"No." His brow furrowed. "I wanted to talk to Mr. Wagner about some articles he's written."

Amelia nodded briskly. "Thank you, Mr. Stone. I'll be sure to let my father know you were here."

His eyes widened. "You're his daughter? I didn't realize—"

"I'm afraid he isn't well," Amelia continued as though he hadn't spoken. "He can't see anyone right now, other than close friends."

"I'm sorry to hear that." He took a step back toward the outer door. "I'll come back when he's feeling better."

Amelia watched him leave, then pivoted and went back to her father's room.

"I'm sorry about that." Homer eyed her with a sheepish expression. "I didn't mean to let my temper get the best of me."

She pasted on a bright smile. "It's all right. I was happy to take care of it."

Deep furrows formed a groove between her father's nose and his downturned lips. "Don't let it bother you, Homer. A visit from Great Western is enough to upset anyone."

Homer nodded his thanks. "I'll go get supper started and do some more work on that piece about the two-headed calf that was born out at the Grinstead farm."

"Brood of vipers," her father muttered when Homer had gone.

"Who? The people at Great Western?" Amelia sat on the edge of his bed and took his hand in hers. "It's a new company in town, isn't it? I don't remember hearing that name before. But we don't need to talk about them if it's going to upset you."

He shook his head. "Probably just as well. Might help get some of it out of my system. They're unhappy about a couple of stories I've written about their intention to start hydraulic mining in the area."

Amelia tightened her grip on his hand. "That man said he wanted to talk to you about some articles."

Her father grunted. "They've asked me not to print any more like that, warning the people of the impact it will have. In fact, they want me to print a retraction."

"A *retraction*?" Amelia sprang to her feet. "Why would they ask for that, unless what you printed wasn't true? And I know you too well for that."

One corner of his mouth quirked up. "Thank you, my dear. That's why I chose John 8:32 for the *Gazette*'s motto."

"'Ye shall know the truth, and the truth shall make you free.'" Amelia quoted from memory, her eyes misting when she thought of the words that had appeared on the *Gazette*'s masthead for as long as she could remember.

Her father nodded. "That's what we print, Amelia. It's what I've always stood by, and what I hope this newspaper will always stand for."

"That's what Clayton Sloan says he admires most about you—your dedication to print the truth, no matter the cost. It's what sets you apart from many other newspaper publishers."

The tight lines of her father's face softened into a smile. "How is Clay? He's been a good friend, letting you help out at the *Denver Journal* from time to time."

"He's doing well. So is the paper. In fact, he's let me write several stories lately. Nothing earth-shaking, but at least I'm getting to put the lessons I learned from you into practice. I wouldn't want to let my writing skills get rusty between my trips to Arizona."

A chuckle shook her father's shoulders. "I can imagine how your mother must feel about you working for a newspaper— even on a casual basis. How is she, by the way?"

Amelia flinched at the change of subject. "Mother is . . . doing well." She tried to keep her tone neutral. From her father's expression, she knew she had failed.

"Still caught up in her social whirl?"

She nodded, hating to see the glimmer of pain that crossed his face, a pain she knew was due to something more than illness.

"Maybe I should have given in and gone back to Denver with her when she left, but I doubt it would have made any difference—except for seeing more of you, of course." His eyes took on a faraway look. "She wanted a better life for you, and I can't blame her for that. But her ideas of a 'better life' and mine couldn't be further apart. I never could fit in with that snobbish social set of hers . . . not that I ever tried very hard."

His breath came out in a long sigh. "I expect she's happier back in her old circle of friends, with her parents' money to keep her in the style she was accustomed to before she married me."

Amelia nodded again, wishing she could say something to take away the hurt in his voice. But he had only spoken the truth. Instead of encouraging her mother to return to her husband when she turned her back on their marriage ten years before, Amelia's grandparents had welcomed her back to Denver with open arms and no recriminations. They had not, however, encouraged divorce, so though living apart, her parents were still man and wife. She wondered—not for the first time—how she could be so closely related to her mother's side of the family and yet share so few of their interests.

She pressed her lips together, holding back the words she longed to say about her mother's social life—and Thaddeus Grayson, who had spent the past few months flitting around her mother like a bee around a flower. She wasn't sure which sickened her more, the sight of him acting that way with a married woman, or the fact that her mother—the married woman in question—didn't make any effort to repulse his attentions.

With her grandparents giving tacit approval to that troubling situation, she had hoped to discuss the matter with her father and seek his counsel. But looking at his gaunt form, she couldn't bring herself to do it now. She would have to wait until his health improved.

Her father hitched himself a little higher up against the pillows. "What are your plans when you return to Denver? Any young men I should know about?" His attempt at a smile didn't quite come off.

"No, there isn't anyone." *Though not for lack of trying on Mother's part.* Amelia leaned forward and stroked his head. "But let's not talk about me going home. I just got here, after all. And I'm not leaving until you're much better. I'll stay as long as you need me."

Homer stepped into the room, wiping his hands on an ink-stained rag. "Doc Harwood is here."

Amelia felt her spirits lighten for the first time since setting foot in her father's sickroom. Finally, someone she could press for answers about his condition!

She rose and patted his hand. "I'll step out and give you

some privacy." She nodded a greeting to the doctor, a tall, gray-haired man, who moved aside so she could exit before he closed the door.

Seeing that Homer's attention was occupied in setting type for the *Gazette*'s upcoming issue, Amelia busied herself straightening loose papers and neatening some of the clutter that typically littered the printing office. From time to time, she darted a glance at her father's door, but it remained stubbornly closed.

She looked around, needing something productive to do. Her eyes lit on the door to her father's office, and she hurried to his desk. Pulling out a fresh sheet of paper, she reached for pen and ink and started jotting notes about the foreclosure she overheard the two women talking about at the station.

She had been scribbling only a few minutes when she heard the sickroom door open, and Dr. Harwood stepped out. Amelia scurried from the office to intercept him.

"I have some questions for you," she began.

"Why don't we talk in the office." Without waiting for a response, he strode into the room she'd just vacated and waited for her to join him. He folded his arms and measured her with a long look. "I don't know how much your father has told you about his condition."

"He mentioned not feeling well several times in his most recent letters, but I didn't realize he'd gotten as sick as this."

The doctor nodded. "I thought that might be the case."

"What's wrong with him?" she demanded. "How long will it take him to recover?"

The doctor's somber expression made her heart constrict, and her voice rose half an octave. "He *is* going to get better, isn't he?"

Dr. Harwood reached out to lay one hand on her shoulder. "Your father has a malignant cancer. I'm afraid it's well advanced by now. Frankly, I'm surprised he's still with us. I think he's been hanging on, just waiting to see you again. Now that you're here—"

"What?" A clutch of dread seized Amelia's throat, and she fought to squeeze the words out. "You're not telling me . . ."

The doctor's gaze softened, and he tightened his grip on her shoulder. "I know this is hard for you to hear, but he's just hanging on by a thread. I'll be surprised if he lasts the week."

Amelia balled her hands into tight fists beneath her chin, trying to grasp the enormity of the doctor's statement. A sob tore from her throat. "But it's too soon! I'm not ready . . ." Her voice trailed off as she recognized the truth reflected in the doctor's solemn gaze and realized the futility of her words. Ready or not, her emotions wouldn't change the situation. Concern for her father—not for her own feelings—had to take precedence.

Lowering her hands to her sides, she squared her shoulders and tried to steady her voice. "What can I do for him? How can I help make him comfortable?"

A brief smile of approval flitted across the doctor's lips. "Homer has some medicine I left that helps ease the pain. He's been doing a fine job of staying on top of things. My advice would be to let him run the paper, and for you to spend as much time with your father as you can. That's the best medicine you can offer him."

He patted her shoulder and withdrew his hand. "I've done all I can do for him, but I'll check back from time to time to see how you're both getting along. And if there's anything you need, just send someone for me. I'll come as quickly as I can." With a final sympathetic look, he gave her a nod and left.

It took several minutes before she could compose herself enough to walk back to the sickroom. Pushing the door open, she stepped inside, trying to conceal her anguish. She took her time settling herself on the ladder-back chair beside the bed, noting her father's pallor and the waxy appearance of his skin. Despite his attempts to set her at ease, he was ill—desperately ill. Why hadn't she recognized the signs before?

The answer was simple enough. *I didn't see it because I didn't want to.*

Her father's lips twisted into a rueful smile. "He told you?"

She should have known he'd see right through her efforts to appear composed. Hadn't he always been able to know what was really going on inside her? Her carefully erected air of calm began to crumble, and she gripped his hand in both her own. "He must be mistaken. He *has* to be! You can't . . ." Her throat tightened, choking off her protest.

He reached up to stroke her cheek with his free hand. "I'm sorry, honey. I wouldn't have planned it this way, but it wasn't left up to me. We have to talk about the future—what we're going to do with the paper, what you're going to do. At least you won't be left completely on your own. You have a home to return to in Denver once this is over."

It isn't a home I want to go back to! Amelia clamped her lower lip between her teeth to keep from saying the words aloud.

"I'd like to keep the paper going as long as we can, so you can get the best price for it," her father went on. "We could ask Clay Sloan to put some feelers out. He might know someone who would be interested."

He laid his palm against her cheek. "I won't ask you to stay indefinitely, but do you think you and Homer could run the *Gazette* until it's sold? I want some of the proceeds to go to Homer. He's been a good helper and a great friend over the years. The rest will be yours."

A spasm crossed his face, and he pulled his hand away to press it against his side.

Amelia started to her feet, but he shook his head and tugged at her hand. "Don't let just anybody have it, though," he continued in a noticeably weaker voice. "I want it to go to someone who cares about the truth as much as you and I do. Something isn't right about Great Western, something even worse than their plans for hydraulic mining, as bad as that is. I need to know whoever is at the helm of the *Gazette* will bring the truth to light."

Amelia leaned forward and blinked back the tears that stung her eyes. "That's enough for now, Papa. I don't want you to wear yourself out."

"Honey, if I rest now, I may never get another chance to tell you." He drew a shaky breath, and his eyelids fluttered. "But I'll admit, I'm pretty tuckered. I wouldn't mind a chance to close my eyes for a bit."

Amelia bent over to tuck the sheet around his shoulders and pressed her quivering lips against his forehead. "I love you, Papa. Always remember that."

"I love you, too, honey." His lips moved again, and she bent lower to catch the faint words. "Look for me at the Eastern Gate."

)X(

Amelia knew she would always remember the next few days as some of the most precious in her life. Every brief scrap of conversation with her father, every tender touch, every loving glance that passed between them, would be emblazoned on her memory forever.

True to his word, Dr. Harwood checked in several times. Pastor Edmonds was a frequent caller, as well, offering spiritual encouragement to them both and bolstering Amelia's flagging spirits by his repeated assurances that she was doing everything humanly possible to bring comfort to her father's final days.

Friends stopped by to say farewell, while Homer put all his efforts into making sure the *Gazette*'s next issue went out on time. Though he looked worn to a frazzle, he insisted he could manage it alone, wanting to give Amelia and her father every possible minute together. Amelia suspected he spent his rare snippets of free time working on a tribute to her father to be printed whenever that day arrived, but she couldn't bring herself to ask if her supposition was correct.

She scarcely left the sickroom for more than a few moments, for fear she might not be there when her father needed her. When the end came, she sat quietly by his side, sandwiching his hand between hers. She watched his chest rise and fall, noting that each faint breath came slower than the one before. Finally she heard one last, gentle sigh . . . and he was gone.

CHAPTER 3

The funeral passed in a haze. With Homer beside her, Amelia sat on a hard pew at the front of the sanctuary of the Granite Springs Community Church. Her mind registered a number of mourners in attendance, though she took no note of individual faces. Pastor Edmonds stood behind the pulpit and spoke in a heartfelt tone, but not one word penetrated her consciousness. Her whole attention remained focused on the simple coffin in front of the minister.

Her head cleared somewhat when the congregation reached the cemetery, and she took her place beside the waiting coffin and the open grave. She scanned the faces around her, recognizing several who had come to pay their last respects.

Emmett Kingston, having closed the general store for the morning, stood beside Thomas Rafferty, the station agent. Both men's eyes were red-rimmed, and they made surreptitious swipes at their noses with pocket handkerchiefs.

Carl Olsen, owner of the livery stable, was there, along with Martin Gilbreth. On Martin's left stood a tall, angular woman Amelia hadn't seen before who kept one hand tucked into the crook of his elbow and patted his arm with the other.

Amelia turned her attention to a small group of men clustered a short distance from the other mourners, beneath the limbs of a solitary pine. None of their faces were familiar to her, so she let her gaze slide past, then jerked it back to the group again when she recognized Ben Stone.

She pressed closer to Homer and spoke in a low tone. "All these people must have known Papa, but some of them are new to me. That woman standing with Mr. Gilbreth, for instance. Did he marry recently?"

Homer snorted and glanced in the direction she indicated. "Martin Gilbreth is as much a confirmed bachelor as I am. That's his older sister. She came out here a few months ago to keep house for him."

Amelia took a second look at the woman and nodded. "Now that you mention it, I can see the family resemblance. What about those men over there?" She tilted her head toward the group by the pine tree.

Homer followed her gaze, and his features took on a stony expression. "It's that bunch of scoundrels from Great Western. They have a lot of nerve, showing their faces here today."

Before he could say more, Pastor Edmonds stepped forward and addressed the mourners. While he read from Psalm 23, Amelia studied the group from Great Western again—five men, wearing identical smug expressions . . . except for Ben Stone.

The disrespect they showed smote Amelia's aching heart like the thrust of a dagger. What kind of men would intrude upon her grief on such a mournful day?

She snapped her attention back to the service when the pallbearers moved into position beside the coffin and carefully lowered it into the grave. Pastor Edmonds said a closing prayer, then dismissed the group of mourners.

He moved closer to Amelia and clasped her hands in his. "Your father was a fine man, and we're all going to miss him. Feel free to call on me if there's anything I can do. And know that you'll be in my prayers."

Amelia nodded and watched him drift off to speak with some of the onlookers. She stooped to pick up a handful of the loose dirt at the grave's edge, then straightened and sprinkled the moist soil onto her father's coffin. "Good-bye, Papa," she whispered.

A shadow fell across the grave, and she looked up to see one of the men from Great Western standing beside her. Her breath caught in her throat, and she took a quick step back.

"Good afternoon, Miss Wagner. I'm sorry for your loss." The sentiments the stocky, dark-haired man expressed were conventional enough, but the sympathetic words didn't match the coldness in his eyes.

Amelia bobbed her head. "Thank you." She looked around for Homer, but he stood some distance away, talking to Emmett Kingston. When she turned to join him, the man at her side raised his hand.

"Allow me to introduce myself. My name is Owen Merrick. I'm the vice president of the Great Western Investment Company. I know nothing can ease the pain of your loss, but I have an offer that might help lighten your burden somewhat."

Amelia could only stare at first, then she finally found her voice. "I'm not sure I understand. . . ."

Mr. Merrick took a step closer. "Being a businessman myself, I understand how trying it can be to dispose of property. For a woman who's alone and grieving . . ." He tilted his head in a show of solicitude and gave her an ingratiating smile. "I'd like to help, and so, on behalf of my company, I'm offering to purchase your newspaper—for a fair price, of course. That way you'll be free to turn your mind to other matters. If you would care to stop by my office tomorrow, we can discuss the terms."

Amelia lifted her chin and tried to keep her voice from wobbling. "This is hardly the time or the place for such an offer, Mr. Merrick. And at any rate, I'm afraid you've wasted your time. The *Gazette* is not for sale."

Not at the moment, at least. And even when she did put the paper on the market, she would never sell it to anyone who had caused her father such grief.

Owen Merrick chuckled. "My dear young lady, you can't intend to run it yourself? Better consider taking my offer while the paper still has some value. Let me know when you've changed your mind." He tipped his hat and joined the rest of the Great Western contingent, who had already started walking back toward town.

As the group moved off, Amelia saw Ben Stone look back over his shoulder. Their gazes met, and the compassion in his eyes tugged at her heart.

Other mourners filed by, murmuring words of comfort. Amelia accepted their condolences, trying to keep her mind focused on giving a polite response while Merrick's stinging words echoed in her mind. Finally she stood with Homer beside her, staring down into the lonely grave.

Homer put his arm around her shoulders and gave her a gentle hug. "Heaven's richer for his passing, but that doesn't make it any easier for those of us who have been left behind."

Amelia didn't respond. She pressed her lips together and swallowed, trying to hold back the tears. Despite her efforts, one slipped from her eye and traced a path down her cheek. With an angry sniff, she reached up to dash it away with the back of her hand.

Pastor Edmonds joined them and patted her on the arm. "Don't try to hold it in, my dear. God understands our broken hearts. Remember, Jesus wept after the death of his friend Lazarus."

Amelia looked up at the kindly minister. Keeping her tone even, she said, "Thank you. I appreciate everything you've done for my father and me." With one last glance at her father's final resting place, she straightened her shoulders and retraced her steps toward town with Homer trailing behind her.

Weeping could come later—she had a newspaper to run.

CHAPTER 4

A re you sure you want this story on the Columbian
Exposition in Chicago at the bottom of the page?"

Amelia looked up from composing a summary of Pastor Edmonds's latest sermon, speaking out against the brothels that carried on their shady business near the south edge of town. She paused a moment to consider Homer's question. He had worked with her father for years and had a finely honed instinct for story placement. But she was the one in charge of the paper now. She had the final say.

"Yes. It may be a big national story, but local news comes first."

A wide grin split Homer's face. "Good. That's what your daddy would have said."

Amelia chuckled at the compliment and went back to work, marveling at the way the ripple of laughter served to dispel some of the tension that had weighed her down ever since she marched back to the *Gazette* from her father's graveside three weeks before. In that time, she had discovered there was a vast difference between being able to perform various tasks that went into producing the paper, and being the one actually at the helm.

She had Homer to consider, as well. His livelihood was as dependent upon the success of the paper as her own. That knowledge doubled her feeling of responsibility.

She glanced down again at Pastor Edmonds's message. Her father would have approved. He had been just as outspoken about the degrading brothel trade in his editorials, while at the same time expressing compassion for the women forced into that sordid life. After putting the finishing touches on the sermon summary, she donned her printer's apron and moved over to help Homer at the press. Taking the brayer from him, she rolled it through the puddle of ink on the marble slab, then applied the ink to the form on the bed of the press while he slid a sheet of newsprint into place. Turning the crank on the left side of the press, he rolled the bed under the platen before pulling on the lever to print the page. Working together, they fell into an easy rhythm.

"There aren't many idle moments for the two of us, are there." Amelia laughed. "Between the paper and the other print jobs that come in, there's more than enough work to keep us busy. However did you manage on your own while Papa was ill?"

"I put in plenty of long hours—that's for sure. But I'm not complaining. Your father was as good a friend as I've ever met. He was there for me when I needed help, and I was happy to return the favor." Homer started to turn the crank again but stopped abruptly when the bed jammed halfway along its track.

Amelia stared at him. "What just happened?"

Homer crouched down to look underneath the apparatus. "Looks like one of the leather belts broke. We won't be printing any more sheets until I get that fixed."

Amelia stooped and saw the end of the dangling leather strap. "What can I do to help?"

"It's pretty much a one-man job. I had Carl Olsen make up a couple of spares so we'd be ready the next time this happened. Why don't you check the pages we've already printed while I tinker with this. If they're dry, you can gather them up so we can print the other side." Catching her anxious expression, he added in a reassuring tone, "I'll have it up and running in time to get the paper out—never fear."

Retrieving a coiled strip of leather from a shelf below the counter, he grabbed a wrench and crawled underneath the press. "'We make a kind of handsome show! Among these hills, from first to last, we've weathered many a furious blast.'"

Amelia smiled. Despite his soothing words and the quoted lines of poetry, the strain in his voice indicated a level of tension equal to her own. Homer always spouted poetry when under pressure.

Or when he'd been tippling. Amelia shook her head, remembering a few unhappy scenes during her youth. But he'd finally sworn off liquor under her father's beneficial influence, with only a few minor relapses since.

She gathered the dry pages and wondered—not for the first time—if she had done the right thing in not putting the *Gazette* up for sale yet. That weighty question had kept her awake well into the night more times than she cared to count.

Watching Homer work, she took note of his worn appearance. Shouldering so much of the load during her father's illness and since his death had taken a toll, even with all the help she could offer.

To be honest, she'd been feeling frazzled herself, and not only from the pressures of running the newspaper. Upon hearing the news of Andrew Wagner's death, her mother insisted Amelia return to Denver posthaste. Every new letter reiterated her demand in no uncertain terms. Reading between the lines, however, Amelia thought her mother's tone sounded more interested in the quest to find her daughter a suitable husband than in having the comfort of Amelia's company while she grieved.

She shrugged off the unpleasant notion. Whatever her mother's reasons for insisting she return, she couldn't just walk away from the *Gazette* and Homer. Her father wouldn't have wanted that.

She heaved a long sigh, wishing she could expel her sense of despondency along with the *whoosh* of air, and then squared her shoulders. Yearning for things to be different didn't make them so. Until she could afford to hire additional help—or find a suitable buyer—they would all just have to muddle along the best they could.

Maybe it would be better for everyone if she took Owen Merrick up on his offer. Homer would then be free to look for other employment. Over the years, he had been her father's staunchest ally and was loyal to a fault. He cared about her, too. She had no doubt he would sacrifice himself to keep on helping her as long as she continued running the paper. And it would be a sacrifice, no doubt about it. The work was hard, and Homer wasn't getting any younger.

And she would be free to behave as a good daughter should

and return to her widowed mother's side. A shudder rippled through her. The idea of going back to Denver wasn't a thought she wanted to entertain.

The door to the street swung open. Amelia fixed a smile on her face when a woman about her mother's age stepped inside. She wiped a smudge of ink off her fingers with a well-used rag and stepped forward to greet her.

Her willowy visitor inclined her head and gave Amelia a gentle smile. "Good day, my dear. I don't believe we've met. My name is Hyacinth Parmenter. My late husband was an avid reader of the *Gazette* while he was alive."

"I'm pleased to meet you. I'm—"

"Oh, I know who you are." Mrs. Parmenter waved away the attempted introduction. "I wanted to give you some time to recover from your loss before stopping in again."

"Again?" Amelia heard a faint clink from behind her and glanced back in time to see Homer scoot farther under the press.

"I used to stop by on occasion to chat with your father. Such a pleasure to find a man of culture in these rough surroundings."

Amelia nodded and tapped her fingertips against the bottom edge of the counter, wondering what prompted Mrs. Parmenter's visit . . . and how soon the woman would leave so she could get back to work. "Is there anything I can do for you today?"

Mrs. Parmenter's face lit up. "It's a matter of what I can do for you." Reaching into her reticule, she drew out a folded sheet of paper and spread it on the counter with a flourish. "I've written a poem I believe will prove edifying to your readers."

Amelia stared at the woman a moment, then bent to study the written lines:

Ode to the Dawn

As golden orb peeks o'er shadowed hills
And lark responds with honey'd trills. . . .

"Oh, my." Her eyes widened as she skimmed the rest of the flowery verse. "I . . . see," she said when she finished. "Thank you, but—"

"I let your father read several of my pieces, and he was most appreciative of the sentiments expressed. During his illness, I brought some of them by to show your assistant, Mr. Crenshaw. I hoped he might want to share them with your readers as a way to provide uplifting thoughts during that trying time. Sadly, he was never able to find space for them, but I thought I might try again, now that you're in charge and some of the burden has been lifted from the dear man's shoulders."

Amelia blinked. "We've already set the type for most of this week's issue. I'm afraid we won't be able to fit it in."

The other woman continued to smile, undaunted by the news. "Then I shall leave this with you for the next issue. I'll bring more in next week, and that way we will be able to stay ahead of schedule." She sent a quick glance around the printing office. "Where is Mr. Crenshaw today? I assumed he would be hard at work, printing tomorrow's edition."

Amelia cast a furtive look over her shoulder, but there was no response from beneath the press. "He's . . . busy. I'll be sure to let him know you were here."

Hyacinth Parmenter smiled her thanks and swept away. The

38

door opened as she neared it, and the new arrival stepped back to allow her to exit before he came inside.

Amelia pushed the poem to one side and moved along the counter to greet Pete Nichols. The owner of the Bon-Ton had placed advertisements for the new café on a weekly basis . . . up until her father died. And he wasn't the only one who had stepped back to see if the paper would survive. That wasn't unusual whenever there was a change in a newspaper's owner-ship, but their dwindling advertising revenues only added to her worries about the paper's future.

"Good morning, Mr. Nichols. How can I help you?"

He pulled off his bowler hat and twisted the brim in his hands, avoiding her gaze. "Morning, Miss Wagner. I'd like to start running my ad again."

Her smile widened. If one businessman took the lead in reestablishing his connection with the paper, other advertisers might follow. "I'm glad to hear that. We'll be pleased to have your custom again."

He glanced at her quickly, then averted his eyes again. "I know I should have come in before now. I just wasn't sure you'd be able to pull it off and keep the paper going after your father was gone. Homer is a good man, but it's a lot for one person to run on his own." Looking at Amelia's ink-stained fingers, he added, "Looks like you're pitching right in, though. I'm glad to see that. We need a good newspaper around here."

Amelia retrieved a sheet of paper and a pencil. "What would you like the ad to say?"

"Just use the same thing I've been running all along." One corner of his lips lifted. "I haven't been open long enough to need many changes yet." He shoved his hands in his pockets and nodded. "I can see you're busy, so I won't take up any more of your time. Just let me know how much I owe you, and expect me to come back soon to have some new menus printed up."

Amelia hummed a light tune as she moved to the press. If she shortened her summary of Pastor Edmonds's sermon, the café's ad could go in that week's issue, providing them with additional revenue. Remembering Mrs. Parmenter's poem, she pushed away a twinge of guilt. The poem was only filler, but Mr. Nichols was a paying customer.

With that decision made, she bent to check on Homer's progress. He lay on his back, with most of his body hidden by the press and only his spindly legs sticking out. "Any luck?"

"Almost there. Thanks for not giving me away to the Parmenter woman."

Amelia leaned back against the counter and grinned. "You didn't seem to be in any hurry to speak to her, *dear man*."

A muffled groan floated out from beneath the press. "I made the mistake of telling her I enjoy poetry. That was before I saw that cloying claptrap she writes. Now she's decided we're kindred sprits."

Amelia chuckled. "It sounds to me like you have an admirer."

A loud snort was Homer's only response. "I meant to tell you, I put the mail on the desk in your office earlier. You might want to look through it." He cleared his throat. "There's a letter lying on top. Looks like it's another one from your mother."

Amelia felt her shoulders tighten. Walking to the office, she scooped up the stack of mail and carried it back out to the counter. If other customers stopped in, she would be able to deal with them and let Homer keep working without interruption. They needed to have the press up and running again as soon as possible if they hoped to stay on schedule.

She sorted through the mail quickly. Homer was right— the letter on top of the stack was indeed from her mother. She set it aside so she could check the other mail first. There might be some important business correspondence awaiting her notice.

Be honest. You just don't want to read her letter. But you'll have to open it eventually.

To her disappointment, she found nothing in the rest of the mail that demanded her attention. With no excuse to put it off any longer, she picked up the envelope with the Denver postmark. She slit the flap, bracing herself for another round of entreaties for her to come back home.

Even without opening the envelope, she knew the kind of phrases she could expect to find. First the tender pleas: *"Please come home, darling. Everyone is asking about you."*

Then the more strident questions: *"How long are you going to persist in this foolishness of trying to operate that paper on your own?"*

Leading up to what her mother would perceive as her most compelling argument: *"Your father is gone. Staying in Arizona isn't going to change that."*

As if she needed any reminder! Every morning she opened her eyes, ready to begin the new day, only to have the jolting memory of her loss wound her afresh.

And despite her pain, she still had to get out of bed and force herself to go on. Her conviction that she could honor her father by continuing his work was the only thing that helped her get through one day to the next.

She tapped the envelope against her finger, sure she had already summed up the letter's contents. Was there any point in even opening it? It would be simple enough to put it away in a drawer, unread.

Simple, but not right. Trying to put aside the resentment she felt over the mounting pressure to comply with her mother's wishes, she pulled the envelope open along the slit she had made, slid out the letter, and unfolded it. After she skimmed the first few lines, she uttered a cry, and the sheets of stationery slipped from her fingers.

Homer pushed himself out from underneath the press and scrambled to his feet. "What's wrong?"

"It's my mother."

Homer hurried over to her, worry creasing his face. "She hasn't taken ill, too, has she?"

"Worse. She's gotten married."

"Married! With your daddy barely in his grave?"

"It's her old sweetheart, Thaddeus Grayson—the man my grandparents would have preferred she married in the first place." Amelia stooped to pick up the scattered pages with fingers that trembled. "He lived in the East for quite a while, but he returned to Denver a little over a year ago. They've been . . . keeping company for some time now. With Papa gone, I suppose they felt it cleared the way for them to wed."

Homer swiped his fingers through his hair, leaving a streak of mingled ink and grease across his forehead. "Hardly seems respectful to your father . . . or respectable, for that matter."

Amelia forced herself to scan the rest of the letter. "She is quite insistent that I come back to Denver. They've established their own household—a lavish one, I'm sure, since he's quite well-off—so we won't be living with my grandparents anymore. She says the three of us will be a family."

"You don't sound any too thrilled about that. But would it be such a bad thing? I know you and your mother don't always see eye to eye, but family is important."

"Not if that family includes Thaddeus Grayson." Ignoring Homer's startled expression, she stepped around him to slip Hyacinth Parmenter's poem into a file for future use. Watching Mr. Grayson dance attendance on her mother had been hard enough to bear, but his attention didn't always stay focused on her mother. After dodging his unwanted advances the few times he'd caught her alone, Amelia had taken to her room any time she knew he would be coming over.

To live in a home where he would be the head of the household, where he could corner her at any moment . . .

Any doubts she had about staying on to run the *Gazette* vanished like the dew on a sunny Arizona morning.

Turning back to Homer, she laid one hand on his slender arm. "I'm not going back. I'm going to stay here and carry on my father's legacy. Between the two of us, we'll make the *Granite Springs Gazette* the finest paper in this part of the territory."

Homer eyed her doubtfully, then patted her hand and smiled. "'If it were done when 'tis done, then 'twere well it were done quickly.'" He dropped her a wink before ducking back under the press, while Amelia chuckled at his playful use of the line from Macbeth.

The door opened again, and a tall woman entered. Amelia recognized her as the one who stood next to Martin Gilbreth at the cemetery.

"Afternoon. I'm Clara Gilbreth, Martin Gilbreth's sister. I expect you're acquainted with him."

Fine lines etched Clara Gilbreth's face, giving her features even more resemblance to the weather-beaten sawmill owner than Amelia had observed at the cemetery.

"Yes, I've known him for several years now. I remember seeing you with him at my father's funeral." Amelia braced herself for the outpouring of sympathy she had come to expect upon every mention of her father's death.

Instead, the other woman merely dipped her head in a brief nod. "I figured you probably did, although I wouldn't have blamed you if you didn't recall. I know how foggy your mind can get when you're burying a parent. I laid both of mine to rest this past winter."

"Both of them?" Tears stung Amelia's eyes. "I'm so sorry."

Clara pressed her lips together and swallowed quickly. "They had a good life and finished the race nearly neck and neck. Ma outlived our pa by only a few weeks, and that's the way they would have wanted it. These things are hard, but the good Lord knows what He's doing. Now they can walk the golden streets hand in hand and never have to say good-bye again."

A smile softened Amelia's lips. "That's a lovely way to look at it. I'm so pleased to meet you. I didn't realize Mr. Gilbreth had a sister."

Clara shrugged. "There's another sister and a brother back in Indiana, but they're both married and have families of their own. When Martin moved out here, we talked about me coming, too. But we decided it was best for me to stay behind to take care of our folks. Now I'm out here to keep house for Martin, since he and I are both on our own."

Amelia's smile broadened. "When I saw you at the cemetery, I thought at first you might be his wife."

The other woman let out a bark of laughter. "Neither Martin nor I ever married, and we're neither one likely to. We're both too set in our ways, and I have a tendency to speak my mind. Most men don't appreciate that in a woman."

Amelia touched her fingertips to her lips to hold back a laugh. Clara's forthrightness might not make her a prime candidate for matrimony, but she found the older woman's attitude refreshing.

"But I didn't come here to tell you my life's story. I wanted to see if you still have a couple of the papers that came out about a month ago. There was a story about the sawmill, and I'd like to send copies to my brother and sister. I should have thought of it earlier, but I hoped you might have some left."

"I'm not sure." Amelia turned and called to Homer, "Do you think we'd have any of those back issues available?"

Homer emerged from under the press wearing a triumphant grin and gave the apparatus an affectionate pat. "She's all set now. Ready to print the rest of this issue." Nodding toward their visitor, he added, "I know the story she means. We don't print a lot of extras, but we might have a couple left over. They'd probably be back in the storeroom. I'll go take a look."

Clara leaned on the counter and eyed Amelia. "What about you? Is running a newspaper something you always wanted to do, or did you just fall into it when your pa died?"

Amelia caught her breath. The other woman could have no idea how close her remark hit home. A flutter of excitement rippled through her at the realization that she would, indeed, be the one running the *Gazette* from now on. "A little of both, actually. I grew up helping my father here and loved every minute of it. I've been doing a bit of work for a paper in Denver and coming back here to spend time with my father in the summers. It always felt like something I was born to do . . . but I never thought I'd be the one in charge."

"Life can take some funny turns," Clara mused. She straightened when Homer returned with two folded copies of the *Gazette.* He cast a sideways look at her when he placed them on the counter, then he scuttled back toward the storeroom.

Clara glanced at the papers and laid some coins on the counter. "Those are the ones I wanted, all right. Now I'd best get out of your hair. I know you have to get the paper out tomorrow, but I may stop in again some day when you aren't so busy. I enjoy talking to you. It's better than trying to make conversation with some simpering female who can only talk about babies or tatting or such."

Amelia watched the door swing shut behind their visitor, then turned back to work feeling like her day had brightened. Clara Gilbreth's visit had been a fresh breeze, sweeping away some of the gloom that had been weighing upon her.

Homer came back carrying a bundle of paper and looked around warily. "Is she gone?"

"Miss Gilbreth? Yes, she just left." Amelia studied him, puzzled. "Why? Don't you like her?"

He thumped the paper down on the counter next to the press. "Old maids like her—or widows like that Parmenter woman—make me nervous. It always feels like they're on the prowl."

Amelia bit back a smile at the thought of scrawny Homer as the target of a gaggle of predatory husband hunters. "You might be right about our local poetess, but has Miss Gilbreth ever said or done anything to make you think she's set her cap for you?"

"No, but I've seen enough of her kind over the years. I know the signs. When women reach a certain age without finding a husband, they turn desperate. I've watched some good men be caught off guard and snapped up like fried chicken at a church picnic when they weren't paying attention."

Despite her efforts, a chuckle gurgled from Amelia's lips. "I don't think you have anything to worry about with her. Besides," she teased, "if she does decide to come after you, I'll be here to protect you."

Homer gave her a baleful look accompanied by a *harrumph*. Then a grin lit up his face. "I guess that would make you my hero, then." He turned on his heel. "Let's both be heroic and get this paper out."

Amelia moved to pull the last printed page from the tympan and hung it up to dry while Homer replaced it with a fresh sheet. Their brief exchange reminded her of the banter Homer and her father shared over the years. It always made her laugh to hear them, and it did the same today.

She had laughed during Clara's visit, as well, and she felt much better for it. How right King Solomon had been when he penned the proverb about a merry heart doing good like a medicine!

X

Several hours later, Amelia folded the last paper and laid it atop the others in the stack with a sense of satisfaction. "That's the last one. We made our deadline."

"We've never missed one yet." Homer stretched his arms wide and rolled his neck from side to side.

Ten-year-old Jimmy Brandt burst through the front door as if on cue. "Are the papers ready to deliver yet?"

"You're right on time." Amelia smiled as she helped their eager delivery boy load the latest issue of the *Gazette* into his ink-smudged canvas bag. "If I didn't know better, I'd think some sort of signal goes up the moment we finish. You always seem to know exactly when to come."

"I must have ink in my veins, the same way you and Mr. Crenshaw say you do. In fact . . ." He puffed out his chest and stood a little straighter. "I picked up a great idea for a story on the way here. I heard Jack Canby tell Danny Morgan someone stole his bag of marbles. That's the third time I've heard of the same happening lately, and I'm pretty sure Skeeter Perry is the one behind it. I think we ought to check into it and print a story that proves he's guilty. What do you think? I'd be glad to write it for you. Then all you'd have to do is set the type."

Amelia bit back a laugh, unwilling to wipe the eager look from his face. "I'll certainly think about it. In the meantime, you'd better get this week's edition out. We need to keep the *Gazette* in business if you're going to be a star reporter someday."

With a grin, the youngster shouldered his canvas bag and hustled off to make his deliveries.

Homer smoothed his cuffs and grimaced when he saw splotches of grease near his elbow. "I guess I should change my shirt and spruce up a bit before I head out to make my deliveries." With a wave of his hand, he headed toward the rear door. "I'll be back in a bit."

Amelia leaned against the counter and drew a deep breath, savoring the sense of a job well done. The moment an issue was finished always brought a sense of respite, even though it was only a momentary break in the continual process of gathering and printing the news.

Lifting the topmost paper from the stack remaining on the counter, she shook it open and scanned the front page. A frown tightened her forehead. Yes, they had completed the job on time, but the week brought little news of any import. The same information could have been gleaned through the local grapevine. That wouldn't be enough to keep subscribers—or advertisers—coming back for more.

She tossed the paper onto the counter and paced the width of the printing office. She and Homer diligently printed every scrap of news they came across, but they needed to do more if they hoped to entice more readers to buy the paper—or advertisers to keep giving their support. The smaller print jobs that came in—restaurant menus, flyers, invitations, and the like—bolstered their income, but they would have to make a success of the *Gazette,* as well, if they hoped to remain afloat financially.

But how was she supposed to do that when Jimmy's tidbit about the marbles theft had been one of the most exciting things in Granite Springs that week? She couldn't very well manufacture news on a whim.

Memories stirred, and her steps slowed. Hadn't her father always maintained that big stories were always there, just waiting to be found? He likened it to someone hunting for ore in gold-rich country. Its presence was certain—all she had to do was keep digging.

All right, then. I'll do it. Advertisers like Pete Nichols might bring their business back to the paper, but they wouldn't stay long if she didn't find a way to revitalize the *Gazette* and give it substance.

The numbness that had enveloped her brain ever since her father's death began to ease its hold, and she felt like she was thinking clearly for the first time in weeks. She needed a story, something worth its weight in gold.

Experienced miners knew where to look by observing rock formations and other signs in the terrain. During her growing-up years, she'd seen plenty of newcomers, watching to see where the old-timers struck pay dirt. Maybe that was what she should do—follow her father's example.

What had her father been working on before he got so sick, and Homer had to take over the writing as well as the printing? She stopped dead in her tracks, remembering Ben Stone's visit to the paper during her father's illness. That had been the first she'd heard of the Great Western Investment Company, and she well remembered the agitation her father had shown at the mention of the company's name.

What was it he'd told her? She squeezed her eyes shut and strained to remember. Something about things not being right at Great Western. A flicker of excitement sparked within her at the memory of her father's words: *"I need to know that whoever is at the helm of the* Gazette *will bring the truth to light."*

The spark burst into a determined flame, and her eyes flew open. She was the one at the *Gazette*'s helm now. She would carry out her father's wishes, uncover the truth . . . and boost the paper's circulation, all in one fell swoop.

Homer strode back in, ready to meet the public in a clean

shirt. He scooped up the stack of papers ready for delivery to local businesses and draped them over his arm. "Once I drop off the last batch, I think I'll hole up and read a bit of Wordsworth . . . unless you need me for something."

"No, take some time for yourself. You've certainly earned it."

As he started for the front door, she called out, "Those stories my father wrote about Great Western—when were those printed?"

"About three months ago. Just before he got so sick." Homer tilted his head and eyed her with a speculative glance. "Why? You thinking about reading them?"

"I thought I might, just to catch up on what was going on before I got here." She laughed. "Looks like we'll both be curling up with our reading this evening, although mine may not be on a par with Wordsworth."

He smiled. "It may not be poetry, but it's some of the finest writing your daddy ever did."

After Homer went on his way, Amelia searched through the bound copies of back issues they kept in the office and located the time period he'd indicated. Carrying them to the desk, she opened the earliest one and scanned the front page. The article she sought was easy enough to find, spreading from one side of the page to the other, topped by the headline: *Friend or Foe? The Not-So-Great Western.*

She scanned the story quickly at first, then went back to read it more slowly. Her father's style was so distinctive she almost felt she could hear him speaking:

Hydraulic mining—the process Great Western intends to inflict on the area around our fair community—is the same despicable process responsible for destroying thousands of acres of rich, California farmland only two decades ago.

Amelia finished the article, then went on to the next issue, which followed along similar lines:

Let us not forget what happened to Marysville, where the mining debris choked the mountain streams and buried the entire town in a sea of brown muck. Do we want that same kind of threat hanging over our beloved Granite Springs?

Amelia's forehead puckered as she read on. The urgency in her father's tone was unmistakable:

Any time a large concern—especially one that has no long-standing ties to our region—goes out of its way to acquire control of a vast number of acres, we have to ask why. Do they have the best interests of our community at heart? This writer doesn't think so. And by what means is this land being acquired? The Gazette *will continue to investigate so the light of truth can shine in Granite Springs.*

Amelia went through the rest of the articles. Then she pushed her chair back and made a slow circle around the office. Her father's prose had been impassioned, compelling. But in expressing his opinions, he had never made any outright claims that Great Western was guilty of any wrongdoing— certainly nothing that would warrant demands for a retraction or an offer to buy the paper. What had gotten the company so stirred up?

And what was the root of her father's obvious animosity toward Great Western? His abhorrence of hydraulic mining and fears for what it might mean for the future of Granite Springs was clear enough. But the recent passage of the Caminetti Bill had made the practice legal again, so the company was within its rights to use the process. As much as her father might dislike the practice, there was nothing illegal about Great Western's actions.

There had to be something more to explain his antagonism. Even on the day of her arrival, he had intimated that something was wrong with the company—something his successor must bring to light. What could it be?

The question stirred her journalistic instincts. She tilted her head and regarded the back issues she had just read. What sparked the drive for her father to print these pieces? She knew her father's methods—he wouldn't have written something like this without compiling a file containing notes, research, and a list of sources.

Maybe these columns were meant to spark interest throughout the community, laying the groundwork before making his full case against Great Western. Amelia paced the office from one end to the other, thoughts flying through her mind at a rapid pace. If she could find his notes and piece them together, she could discover the truth her father sought and make it known. It would be a fitting way to carry on his legacy.

And it might provide exactly the boost the *Gazette* needed to sell more papers. A sense of elation swelled within her. Maybe she had struck gold, after all.

CHAPTER 5

"B en, could you step in here for a moment?"

Ben Stone lifted his head at the sound of Owen Merrick's voice and got to his feet. "I'll be right there, sir."

He straightened his tie, slicked back his hair with the palms of his hands, pulled his jacket from its resting place on the back of his chair, and slipped it on as he crossed the distance to Merrick's office with quick strides. A summons to his boss's inner sanctum didn't happen every day.

After three months in the employ of Great Western, he still felt as if he was trying to find his place within the company. His work was beyond reproach—he took pains to make certain of that—but for all his striving, he'd never received the level of trust Merrick gave Eddie Franklin, his co-worker.

It wasn't for lack of trying, though. Ever since his arrival in Granite Springs, he'd done his best to negotiate land purchases. Was it Ben's fault if few of the locals seemed interested in selling? Franklin seemed to have found a way to make some inroads, though. How he managed it, Ben didn't know, but his success along that line made him Merrick's favored employee, to the point that Ben found himself relegated more to researching ownership and writing up contracts. *Little more than a clerk.* His lips twisted at the idea.

A new thought struck him, and his steps slowed as he reached the doorway. Could something be wrong? A knot tightened in his stomach. As hard as he worked, he still had a lot to learn about Great Western's business. Had he unwittingly committed some infraction? And if so, would he merely be reprimanded, or sent packing? *Please, not that!* The idea of returning to the East wasn't a possibility he wanted to entertain.

Pausing only long enough to breathe a quick prayer and compose his features before crossing the threshold, he stepped inside. "Yes, sir?"

Owen Merrick looked up from behind his gleaming mahogany desk and waved Ben to a wooden chair facing him. Ben took the seat indicated and settled back against the uncomfortable wooden slats, trying to appear more at ease than he felt.

His employer leaned back in his black leather chair and regarded Ben with a thoughtful gaze. "How do you like it out here, son?"

Ben blinked at the unexpected question. "It's a fine place. I'm very happy to be here."

"You aren't homesick for the East? Granite Springs is a nice enough spot, but it certainly doesn't have the amenities you grew up with in your father's home."

Ben swallowed hard. From the line his employer was taking, it sounded like the ax was about to fall, and he couldn't imagine why. He scrambled to think of any mistakes he might have made. What could he have done wrong? And once that was made clear, would he be given a chance to make it right,

or would he be summarily dismissed? Merrick had a reputation for running a tight ship. Even though Ben had known the
man all his life and felt reasonably comfortable in his presence,
his employer had an undeniable core of steel when crossed.

"It's certainly different from Montgomery County, but it's
a good place in its own right . . . for a man who wants to rise
to the challenge."

Merrick nodded. He pursed his lips and leaned forward
again. "What I'm about to say is a little difficult."

Ben steeled himself for whatever was about to come.

Tenting his fingers, Merrick tapped the tips together and
looked at Ben with a solemn expression. "We're entering a time
when investors might look askance at negative talk about our
company—the kind of talk that has recently been printed in
the local newspaper in opposition to hydraulic mining. There
will always be those who don't share our vision for the future
and are determined to stand in the way of progress, but few of
them speak from such a position of influence. Having stories
in circulation that imply a sizable opposition could be enough
to make investors wonder if they'll receive a timely return. If
those concerns aren't relieved, they may choose to put their
money elsewhere."

Ben nodded. "You mean the stories you asked me to speak
to Mr. Wagner about several weeks ago. I knew you wanted
him to retract something he'd written, but I haven't seen the
articles myself."

Merrick slid open the bottom desk drawer and pulled out
a stack of newspaper clippings, then handed them to Ben.
"These came out about the time you started working for me.
There was so much for you to learn as a new employee, I didn't

want to distract you at that point. But I think now is the right time for you to see what we're up against."

Ben picked up the articles and read them with a growing sense of disbelief that quickly turned to outrage. When he finished, he laid them back on the desk and looked at his boss. "But . . . but these articles make it seem like Great Western is out to destroy this area rather than to help it prosper!"

Merrick's face grew stern. "Exactly. And it's bad enough to see such nonsense in print locally, but it has come to my attention that portions of these articles have been reprinted in papers in Denver and back east."

Ben stared at his employer. "What!"

"I faced Wagner with it head on. I tried to appeal to his sense of honor, but to no avail. The man was utterly inflexible. Once he got the notion in his head that we were up to no good, there was no reasoning with him."

Ben set his mouth in a hard line. "Or maybe reason didn't matter to him. I've seen several instances in the East of newspapers engaged in fear mongering, just so they could boost their circulation."

A sorrowful expression crossed Merrick's face. "Ben, you know the good we're trying to do here. We're succeeding for the most part. But if our investors back east read this drivel— and pull their funding because of it—we might have to cease operations. And that would mean the end of all the plans we have to bring growth and prosperity to this entire area."

Ben sat straight up in his chair. "That's outrageous! Those stories should never have seen the light of day. At the very least, Wagner should have printed a retraction."

Merrick spread his hands wide. "As I told you, I tried to

reason with him. But the more we talked, the more he dug in his heels. I don't like to speak ill of the dead, but I have to admit it's a relief to know we don't have to worry about him anymore. However, the paper didn't die with him. His daughter has taken over the *Gazette*."

"Do you think she might be willing to see reason and print a retraction? Or are you concerned she may pick up the articles where her father left off?"

"I hope she may prove to be more reasonable than her father. From what I've been able to learn, she spent the last ten years in Denver, but she lived here as a child and has returned to visit every summer. She obviously has a heart for this place. If she cares about the people here, she won't want to jeopardize their future by shutting us down."

"That would make sense." Ben felt a glimmer of hope.

"But there is also the possibility her father's influence might cloud her perspective. She may be more interested in taking up his mantle without considering the consequences to her community.

"Something needs to be done." Merrick eyed Ben steadily. "And I believe you're the man for the job."

Ben started, then he leaned forward. "What is it you want me to do?"

Merrick smiled and cleared his throat. "I'm hoping Miss Wagner can be convinced to set the record straight, print a retraction. And that's where you come in."

"You want me to speak to her about it?"

"Not straightaway. This calls for a more delicate approach." Merrick's smile widened. "As I told you, her father and I butted heads more than once, and the man took an unreasoning dislike to me. From the response I got when I spoke to her at his funeral, it would appear she feels the same way. And that isn't surprising, since all she has to go on is her father's skewed perception. She needs a fresh look at Great Western, and that's what I want you to give her."

Ben scooted forward in his chair, his heart quickening. "How can I help?"

"You're close to her in age. It should be easy for you to build a rapport with her and let her see you as a friend. Don't bring up anything about the articles—not at first. Help her see the good in what we do. Convince her that Great Western is a company that will benefit not only this community, but the territory at large."

Ben took a moment to digest what he'd just heard. "I don't know, sir." He took a deep breath and went on, wondering if he was about to bungle an opportunity to win his employer's confidence. "I'm not sure I would be comfortable doing that. It sounds a bit like subterfuge."

To his great relief, Merrick's eyes shone with understanding. "It's to your credit that you feel that way. Your honesty is one of the reasons I picked you for this job. I'm not asking you to deceive Miss Wagner—quite the contrary. I'm asking you to help her see things as they really are."

Ben nodded slowly. "All right, then. How do you want me to go about it? How soon do you want results?"

"This is a matter of some delicacy. It isn't something we can rush. I want you to take all the time you need to build a relationship with the young lady and let her know she can trust you. Once that trust is established, she may be willing to print a retraction . . . or even better, write a story in our favor. Until then, we'll shift some of your duties to the other fellows in the office. I want most of your attention focused on the pursuit of Miss Wagner."

"Pursuit?" Ben drew his brows together. "That almost sounds like you're asking me to initiate a courtship."

Merrick shrugged, and a smile flitted across his face. "Would that be so bad? She's certainly attractive enough. It shouldn't be too much of a hardship for you to spend time with her."

Merrick's smile broadened to a grin. "Ah, if only I'd been charged with a task like this when I was starting out!" He leaned back and gave Ben a wink. "Be sure to let me know how things progress."

Ben nodded and rose to leave. As he reached the door, Merrick's voice stopped him.

"Remember, Ben, this is important. Don't let me down. This could be the making of you . . . and your future."

X

As soon as the door clicked shut behind Ben, another door in the rear of the office swung open and Eddie Franklin slipped into the room.

The tall, lean man eyed the closed door, then turned to Merrick. "So you've sicced him on the girl?"

Merrick nodded.

"Do you think it'll work?"

"Of course it will. And keeping her occupied by young Stone serves a dual purpose. Her father only scratched the surface of what we're doing—thank goodness—and we need to make sure his daughter doesn't stumble onto anything that would interfere with our plans."

"Stone hasn't a clue just how important this is. Do you think he's up to the job?"

Merrick glared at his underling. "He's loyal to the company, and that's what matters. If it doesn't work out the way we hope, we can always find another way to deal with the problem. It didn't take much to take care of Rogers and old man Smith when they wanted to stir things up. They could have caused any number of complications. . . . But they aren't around to trouble us anymore, are they?"

Franklin's eyes narrowed. "You're thinking about getting her out of the way?"

Merrick's jaw tightened. "Don't be so shortsighted, Eddie. Violence is not the only avenue available to us. Intimidation can be just as strong a deterrent, if applied judiciously."

Franklin rubbed the back of his neck. "I don't know about this plan of yours. What if Stone catches on? What then?"

"Why should he? You've seen the girl—she's certainly comely enough. If I were in his shoes, I know I wouldn't be averse to spending as much time with her as I could. He'll be so busy staring into those blue eyes of hers, he won't think twice about anything else."

"I hope you're right."

"You worry too much, Eddie. Go on about your business and relax. I have everything under control." Merrick watched as the man exited through the rear door, then turned back to his desk, trying to tamp down his irritation. It wasn't easy to be a man of vision, especially when those he worked with seemed so blind to the possibilities at their fingertips, just waiting to be grasped.

"What if Stone catches on?" Eddie's question teased at his

mind, and he brushed the bothersome thought away as if it were a pesky fly.

Ben was a smart young man, no doubt about it. But in many ways, he was like his father, trusting his friends—or those he saw as friends—too easily. He had jumped at the chance to join Great Western here in Arizona, looking upon his father's boyhood companion as a kindly mentor.

Merrick chuckled. No worries about Ben Stone. He had the boy in the palm of his hand. Why should Ben ever look beyond the genial, caring surface?

His father never did.

CHAPTER 6

"S o you actually saw the mountain lion go after the Evanses' chickens?" Amelia held her pencil poised over her notebook and waited for Emmett Kingston's answer. When Jimmy had burst through the door of the *Gazette* with news of the lion sighting, she had found it difficult to muster up much excitement. On the other hand, it might be the most newsworthy story of the week.

The storekeeper strode out the front door of his mercantile with Amelia on his heels. Taking a stance in the middle of the boardwalk, he pointed south, toward the neat frame houses lining the near end of Sheridan Street. "I was sweeping the porch early yesterday morning, when I heard chickens squawking. Since the store is right on the corner, I have a clear view of the Evans property. I saw this big cat trotting away with one of their hens in its mouth. He headed that way, farther down the street, and then went right in front of . . . of . . ." He shot a nervous glance Amelia's way and trailed off.

Amelia followed his gaze and understood his discomfiture at once. The town's brothels lay at the far end of Sheridan. She nodded, keeping her expression neutral. "Did you see where it went after that?"

Emmett gave her a grateful look and went on. "Nope. As far as I know, it headed on back to the woods." He shook his head, as if reliving the memory. "I haven't seen a mountain lion in town for years, and never one that size. Who'd think I'd spot one right down the street, and in broad daylight?"

Amelia scribbled frantically in her notebook, then looked up at the store owner. "I think that's all I need. Thank you for your time."

"My pleasure, Miss Amelia." Emmett tugged at the waist of his apron. "By the way, I just wanted to tell you how glad everyone is that you decided to keep the paper going. You *are* staying on permanently, right?"

"Yes, that's my plan."

"That's good to know." He cleared his throat. "It's probably none of my business, but as a businessman, I know how tight money can get from time to time. Not saying that's the case with you, but if you ever do find yourself in a bind, I thought you should know Great Western just purchased a couple pieces of land near that property your father bought out near Sawmill Road. If you're in need of cash, you might want to talk to them."

Amelia's jaw dropped. "What property are you talking about?"

Emmett's face reddened. "I'm sorry, I figured you knew. He bought it from Virgil Sparks when he was getting ready to head back to Arkansas. Great Western made an offer on the place, but Virgil didn't like those folks any better than your father did. I don't think your dad planned to do anything in particular with it. He just wanted to keep it out of Great

Western's hands. Like I said, it's none of my business, but I thought I'd mention it, just in case the information might come in handy someday."

"Thank you," Amelia said. "Things aren't that tight right now, but I'll be sure to keep it in mind." *For more reasons than one.* Maybe Emmett could help clarify her father's distrust. "Do you know why my father was so set against Great Western? I know he despised the practice of hydraulic mining, but was there more to it than that?"

Emmett shifted from one foot to another and appeared to turn the question over in his mind. "Can't say that I do. He was always talking about how they could destroy this whole area, like what happened over in California. But I really don't know anything beyond that."

Amelia thanked him again and tucked the pencil and notebook back in her reticule, making a mental checklist of the things she still needed to accomplish that day. The afternoon train was due to arrive momentarily. She could stop by the station to take note of new arrivals before she went back to the newspaper to write up her story on the mountain lion and warn residents to be watchful.

And that would probably be the most exciting item on this week's front-page news. She grimaced, then realized Emmett Kingston was still speaking.

" . . . thinkin' I ought to put another ad in the paper. I got a new shipment of ladies' hats and dresses day before yesterday, and I need to let folks know about it."

Amelia brightened. "We'll be happy to accommodate you. Just stop by the paper. I'll be out and about for a while, but Homer is there now. He can work with you to set up the ad."

"Maybe I'll wait 'til you get back." Emmett shoved his hands in his apron pockets and rocked back on his heels. "No offense to Homer, but this one needs a woman's point of view."

"Why don't we work on it tomorrow morning? That will give us time to have it ready for this week's issue."

"Sounds good." Emmett turned back toward the store. "I'll see you then."

Bidding him good-bye, Amelia started toward the station, trying to keep her excitement from showing.

Why was Great Western interested in Virgil Sparks's property and the land around it? As far as she could remember, that area had been used for nothing but farmland. Had her father discovered some other plan that would be detrimental to the region and purchased the property to keep Great Western from moving ahead? Was that the truth he hoped his successor would uncover?

Amelia's pulse quickened. The Sparks place lay only a couple of miles beyond the sawmill—barely an hour's journey by buggy. She would have to make plans to go out there one day soon and see what she could discover. Perhaps it would be her chance to gain her first tangible piece of evidence of what had been preying on her father's mind.

Her steps slowed, and she halted to check the sun's position in the western sky. *Why wait?* The train would arrive any minute, but Thomas Rafferty would be glad to fill her in about new arrivals later. She knew how much he enjoyed his role as a ready source of information.

She swung around and headed for the livery. A few steps later, she stopped to reconsider. While she felt perfectly safe strolling the streets of Granite Springs on her own, the area beyond the sawmill was only sparsely settled. Would venturing out there alone be a wise thing to do?

But she was a journalist, and a journalist followed the story. How many times had she heard her father say that? The answer to her questions might lie within easy reach. She needed to go out and take a quick look around. She ignored her misgivings as she checked the sun's position again. A few minutes for Carl Olsen to get the buggy ready, then an hour out and another hour back—less, if she kept the horse to a brisk trot. That left enough time to do some investigating and still be back in town before sunset.

With her mind made up, she angled across First Street and headed toward the livery. A man stood leaning against the corner of the Great Western building. As she drew nearer, he stepped out, and she recognized Ben Stone.

Her steps faltered. She had no desire to converse with anyone from Great Western. Maybe later, when she had gathered more information and could formulate specific questions, but not now. Avoiding his eyes, she focused on a point farther along the street and picked up her pace.

To her chagrin, he stepped off the boardwalk and tipped his hat. "Good afternoon, Miss Wagner."

Amelia drew herself up and hitched her reticule higher on her arm. "Good day to you, Mr. Stone." She sidestepped, intending to sweep past him. Instead, he turned and fell into step beside her.

She swallowed back an indignant *huff*. Why couldn't he have taken the hint? True, he wasn't doing anything wrong; he had as much right to walk down the street as she did. But the man worked for Owen Merrick, and she didn't trust Great Western's vice president one bit.

On the other hand . . . She tried to tamp down her impatience and shot a quick glance to her side as they stepped up onto the boardwalk, remembering the look of compassion she had seen on his face at the cemetery. But a fleeting expression didn't necessarily reflect what lay within a man's heart.

He cleared his throat, and her shoulders tensed. The obtuse man obviously hadn't picked up on her lack of desire to speak with him. What was she supposed to do to make her feelings clear, swing her reticule at his head? Tempting as the idea seemed, she pushed it aside and walked faster.

"I hear the Ladies Auxiliary is holding a poetry reading at the church next Saturday."

"Oh?" Amelia kept her tone cool.

"I was wondering if you might like to attend it with me."

Amelia stopped dead and gaped up at him. "I . . . Thank you, but I believe I'll be attending with Mr. Crenshaw."

"Oh." Her unwelcome escort seemed at a loss for words. "Well, then . . . I hope you have a pleasant time. Perhaps I'll see you there."

Amelia dipped her head in a curt nod. "Perhaps. Excuse me, but I must be going now. There are some matters I must attend to." She moved on quickly, relieved when he didn't follow as she walked toward the livery at the corner of First and Railroad. She would have to remember to mention to Homer that he would be escorting her to the poetry reading . . . if he wasn't put off by the prospect that Hyacinth Parmenter would probably also be in attendance.

Her steps slowed when she came to the weathered, board-

and-batten building with *Olsen's Livery* lettered over the door. The rich scent of hay and horses filled her nostrils when she stepped inside. "Mr. Olsen?" she called.

The owner of the livery appeared from one of the farther stalls with a pitchfork in his hand. His face lit up when he saw Amelia. "Well, hello, Miss Wagner. What can I do for you?"

"I apologize for the short notice, but could you hitch up my father's horse and buggy for me?"

"Sure, I'll have it done in a jiffy." Mr. Olsen glanced outside and looked back at her with a trace of a frown. "You aren't going to be gone long, are you? The days are growing longer, but it's a little late to start on a lengthy drive."

Amelia smiled. "Don't worry. I'll only be gone a couple of hours."

Looking relieved, he pulled a harness from its peg on the wall and headed to the stall that housed Smokey, the dapple-gray gelding her father had purchased three years before. He slipped the bridle over the horse's head and led him back to the center of the alleyway.

While he finished putting on the harness, Amelia walked over and ran her palm down the gray's sleek neck. Smokey whickered and nosed at her hand, looking for a treat.

Amelia laughed and stroked his velvety nose. "I'm sorry, boy. I didn't bring anything with me this time."

Carl Olsen led Smokey outside, where he made short work of hooking him up to the shiny black buggy. Extending a work-worn hand, he helped Amelia up into the seat and handed her the reins.

"Thank you so much," she said. "I'll see you in a couple of hours."

She clicked her tongue at the gelding and guided him along First Street before turning left onto Jefferson Road, leading out to the sawmill. Smokey covered the dusty ground at a smart clip. With every turn of the wheels, Amelia felt her spirits rise, and a sense of peace seeped into her mind. How wonderful to be free—if only for a brief time—of the responsibilities for keeping the paper afloat!

Fragrant, pine-covered slopes rose above the road on her right, while off to the south, the rolling Bradshaw Mountains loomed in the distance. The warm sunlight, the twittering birds, and the white puffy clouds scudding their way across the late afternoon sky combined to bring back memories of carefree childhood days, before her parents' marriage fragmented and her family was torn apart.

As if sensing her nostalgic mood, the gelding's pace slowed, and Amelia turned her attention back to the moment. She and Smokey were on a mission. This was no time for woolgathering.

She slapped the reins against the gelding's hindquarters, moving him back into a brisk trot. Sitting erect with both hands on the reins, she tilted her head slightly, the better to enjoy the light breeze that fanned her face.

She and the horse noticed the snake at the same time—a long, mottled brown shape that slithered to the edge of the road and coiled itself into a threatening posture, head up and ready to strike. A sharp rattle buzzed through the air.

Smokey let out a sharp whinny and sprang to the left, jerking the buggy and throwing Amelia off balance. She recovered quickly, guiding him over to the far left side of the road and leaving the rattlesnake behind.

"Good boy. You didn't let him spook you." She kept her tone low and soothing. After a fearful glance over his shoulder, the horse nickered and went on his way, though his high-stepping gait gave proof of his agitation.

The road curved, and a stretch of dense cedar growth came into view. Amelia's lips curved into a smile, remembering the happy hours she had spent exploring the heavily wooded grove with her best friend, Callie Jacobs, and her siblings. The dark tangle of trees formed a nearly impenetrable thicket, providing the perfect setting for countless games of hide-and-seek.

A wistful sigh escaped her lips. Those days were long gone. Like herself, her friends had grown up and moved on. Callie now lived in Phoenix, where her husband managed a hotel, and her sister had moved to Tucson. Their oldest brother headed to California, where he'd planted orange groves in the San Bernardino Valley. A few other schoolmates still lived near Granite Springs, but they were married now and busy with families of their own.

A sudden jarring brought her back to the present. The buggy jounced into the air and thudded back to earth, where it began swerving from side to side. Amelia let out a yelp and looked back over her shoulder, berating herself when she saw a large rock in the road. She should have been paying more attention.

Smokey, already jittery from the encounter with the snake, put on a burst of speed. Amelia tugged on the reins, fighting to keep the vehicle under control as the buggy careened from one side of the dusty road to the other.

She seesawed on the reins, hauling back on them for all she was worth. The buggy bounced again, and she saw one of the wheels roll past her and veer off the road to the right. Without warning, the buggy tilted to one side and the tip of the axle jammed into the dirt, bringing the vehicle to an abrupt halt.

With the buggy thus anchored, Smokey had no choice but to stop. He pranced and snorted while Amelia clung to the slanting buggy seat with one hand and the reins with the other.

It took her several moments to catch her breath and send up a quick prayer of thanks that she hadn't been injured. *But what about Smokey?* With the hand holding the reins, she reached for the brake handle, then realized there was little point in setting it. The buggy wasn't about to go anywhere. Looping the reins around the brake, she slid down to the end of the seat and lowered herself to the ground.

Smokey pawed the dirt with his front hoof when she approached, sending up clouds of tawny dust. Amelia stroked his neck and murmured calming words. After a few minutes he settled somewhat, though his eyes still flared wide. She ran her hand down each leg, assuring herself the horse had escaped injury. With that done, she walked back to assess the damage done to the buggy.

The axle wasn't broken, as far as she could determine. That was a relief, but what was she to do now? She couldn't move the buggy in its present condition. And even if she could find the wheel and somehow fashion a lever, she couldn't lift the buggy to replace the wheel on her own.

She eyed Smokey and pursed her lips. Could she unhook the buggy and ride him back to town? If she did manage to get him loose, would he stand still long enough for her to find a way to mount? She shook her head, dismissing the idea. It wouldn't be worth the risk. If the horse ran off, she would be utterly stranded.

Shielding her eyes, she checked the sun's position. It had dropped nearly a handspan lower in the sky since she'd left the livery. She chewed on her lower lip. If she left Smokey and the buggy and walked back to Granite Springs, it would be nearly dark when she arrived. Then she would have to ask Mr. Olsen to come out to retrieve her horse and repair the buggy. He'd be out there half the night.

Her shoulders slumped. Look what her impulsive decision had cost her! It wouldn't be right to leave poor Smokey out there alone. He'd already been spooked enough. No telling what danger he might get himself into if she left him on his own. She would either have to stay with him until someone happened to come along, or figure out a way to ride him back to town.

Or . . . she took a deep breath. If she could get Smokey free of the buggy, she could lead him. It would still be late when she arrived, but at least she would be sure the horse was safe. Stepping over to his side, she lifted her hands and started fumbling with the harness when the gelding flicked his ears backwards. He nickered again, and his eyes grew wide.

Amelia took a step back and scanned the ground. Had Smokey's keen senses detected another snake?

A moment later, she heard the faint *clip-clop* of hooves on the packed dirt road, somewhere beyond the curve. Her heart leapt. A rider was coming!

She took a stance in the middle of the road, ready to greet her potential rescuer. Then caution asserted itself. What was she thinking? She had no idea what kind of person might be coming her way. Without further deliberation, she left Smokey standing in the road and faded back into the close-set cedars.

CHAPTER 7

Amelia ducked under a low branch and moved back into deeper cover. The hoofbeats grew nearer, but the thick tangle of branches screened the approaching figure. The rider must have spied the wreck, because she heard the horse pick up its pace.

When he reached the disabled buggy, the rider stopped and dismounted. Holding her breath, Amelia peeked between the cedar branches and could make out a figure rushing to the buggy and looking inside. He turned around and cupped his hands around his mouth. "Miss Wagner! Where are you? Are you all right?"

Relief flooded Amelia when she recognized Ben Stone. Had it only been an hour before that she was ready to swat him away with her reticule? Now he seemed more like a knight in shining armor, come to rescue her from her plight.

Pushing the concealing branches aside, she stepped out of her hiding place. "I'm over here."

Ben rushed to her side, concern written on his face. "Are you hurt? Were you thrown from the buggy?"

Heat tinged Amelia's cheeks. "I heard you coming, but I

didn't know who it was. I wanted to be sure it was safe before I showed myself."

A light glowed in Ben's eyes. "I'm glad you're all right . . . and that you felt you could trust me." Turning back to the buggy, he walked over and bent to study the axle. "The cotter pin is missing."

Amelia frowned. "How could that have happened? Did it break? And what can we do about it?"

"I have an idea that may work." He turned around in a slow circle. "Do you have any idea where the wheel went?"

Amelia pointed toward the right side of the road. "It rolled off that way."

He disappeared into a dense clump of manzanita and buckbrush. A moment later he reemerged, carrying the wheel by its spokes. Back at the buggy, he leaned the wheel against the side and set the brake. Then he squatted next to the axle and gripped the underside of the buggy. "When I pick this up, can you slide the wheel onto the axle?"

Amelia nodded, and he began to lift. She could see the muscles in his shoulders stretch the fabric of his shirt as he strained to raise the buggy high enough. She watched for the moment as the axle lined up with the hub of the wheel, then she wiggled the wheel onto the shaft.

"Is it in place yet?" he asked through gritted teeth.

"It's on as far as I can make it go."

He eased his grip, not turning loose completely until he assured himself the wheel would support the buggy's weight.

Amelia looked up at him. "Now what? How can we keep it from coming off again?"

"Give me a minute, and I'll show you." Ben eyed the hole

where the cotter pin had been, then he walked over to a scrub oak. Pulling out his pocketknife, he cut off a small branch. As he walked back to the buggy, he began whittling the smaller end. After tapering it down, he jammed it into the hole and tapped it into place with a rock.

"There you are." He stood back, admiring his work.

Amelia tilted her head. "Are you sure that will work?"

"If we take it easy, it should hold long enough for us to get back to town." When Amelia eyed him doubtfully, he chuckled. "What do you think they used on the old Conestogas that rolled all the way across the prairie?"

"Surely they used something more sturdy than a twig."

"Granted, but it's the same principle. If it worked for them, it should work for us . . . at least as far as Granite Springs." Ben walked back to lead his own horse to the buggy and tied it to the rear.

Amelia stared at him. "What are you doing?"

He shrugged. "You didn't think I was just going to send you off on your own, did you?"

She opened her mouth to protest, then reconsidered. What if the improvised pin broke on the way back? Who knew how long it would take for someone else to come along. Did she really want to be out alone on this road after nightfall? Catching up her skirt in one hand, she scrambled into the buggy, not waiting for him to help her up.

Without comment, he circled around to the other side and took his seat before gathering the reins and setting Smokey off at a walk. Amelia sat rigidly upright, hands folded primly in her lap. Being stranded had unnerved her enough to let her guard down when Ben arrived, but now that the danger was over . . .

The buggy wheel dipped down into a rut in the road and bounced back out again. Amelia held her breath, but the substitute cotter pin held fast. The slight pitch of the buggy jostled Ben to one side, and their shoulders brushed. Amelia drew in a quick breath and slid as far to the right of the seat as she could.

"I'm sorry your journey was interrupted," Ben said. "What brought you out this way?"

Amelia flicked a glance at him, then looked away. "I wanted to check into something, but I guess I'll have to do that another time." She slid her right hand from her lap and clutched the edge of the seat to steady herself against the swaying motion of the buggy.

Ben held the reins in a sure grip and kept his eyes on the road ahead. "I admire you for taking on the newspaper. That's quite a venture for anyone—especially a woman alone. But you seem to be up to the challenge."

Amelia eyed him narrowly, trying to decide whether his tone held sincerity or sarcasm. To her surprise, she saw only honest admiration in his gaze.

"Your employer doesn't seem to share your opinion. He offered to buy the *Gazette* before I had a chance to run it into the ground."

He whipped his head around to face her fully. "He did? When?"

"The day of my father's funeral. Just after they lowered his casket into the ground." Speaking the words aloud brought back the bitter memory of that unhealed wound.

Ben's eyes shadowed, and he shook his head. "I'm sorry. I'm sure the offer was made in good faith, but his timing was deplorable."

So even Owen Merrick's own employee recognized how rude and thoughtless his actions had been. Amelia allowed herself to relax enough to let her shoulder blades touch the back of the padded seat while the buggy rolled along. After the tension of the past few weeks, it felt good to allow someone else to take over and relieve her of even this small responsibility.

The breeze stirred the curls at her temples, soothing her even more. Under different circumstances, an evening buggy ride with the soft, pastel hues of approaching sunset threading their way across the sky and a handsome man beside her would have been heavenly. But this man worked for Great Western.

Watch yourself, Amelia. Much as she'd been enjoying Benjamin Stone's company, she didn't dare let down her guard completely. Just because he had helped her in her recent plight, it didn't mean his motives were pure. She pulled herself erect, and they rode the rest of the distance to town in silence.

When they pulled up in front of the livery, Carl Olsen hurried out to greet them. He slid to a stop, and his mouth dropped open when he spotted Ben driving the buggy and his horse tied behind. Recovering quickly, he turned his attention back to Amelia. "So, you went out for an evening drive . . . ?"

Amelia felt her face flame. Up to now, she was just grateful to have made it back to town safely. Until she saw the goggle-eyed look on Mr. Olsen's face, she hadn't considered what other people's reactions might be at seeing her in Ben's company. She forced herself to answer calmly. "I had a bit of a mishap with the buggy wheel, and Mr. Stone was kind enough to rescue me."

Ben stepped to the ground nonchalantly, as if coming to

the aid of damsels in distress was something he did every day of the week. As he walked around the back of the buggy, he patted the right wheel. "'A bit of a mishap' may be an understatement. This wheel came off while Miss Wagner was driving. It's a good thing she wasn't seriously hurt."

While the livery owner bent to examine the damaged wheel, Ben moved forward to help Amelia down. Her mouth went dry when his strong hands spanned her waist, and her breath left her lungs in a *whoosh*. Seemingly unaware of her response to his touch, he walked over to explain about the cotter pin and point out his improvised solution.

Mr. Olsen placed both hands on the wheel and wiggled it back and forth. He examined the makeshift cotter pin, and his face reddened. "I don't know how I could have missed that the pin was damaged." He straightened and faced Amelia. "I'm sure glad you weren't hurt. I'll go over every bit of this buggy and make sure it's in top shape before you take it out again."

"Thank you," said Amelia. "I wouldn't want to put my guardian angel to the test too often."

"It will be dark soon," Ben said. "May I escort you home?"

Amelia frowned. "What about your horse?"

"He'll be fine. I'll only be gone a few minutes."

She didn't really need an escort now that she was back in town. But in the face of Carl Olsen's curious gaze, she decided not to argue. It was obvious the livery owner had questions about her encounter with Ben. No point in giving him more reason to speculate.

Ben smiled and offered his arm. Amelia hesitated, then she tucked her fingers in the crook of his elbow. Their heels thudded softly along the boardwalk until they reached the *Gazette* building, where a single light shone inside the printing office. Ben opened the door, and Amelia walked in first.

Homer looked up from setting a column of type. "There you are. I wondered where you'd gotten off to." His smile faded when Ben stepped in behind her.

Removing his hat, he nodded to Homer, then turned to Amelia. "I'm glad we got you home safe and sound. I hope the rest of your evening goes better." With that, he nodded again to Homer and took his leave.

Homer strode across the floor while Amelia busied herself with the lock. His head swiveled back and forth, looking first at her, then out the front window. "Safe and sound? What was that all about?"

Amelia sagged back against the door. "I wanted to check on something out at the old Sparks place, so I started out there in the buggy. But the wheel came off while I was passing the cedar thicket. If Mr. Stone hadn't come along and helped me, I might still be stranded out there."

Homer's eyes bulged, and he sputtered like a teakettle on the boil. "What were you thinking, taking off that late in the day?"

"Emmett Kingston told me Papa bought that land. It's the first I'd heard about it, so I thought I'd go out and take a look." Amelia removed her hat and hung it on the coatrack near the door, hoping the move would keep Homer from seeing the flush that tinged her cheeks at the reminder of her foolishness. "It seemed a good idea at the time." Smoothing her skirt with her hands, she turned back to face him. "But I'm fine. And Carl Olsen feels terrible about it. He couldn't apologize enough for not having noticed it was damaged."

"Unless the problem was man-made."

She shot a sharp glance at him, startled at the frown that darkened his face. "What do you mean?"

"What was young Stone doing out there? Seems to me it was awfully convenient that he happened to come along just when you needed help."

"I didn't ask what he was doing there. You aren't suggesting he had something to do with the cotter pin, are you?"

Homer snorted. "I wouldn't put it past any of that Great Western bunch. He may not be as bad as Merrick or some of the others, but you can't lie down with dogs and not get up with fleas."

Amelia was too tired to argue. The keyed-up emotions that had sustained her throughout her adventure seeped away, leaving her empty and exhausted. "We can talk about that another time. I'm just glad he came along when he did." She stood on tiptoe to brush a kiss on Homer's lined cheek. "Lock the back door when you leave, will you? I'm turning in for the night."

Upstairs in her room, she went through the motions of getting ready to retire and tumbled into bed, letting out a blissful sigh as she stretched out on the sheets and her head sank into the pillow. Worn out as she was, her mind kept drifting back to her panic when the wheel sailed off, and the relief she felt at Ben's timely rescue.

Homer might have found the coincidence to be suspicious, but if Ben hadn't come along, she would have had to deal with a most unpleasant—and possibly dangerous—situation on her own. She was grateful for his chivalrous assistance.

Her eyelids drifted shut, only to fly open again an instant later, remembering her earlier encounter with Ben Stone that afternoon. He'd extended his invitation to the poetry reading, and she had turned him down abruptly before walking off to leave him standing alone on the boardwalk.

Amelia pushed herself up on her elbows and stared into the darkness. She had made no mention of leaving town, she was sure of it. Nor had she spoken of going to the livery.

By the time he came upon the wrecked buggy, she was well hidden in the tangle of cedars, yet he'd immediately called her name and asked if she was all right. Her chest tightened, and she struggled to draw a breath.

Ben had asked her what she was doing out on that lonely road . . . but he never explained his own reason for being there. What brought him out to the scene of the wreck?

And if Ben had nothing to do with the accident, how could he have known whose buggy it was?

※

Ben pulled the saddle from his horse. The leather creaked as he set it atop the saddle rack. After slipping a canvas feedbag filled with grain over the animal's head, he took the currycomb from its hook on the wall. He ran it along the horse's back with long, smooth strokes, while the sound of steady munching filled the quiet of the dim barn.

"I hope you enjoy your dinner, boy. It's too late for mine." Mrs. Taylor, the proprietress of his boardinghouse on the outskirts of town, made it clear from the outset that the evening meal would be served punctually at six. If her boarders didn't make it to the table on time, they would be responsible for getting their supper elsewhere. He had missed that deadline by a couple of hours.

Removing the empty feedbag with a pang of envy, he led

the horse to its stall and threw a forkful of fragrant hay into the enclosure. His stomach growled as he slid his hands into his pockets and strolled outside the barn. A few lights still gleamed from within the boardinghouse, but Ben didn't feel ready to go inside just yet.

Walking over to the split-rail fence that marked the edge of Mrs. Taylor's property, he leaned against the top rail and tipped his head back to look up at the inky night sky. The clouds he'd seen earlier had disappeared, leaving the sky looking as though it had been swept clean to afford a perfect view of the stars overhead. From where he stood, he could pick out Orion, the Seven Sisters, and Cassiopeia in their stately march across the sky.

He let out a long sigh, wishing his own path could be as sure as theirs. When he'd accepted the assignment to strike up an acquaintance with the *Gazette*'s new editor, the task had seemed simple enough. But he hadn't anticipated the difficulties that might arise.

When Amelia Wagner abruptly refused his invitation and sailed off down First Street without a backward glance, the rebuff had stung. What had he done to warrant that kind of reaction? From what he'd learned during their drive in the buggy, she held a fair amount of resentment about Owen Merrick's offer to purchase the newspaper. Ben could see her point on that. The overture had been ill-timed, indeed. *But I'm not Merrick.*

It was obvious Homer Crenshaw didn't like him, either—or anyone who worked at Great Western. Maybe his attitude had influenced hers. But Ben hadn't approached her on a business matter—which made her refusal seem all the more personal.

When she told him she had things to attend to, he assumed she was on her way back to the newspaper, or perhaps to the café for an early dinner. Instead, she'd marched straight to the livery stable.

That move had puzzled him, so he'd taken up a post in a nearby alleyway and waited. Fifteen minutes later, she reappeared, driving a dapple-gray gelding. With his curiosity thoroughly piqued, he ducked back into the alley and trotted along on a course parallel to hers, hurrying to keep the buggy in sight, and watched her turn onto the road that led southwest out of town.

The only business along Jefferson Road was the sawmill, which had already closed for the day. Try as he might, he hadn't been able to think of any logical reason for an evening visit. But whatever her destination, that route was the only way she could take back to town.

Sprinting back to his boardinghouse, he'd hurried to the barn and saddled his horse, then followed the same route she had taken. She had to return to town sometime. And if he just happened to be on that road when she drove back, it would give him the opportunity to strike up another conversation.

When he'd rounded the curve and saw the buggy canted to one side at a crazy angle on the edge of the lonely road, a surge of panic had coursed through him, wondering if she'd been thrown out and injured . . . maybe even killed?

He'd wanted to whoop with relief when she came straggling out of that dense stand of cedars—even more so when she seemed to welcome his presence. She hadn't even raised an objection when he stated his intention to drive the buggy back to town.

And he had to admire her presence of mind. She hadn't flown into hysterics at being stranded, which would have been the first reaction of most women of his acquaintance. His admiration for her had only grown when she told him about her plan to unharness her horse and lead it back to town. Amelia Wagner was one determined woman—and one he was eager to know better. He didn't need an assignment from his boss to convince him of that.

He smiled, remembering the look of her glossy brown curls dancing around her heart-shaped face, and the way her wide blue eyes shone when he'd managed to repair the buggy wheel. Even though following his boss's order was the initial reason for striking up an acquaintance, it was going to be very easy to spend time in Amelia Wagner's company.

CHAPTER 8

Amelia could hear the rhythmic clank and squeal as Homer worked the treadle of the Peerless press. She stared down at her freshly-penned lines.

> We appreciate the support shown by the citizens of Granite Springs during this difficult time. Though under new management, your new editor wants to assure you the Gazette will continue its founder's commitment to shine the light of truth on local happenings, with a view toward bettering our community.

Had she captured the proper tone in her first editorial since taking over the paper? What about the length? The piece was concise and to the point, but there was so much more to say, so many things that she wanted to share with her readers.

The sound of the press ceased, and Homer's head appeared in the open office door. "Is your editorial ready to go? I just finished that new round of tally sheets for Harlan Griggs over at the Brass Rail, and I'd like to finish setting the front page while they dry."

"I'm almost finished. Just a minute more."

"'Once more unto the breach, dear friends, once more.'" Homer thrust his arm forward in dramatic fashion as he turned back to the printing office.

Amelia wrinkled her nose, wondering if she detected a faint whiff of alcohol mingled with the smell of printer's ink. Had Homer been tippling? She thought back to the line he'd just quoted from Shakespeare's *King Henry V* and the wide swing of his arm that accompanied it and nibbled on her lower lip. It was nothing out of the ordinary for Homer to throw out a line of poetry, but his gestures always became more flamboyant when he'd been nipping at the bottle.

A tendril of worry threaded its way up her spine. When her father first met Homer, he recognized the man's redeeming qualities despite his bent for heavy drinking. He'd taken Homer under his wing, helped him sober up, and introduced him to the Lord when Amelia was a small child. From that point on, Homer turned his back on alcohol . . . for the most part. Amelia had several vivid memories of times when he slipped back into his old ways when under pressure.

But they were both under pressure now. She pressed her lips together and tried to rein in her impatient thoughts. At the moment, her main objective was getting this week's paper out. She could question him about his drinking later.

She took a moment to scan the editorial once more, then picked up her pen and rolled it between her fingers. How should she sign the piece? Everyone in Granite Springs knew that Andrew James Wagner was no longer the proprietor of the *Gazette,* but this would be her first official declaration that she was now the one at the helm.

She chewed her lip again while she turned over several possibilities in her mind. Then she smiled. Her father had always used his initials: A. J. Wagner. And her name was Amelia Jane.

Dipping her pen in the inkwell, she scrawled *A. J. Wagner* across the bottom of the page with a flourish. It was a way of blending the old with the new, one more proof that the *Gazette*'s mission had not changed.

Taking the paper to the printing office, she picked up a composing stick and carried the shallow metal tray to the type cabinet. "What's left to set up for the front page?"

"It's nearly done." Homer glanced at the written page in front of her and grimaced. "I was hoping that editorial would be longer. It would have given us an excuse to leave out that Mrs. Parmenter's treacly excuse for a poem."

Amelia hid a smile. "It is a bit much, isn't it?"

"'Golden orb and honey'd trills.'" Homer snorted. "The *Gazette* has a reputation as a respected newspaper. I don't know why you agreed to print that tripe in the first place."

"The *Gazette* is also a voice of the community. And Hyacinth Parmenter's voice is going to be telling all her friends to buy a copy of the paper that showcased her masterpiece. Think of it as a good business move."

"Once you let her start, you won't be able to stop her. She'll expect you to keep right on printing more every week."

"As a matter of fact"—Amelia reached under the counter and drew forth a sheet of paper—"she dropped this off yesterday so we'd have plenty of time to work it into the next issue."

Homer moved closer and bent to read the flowing script: "'White, woolly clouds mass o'er the land, and skip along like gamboling lambs.'" His mouth dropped open. "Have mercy."

"She obviously has a love of verse." Amelia gave him a teasing grin. "Maybe all she needs is a guiding hand. Someone who could explain to her the intricacies of true poetry. Maybe you should take her under your wing. . . . You could think of it as doing a service to the community."

Homer glowered at her. "Not on your tintype, missy."

Amelia laughed, and then her face grew somber. While she fitted the small pieces of type into the composing stick, she asked, "Why didn't Papa ever tell me about buying that property from Virgil Sparks?"

Homer shrugged. "Maybe with more important things on his mind, he just didn't get around to it. The main reason he bought that land was to help Virgil out. At first, he thought he might hold on to it for a couple of years and see if it would increase in value. When he found out Great Western was interested in it, he started looking at it like a game of checkers, where he was able to keep them from gobbling up everything in that area."

Amelia nodded. That would explain why her father wanted to keep control of the property. But it didn't answer the question of why Great Western was so interested in that section.

))(

By the end of the afternoon, the week's edition was folded, stacked, and ready to deliver. Amelia let out a sigh of relief and started to swipe her hand across her forehead to push back a tumble of curls, but she stopped when she realized how smudged her fingers were.

Homer kicked a heap of paper scraps to one corner of the floor and picked up a rag to clean his hands. Maybe now was the time to ask him about the alcohol she thought she smelled earlier. She took a step forward and cleared her throat.

Before she could speak, the front door burst open, and Jimmy Brandt arrived, right on cue. "Is the paper finished?"

Amelia sighed and forced a smile. "Perfect timing, as always." She helped Jimmy load his canvas bag and watched him and Homer set out on their delivery rounds. She would have to bring up the drinking another time . . . if she had been correct in her assessment. Homer hadn't seemed impaired in the least, so maybe it hadn't been alcohol she smelled.

She wet a rag with coal oil and began cleaning the type. Just as she completed the task, a movement outside caught her eye, and she recognized Clara Gilbreth passing by. Hurrying over to the front window, Amelia tapped on the glass to catch the other woman's attention and went outside to greet her.

Clara looked at Amelia in surprise. "I thought you'd be hard at work getting the paper out."

"We just finished. Jimmy and Homer are out making deliveries, and I'm ready to take a breather as soon as I clean the ink off my hands. Would you like to walk to the café with me and help me celebrate with a cup of tea?"

A grin creased Clara's face. "If you're willing to stop at Kingston's store first. I need to pick up a packet of pins."

As they walked to the general store, Amelia spotted Jimmy darting from one house to another along the residential section of Jefferson Road. Once Clara finished her errand, they headed toward the café.

"I heard a whisper around town." Clara shot her a sidelong glance as they walked down First Street toward the café. "Something about you having trouble on the road out near the sawmill the other night. Or was it more like a fortuitous encounter?"

Amelia sucked in her breath and tried to answer in a casual

tone. "It was nothing, really. I was just taking a drive, and the buggy lost a wheel. Mr. Stone happened to come along just then, and he was nice enough to mend the wheel for me so I could get back to town."

"So it wasn't a planned meeting, like some folks are saying?"

Amelia's eyes flared wide. "No, not at all." She thought she had managed to convince Carl Olsen their meeting was accidental, but apparently he'd wasted no time in spreading his version of her mishap to eager ears. If Clara had heard the tale already, it was a sure thing everyone else in the Granite Springs community knew of it by now.

Most likely with numerous embellishments.

But what could she expect? She'd been raised in this town. She knew as well as anyone the loquacious livery owner served as a hub of information that rivaled the *Gazette*.

A new thought popped into her head. Had Ben heard this version of their encounter? And if so, how did he feel about being the focus of local gossip? She cringed, trying to imagine his reaction.

Clara waited to speak until they reached the café and ordered their tea. "I didn't mean to stir things up. No one is trying to start a scandal, if that's what you're worried about. Everyone around here knows you've been through a rough patch, and the idea of you finding some happiness makes them happy, too."

The tea arrived just then, and Amelia busied herself stirring sugar into the steaming brew in the blue willow cup, giving herself time to ponder what her friend had said. Did being around Ben make her happy? They'd only spent a short time together, but the mere memory of him sitting beside her on the buggy seat set her heart beating at a faster rate. She tried to steer her thoughts away from Homer's suspicions and the confusion they engendered.

A change of subject seemed in order. "How are things going at the sawmill?"

Clara took a brief sip of tea, then smiled as she set the cup down in the saucer. "Couldn't be better. Martin got a new contract, and everything is buzzing like a bunch of bees around a hive."

She glanced down at the table, then looked back up at Amelia. "I don't mean to pry, but something's been puzzling me."

Amelia eyed her, wondering what was to come next. "Go ahead."

"Martin told me you've been living in Denver with your mother for quite a while. I'm wondering how that happened, with your pa being out here. I know it's really none of my business, but like I told you, I tend to speak what's on my mind."

Amelia added another spoonful of sugar to her tea and watched the spoon swirl the amber liquid around in the cup. "When my parents married, my mother thought she was getting someone who wanted to make a difference in the world. In her mind, that meant forging friendships with politicians and leaders of society. But Papa planned to make a difference in another way. We moved out here when I was quite small so he could start the *Gazette* and have a part in opening up a new section of the country."

"How did that set with your mother?"

Amelia lifted her shoulders in a tiny shrug. "She put up with it for a while, long enough to realize that unlike most newspaper editors, he wasn't willing to be used to further the agenda of some political faction. He had a mission to make the truth known, and he wasn't going to use his position as a stepping-stone to bigger and better things. When I was thirteen, she insisted we all return to Denver so I could have the opportunities for a cultured life, the kind she felt a young lady ought to welcome."

Clara studied her with a knowing expression. "Something tells me it didn't work out exactly the way she planned, since Martin says you made it a point to come back here every summer. And now you're staying on."

Amelia chose her words with care. "Denver has a lot to offer, although the things I enjoy about it aren't the same things my mother takes pleasure in. She expected me to be thrilled with coming-out parties, balls, and the rest of the social whirl. Instead, I got involved with a ministry to the underprivileged through my church. That was far more fulfilling to me than any of my mother's parties.

"And then"—she smiled—"I got in touch with one of my father's friends, an editor at one of the Denver newspapers. He knew I had worked alongside my father, so he let me come in and help out from time to time."

Clara's faded blue eyes twinkled. "I'm guessing that didn't set too well with your ma."

"You'd be right about that. But I love everything about the newspaper world. Papa always used to say he was born with printer's ink in his veins. He must have passed that along to me." She glanced out the window and watched a ranch hand driving a buckboard loaded with spools of barbed wire away from the depot. "I inherited his love for Granite Springs, too. Staying here was the right decision for me. This is where I belong."

Clara bobbed her head. "It's good for a body to know where they belong. Lots of folks spend too many years trying to figure that out, and some of them never do get it right." She pushed her chair back from the table. "And fixing Martin's dinner is what I ought to be doing right now. I'd best be moving along."

After paying for their tea, they started back in the direction of the paper. Amelia smiled when she noticed a number of people standing along the boardwalk, reading the *Gazette*. Several of them glanced up long enough to smile and nod, then went back to their reading. A thrill of pride rippled through her at the sight.

They crossed to the other side of the street and passed the Great Western building. Amelia slowed a bit and peered through the plate-glass window, wondering if she might catch sight of Ben.

Clara's voice cut into her thoughts. "What are you planning to do with your evening?"

Amelia pulled her attention away from the office building and turned back to her friend. "I have work to do in the newspaper office. Then I thought I might read for a while before I retire."

"That sounds like a grand idea. Nothing like curling up with a good book after a hard day's work."

Amelia nodded, although her plan didn't involve a book. This evening, she intended to go through her father's files and read over his notes.

Stepping down to cross the alley that ran between the offices of Black & Landry, Attorneys-at-Law, and the *Gazette*, Clara stopped dead in her tracks and stared over the top of Amelia's head. "What on earth?"

Amelia whirled around and gasped at the sight of a man sprawled facedown in the alleyway. Horror filled her when she recognized the wispy white hair.

It was Homer.

CHAPTER 9

A melia hiked up her skirt and raced down the alley. She
skidded to a halt at Homer's side and dropped down
next to him, heedless of the loose gravel that dug into her knees.

She pressed her fingers against his neck, praying she would
find a pulse. A sob of relief tore from her throat when her
fingertips detected the reassuring sign of life. Then she caught
the unmistakable odor of alcohol, much stronger than before.

No. Rocking back on her heels, she looked down the alley
and retraced Homer's route in her mind. His last stop in delivering the *Gazette* would have been Zeke Miller's boardinghouse,
which sat next door to the Brass Rail Saloon. It would seem
Homer had stopped by one of the town's watering holes for
a libation on his way back to the newspaper.

So I didn't imagine it earlier. A shadow fell across Homer's
limp form, and Amelia looked up to see Clara standing over her.

"Is he dead?"

"No, I'm afraid—"

Before she could say more, Clara knelt beside her. At that
moment, Homer stirred and let out a moan. Pungent fumes

95

wafted up, enveloping the two women. "Ah." Clara raised one eyebrow. "We'd best get him inside, then."

Amelia stared openmouthed, amazed at the way her friend was taking the situation in stride. She looked down at the unmoving man. "I suppose you're right. But how?"

Clara reached over and clapped Homer on the back. "Come on. You need to get up."

Homer's eyes flickered open, then fluttered closed again.

Clara grabbed his shoulder and gave it a good shake. "We can't get you inside on our own. You need to help us."

With a groan, Homer scrambled to his hands and knees, then stumbled to his feet.

Clara stepped up beside him. "If we each get under one arm, can you manage?" Without waiting for a reply, she gestured to Amelia.

Amelia moved to Homer's left side and drew his arm across her shoulder, gasping when her knees buckled under his weight.

"Where does he live?" Clara's strained voice gave evidence of Homer weighing her down, as well.

"He has a little cabin out back, but I don't think we can get him that far. Let's take him through this rear door. It's the one we use for deliveries."

Step by halting step, they staggered along the alley. Amelia shot a quick glance over her shoulder, hoping no one was there to witness their weaving progress. To a casual observer, it might look like all three of them had spent the afternoon at the Brass Rail.

When they reached the alley door, she fumbled with the latch and kicked the door open with her foot. "In here." She nodded toward the improvised sickroom her father so recently occupied. She and Homer had returned the shelves and most of the storage items to their places, but the bed still took up space against one wall.

She and Clara maneuvered Homer over to it, then let him slip out of their grasp. He sprawled across the mattress and lay there, moaning.

Amelia stared down at her old friend, compassion and anger warring within her. She should have spoken to him earlier, as soon as she caught that faint smell of alcohol on his breath.

How would Papa deal with this? Homer had been a heavy drinker when her father took him under his wing, but he'd looked beyond the surface and recognized Homer's value—not just as a help around the newspaper but as a human being worthy of God's love and forgiveness . . . and thus, his own.

His occasional lapses over the years hadn't pleased her father, but he'd seemed to take them in his stride. She was not her father, though. How could she love somebody like a dear uncle on one hand, and at the same time want to shake him until his teeth rattled?

She looked over at Clara, mortified that her friend had witnessed Homer's backsliding. "Thank you for your help. I never could have gotten him inside on my own. I'm sorry you had to see him like this."

Clara brushed off the incident. "I had an uncle with the same problem. It isn't the first time I've had to help someone home after he's been on a bender. My uncle was a fine man, though, when he wasn't bending his elbow too much."

She bent over Homer and frowned. "Looks like he whacked his forehead on the ground when he passed out."

Moving closer, Amelia could see the knot forming near

Homer's temple. "I'll get a cloth and a basin of water." She went to the kitchen to retrieve the supplies, along with some bandages. Annoyed as she was at Homer's drinking, he still needed care.

Carrying the items back to the storeroom, she set the basin on a nearby shelf and started dabbing at the wound. Homer flinched and tried to swat her hand away.

"I'm sorry. I know this is going to hurt. You have quite a lump already. You must have struck your head when you passed out."

Homer looked up as if trying to focus on her face. "Didn't pass out. Not on my own, anyway." He planted his hands on the mattress and eased himself back up against the wall at the head of the bed. "I was walking down the alley, and something smacked me on the head."

He probed the discolored knot with his fingers. "This is tender, all right, but where it really hurts is up here." He raised his hand, indicating the top of his head.

Amelia set the rag on the edge of the basin and used her fingers to part his hair with a gentle touch. She sucked in her breath when she saw a line of blood along his scalp.

Clara leaned close. "Must've been quite a wallop. And it didn't come from hitting his head on the ground."

Amelia's eyes widened. "What did that, Homer? Was anybody else around?"

"Only me in the alley, as far as I could see. It doesn't make a bit of sense, but I know it happened."

Clara's lips tightened. "Things like that don't just happen out of the blue. I think I'll go outside and have a look around."

Amelia waited until she heard the alley door open and close, then she drew a deep breath and summoned up her courage. "Homer, this has to stop."

He looked up at her with a puzzled frown. "What? Getting beaned on the head? I'll agree to that."

"I'm talking about your drinking. You and I both know—" She broke off when Clara stepped back inside, carrying Homer's hat in her hand.

"I found this in the alley, not too far from where he was lying. This was off to the side." She held out an oblong brick. "You can see the scuff on his hat where this hit him. Wearing the hat is probably all that kept that brick from busting his skull open."

Remorse flooded Amelia when she took the heavy brick in her hands. Here she'd been thinking terrible things about Homer, when he'd been the victim of an accident.

Still, there was that telltale smell of alcohol on his breath.

As if reading her thoughts, Homer reached for her hand. "I'll admit I did stop in the Brass Rail on my way back here, just by way of celebrating the paper going out on time. But it was only one drink, and a small one at that." His lips stretched into a thin line, showing how much it cost him to make even that small admission.

Amelia squeezed his fingers. "It always starts with one. You don't want it taking over your life again, do you? I hate what it can do to you. So did Papa."

He pulled his hand away, avoiding her eyes. "I know he did . . . but he understood how it could happen. It's just the way I let off steam when things get a little tense. You have to admit there's been plenty of pressure around here lately."

The bell over the street door jingled, saving Amelia from making a response. A voice called out, "Hello? Anybody here?"

Amelia's spirits brightened when she recognized Ben's voice.

Clara moved toward the door. "Want me to tell whoever's out there to come back later?"

Amelia smoothed her skirt and stepped forward. "No, it's all right. It's Mr. Stone. I'll go see what he wants." Ignoring Clara's knowing look—and the grunt from Homer on the bed—she walked out into the printing office.

Ben grinned when she came into view. "I saw Jimmy out on the street with the latest issue. I know how busy things can get when you're putting it together, so I thought this might be an opportune time for you to take a break. Would you like to have dinner with me at the Bon-Ton?"

Amelia's heart skipped like one of Hyacinth Parmenter's fluffy lambs. Then her thoughts turned to Homer, and she came back to earth with a thud. "I'd like to, but I won't be able to this evening."

The hopeful smile faded from Ben's face. "Oh. Well, maybe some other time. I'm sorry if I disturbed you."

"No, really! Something dreadful just happened to Homer. Come on, you can see for yourself."

She led him back to the storeroom. Homer still sat at the head of the bed, but now a white swath of bandages encircled his forehead. Clara looked up from rolling up the rest of the cloths. Her eyebrows rose when she saw Ben. Homer merely glowered.

Ben took in the sight, then looked back at Amelia. "What happened?"

Amelia picked up the brick and held it out to him. "This fell on him while he was walking down the alley. If he hadn't been wearing his hat, it could have been much worse."

Ben took the brick and turned it over in his hand with a

thoughtful expression. He looked back at Homer. "That must have been quite a wallop you took."

His obvious concern took some of the starch out of Homer. "Yeah, it felt like a mule kicked me." Then he seemed to remember who he was talking to, and his expression stiffened again.

Undeterred, Ben set the brick aside and leaned over the stricken man. "Is your vision blurred? How many fingers am I holding up?"

"What do you think you're doing?" From the distrustful expression on Homer's face, Amelia knew he would have scooted back out of Ben's reach if the wall hadn't been behind him.

Ben persisted. "How many fingers do you see?"

"Three. Does that make you happy?"

Without answering, Ben bent closer and studied Homer's eyes. "Both pupils are the same size. That's a good sign."

Amelia exchanged a puzzled glance with Clara and turned back to Ben. "Have you had medical training?"

"I was on the boxing team at my college. This isn't the first time I've seen someone get a knock on the head. I've watched the team trainers check for concussion often enough."

He moved his hand back and forth in front of Homer's face. "I want you to follow my hand, but just move your eyes, not your head."

Homer fixed him with a baleful glare but did as he was bidden. Ben observed him closely, then leaned back as if satisfied. "I'm pretty sure there's no concussion. It wouldn't hurt to call in Doc Harwood, but I think you're going to be okay. You're going to have one nasty headache for a while, though. If I were you, I'd get some rest, and not do anything strenuous for a day or two."

He stepped back and looked around him with a bemused expression. "Is this your room?"

"No," Amelia said. "This is normally our storeroom. We had it set up as a sickroom when my father . . ." Emotion clogged her throat, and her voice trailed off.

Homer scooted toward the edge of the bed. "I have a little cabin out back. I'll go along now and do a little reading before I turn in for the night." He swung his legs over the side of the bed and pushed himself up. His body swayed the moment his feet touched the ground.

Ben moved swiftly to his side. "Let me help you."

When Homer tried to shrug him away, Clara planted both hands on her hips. "You had enough trouble getting this far with both Amelia and me dragging you along. You aren't going to make it home on your own, unless you plan to do it on all fours."

Homer tried once more to hold himself erect, then gave in. Muttering under his breath, he draped one arm across the younger man's shoulder, and the two of them made their way out the alley door.

Clara watched their slow progress and shook her head. "That poor man. Just like my uncle—salt of the earth, except when he'd been tippling. Well, I'd best be getting on my way. Martin will be wondering where I am."

Amelia followed her to the front door. "Thank you so much for helping. I never would have been able to manage on my own." She watched her friend walk away down First Street, then closed the door and bolted it.

Returning to the other end of the building, she opened the rear door and peered out into the alley. There was no sign of

Homer . . . or Ben. A pang of disappointment caught her by surprise. It would have been nice to go to dinner with him. Maybe he'd ask her again sometime. She closed the door and locked it, then went to straighten up the printing office.

She carried a stack of blank paper back to the storeroom, then set about sorting the pieces of type back into their cases. She and Homer usually tended to that chore together, but tonight was anything but normal.

Poor Homer! To have a brick topple onto his head and then be scolded for taking a drink. Remorse nipped at her again for adding to his troubles.

But he *had* been drinking. Maybe only a small amount, but wasn't that the way it always started? A knot formed in her throat, and she tried to swallow it back. Her father had always been able to get Homer back on the straight and narrow after one of his lapses. But her father wasn't here anymore. Would Homer listen to her?

She couldn't run the paper on her own. She needed Homer, not only as an employee, but as a friend. One she could depend on.

※

Ben pulled the door to Homer's cabin shut behind him and stepped out into the alley. Despite his earlier assurances, he wanted to make certain Homer hadn't been hurt worse than they'd thought, so he stayed long enough to assure himself that all was well. Or as well as could be expected after being hit on the head by a brick.

Walking back along the passage between the *Gazette* and the Black & Landry building, he studied the dusty ground until he came upon the scuffed area where Homer must have fallen and the footprints of the women where they'd helped him up.

He tilted his head and studied the building opposite. The brick in its walls matched the one Amelia had shown him earlier. He tipped his head back and scanned the upper edge of the wall until he spotted an empty space in the top row of bricks.

He frowned and took a closer look. The attorneys' office building wasn't that old. Certainly not old enough for bricks to be falling out. And it was odd that none of the adjoining bricks had shifted out of place. Odder still that one would tumble down like that at the precise moment Homer was walking along the alley.

That would be quite a coincidence. And Ben didn't believe in coincidences.

Retracing his steps, he rounded the back of the office building and narrowed his eyes when he saw a ladder leaning up against the far corner. Tucking his thumbs in his belt with a nonchalant air, he took a long look around. The attorneys' office was closed for the evening, and no one else stirred in the vicinity of the alley. A smile curved his lips. That meant there was no one around to object if he did a little investigating.

Without further hesitation, he climbed the ladder and crossed the flat roof to the spot where he'd noticed the missing brick. Kneeling down, he spotted chips of mortar scattered about . . . and a hammer lying off to one side.

Ben puckered his lips and let out a low whistle. Picking up the hammer, he rocked back on his haunches, deep in thought. His earlier supposition had been correct. That brick hadn't fallen on its own.

CHAPTER 10

A knock at the alley door startled Amelia as she redistributed the type back into its California-style case. She tipped her head to one side and frowned. People didn't usually come to the back door, especially so late in the day.

Who could it be? She opened the door cautiously, and her knees grew weak with relief at the sight of Ben standing there. His boyish smile sent a flood of warmth through her, and she couldn't hold back a grin of her own.

"Did you get Homer settled?"

"Yes, and I spent a little while visiting with him. He was resting comfortably, but I think he was happy to see me leave." He chuckled. "Since he seems to be doing all right, I wonder if you'd reconsider that invitation to have dinner with me."

Before she could respond, Amelia's stomach growled audibly. Her cheeks flushed as she pressed her hand against her waist, but Ben only laughed.

"Is that a yes?"

"I suppose so." She laughed, as well, in spite of her embarrassment. "Except for a cup of tea with Clara earlier, I haven't had anything since breakfast. Let me get my reticule."

She sped upstairs to gather up her bag and gasped when she glimpsed herself in the mirror. She took a moment to rearrange her hair and cast a longing glance at the wardrobe. If only she had time to change into a more suitable dress! But that would take too long. Ben had been thoughtful enough to extend his dinner invitation twice in one evening. She didn't want to keep him waiting.

Looping the reticule over her arm, she trotted down the stairs to where Ben stood leaning against the wall near the type cabinet. He straightened when she reached the bottom step, and the glow in his eyes made her forget her worries about her appearance. He extended his arm and escorted her outside, waiting patiently while she closed and locked the door behind them.

He matched his stride to hers as they strolled down the boardwalk, their heels echoing in unison on the weathered wood. Several shopkeepers, locking their front doors for the night, nodded as they walked past.

"I'm glad you're able to take some time off after such a busy day."

The tension of the afternoon seemed to roll off Amelia's shoulders. How long had it been since she had gone out for a meal with no purpose in mind but relaxing? Concerns for the paper could wait until tomorrow. For this evening, at least, she wouldn't worry about business matters or what her next story might be. Tonight she would just enjoy Ben's company.

At the Bon-Ton Café, he reached out to open the door. It swung open before his fingers touched it, and Carl Olsen walked outside, nearly colliding with them. He muttered a quick apology, then did a double take when he recognized them. A smile creased his face, and he gave Amelia a wink and walked back toward the livery.

She felt a blush stain her cheeks. The garrulous livery owner would be sure to add this sighting to whatever stories he was already spreading about their supposed relationship. Squaring her shoulders, she gave Ben a smile and stepped through the doorway, determined not to let the encounter ruin their evening.

Ben stopped beside her. "Would you like to sit near the window or farther back in the dining area?"

She started toward the window, where they would be able to look out and watch people pass by, but pulled herself up short at the realization that it would mean everyone going past could see her dining with Ben.

Smiling, she indicated a table toward the rear of the room. "How about back there?" When he nodded, she turned and led the way, relieved he hadn't objected. Having Carl Olsen spread the tale would be enough. They didn't have to put themselves on display for everyone who walked by.

After they placed their orders, Amelia looked around at the café's décor. "Pete Nichols has done a good job fixing the place up. The new tablecloths and a fresh coat of paint make it look very homey."

Ben followed her gaze. "I wouldn't know whether it's an improvement on the old café or not, but it does look inviting."

The corners of her lips tugged upward. "It's an improvement, trust me. The previous name was the Coffeepot, and the owners took that very much to heart, with rusty old coffeepots hung up on the walls for their décor." His comment sparked her curiosity. "How long have you been in Granite Springs?"

"About three months." He paused to let their waitress set

plates of roast beef and boiled potatoes in front of them. "I just moved here in the spring. But I take it you have quite a history here. Is that right?"

Amelia nodded while she cut her potato open and topped it with a pat of butter. "My family came here when I was quite young. I've been living in Denver for the past ten years, but I made it a point to come back here and spend every summer with my father."

She waited for the inevitable questions, but he didn't press for more details. *Thank goodness.* She enjoyed Ben's company, but she wasn't ready to launch into an explanation about her mother breaking up their family. But was it all her mother's doing? For the thousandth time, she wondered what her life would have been like if her father had consented to relocate to Denver.

Pushing aside the all-too-familiar pang of grief for what might have been, she focused her attention back to the meal and her companion. Savoring a bite of the succulent roast beef, she followed it with a swallow of lemonade before asking, "What about you? Have you always lived in the West?"

Ben shook his head. "This is my first experience out here. I was born in Pennsylvania and raised in Maryland, just outside Washington, D.C."

Amelia's eyes grew round. "What a thrill it must have been to grow up in the midst of so much history!"

A wide smile crossed his face. "It was. In fact, I went to college in our nation's capital—the University of the District of Columbia."

She tilted her head. "I remember you saying you were on your school's boxing team."

"And the rowing team. I enjoyed the physical effort, as well as the teamwork. I graduated a little over a year ago and tried a couple of different jobs before Mr. Merrick offered me a position out here."

A chill seemed to sweep over the table at the mention of Owen Merrick's name. Amelia knotted her fists in her napkin and tried not to react.

Ben didn't appear to notice her discomfort. "He and my father have been friends since they served in the Union Army together. In fact, he once saved my father's life. I wouldn't be here today if it weren't for him."

Amelia reached for her glass and took another long swallow of lemonade. "You must be grateful to him for that."

"That's for sure." His smile broadened. "The offer came at a time I needed some direction, and my father encouraged me to accept the job. He said it would be a good opportunity, one that could open a lot of doors later on."

Ben stared into the distance for a moment, then nodded and looked back at Amelia. "He was right. I love it out here. With this job, I've gotten to do quite a bit of traveling around the area, and I think Granite Springs is a perfect location. Grand vistas, wide open spaces, a warm climate, and plenty of potential for growth—everything a man could want is right here."

Seeing the sparkle in his eyes and hearing the excitement in his voice, Amelia felt her tension melt away. That same exhilaration swept over her whenever she returned from Denver. Ben's words spoke to her soul and echoed the joy in her own heart.

The rest of the meal was filled with more talk of Granite

Springs and the area she loved so much. By the time they started back to the newspaper, dusk had begun to settle over the town like a soft blanket. Lights flickered through curtained windows, and they had First Street nearly to themselves.

They walked along in a companionable silence that filled Amelia with contentment. Farther along the street, a clatter of wheels announced a buggy heading toward the livery. The sight stirred a memory, and Amelia's sense of well-being evaporated.

Her steps slowed, pulling Ben to a halt. She looked up at him, hating to shatter the peaceful mood but wanting an answer to the question that had been niggling at her mind. "I need to ask you something. The other night, when you rescued me, you called my name before you ever saw me. How did you know I was out there?"

Something flickered in his eyes, and Amelia felt her stomach tighten.

His gaze darted away for a moment before he met her eyes. "I'm a little embarrassed that you found me out." When she blinked and stepped back, he hastened to explain. "After you walked away from me that afternoon, I watched you go to the livery. Not long after that, I saw you drive out of town in the buggy. It may not seem gentlemanly, but I ran to get my horse and followed, hoping I might get a chance to meet you on the road and talk to you. I wanted to get to know you better, and that seemed like a good opportunity." He shrugged. "And as it turns out, I'm glad I did. I'd hate to think what might have happened if you had been stranded out there on your own."

Amelia studied his face, then broke into a smile. "I'm glad you did, too."

She tucked her hand back into the crook of his elbow, and they went on their way, her equanimity restored. Homer had been mistaken. Ben had nothing to do with the buggy breaking down, or any ulterior motive in coming across her when he did. He'd only wanted to spend time with her.

A light sigh drifted from her lips. Ben might work for Owen Merrick, but that didn't mean they were cut from the same cloth. Everything she had seen about Ben portrayed him as a man of honor, and one who enjoyed her company just as much as she enjoyed his.

Ben slid his hand up her arm to cup her elbow when they stepped down to cross the street. When he helped her step back up onto the boardwalk on the other side of Sheridan, his face took on a solemn cast. "Does Homer have any enemies?"

Startled from her happy reverie, Amelia could only gape at him. "What? Why, no, I don't think so. Why do you ask?"

He drew his brows together as if in deep thought, and they walked on several steps before he answered. "After I left him, I took a look at the building next to yours. Something didn't set right with me. It's a relatively new building, far too new for bricks to be coming loose and falling off."

The statement only deepened her bewilderment. "I'm not sure I understand."

"When I went behind the building, I found a ladder up against the back wall, so I climbed up to take a look around."

Something about his tone filled her with foreboding. She felt her heart begin a heavy thudding in her chest. "And what did you find?"

Even in the gathering gloom, she could see the tautness in his face. "Chips of mortar were scattered around the empty space where that brick had been. And there was a hammer lying nearby."

She pressed her hand against her throat. "What are you saying?"

"I'm saying that brick didn't come down on its own. Someone pried it loose and dropped it down on Homer."

※

"Be sure to lock the door behind me." Ben stretched his hand toward Amelia, then arrested the movement and stepped outside the alley door. "I'm glad you were able to dine with me. I hope we can do it again some time."

He cleared his throat and opened his mouth as if he wanted to say more, but settled for a sorrowful smile. "Good night."

He waited for Amelia to shut the door, and she didn't waste time in complying. It wasn't until she shot the bolt into place that she heard his footsteps move away down the alley.

Leaning against the door, she closed her eyes, reliving the past few minutes. Ben's revelation about a deliberate attack on Homer had shaken her more than she'd wanted to let on, although she suspected her horrified cry left no doubt in Ben's mind about how shocked she was.

Pulling herself together, she made her way to the printing office, where she lit one of the gas lamps and went back to the never-ending chore of redistributing the type. Though her hands stayed busy, her thoughts were free to review his startling announcement over and over again.

His blunt words sent a shiver of apprehension through her. Could he be mistaken, or was there something to it?

She shook her head as she dropped one piece of type after

another into its place in the case. Though she didn't know Ben well, he seemed to be a steady man, not the type to jump to conclusions and make unfounded accusations.

From the way he described the scene on the rooftop, dropping that brick had to have been an intentional act. But would any random passerby have sufficed, or was the brick meant for Homer?

While others did use the alley as a shortcut from time to time, it was by no means a heavily traveled thoroughfare. But Homer followed the same path every week after making his last delivery. That would mean someone climbed up on that building to loosen the brick, then watch and wait . . . ready for the moment Homer came along.

Amelia clamped her hands against her waist as a wave of nausea overtook her. What kind of person could do a thing like that?

Ben asked whether Homer had any enemies, but she couldn't imagine anyone disliking the gentle man. She closed her eyes, trying to think. Had he said or done anything to antagonize a member of the community? Could someone be upset about something Homer wrote while her father was ill?

She shook her head. The men of Granite Springs wouldn't hesitate to settle a disagreement with a fistfight—in dire cases, even gunplay might be involved—but not this kind of anonymous sneak attack.

Could it have been some sort of misguided childish prank gone wrong? She thought about Jimmy and his friends, and the other youngsters in town. No, it simply didn't add up. None of the boys she knew were capable of anything like that.

She hadn't been back in Granite Springs all that long. Maybe there was someone new in town, someone she didn't know yet.

A new thought struck her. If Ben was right, and the falling brick had been a deliberate attack on Homer, was he in danger even now?

She started toward the back door, ready to run to Homer's cabin and check up on him. Then she halted and forced herself to relax. When Ben dropped her off, he assured her he would go over to check on Homer once more before returning to his boardinghouse for the night. If he found anything amiss, she was sure he would let her know.

She turned back to her work. If Ben said he would do it, she knew she could rely on him. In the short time she'd known him, he'd never hesitated to step in and help when needed. When she was stranded, he'd fixed her buggy and escorted her back to town, treating her in the most chivalrous manner possible.

And look at the way he treated Homer tonight, despite the older man's obvious dislike. The fact that he'd come seeking her company later on wasn't lost on her, either. A shiver of pleasure rippled through her, helping to dispel her unease. Ben was a nice man, a good man. Her fingers stilled.

And he worked for Great Western.

She sagged against the type cabinet, remembering the strong reactions the very mention of the company's name brought about in both her father and Homer. Then there were those articles her father had written, and Owen Merrick's insistence that he print a retraction.

Just being around Owen Merrick made her skin crawl, but according to Ben, the man had been a hero, once saving his father's life. Maybe that abrasive behavior was just part of his personality. Being obnoxious didn't necessarily make him a villain.

Ben was a man of integrity. Everything she saw of him convinced her of that. Despite Homer's oft-voiced misgivings, she had seen nothing to indicate otherwise. A man as honest as she believed Ben to be wouldn't work for a company involved in skullduggery.

But her father was a man of strong integrity, as well. How could two men on the side of truth have such divergent opinions about the same issue?

Walking into her father's office, she stood facing the file cabinets lined up against the far wall. She searched through the drawers until she found a thick file labeled *Great Western*. Pulling the file from the drawer, she tucked it under her arm and started upstairs. Perhaps his notes would yield the answers she sought.

CHAPTER II

The next morning, Amelia came down the stairs with a light step, refreshed after a good night's sleep. More sleep than she planned on, she reminded herself, with a rueful glance at the stack of papers she carried under her arm.

Her intention the night before had been to go through every document, every scrap of information on Great Western in the thick file, but she had fallen asleep before she got through the first few pages. She set them down on the desk in her father's office, promising herself she would take time to go through them more thoroughly at the first opportunity.

Homer stood next to the Peerless press, setting up Pete Nichols's new menu for the Bon-Ton. Amelia smiled when she noticed he had abandoned the swath of bandages Clara applied the night before.

"How are you feeling this morning?"

"Not bad, except for a whale of a headache."

She stepped closer and examined his head. "The swelling seems to have gone down on your forehead. That's good."

He gave a quick nod, then grimaced. "I put some arnica

ointment on it before I turned in last night. It's still sore, but nothing that'll keep me from doing my job."

"I'm grateful the brick didn't do any more damage." She watched him work a moment, then asked, "Can you think of anyone who is angry at you? Angry enough to try to hurt you?"

He drew back his head and winced again. "What are you getting at?"

"Ben doesn't think it was an accident." She went on to explain what he had found up on the rooftop.

Homer's eyes narrowed, and his bushy, white brows drew together. "You mean somebody waited up there for me to come along, and then dropped that brick down on me?"

"That's what it looked like to him, and from the way he described things, I think he may be right. It may have just been some misguided prank, but even so, the results could have been a lot worse. I can't imagine anyone wanting to do you harm, but just in case, promise me you'll be careful."

Homer nodded. "I'll keep an eye out for trouble." When he turned back to his work, Amelia heard him mutter, "If someone is out to get me, they're the ones who'd better watch out."

She cast a worried glance at her friend. Homer's spindly frame didn't inspire confidence in his ability to take on an assailant, but at least he would be on his guard. With no pressing duties at the moment, she walked back to the office and settled herself at the desk.

Pulling the file toward her, she spent the next thirty minutes sorting its contents into neat stacks. She found handwritten drafts of the articles she'd already read, along with notes on hydraulic mining and a few scribbled sheets containing little except hastily jotted notes that bore little meaning to her. At the bottom of the file, she found an assortment of clippings from eastern newspapers.

Intrigued, she went through the clippings one by one. Each of them contained some mention of Owen Merrick. In one, he was named as the recipient of an award for public service. In another, he had been appointed to the board of directors of a shipping company in Virginia. Others mentioned his name briefly as an attendee at some party or political function. None of them gave indication of him being involved with any underhanded activity.

Amelia frowned and went over each clipping again, looking for any incriminating detail, but she found nothing.

Propping her elbows on the desk, she rested her forehead in her hands. There had to be some reason for her father's antipathy toward Merrick, but the clippings gave no clue about what that might be.

She slid the clippings back into the folder, then sorted through the scribbled notes once more. Ten minutes later, she pushed away from the desk with a frustrated groan. The scattered words must have had some meaning for her father, but try as she might, she couldn't make sense of them.

Her stomach clenched, and a sinking feeling swept over her. Did her father's dislike for Great Western stem from nothing more than a clash of personalities between him and its vice president? If Owen Merrick's grating manner affected her father the same way it did her, she could understand his distrust. But it would be totally unlike her father to voice his dislike in print for no other reason.

He had been ill, she reminded herself—grievously ill. Could the sickness that claimed his life have altered his thinking somehow, making him see wrongdoing where it didn't exist?

She glanced out into the printing office, where Homer moved around the Peerless press, performing his weekly maintenance. He wouldn't need her help any time soon. Rolling her neck from side to side to loosen the tight muscles, she scooted forward again and turned back to her father's notes.

One of the scraps of paper bore a list of names, although there was nothing to indicate their significance. She went over them again, her attention quickening when one notation caught her eye: *V. Sparks.*

Did that refer to Virgil Sparks, the same man who sold his property to her father rather than let it go to Great Western?

Excitement stirred within her. If that was the case, perhaps the other people on this list also held grievances against Great Western. And if so, they were people she should talk to. Once she learned their stories, perhaps she could finally start putting the pieces of this puzzle together.

More than anything, she needed to learn the truth. She owed that to her father, to herself, and to the readers of the *Gazette.*

Scooping the rest of the papers back into the folder, she replaced it in the file cabinet and marched out to the printing office with the list of names in her hand. Walking up to Homer, she said, "I need to ask you something."

He set down the oilcan he held and looked at the paper she held out to him.

"Do you have any idea why my father kept this list of names? I found it in the file he had on Great Western."

He took the list from her and studied it, his lips moving as he scanned the handwriting. His brow puckered, and he stared across the room as if deep in thought. Finally he spoke. "It's

119

an odd list, if you ask me." He frowned. "None of those folks live here anymore."

Amelia's newfound excitement at having a lead to follow plummeted like a bird falling out of the sky. "They've moved away? All of them?"

Homer nodded. "All within the last six months or so." His gaze sharpened, and he focused on the list again. "That's interesting."

Hope fluttered feeble wings, and Amelia caught her breath. "What is?"

"As you know, Virgil Sparks sold that piece of land to your daddy. But the rest of them—the Seavers, Gabe Rogers, old man Smith—all sold out to Great Western before they left town."

He jabbed an ink-stained finger at the top name on the list. "The Seaver family was one of the first to leave. There was talk of a new gold strike up in Idaho, and Ephraim couldn't wait to pack his family up and light out. Now that I think about it, your father tried to contact him, sent a letter to wherever it was they went, but it was returned."

"What about the others? Did he try to contact them, too?"

Homer handed the paper back with a regretful shrug. "He didn't always fill me in on everything he did. I honestly don't know."

"Where did the Seavers live? Do they have any neighbors who might still be in contact with them?"

He shook his head. "Sparks's place was on one side of them. Rogers and Smith were out past them. Seavers had youngsters at the school, though. Maybe the teacher knows something."

It was a slim lead, but it was all she had to go on. Checking to make sure her pencil and notebook were tucked inside her reticule, Amelia went on her way and soon reached the schoolhouse.

She waited at the back of the room until the students were busy with their slate work and Rose Thompson, the young schoolteacher, was free to talk with her.

"I'm afraid I can't be of much help," the slender blonde said in response to Amelia's question. "I haven't heard a word from the family since they left last winter. If you do find a way to contact them, would you please send them my regards? They were sweet children, and I miss them."

Amelia thanked her and left, wondering where she should turn next. As if in answer, she spotted Owen Merrick's stocky figure striding in her direction on the opposite side of the street.

"Go to the source." Amelia jumped and clutched her reticule to her side. It was almost as if her father's voice had spoken in her ear. One of his main precepts had been the importance of getting information directly from the subject of a story, rather than relying on hearsay.

Heat scalded her face at the memory. How could she have forgotten such a basic principle? She hadn't forgotten, she admitted to herself. Based on her father's attitude and her first impression of Merrick, she had chosen to ignore it completely. Owen Merrick was the last person she wanted to talk to.

But her personal feelings didn't matter. Was she a journalist or wasn't she? Squaring her shoulders, she stepped down off the boardwalk and crossed the street to intercept him.

Steeling herself, she forced a polite smile to her lips. "Good day, Mr. Merrick. Might I have a moment of your time?"

A look of astonishment crossed his face, quickly replaced by a triumphant grin. "Why, Miss Wagner! How lovely to see you on this fine morning. May I hope this means you've decided to accept my offer to purchase the *Gazette*?"

Caught completely off guard, Amelia could only gape at him. It took a moment to find her voice. "I'm afraid you're mistaken. I merely wanted to ask you some questions."

The genial look vanished, and he lifted one eyebrow slightly. "Oh?"

Now that the moment had arrived, Amelia found herself scrambling for the right question. Depending on Merrick's reaction, she might only have one chance to get the information she sought. What did she want to know most?

"What was the problem between you and my father? Why were the two of you so at odds?"

A glimmer lit Merrick's eyes for a moment, then his expression smoothed. "You don't know? I'm surprised he didn't tell you."

"I was always taught to get both sides of a disagreement," she said, hoping he wouldn't press her for details she didn't possess.

"I've never been one to speak ill of the dead . . . or to malign someone who didn't have a chance to answer back." He fixed her with a meaningful glance that brought a flush to her cheeks. "And now if you'll excuse me, I—"

"Just a minute." Amelia pulled out her pencil and notebook and took a quick step to one side, planting herself squarely in his path. "There's one more thing I'd like to know. I'm aware that Great Western has plans to engage in hydraulic mining, but does the company intend to stay in Granite Springs long enough to repair the damage that process is sure to create? Or are you merely here to plunder the area and then move on?

You'd be within your legal rights to do so—as deplorable as that might be—but my readers would like to know what they can expect."

He'd stared at her throughout her inquiry, and for a moment silence hung in the air when she ended. Then he smiled, looked around as if checking to see if anyone else was within hearing distance, and began. "Our goal is for the betterment of the area. We want to improve the economy of the entire region. As for specific plans, I can't discuss them with you right now. We're at a critical stage in our operations, and I don't want to jeopardize them by speaking too soon. Suffice it to say that the end results will be good for Granite Springs, for Arizona, and the whole West."

Amelia tapped her pencil against the notebook. "I'm afraid my readers will want more than vague assurances."

Merrick's smile faded, and his lips tightened into a thin line. "And I'm afraid that's all you're going to get from me."

She met his gaze straight on, hoping he didn't notice the way her fingers trembled. "In that case, I'll have to keep digging. My readers need to know the whole truth, and I mean to find it."

He fixed her with a steely gaze and spoke in a tone to match. "Just remember, Miss Wagner, if you keep on digging, you may not like what you turn up." Pivoting on his heel, he strode away in the opposite direction.

Amelia stared after him. What did he mean? His parting comment sounded like a thinly veiled threat, though she couldn't imagine what he meant by it. Could it have anything to do with the property her father bought from Virgil Sparks?

She took a moment to pull herself together. Their brief altercation had shaken her more than she cared to admit, but confrontations like that were part and parcel of a reporter's life. She couldn't let that deter her from her pursuit of news.

Speaking of which . . . She walked along First Street, looking for anything newsworthy.

Spying a large poster in the front window of the Odd Fellows Hall, she walked over to inspect it. The hand-lettered sign announced an upcoming concert by the military band from Fort Whipple. Amelia wrinkled her nose. The uneven writing conveyed the information clearly enough, but she and Homer could have done a much more professional job on the Peerless. Nevertheless, it was news. She jotted the information in her notebook and glanced down the street, alert for further inspiration.

Farther down the block, she spotted a familiar figure. She broke into a smile at the sight of Ben Stone, remembering the pleasant meal they shared the evening before. At the same moment, he caught sight of her and raised his hand in greeting.

She watched him hurry toward her, trying to quell the sensation that a swarm of butterflies had taken up residence in her stomach. Ducking her head to tuck her notebook and pencil back inside her reticule, she used the opportunity to gather her thoughts before he joined her.

"I was hoping I might see you this morning," he said.

Amelia forgot her butterflies when her heart picked up speed and started racing like a runaway horse. "It's good to see you, too. Thank you again for last night. I enjoyed the time we spent together, and I so appreciated your help with Homer."

"How is he today?"

"Much better. He's working, as am I." She slanted a teasing look up at him. "What about you?"

To her surprise, a flush tinged his cheeks. "I just needed to step out for a few minutes to run an errand. Seeing you was an unexpected bonus."

"It seems like everyone from your company is out and about today. I saw your employer just a few minutes ago." The reminder of her conversation with Owen Merrick brought her back down to earth with a thud. So much for going to the source to get both sides of a story.

Her eyes widened, remembering another of her father's sayings—*"If you can't access the source itself, get as close to the source as you can."*

She looked up at Ben, wondering how he would feel about the idea that had just sprung into her mind. "Do you have to get right back to your office, or could you spare a few minutes to talk with me?"

The light in his eyes warmed her through and through. "I can't think of anything I'd like more. Do you want to sit on one of the benches here in front of the general store?"

"No. What about . . ." Amelia's mind whirled, trying to come up with the best place to broach her improvised plan to Ben. The newspaper office? No, Homer would be there. Last night's episode ought to have softened his attitude toward Ben, but if he overheard them talking about Great Western, no telling what his reaction might be.

She scanned the buildings along the street. The café? Too many listening ears. She needed someplace that offered more privacy.

"Maybe we could walk up to the grove of trees near the spring. It's quiet there. I hope you don't think that's too forward of me," she added when she saw his look of surprise.

"Not at all. It would be my pleasure to escort you there." He held out his arm, and they followed the road past the north end of town.

When they reached the bubbling pool of water that gave Granite Springs its name, Amelia stopped beneath a walnut tree and leaned back against the rough trunk. "I'd like to ask you to do something for me."

Ben rested one arm on a low-growing limb and bent his head toward her. "I'll be glad to help in any way I can."

The look he gave her sent a shiver up her spine, and she had to glance away in order to concentrate on what to say next. "As you know, my father wrote some articles that portrayed Great Western in a less than flattering light."

A flicker of surprise shone in his eyes, and he drew himself up slightly. "Yes."

"And you're probably aware that Owen Merrick wanted him to retract what he'd written."

Ben straightened and tucked his thumb in one pocket. "You have to understand. This company relies on investors for its operating capital. Stories that stir up unfounded fears among the public—like the ones your father wrote—could have a great impact on their decisions about future investments with us. Or even create a sense of unease that would cause them to withdraw money they've already invested."

Amelia leaned forward, willing him to understand. "But you didn't know my father. The motto he chose for the *Gazette* is taken straight from the Bible: 'Ye shall know the truth, and the truth shall make you free.' Those weren't just idle words to my father. They spoke of who he was and what he lived for."

She waited a moment to let her words sink in before continuing. "He never would have printed those stories had he not believed in their accuracy one hundred percent."

Ben's features softened. "I'm not calling his honesty into question. I have no doubt your father was a fine man." His voice took on a gentle tone. "But even a good man can be mistaken."

The statement hit Amelia like a blow. Wasn't that exactly what she'd been thinking earlier? But she wasn't ready to admit that to Ben.

She folded her arms. "Let's assume for a moment you're right. Not that I'm saying you are, but it seems to me we're both interested in making the truth known. In order to do that, we need more information. Your employer holds one point of view; my father held another. They can't both be right. I'd like you to help me learn the truth—whatever it may be—so we can set the record straight."

Ben drew his head back slightly. "What, exactly, are you asking me to do?"

She spread her hands wide, then let them fall to her sides. "I'm not sure what I'm asking. I know my father was concerned about what Great Western's long-term plans might be. They're obviously buying up a lot of land, but to what purpose? And how are they acquiring it? You know your boss and the other people in the company. You know how business is transacted there."

Ben nodded, but his features took on a wary expression.

She took a deep breath and plunged ahead. "I told you I saw your boss earlier, but I didn't tell you I'd spoken to him. When I asked him that question, he cut me off and refused to discuss it. But when a company's true plans aren't made known, it gives rise to speculation, which may or may not line up with facts. An investment company is in business to make a profit—but at what cost to others? Great Western already plans to flush gold out of the rock with high-pressure nozzles. What's the next step—clear-cutting tracts of timber from the hillsides? Things like that will affect this area for decades to come. Surely you can understand why people around here are concerned."

Ben raked his fingers through his hair. "I can't tell you anything specific about what the future holds. I'm responsible for researching the ownership of certain properties the company is interested in, and then contacting those owners to try to negotiate a purchase. I'm told which properties to look into, but I haven't been with Great Western long enough to be privy to all their plans."

"But don't you want to know what they are? Think about it—a company with enough backing can buy up land, squeeze every penny of profit out of it, and then go on its way with money in its pockets. But the people who have built their lives here would be left with nothing, surrounded by devastation. You wouldn't want to be a part of something like that, would you?"

"Of course not," he sputtered.

"Then help me. Please. Your boss wouldn't confide in me, but there isn't any reason he shouldn't tell you what his intentions are. And if he won't . . . maybe you could keep your eyes and ears open, see what you can learn."

Ben's eyebrows soared toward his hairline. "You're asking me to spy?"

"No, of course not!" Her conscience pricked her. "Not exactly, anyway." She lifted her chin and tried to look more confident than she felt. "The people of Granite Springs deserve to know how they'll be affected by whatever Great Western plans to do."

"It certainly sounds like spying to me. For someone who's interested in the truth, that strikes me as rather underhanded."

He was going to say no. She could see his answer written in the taut lines of his body and the stern expression on his face.

She scrabbled in her mind for something more to say. "Gaining information isn't wrong in itself. Think about what Joshua did in the Bible."

The look on Ben's face would have been comical if the situation hadn't been so serious. "Excuse me?"

"Don't you remember? He sent two men—the ones Rahab hid in her house—to find out about the defenses of Jericho."

He nodded, still looking confused. "When God was planning to destroy the city, they—" He broke off, and his eyes narrowed. "Is that what you're planning to do, come up with some way to tear down Great Western?"

Amelia laid her hand on his arm, afraid she had pushed him too far. "I'm not trying to harm the company. This is not a vendetta, I'm merely trying to find out the truth." She squeezed her eyes shut, then looked up into his face. "And if it turns out that my father was mistaken and Great Western has only beneficial things planned for their work in this area, I will be glad to print a retraction."

Do I really mean that? Taken off guard by her own statement, she pondered the question while she waited for Ben's response. Could she admit publicly that her father had been wrong?

Taking in a deep breath, she let it out again on a shuddering sigh. She could. It would kill her to do it, but it would be the right thing—the same thing her father would do if he were still alive.

Before Ben could answer, footsteps crunched along the pathway through the grove of trees. Amelia spun around to see Martin Gilbreth approaching.

His weather-beaten face lit up when he saw Ben. "There you are. Emmett said he saw you headed up this way. I wanted to let you know I've decided to sell that property your company's interested in. I didn't mean to interrupt you, but I thought we probably ought to take care of it right now . . . before I change my mind," he added with a grin.

Ben stepped toward Martin, removing his arm from Amelia's grasp. "You aren't interrupting. We were almost finished here." Tipping his hat to Amelia, he turned away and the two men started back down the street.

"Ben!" she called. "That favor I asked of you . . . ?"

He halted and turned back to face her. The compassion in his eyes sparked hope in her heart, but his words dashed it to pieces. "I'm sorry. I'm not going to be able to help you. Not like that."

CHAPTER 12

Ben opened the door of the Great Western building and ushered Martin inside. In the far corner of the spacious room, Owen Merrick leaned over Josh Brady's desk. The two looked up when Ben and Martin entered.

A smile of welcome lit Merrick's face. He crossed the room with rapid strides and enveloped Martin's fingers in a hearty handshake. "Mr. Gilbreth! How nice of you to stop by. Have you decided to accept our offer?"

Martin gave a quick nod and tucked his thumbs in his belt. "I caught up with Ben just now and asked him to draw up the papers, since he's the one I originally talked to about it."

Merrick clapped him on the shoulder. "I'll let the two of you get on with it, then."

Ben led Martin back to his desk and seated him in a wooden visitor's chair. He slid open his desk drawer and pulled out the necessary forms. "I'm delighted you came to this decision, but I must say I'm surprised. You seemed totally against it the last time we spoke. What changed your mind?"

Martin shrugged and settled back in the chair. "The more I thought about it, it just didn't make sense to hold on to that piece. I've already harvested the marketable lumber, and it's so far from the sawmill, there isn't much else I could do with it. Might as well make a little profit on it. I could use that capital for the sawmill right now."

Ben reviewed his file on the Gilbreth property and made quick work of filling in the forms on the contract. "If you'll read through this and sign here," he pointed to a line at the bottom of the page, "I'll go get the bank draft from Mr. Merrick."

After Martin perused the papers and signed his name, Ben carried the contract to Merrick's office. The company's vice president scanned the paperwork, then filled out the bank draft for the amount agreed upon and signed his name with a flourish. Handing it to Ben, he said, "I need to speak with you as soon as Gilbreth has gone."

"Of course." He carried the draft back to his desk and handed it over to Martin, who looked at it with a lack of enthusiasm Ben found surprising.

"Is everything all right?"

The older man nodded as he folded the paper and tucked it into his shirt pocket. "I still think it's worth more than this, but we've talked about that before. I need the capital to move forward with an expansion at the sawmill, so I'll take what I can get and be satisfied." He pushed himself out of the chair and held out his hand.

Ben returned the handshake. "I'll make sure all the papers are filed with the county recorder in Prescott. It's been a pleasure doing business with you."

After showing Martin to the door, he started back to his desk, then remembered his conversation with his boss and changed course to Merrick's office. He tapped lightly on the frame of the open door. "You wanted to see me?"

"Ah, yes. Come in, my boy. And close the door behind you." When the door latch clicked into place, he tented his fingers and peered over them at Ben with a pensive expression. "Have a seat, son. I'm happy you closed the deal with Martin Gilbreth, but how are things progressing with Miss Wagner? I don't want to see you getting distracted from the task I entrusted to you."

Ben shifted on his chair, feeling like an errant schoolboy under Merrick's penetrating gaze. "I was talking with Miss Wagner when Martin walked up. Since I was the one who initiated the negotiations for his property, it was reasonable for him to expect me to complete it for him."

"I see." Merrick pondered a moment, then broke into a broad smile. "You're doing a fine job, Ben. It's a good sign that Gilbreth sought you out instead of just walking in on his own. It shows people around here are getting to know you and trust you. And it's nice to know that even after what has been printed in the *Gazette*, people still have faith in Great Western." His tension seemed to slip away, and he leaned back in his chair. "Your father would be proud of you."

Ben's chest expanded at the compliment. "Thank you, sir."

"Speaking of Miss Wagner, remember that I want to stay up to date on what's happening. Do you have anything to report?"

"Not really." *Except that she just asked me to spy on Great Western.* "I've been spending time with her, getting to know her as you directed."

"Good, good." Merrick's gaze sharpened. "What about those articles her father wrote?"

Ben fought the urge to squirm like a bug on the point of a

pin. Trying to fulfill his promise to keep tabs on a woman he was beginning to care for in a decidedly non-business sense made him feel as if he were walking a tightrope, where any misstep might mean disaster. How had he gotten himself into such a tangle? He chose his words with care. "I haven't asked her to print a retraction yet. I thought it best to develop a relationship first. And I know she's curious as to what our long-range plans are." He held his breath, waiting for an answer.

A glint of anger flitted across Merrick's face. Then his features smoothed out so quickly, Ben wondered if he had imagined it.

Merrick pursed his lips. "I'm sure you're taking the right tack. Carry on."

Ben returned to his desk, feeling rebuffed by the abrupt dismissal. He filled out the rest of the paperwork on the Gilbreth sale and set it atop the stack of documents that needed to be taken to the county recorder's office in Prescott.

With that chore finished, he leaned back in his chair and stared around at the quiet activity in the office. He watched Josh Brady and Eddie Franklin go about their business, finding it impossible to believe there was anything underhanded about Great Western's activities.

When he rejected Amelia's request to do some spying on her behalf, he felt he'd taken the high road. But how different was that from agreeing to strike up a friendship with Amelia for the purpose of swaying her opinion in favor of Great Western? He groaned and pinched the bridge of his nose between his thumb and forefinger.

How did he get himself in this crazy situation? More important, what kind of man was he to be so easily talked into doing such a thing?

He shook his head, remembering Amelia's reference to Joshua. He felt about as far from a Bible hero as anyone could get. If someone asked him to characterize himself as a biblical character, he had to admit he bore far more resemblance to Jonah.

His similarity to the rebellious prophet was something he tried to avoid thinking of, but he couldn't escape the parallels that existed in their lives. Hadn't he heard God's voice and run in the opposite direction, just as Jonah had? When the opportunity arose to join Great Western, he had wasted no time in traveling to the other end of the country, trying to evade the call God placed on his life.

Ben straightened in his chair, willing himself to stop brooding. Surely the God who formed the heavens and the earth was big enough to use him anywhere, even in this tiny Arizona community.

And God *was* using him. He could see the proof of that every day. Take the transaction he had just completed. That sale benefited not only his employer, but Martin Gilbreth, as well. With the money gained from the sale of his land, Martin would be able to implement his plans to build his business, which in turn would provide more jobs and help the entire community.

He squared the stack of papers on his desk, feeling the satisfaction of a job well done. And he was just one of the employees here. How many others had Great Western already helped during their brief time in Granite Springs?

He walked to the front window, taking in the bustle of activity along First Street. The town was growing, and Great

Western was a part of that. What could have possessed Andrew Wagner to try to undermine the company?

The question brought his conversation with Amelia back to mind. He blew out a huff of air, remembering what she had asked of him. He cocked his head to one side as a thought struck him. What if he did the requested digging and turned up tangible proof that her father's concerns had been groundless?

That would mean Amelia could lay her doubts to rest and print the promised retraction, which would make Owen Merrick happy. Ben would be released from his obligation to try to sway Amelia's opinion of the company and would be free to pursue a friendship with her, without feeling like he was caught in the middle.

He smacked his fist into his palm, elated at finding such a simple solution. If he could pull that off, it would solve all his problems.

Grinning, he walked back to his desk and retrieved his jacket. It was time to get back to work. Mr. Merrick had been very clear about expecting him to spend more time with Amelia.

And there was nothing he wanted to do more.

CHAPTER 13

Amelia bent over the jumbled stack of papers on her father's desk and rubbed her eyes, hoping the action would bring the printed words back into focus. Over the past week, she had expanded her search in her quest to learn more about Great Western, poring over every issue of the *Gazette* since the company started doing business in Granite Springs nearly a year ago.

So far she had learned that Owen Merrick came from the Washington, D.C. area, he'd arrived with a substantial amount of cash to finance the company's initial operations, and he seemed to be held in high regard by his acquaintances in the East—points worth noting, but nothing that helped move her investigation forward.

If only Ben had agreed to help her! She heaved a sigh. Another week had come and gone without making any headway. Another issue of the *Gazette* would go to press tomorrow without the big story she hoped for.

A quick glance at the clock on the wall facing the desk told her it was after three o'clock. She stretched wearily, trying to straighten the kink in her neck. Had she really wasted the entire afternoon chasing down a rabbit trail?

And where was Homer? He'd volunteered to go out in search of news to fill the front page—"just in case nothing pans out for you here." Intent in her search, she'd let him go without making any objection. But that had been hours ago.

She felt a twinge of guilt at the thought of saddling him with news gathering along with his regular chores. The first day she arrived, he had looked almost this harried, trying to run the paper on his own and look after her father, as well. Her heart had gone out to him then, yet here she was, putting him back in a similar predicament.

But she had to find out what was going on with Great Western. Her father's words on the night of her arrival were permanently etched in her memory. He had seemed so certain that something was amiss with the company, something even more nefarious than his articles on hydraulic mining brought to light. If his suspicions were correct, she had a duty as a journalist to uncover it.

She looked at the notes she had jotted down, then tossed them back onto the desk with a frustrated moan. The answer—or at least a lead—had to be there. She just wasn't seeing it.

Shoving her chair away from the desk, she rose and started to pace the office. Something was wrong at Great Western. She felt it in her bones. Why else would her father's articles have upset Owen Merrick so much? After reading through them numerous times, she could see how her father's words might have stepped on Merrick's toes, but they were hardly enough to bring about a demand for a retraction. Or an offer to buy out the paper, for goodness' sake!

Thinking of Merrick, her steps slowed as she considered the cryptic comment he made the week before, when he warned her against digging deeper. What had he meant by that? Had it only been an angry man's way of lashing out because he didn't like being cast in an unflattering light? Or was it intended as a serious attempt to shut down the truth?

A dull throb took up a steady beat in her temples, and she pressed her fingertips against her forehead to ease the pounding. Trying to find the answers she needed was like working a jigsaw puzzle without any idea what the completed picture was supposed to look like.

If only her father's notes had been clearer! Such haphazard documentation was totally unlike him. Again, she wondered if his illness might be the cause of that lapse. When she was younger, he had been a model of organization, able to put his finger on the facts he needed at a moment's notice.

And once he'd started on a story, he never gave up until he was finished. Amelia chuckled, remembering how Homer had once compared him to a rat terrier, saying that once her father got his teeth in something, it was impossible to make him let go.

Homer had been right. How often had she heard her father tell her to chase a story down and keep digging until it yielded all its secrets?

"I know that's what I need to do, Papa." She whispered the words aloud, as though he were in the room with her. "But how am I supposed to dig when I have no idea where to look? I wish you were here so you could make sense of this for me."

What more could she do? Besides going over the pages in her father's files, she had talked to Martin Gilbreth the day he asked Ben to accompany him to the Great Western office.

In response to her questions, Martin had affirmed he sold his property to Great Western of his own free will. In addition, he had given her the names of several others who had sold to Great Western in recent weeks. Those she was able to contact said much the same thing, leaving her back where she had begun.

She drew in a deep breath and let it out slowly. For the moment, she had done everything she could think of. Unless some new inspiration struck, she needed to come up with some inside information. And given Ben's unwillingness to help in that department, she had no idea how to go about obtaining that.

The street door opened, and Homer walked in. While he hung up his hat and jacket, Amelia hurried to greet him, trying to appear more cheerful than she felt.

"You've been gone quite a while. Does that mean you managed to turn up something interesting for the front page?"

He pulled a notebook from his shirt pocket and flipped it open. "I heard talk about a man named Copeland going missing down in Prescott. Sounds like there's been quite a stir, since he's on the board of directors for the Peavine. I don't have all the particulars, but we can make mention of it in tomorrow's issue and add more in the next."

He consulted the notebook again. "There are a few snippets here and there we can use to fill space. And I spent quite a bit of time talking to Walt Ingram and Emmett Kingston about the upcoming concert at the Odd Fellows Hall. They gave me plenty of details, so we can use that for the lead story." He shot her a sidelong glance. "Unless you turned up something on that piece you've been working on."

Stung by the reminder that Homer's efforts had produced more than her own obsessive research, Amelia looked away.

"I don't have a thing. Not one single thing to show for all the time I've wasted on Great Western. I'm sorry I've let myself get so focused on this. You shouldn't be out trying to do my job as well as your own."

He gave her a clumsy pat on the shoulder. "Don't you worry about it. Your daddy was on to something—you and I both know that. It'll come to light one of these days. Just wait and see. Then maybe we can send that whole brood of vipers packing."

Amelia swung around to face him. "You can't lump everyone who works at Great Western into that category. Not until we find out what's going on and who all is involved."

Homer propped his notebook up on the type cabinet and gave his notes a quick glance. "You're talking about that young Stone fellow, aren't you?" Picking up a composing stick, he started setting type in place, putting the story together while he worked rather than taking the time to write out a first draft on paper.

Amelia pulled her printer's apron from its hook on the wall and tied it around her waist. If Homer was willing to do her work for her, the least she could do was help him in return. "What are you using for a headline?"

"How about 'Fort Whipple Band Coming to Town'? It's simple and to the point."

She nodded and watched him reach for a set of larger type. "Ben isn't like Owen Merrick. I simply can't believe he's involved in any wrongdoing."

Homer grunted. "I know he's handsome enough to turn a young girl's head, but he's still part of Great Western, and I don't trust a one of them."

"But look at the way he helped me with the buggy, and how willing he was to help when you got hit on the head."

He ran his fingers through his shock of white hair as if reliving the memory of that night. "I'll allow he was helpful enough. But maybe he was just trying to worm his way into our good graces."

At that moment, the bell over the street door jangled, and the object of their conversation walked inside. Amelia couldn't hold back the grin that spread across her face.

The warmth of Ben's smile chased away her weariness. "I had to take something down to the station, and I thought I'd stop in to see you while I was out. It looks like you're both busy."

"We are, since the paper goes out tomorrow. It always gets hectic at this point in the week."

He glanced from Amelia to Homer to the press. "Is there anything I can do to help?"

"Well . . ." Amelia looked around, ignoring Homer's muffled grunt. "The inside pages are set and ready to print. You could help me with that while Homer finishes setting the lead story."

Ben grinned. "Just tell me what to do."

She showed him how to fit the paper into place while she rolled the brayer across the marble stone and inked the set type. With Ben's help, she lowered the tympan holding the paper onto the bed of the press and motioned for him to turn the crank, rolling the bed forward.

"Like this?" he asked.

Amelia nodded and reached out to pull the lever that pressed the paper against the inked type.

She smiled up at him while she peeled the printed page from

the tympan and turned to hang it up to dry on one of the clotheslines stretched along the rafters around the perimeter of the ceiling. "That's the first one. From here on out, I'll handle the inking, and you're in charge of operating the press. We only have two hundred and forty-nine more to go."

With a laugh, Ben set the next page in place, and they repeated the process until Amelia called a stop.

Placing her hands against the small of her back, she twisted from side to side. "I don't know about you, but I could use a break."

"You're the boss." Ben's playful tone made her laugh as he leaned back against the counter.

Homer set his composing stick down and started for the kitchen. "I need a drink of water. I'll bring some back for the three of us."

Amelia couldn't help but smile at the way he'd accepted Ben's presence. As soon as he left the room, she moved closer to Ben. Keeping her voice just above a whisper, she asked, "Have you learned anything about the company's plans?"

His mouth tightened, making her regret her impulsive question. "I told you I wasn't going to spy on my employer." When her shoulders sagged, his expression softened, and he added, "But if I happen to hear of anything that might help, I'll let you know."

Homer returned with three glasses of water, and they drank their fill before returning to work. When the last of the inside pages had been hung up to dry, Amelia surveyed all they had accomplished with a sense of satisfaction.

"I don't know how to thank you for your help. You've lightened my load considerably."

"You don't have to thank me," Ben told her. Then his eyes twinkled. "But if you really feel you need to pay me back, how about having dinner with me at the Cosmopolitan this evening?"

"I wish I could." When she saw the light in his eyes fade, she hastened to add, "I hate to say no, but we still have a lot to do to get the paper ready to go out tomorrow."

He accepted her explanation with good grace. "Another time, perhaps. I was glad to help, by the way. There's a lot more that goes into producing a paper than I realized."

After he left, Amelia turned to Homer. "So what do you think now? He only stopped by to say hello. He certainly didn't need to spend all that time helping out. Seems to me like that kind of effort goes above and beyond the call for someone trying to worm his way into our good graces."

"It does, at that." Homer finished tightening the type for the front page into the chase, ready to be printed the next morning. "To all appearances, the man's an upstanding fellow."

Buoyed by his words, Amelia smiled as she reached for a rag to clean her hands. As she leaned past Homer, she could barely hear the words he muttered under his breath. "But I've been fooled before."

CHAPTER 14

Here's the paper, Mr. Stone. Right off the press."

"Thanks, Jimmy."

The young newsboy bounced on his toes. "Anything going on around here that would make a good story for Miss Amelia?"

Ben shook his head. "Nothing exciting, I'm afraid. It's pretty much business as usual."

Jimmy screwed his mouth to one side. "And if you knew anything, you'd probably tell her yourself. You've been spending an awful lot of time around the newspaper office."

Ben chuckled as he pulled a dime from his pocket and tossed it up. The young newsboy snatched it out of the air with a grin. With a quick wave, he scooted out the door of the Great Western building and turned left onto First Street.

Ben tucked the newspaper under his arm and watched Jimmy scamper away on his appointed rounds. So the latest issue of the *Gazette* was on the street. The weekly pressure would be off Amelia's shoulders, for the moment at least. She had been too swamped with work to go out with him the night before, but she just might be free this evening. Tossing the paper onto his desk, he slipped into his jacket, reached for his hat, and sauntered out the door.

He could see Jimmy popping in and out of doorways farther along First Street. That must mean Homer would be out making his deliveries, too. Ben grinned at the knowledge that he'd be able to talk to Amelia without the distraction of Homer's disapproving gaze.

He wasn't sure what he'd done to earn the older man's distrust, but perhaps that dislike wasn't personal. Before Amelia arrived in Granite Springs, he hadn't had much interaction with Homer Crenshaw or Andrew Wagner. But neither of them made any secret of their antagonism toward Great Western. In Homer's mind, that apparently extended to all the company's employees.

At least Amelia didn't seem to share that distaste where Ben was concerned. His spirits rose, remembering the way she invited him to pitch in and help the night before. To his surprise, he'd enjoyed the activity almost as much as spending time with Amelia. After months of doing little but paperwork, it felt good to do something more physical.

Making his way to the *Gazette* office, he swung the door open and stepped inside. Amelia looked up from sweeping the floor when the bell jangled. Without hesitation, she propped the broom against the wall and stepped forward to greet him with a pleased expression. "What brings you here this afternoon?"

Ben swept off his hat and turned the brim between his fingers. "I hope I'm not interrupting. I saw Jimmy out delivering papers, so I thought this might be a good time to talk to you."

"It's perfect. The evening after the paper goes out is one of the few moments I have all week long to catch my breath."

So his timing had been right, as he'd hoped. "In that case, I'd like to extend another invitation to have dinner with me."

Her eyes flew open wide. "Right now?" She put her hand up as if to straighten her tangled brown curls, but stopped when she noticed the ink stains on her hand. She wrinkled her nose and thrust her hands behind her back.

Ben couldn't help but grin. "I was thinking more along the lines of later this evening. Would six o'clock work for you?"

She gave him a radiant smile that seemed to light up every corner of the printing office. "That would be perfect. It will give me time to put things in order and make myself present-able." Her brilliant blue eyes sparkled as she locked her gaze on his. "Thank you. I'm looking forward to it."

"So am I. I have a little work to finish up, and I'll meet you here at six."

Back at the office, Ben looked at the mound of papers on his desk. Lately, he'd been so lost in thoughts of Amelia, he had neglected to keep things organized as well as he usually did. This would be a good time to rectify that.

He busied himself with sorting papers into neat piles, ready to be slipped into the appropriate folders. Pulling open one of the drawers in the first file cabinet, he stopped and stared down at the documents in his hand.

Was this the work he wanted to do for the rest of his life? After the satisfaction he'd felt in helping Amelia and Homer at the *Gazette*, shuffling papers suddenly seemed tame in comparison. Thinking back to the visit Owen Merrick made to his father's home early in the spring, Ben remembered his excitement at being offered a position with Great Western. At the time, it seemed like an opportunity full of promise. What had changed in only a few short months?

Sensing his eagerness to relocate—if not the reason behind it—his father had encouraged Ben to take the job. Owen Merrick had been Paul Stone's trusted friend ever since saving his life just after the Battle of Spotsylvania Court House. He knew his former comrade-in-arms would take good care of his son.

Coupled with Ben's own desire to leave, his father's urging had been all it took for him to jump at the opportunity presented and accompany Merrick to Arizona.

It had proven to be a good move. He'd been happy in Granite Springs . . . hadn't he? Negotiating deals that benefited both the company's investors and the people who sold land to Great Western satisfied his desire to be of service. To all appearances, Merrick seemed sufficiently pleased with his work and showed more trust in him all the time. After all, he'd handpicked Ben for the task of winning Amelia's favor. That had to count for something. As long as he continued to measure up to his employer's standards, a bright future with Great Western was his for the taking—if he wanted it.

He glanced around the office, noting that his co-workers showed signs of getting ready to leave for the day. A thought struck him—the building would soon be empty. If he lagged behind after everyone else had gone, it would give him a chance to do a little looking around and see if he could come up with the answers Amelia sought.

Eddie Franklin walked out the front door first, followed by Norman Dickerson. Josh Brady lingered after the others had gone, but eventually he left, too, giving Ben a wave of his hand.

Now's the time. An opportunity like this might not present itself again. Rising from his desk, he crossed the floor to the set of file cabinets behind Josh's desk, where the company ledger was kept. He halted in midstride when he heard low voices coming from behind the closed door to Merrick's office.

He stood for a moment, like a small boy with his hand caught in the cookie jar, then started to retrace his steps. He'd gotten halfway back to his desk when the door to Merrick's office swung wide, and his employer stepped into the room. "Josh?" he called.

Ben cleared his throat. "I'm afraid he's gone for the day, sir. He left just a few minutes ago."

"Ah, Ben!" Merrick's face brightened. "I didn't realize you were here. Come in, my boy, there's someone I'd like you to talk to."

Ben straightened his collar and followed his boss to the inner office, where a tall, distinguished-looking man stood beside Merrick's desk.

Merrick swept his arm toward the visitor. "I believe you know Thaddeus Grayson."

It took a moment for the name to register, then Ben stepped forward and extended his hand. "Certainly. I met you once at a function in Washington—at Senator Drake's home, if I remember correctly."

Merrick stepped over to join them as the two shook hands. "I was sure your father and Thaddeus moved in the same circles. Thaddeus is the head of the Colorado Mining & Exploration Company in Denver . . . and the owner of Great Western, as well."

Ben struggled to keep his surprise from showing. "What a pleasant surprise, sir. I didn't realize we had this connection."

Both Merrick and Grayson chuckled. "You have more than that in common, Ben," Merrick said.

Ben shot a quizzical look at the smiling men.

Grayson rocked back on his heels and tucked his thumbs in the pockets of his pearl-gray vest. A jovial smile lit his face. "I hear you've been keeping company with my stepdaughter."

"Your stepdaughter?" Ben echoed. Who could he mean? There was only one woman he'd been spending time with in Granite Springs. But surely . . . "You mean Miss Wagner? Amelia?"

A deep laugh rumbled from Grayson's broad chest. "That's right. I recently married my childhood sweetheart, who happens to be Amelia's mother."

Ben's jaw sagged. Amelia didn't talk much about her family in Denver, and she had never mentioned a stepfather. "Does she know you're in town?"

"Not yet. I just arrived on the afternoon train, and I came straight to the office to discuss certain matters with Owen."

Ben's mind whirled, trying to assimilate this new information. He realized Merrick was speaking and pulled himself back to the moment. "Sir?"

"I was just telling Thaddeus you've been spending quite a bit of time with Miss Wagner. Isn't that right?"

Ben nodded, still feeling a bit dazed. "That's correct. As a matter of fact, we're having dinner together at the Cosmopolitan this evening."

A spark glinted in Grayson's penetrating eyes. "Why don't I join you? I need to speak to Amelia about some family matters."

Ben floundered for a reply. "I . . . I suppose that would be all right. I planned to call for her at six."

Grayson consulted the clock on the office wall and nodded. "Perfect. That will give me enough time to get settled in my room at the hotel before meeting you at the restaurant."

Ben swallowed and nodded, hoping to mask his dismay at having his plans for the evening rearranged. "I'll go back to the newspaper now and let her know you'll be dining with us."

Grayson's eyes crinkled at the corners. "No, my boy. Why don't we keep that to ourselves? I'd rather let it be a surprise."

)(

Once the door closed behind Ben, Merrick turned to Thaddeus Grayson. The affable expression had vanished from the other man's face, and he stared after Ben with a speculative gleam in his eye.

"So this is the young fellow you have working to win Amelia's trust?"

"That's right." Merrick's clipped words matched the other's tone. "And he's doing a fine job. There hasn't been a hint of negative comment in the *Gazette* since I gave him the assignment."

"And you think that's evidence that everything has been taken care of?" Grayson's lip curled. "Our plans aren't secure as long as that paper is in operation."

Merrick bristled. "Her father is dead. She's asked a few questions—but without any solid answers, where can she go? A budding friendship with young Stone should help allay any suspicions she may still harbor. In fact, I haven't given up hope of getting a retraction, if things develop between the two of them the way I expect they will."

Grayson shook his head and gave him a dour look. "You don't know the girl like I do. She has every bit of her father's tenacity. If she comes across any incriminating information he may have left behind, this whole thing could blow up in our faces."

He turned and fixed Merrick with a menacing glare. "It's taking too long. We need to have that newspaper shut down."

"You've always been impatient. I prefer taking a more subtle approach."

Grayson's eyes took on the color of cold steel. "I am a man of action. I like to have things cut and dried."

Merrick willed himself not to take a step backward. He didn't consider himself a coward—far from it! But he'd heard more than one story about people who had crossed Grayson in the past. He cleared his throat and forced a stern note into his voice. "Be careful. You know what the West is like. If you harm a woman, you'd be signing your own death warrant."

Warmth returned to Grayson's eyes, and one corner of his lips curled upward. "Who's talking about hurting her? There's more than one way to neutralize a problem."

CHAPTER 15

Amelia tucked one wayward curl in place and stepped
back to survey her reflection in the dresser mirror.
The light-blue shirred bodice with its matching box-pleated
skirt set off her eyes to perfection. She tugged at her right
sleeve, teasing its fullness into a more rounded shape, and
gave a satisfied nod. Fashionable, but not too fussy—exactly
the effect she'd hoped to create. She didn't want to make too
much of one evening meal together. It was only dinner with
a friend, after all.

But as much as she kept reminding herself of that fact, she
couldn't quell her excitement at spending more time with Ben
and getting to know him better. Perhaps for this evening, at
least, they could set aside concerns about the newspaper and
Great Western.

Unless Ben had discovered some news about the company.
Her mood sobered. If he had, would he be willing to share it
with her? And would she be ready to hear it?

If the facts didn't bolster her father's position, then what?
The mere idea of printing a retraction made her feel disloyal,
but her father had demanded as much honesty from himself

as he had expected from others. She knew he wouldn't have twisted the facts deliberately, but if he learned he'd been misled, he would have been the first to admit it and set the record straight. A retraction, if one was called for, would not dishonor his name. Quite the opposite!

With that reassurance, she gave her hair one final pat and headed down the stairs to be ready when Ben arrived. If they could find the truth—no matter where it might lead—perhaps they could move forward into a friendship unmarred by suspicion on either side.

At the foot of the stairs, she pulled up, surprised to find Homer sitting near the Peerless press, with a book of poetry on his lap. "I thought you'd gone home already."

He shrugged. "I went out and grabbed a sandwich at the Bon-Ton. Thought I'd bring it back here and read for a while." He pursed his lips as he took in her appearance. "You're getting ready to go out with young Stone?"

"That's right." Amelia lifted her chin, refusing to let Homer's obvious disapproval put a damper on her evening. She moved to his side and laid her hand on his shoulder. "Don't worry. I know you don't trust him, but I'm not some naïve, dewy-eyed schoolgirl. I'll keep my eyes open."

His expression softened. "I didn't doubt that for a minute. You've been through enough hard times lately, and I just don't want you to be hurt." He shifted on his chair. "What time do you think you'll be getting back?"

The question caught her off guard. And had she just detected the faintest whiff of alcohol? She narrowed her eyes and studied Homer's face. His eyes were clear, and he gave no other indication he'd been drinking.

Should she say anything? She pondered the thought a moment, then decided against it. The last time she took him to task, he'd been injured, not inebriated. She didn't want to accuse him unjustly, especially when a confrontation would be sure to spoil her evening with Ben.

Homer's eyes were still fixed on hers, awaiting an answer.

"When will I be home?" she floundered. "I'm not sure. If we take our time over dinner and talk a bit, I expect it will be at least an hour, maybe more."

Homer gave a short nod. "I'll be here when you get back."

She jerked her head back. "You're waiting up for me? But what if it's later than that?"

"I'll be here, no matter what time it is." Homer set his poetry book aside and pushed himself up off the chair. "I want that young man to know someone is keeping an eye on you, even if your daddy isn't around to do it anymore."

The bell over the door jangled, and Ben stepped inside. Amelia shot a warning look at Homer as she moved forward to greet him.

"You look lovely." The way Ben's eyes lit up at the sight of her sent warmth flooding through her veins. Then he looked past her and nodded to Homer. "Good evening, Mr. Crenshaw. It's good to see you." He walked over to the older man and held out his hand.

After a moment's hesitation, Homer accepted the handshake and cleared his throat. "Evening. I hope you two have a pleasant meal."

Amelia stifled a laugh as she picked up her reticule. She had to give Homer credit. His words sounded gracious enough, but she knew the effort it cost him. She sent an appreciative smile his way as Ben held the door open for her to step out onto the boardwalk.

"It's a lovely evening, isn't it?" Ben asked.

Amelia murmured agreement. A gentle breeze stirred the air, carrying the scent of fresh-cut lumber from Martin Gilbreth's sawmill and the pungent tang of the pine trees farther up the slopes. She tucked her hand into the crook of Ben's arm, feeling the texture of his broadcloth jacket beneath her fingertips.

Ben smiled down at her and laid his other hand atop hers for a moment. Amelia met his eyes and caught her breath at the intensity of his gaze. "Yes, I'd say it's just about perfect."

Oddly, his pleasure seemed to fade and his steps lagged as they moved farther along the boardwalk. She looked up at him and studied his face. "Is anything wrong?"

He offered a smile that seemed forced. "There's a bit of a surprise waiting for you at the restaurant."

Her interest quickened. Maybe he had come across some information about Great Western, after all. And from his solemn expression, she suspected it might help substantiate her father's articles. "A surprise? What is it?"

He laid his hand over the spot where hers rested on his sleeve and squeezed her fingers. "You'll find out soon enough. Let's wait until we get there."

Amelia could hardly contain her anticipation until they reached the Cosmopolitan and Ben ushered her inside. She laughed at herself, knowing she was as excited as a young child on Christmas morning.

As they entered, she smiled up at him. "All right, we're here. What's the surprise?"

Instead of answering, Ben scanned the room. "This way."

Taking Amelia's arm, he led her toward the rear. She nodded to the other diners as they threaded their way past tables covered in crisp, white linen. Finally he indicated a table where a silver-haired man sat with his back to them.

Amelia turned a quizzical look at Ben as the other man rose. Ben cleared his throat and said, "I don't believe an introduction is necessary."

The table's occupant turned to face them. An icy hand seemed to clutch at Amelia's heart when she stared up into the face of Thaddeus Grayson.

She swayed slightly and tightened her hold on Ben's arm to steady herself.

A chuckle rumbled from Grayson's chest. "Ah, I see we managed to pull off our surprise. Well done, Ben. You know how to keep a secret." Turning back to Amelia, he ran his eyes down the front of her dress and back up again. "How delightful to see you, my dear."

He leaned over and kissed her on the cheek, then lifted his eyebrows in mock surprise. "What? No congratulations for your new stepfather?"

Amelia knotted her hands into fists to hold them back from scrubbing the unwanted contact away. At last, she found her voice. "What are you doing here? What is this all about?"

She swiveled around to look at Ben, who looked as confused as she felt.

"Why don't we discuss it over dinner?" Grayson extended his hand toward the table and favored them both with an affable smile.

Share a meal with this man? *No!* Amelia cast a longing glance at the front of the restaurant. More than anything, she wanted to bolt for the door, but her wobbly legs refused to cooperate.

She followed Ben's lead as he held a chair for her and settled her into the place opposite Grayson's, then took the seat to her left.

A moment later, their waitress appeared. Grayson beamed at her. "An order of your finest steaks, all around."

Amelia couldn't find the energy to object to him making the choice without consulting them first. She went back to staring between him and Ben, a whirl of thoughts cascading through her mind.

"So you two know each other?" She had to concentrate to force the words out.

Ben opened his mouth to answer, but Grayson cut in. "Ah, yes. I met Benjamin several years ago while I was working back east. He struck me as a bright young man, and I'm pleased to see he's fulfilling that promise. I'm only sorry I didn't take him under my wing back then. He could have been working for me in Denver instead of here at Great Western with my friend Owen Merrick."

Amelia stared at Ben as if seeing him for the first time. He seemed distant somehow, as if she was peering at him through the wrong end of a telescope. She had spent much of her time lately wondering if her father had been misled, but was she the one who had been deceived?

That open face, the steady gaze she had begun to trust— nothing she had learned of Ben seemed to fit the type of man she knew Grayson to be. But was that the real man, or all part of an act? She knew Grayson's ability to put forth one face in public, while a completely different persona emerged behind closed doors.

Their waitress appeared, bearing plates of succulent-looking steaks. Amelia stared at the sizzling meat and accompanying side dishes, but her appetite had fled. The waitress set a cup of tea before her, and Amelia took a long sip. Drawing strength from the reviving brew, she mentally shook herself and felt her journalistic instincts kick in.

She didn't want to believe the worst of Ben, not on circumstantial evidence alone. A mere acquaintance with Thaddeus Grayson didn't make him guilty by association. Her father's training taught her to ask questions and look at things objectively. She needed to put aside her dislike of her stepfather and step into the role of a reporter, ready to observe them both.

After taking a tiny bite and fortifying herself with another sip of tea, she forced herself to meet Grayson's eyes. "You've never really told me much about your work."

A smile lit his face, as though pleased by her apparent capitulation. "You've probably heard quite a bit about it already from young Ben, here."

When she stared at him, stupefied, he chuckled and added, "I am the owner of several businesses committed to playing a part in the expansion of the West—including the Great Western Investment Company. It's an exciting time, my dear, one filled with opportunities."

Amelia could only stare at him. That meant Ben worked for her stepfather! The revelation made her thoughts reel. Keeping her voice steady, she said, "So business brought you here?"

He turned a burning gaze on her, and she looked down at her plate. "For the most part, but something a little more personal drew me to Granite Springs, as well."

She yanked her head up and looked at him again. "What do you mean?"

Grayson laid his fork on his plate with a soft clink. He leaned across the table toward her, his face suddenly serious. "It's your mother, Amelia."

Her hand flew to her throat. "What about Mother? Is she ill?"

Her stepfather sighed. "She's been under a lot of stress lately, what with the shock of your father's death and all the preparations for our wedding."

Amelia's lips twisted. As quickly as they had married, the wedding couldn't have needed too much preparation. Surely her mother, even with her love of being the center of attention, wouldn't have insisted on a lavish ceremony, with her first husband so recently departed.

Grayson leaned even closer. "She's been worrying herself sick . . . over you."

Over me, or how my prolonged absence might be perceived by her society friends? Amelia felt a quick twinge of guilt. Maternal feelings must exist somewhere in her mother's nature, although she would be hard-pressed to come up with many examples.

She drew herself up. "Please tell Mother she doesn't have anything to worry about. I'm doing quite well here, and I'm very happy." Clenching her hands in her lap, she shot a pleading look at Ben. If only she could find a way to get out of this miserable situation!

His brow puckered, as if he realized she was sending an unspoken message but wasn't sure what she wanted him to do.

Grayson went on as though she hadn't spoken. "She's beside

herself, thinking about you on your own out here, alone and unprotected."

Amelia nearly scoffed aloud. He was the last person who should bring up such ideas. Nobody ever worried about her needing protection back in Denver . . . from him.

She looked back down at her plate, thinking about the lovely evening she had anticipated, sitting across the table from Ben and staring into his eyes. But Thaddeus Grayson's unwelcome appearance had turned her plans to dust. There had to be a way to call a stop to the evening. She couldn't take much more of this.

Something nudged the toe of her shoe, and she glanced at Ben. Was this a way of sending her unspoken support? To be fair, whatever he did or didn't know about Grayson's business, he couldn't possibly be aware of her troubled relationship with the man who had become her stepfather. She could understand his confusion and not wanting to make a scene in a public place.

To her surprise, Ben's eyes remained fixed on his plate while he sliced off another bite of his steak. The pressure on her foot increased, then moved up higher along her ankle.

When Ben still gave no sign of awareness, she flicked a glance back at Grayson. The glint in his eyes and the half smile on his lips confirmed her suspicions. She yanked her foot back. "What do you think you're doing?"

Ben jerked his head up, and Grayson arched his eyebrows. "What do you mean? I'm just a man looking out for the welfare of my stepdaughter. I can't tell you how much your mother and I look forward to the day you move back to Denver and share our home."

The small bit of food she'd managed to eat threatened to

make a reappearance. She pressed her napkin against her lips and looked at Ben. "I'm not feeling well. Would you please excuse me?"

"Of course." He jumped to his feet. "Let me escort you home." He looked around as if trying to catch the waitress's attention.

Grayson waved his hand. "No, no. I'll take care of the bill. The important thing is to make sure Amelia is taken care of."

Ben hovered over her on their walk back to the *Gazette* in a way that reminded her of a concerned mother hen. "I'm sorry you aren't feeling well. Was something wrong with your meal?"

Amelia tucked her hands close to her sides. "No. It was the company."

Ben's eyes widened, and his face went slack. "Are you talking about your stepfather, or me, or both? I already picked up on the fact that your stepfather's surprise wasn't a welcome one."

"I shouldn't blame you for that. You couldn't have known."

"Known what?"

Amelia glanced up at him, then looked away. "My mother and Thaddeus Grayson have known each other for years—most of their lives, in fact. He began to squire her around when he moved back to Denver, about a year ago."

"But your father—" Ben broke off and looked as if he wished he could take the words back.

"That's right." Amelia sighed. "They were seeing each other while my father was still alive, long before he took ill. And they didn't waste any time jumping into marriage after his death."

Her voice shook, and she pressed her lips together until she regained control. "But I wouldn't be in favor of this marriage, no matter how long they waited. Thaddeus Grayson is not a man I admire."

When they reached the *Gazette,* Ben paused before opening the door. Amelia searched his face, wishing she knew what lay behind his solemn gaze. "This 'surprise,'" she said, "was it your idea or his?"

Ben started and shook his head emphatically. "Are you asking if I invited you to dinner tonight for the purpose of meeting him? The answer is no. I only met Grayson once, years ago. And that was just in passing. I had no idea he was in town until after I talked to you this afternoon. And I certainly never dreamed there was any connection between the two of you before he told me today."

He raised one hand and trailed the backs of his fingers along her cheek. "I'm so sorry our evening was ruined. This wasn't the way I planned for it to go."

Her eyes fluttered closed at his touch, knowing she would have enjoyed the contact more had her emotions not been in such turmoil.

"Perhaps another time?"

She opened her eyes to study his face again. A small smile tugged at the corners of her lips. "I'd like that. Thank you for seeing me home. Good night."

※

Homer looked up from his book when she walked in and closed the door behind her. His bushy eyebrows shot up. "Back so soon?"

Amelia set her reticule on the counter. "Things didn't go quite the way I expected."

Homer stood and laid the book on the floor next to the press. His face took on a stormy hue. "Did that scoundrel do something out of line? I'd be happy to pay him a visit and give him a piece of my mind—or more, if he needs it."

Despite her taut nerves, a laugh gurgled from Amelia's throat. She walked over to give her protector a hug, feeling her tension begin to slip away. "Nothing like that. Ben was a perfect gentleman. It's just that . . ." Her shoulders tightened. "My stepfather is in town." Reaching for her reticule, she pulled out a lace-trimmed handkerchief and scrubbed at the spot on her cheek where Grayson had kissed her.

Homer pushed his chair toward her. "You need to sit down?"

She shook her head. "No, I could hardly hold myself up when I first saw him, but I'm fine now." In fact, she felt suddenly energized. Tossing her handkerchief beside the reticule, she strode to the opposite end of the printing office, then pivoted and retraced her steps.

Homer watched her, tilting his head to one side. "I know you're unhappy that he married your mother, but is there something else? Did he say something that upset you?"

His question jolted her to a halt. She had known Homer nearly all her life and trusted him more than anyone but her father. The words she couldn't bring herself to say to Ben came spilling out. "It isn't so much what he says as the way he says it. And the way he looks at me."

She stopped short. Not even to Homer could she explain how she felt when Thaddeus Grayson's gaze raked across her. Like this evening, when he made a show of complimenting her appearance, eyeing her as though looking through her dress, not at it.

Homer scratched his head. "I thought it was your mother he was focused on."

164

"Oh, he's interested in her, all right—her money and status, anyway."

When she trailed off, Homer set his lips in a thin line. "I'm guessing there's more to this than you're telling me."

"Let's just say he isn't an honorable man and leave it at that. He certainly knows how to squire my mother around and make her feel special, but I can't believe their marriage vows will mean anything to him. He had no qualms about pursuing my mother while she was married to my father. Now that she's married to him, I have no illusions it will keep him from dallying with other women."

Or away from me. Nothing, not even his supposedly single-minded pursuit of her mother, had stopped his unwelcome advances before. And just like tonight, they had often been made in full view of other people, without anyone but her aware of what was happening.

"Where did you see him? Did you run across him while you were on your way to the restaurant?"

"No." She uttered a shaky laugh. "He'd already spoken to Ben. He was waiting for us there."

"What!" Homer's voice cracked. "What was that young pup thinking, to set that up without telling you?"

"He had no way of knowing." Speaking the words aloud made her more convinced than ever that it was true. She knew her stepfather's duplicity all too well, but everything she had seen of Ben spoke of him being the man of honor she believed him to be.

Homer shook his head. "I hope you're right. But as for this Grayson fellow . . . ." He marched over to snap the lock in place on the front door. "I want you to keep this place locked up tight as a drum when I'm not around. Do you hear? And that won't be very often. I plan to stick around here like a burr. That stepfather of yours isn't going to bother you, as long as I'm here."

Amelia gave him a hug and a peck on the cheek, then made her way up the stairs to her room. Unbuttoning the light-blue bodice and skirt she'd donned with such anticipation, she hung them in her wardrobe. Then she pulled her nightgown from its hook and held it to her chest.

Homer had meant every word of that promise. And she felt sure Ben would never allow anyone to take advantage of her.

But neither of them would be able to stay at her side every moment. And from the look in Thaddeus Grayson's eyes tonight, she knew he would somehow find a way to get her alone.

CHAPTER 16

Amelia woke up the next morning with a renewed sense of purpose. The shock of seeing her stepfather, coupled with fear and disgust stirred up by memories of their earlier encounters, had so paralyzed her thinking, she hadn't been able to look beyond her immediate reaction and consider the bigger picture.

While she dressed, she reviewed the ideas that teased at her mind throughout the night. Her stepfather implied a long-standing relationship with Owen Merrick. He obviously trusted the man, to put him in charge of his operations in Granite Springs. Knowing of Thaddeus Grayson's connection to Great Western, she felt more convinced than ever that her father had been on to something.

Picking up her hairbrush, she spent the next few minutes trying to smooth her stubborn dark curls into some semblance of order. *How could I have doubted Papa?* Sick or not, he had an unerring instinct for a newsworthy story.

She trotted down the stairs to the small kitchen and set a kettle of water on the stove to heat water for a cup of tea. A note propped near the stove caught her eye:

Heading out to see what news I can turn up. Keep the doors locked until I get back.

A twinge of impatience shot through her. *I'm not a little child.* The spark of irritation faded almost as quickly as it arose, however, and a smile curved her lips at the reminder that Homer was only looking out for her safety. Hearing the teakettle whistle, she poured boiling water over the tea leaves and started back to the office with her cup and saucer in her hand. A knock at the alley door interrupted her.

Amelia frowned and set the cup and saucer down on the sideboard next to the stove. *Who could that be?* Homer had his own key, so he wouldn't bother to knock. They weren't expecting any deliveries. There was no reason anyone should be coming to the rear of the newspaper office.

Treading softly, she crept to the door and pressed her ear against the planks. Had her stepfather seen Homer leave and decided to pay her a visit?

Another knock, a louder one this time, rattled the door. Amelia squeaked and jumped back as though she'd been stung by a bee.

"Hello! Is anybody there?"

Her knees sagged in relief at the sound of a woman's voice. Hastening to the door, she turned the lock and swung it open. Her eyes widened when she recognized Millie Brown, proprietress of Granite Springs's most notorious brothel.

"I need to come in." When Amelia didn't respond immediately, the other woman narrowed her eyes. "We need to talk, and I don't think you want folks to see me standing outside your door."

Amelia stepped aside to let the brassy blond woman sashay

past her. She studied her unexpected visitor while she busied herself with the lock. What on earth was Millie Brown doing at the *Gazette*? She couldn't think of a single reason the woman would want to speak with her. Unless . . .

Her father had written a number of editorials about the plight of fallen women who found themselves reduced to a life of sin. Perhaps his words had touched Millie's heart, and she'd come seeking help.

Amelia stretched out her hand. "What can I do for you?"

"I'm here to talk business."

Amelia gaped at the brusque words. "Excuse me?"

Millie planted one hand on her ample hip and regarded Amelia with a look of impatience. "Business." She enunciated the word with care. "Your father is dead, and since you're his heir, that means I need to speak to you."

"My father? But what—"

"Your father, my partner. He owned half my business." Millie's painted lips curled into a scornful smile. "I take it he didn't tell you?"

Amelia tried to make sense of the other woman's statement while the room seemed to spin around her. "You're saying . . . No, that isn't possible!"

Without bothering to respond to her outburst, Millie continued. "I'm not surprised. Most men don't want their womenfolk to know everything they've been up to. Your father fronted the money when I started the business. It's worked out well for both of us, but now that he's gone, I'd like to own it outright. I figure his share is worth two thousand dollars."

Opening her black satin reticule, she drew out a wad of bills and thrust it toward Amelia. "Here, it's yours."

Amelia stared at the tainted money in the woman's hand. "Stop! I don't believe you. My father wouldn't have been involved in anything like that."

Millie shrugged. "I thought you might not take my word for it, so I brought proof." Tucking the cash back into her reticule, she pulled forth a folded sheet of paper and held it out. "Read this."

Feeling as though she had just walked into a nightmare, Amelia took the paper and spread it open. She scanned the page quickly, then went back over it again, more carefully this time. The document appeared to be a deed to the building that housed Millie Brown's establishment, with Millie and Andrew Wagner listed as co-owners of the business. Tears stung her eyes when she saw the familiar signature at the bottom of the page: *A. J. Wagner.*

No, it can't be true. In a daze, she folded the paper again and pressed it between her hands. Millie reached over and snatched it from her fingers.

"I'll have that back, if you please. You don't need both copies."

"Both?"

"Your father had his own. There's no reason for you to have mine, as well."

Amelia ran her fingers through her curls, trying to sweep the web of confusion from her mind. "There has to be some mistake."

Millie Brown lifted one shoulder. "Don't take my word for it, go look for yourself. He kept it in the bottom drawer of one of those file cabinets of his. I saw him put it there with my own eyes."

Amelia stared at her for a long moment, and then she pushed her way past the other woman and hurried to her office. Millie sauntered along in her wake.

"Which cabinet?" Amelia demanded. "Show me."

"That one." Millie pointed to the cabinet on the far right. "Bottom drawer."

Dropping to her knees, Amelia yanked the drawer open. She had looked through every cabinet when she started her research on Great Western, but this drawer contained only three files, none of them pertaining to the company. She'd seen no reason to explore them in detail.

Reaching into the drawer, she pulled the files into her lap. The first one contained a handful of receipts, nothing more. The second held a number of proofs from old print jobs. The third . . . Amelia flipped open the cover and froze when she saw only one paper inside—a document identical to the one Millie had shown her.

She picked it up and stood, spilling the contents of the other folders onto the floor. Her lips quivered as she stared at the incriminating words above her father's signature, and then she let the page slip from her fingers and flutter to the floor. "This can't be right," she whispered. "I simply can't believe it."

Millie's smile reminded her of a purring cat. "I hate to be the one to burst your bubble, but your daddy was a man like all the rest. Believe it or not, it's true." Looping the reticule higher on her arm, she turned toward the door. "Take a little time to let it sink in, and send me word when you're ready to make a deal. Don't worry, it'll stay our little secret."

Her footsteps thudded across the wooden floor, and Amelia

heard the alley door open and close. She managed to get to the door and turn the lock, then she slumped back against the wall.

Her father, a silent partner in that abominable trade? Ridiculous! Yet she had seen the document Millie Brown produced and found a matching one tucked away in her father's files, both bearing his signature.

Pushing herself upright, she staggered back to the kitchen and poured out her cup of tea, now stone-cold. There was no point in warming it up again. She wouldn't be able to keep it down even if she did manage to swallow it.

She made her way to her office in a haze and sank into the chair behind the desk. Her father's chair.

A low moan escaped her lips as she trailed her fingers along the armrests, following the grooves his own hands had imprinted there over the years. How well did she know her father after all? She would have staked all she held dear on his unwavering integrity, but Millie Brown's revelation shattered everything she thought she knew about him into a million pieces. Cradling her head in her hands, she let the tears flow.

"The truth shall make you free." The familiar words echoed in her mind.

Sobs shook her shoulders. Free? How was that possible? If what that odious woman said was true, then everything she'd believed about her father was based on lies. How could she call it freedom when she felt like she'd been weighed down by chains of shame and doubt?

"Seek the truth." The thought filtered into her mind.

Amelia lifted her head at the reminder of her father's familiar maxim. She had lived by that creed all her life, but today's truth wasn't one she wanted to pursue. She had seen the evidence of Millie Brown's claim, held the incriminating paper in her own hands.

What truth *did* she want to follow? If her father wasn't the man she'd always thought him to be, at least she could cling to the knowledge that she was a child of God, whose sins had been washed away. All her sins, big and little. And what a relief that was!

"And forgive us our debts, as we forgive our debtors."

The words from the Lord's Prayer struck her like a blow. Could she forgive her father for not being the person she believed him to be? More than once, she'd heard Pastor Edmonds say forgiveness didn't imply approval for what a person had done. It was more like the cancellation of a debt, making the choice not to harbor ill feelings for being wronged.

She might never know all the facts about her father's involvement in this matter. But she knew beyond a doubt that he had loved her. And she knew he had unerring instincts for discovering a news story worth pursuing. That much, she could believe without question.

And the pursuit of truth still mattered now, just as much as it ever had. She swept her fingers across her cheeks to wipe away the tears. She wouldn't let Millie Brown's stunning announcement distract her from her mission: to learn the truth about Great Western.

Taking a deep breath, she straightened in her chair and tried to concentrate. Her father had voiced concern over the company's plans to use hydraulic mining, thereby defacing the area around Granite Springs. But he'd also implied something else was going on, something he hadn't been able to uncover before his death.

She drummed an impatient tattoo on the desktop with her fingertips, forcing her thoughts in order. Hydraulic mining required quantities of heavy equipment, shipped in by train. What if other shipments had arrived, as well, something that might give her a clue as to some other direction the company might take?

Her lips curved. If that were the case, there was one person who would be sure to know all about it.

Reaching for her notebook, she rose from the desk. Her eyes lit on the deed, lying atop the other papers she had scattered on the floor earlier. With a sigh, she knelt to scoop up the papers and return them to their respective folders.

Picking up the deed with her father's signature, she wavered for a moment, then slipped it back into its hiding place. At some point, she would have to decide what to do with the bombshell of information Millie Brown had dropped into her lap. But she could only deal with one crisis at a time.

CHAPTER 17

Pausing only long enough to wash the traces of tears from her face, she scribbled a note to Homer and hurried to the station. When she spotted Thomas Rafferty stacking crates at the edge of the platform, she quickened her pace and called out to him.

"Good morning! Could I interrupt your work for a moment?"

The station agent straightened slowly and pressed his hands against his lower back. "I can always make time for you. It's a welcome respite after pushing these heavy crates around. What can I do for you?"

Amelia glanced around to make sure they wouldn't be overheard. Keeping her voice low, she asked, "I'm interested in learning about any large shipments that may have arrived for Owen Merrick—or Great Western."

Rafferty rubbed his hand across the back of his neck and frowned. "They've had quite a bit come in over the past few weeks. A car full of pipe and hoses and nozzles showed up about ten days ago. I'm not quite sure what that's all about."

Amelia nodded. "That would be some of the equipment

they need for hydraulic mining," she told him, drawing on the information she had gleaned from her father's notes.

Thomas Rafferty squinted. "But I thought that was outlawed some ten years back, after they saw all the damage it did over in California."

"It was, until the Caminetti Mining Bill passed. It's a viable option once again for mine owners operating on a big scale."

Rafferty drew his head back. "I'm sorry to hear that." He looked up at the hills around them and shook his head slowly. "I can't even picture what it would be like if the mountainside was scarred up, with nothing but bare rock where all those big trees are."

Amelia took a breath and chose her words carefully. "They've bought up a lot of local land, and they can do whatever they want with it. As much as I hate thinking about that, my father seemed to feel they might be planning something even worse. Have you seen anything that might help give us a clue as to what it is?"

The station agent pulled off his cap and scratched his head. "I can't say that I have." Replacing the cap on his head, he added with a determined look, "But you can bet I'll be keeping my eyes open."

He grinned at her. "I suppose you'd like me to let you know if I spot something that might fit the bill?"

"I'd appreciate that very much." Amelia laid her hand on his arm and leaned closer to him. "And if you don't mind, let's keep this just between us."

Rafferty's grin broadened, and he lowered one eyelid in a conspiratorial wink. "You sounded just like your dad right then. And the answer is yes—I kept a confidence for him more than once, and I'll be glad to do the same for you."

Amelia squeezed his arm in thanks and let him get back to his work. Walking along the edge of the platform, she eyed the bustling activity in town. The scene reminded her of the day she arrived. She had been standing in almost that same spot, waiting for her father to come meet her.

A pang of grief smote her when she recalled her bright anticipation for this visit and how differently things had turned out from what she'd expected.

She looked around, remembering the day she arrived in Granite Springs and the last moments of carefree normalcy before her world fell apart. She smiled when she recalled the cowboy who mistook her for an eastern tenderfoot, the gossiping matrons who moved away when they thought she'd overheard them, and that mischievous little boy careening along the street with his hoop.

Something about the women jarred her memory, and she frowned. She *had* overheard part of their conversation, even made a note of it as a possible story lead. Her frown deepened. What had they been saying?

Something about a foreclosure, she recalled. She intended to look into it further at the time, but her interest in the potential story had been pushed aside by the discovery of her father's illness.

Now the revived memory picked at her thoughts, refusing to leave her alone. What exactly had they talked about? She dug in her reticule and pulled out her notebook. Thumbing through the pages, she let out a small cry of triumph when she came across the entry she sought.

It wasn't much to go on, though. Merely a quick note about a foreclosure on Bart McCaffrey's property.

She tapped her finger against the penciled words. If memory served, one of the women chalked the foreclosure up to poor business sense. But could there be more to it than that?

Tucking her notebook away, she tightened the drawstring of her reticule and set off toward the bank. It might or might not lead to a newsworthy story, but it was worth checking out.

She walked along Railroad Street, then turned up Second. As she rounded the corner, she nearly collided with a man striding along quickly in the opposite direction.

"Oh!" Amelia stumbled to a stop. She drew herself up when she recognized Owen Merrick. "Pardon me," she said coolly, intending to sweep past him without further comment.

To her surprise, Merrick tipped his hat and smiled. "Good morning to you, Miss Wagner. Out looking for more rumors to spread so early in the day?"

She lifted her chin and glared at him. "If you're asking whether I'm going about my duties as a journalist, the answer is yes."

"More of that digging we talked about earlier?" One corner of his mouth tilted in a sardonic smile. "Just remember what I said: You may not like what you turn up. People who live in glass houses shouldn't throw stones, you know." With another tip of his hat, he turned on his heel and went on his way.

His words took her breath away as effectively as a blow to the stomach. Amelia's mouth fell open, and she struggled for air as she stared after his departing figure.

She had sensed a veiled threat in his previous warning to stop asking questions about Great Western, although she'd had no idea what he'd meant by it. This time his words filled her with dread. *He knows!*

Her certainty grew as she recalled his mocking smile and the smug look in his eyes. Somehow Owen Merrick had learned about her father's dealings with Millie Brown. And he meant to use that against her if she continued to investigate Great Western.

Which meant there must be something he didn't want her to uncover.

She stood frozen like a statue for a few moments, as fear of exposure warred with her sense of duty. The revelation of her father's involvement with a local brothel would do irreparable damage to the reputation he had built. But allowing herself to be blackmailed would mean withholding truth that might be vital to the well-being of Granite Springs and its citizens.

That realization snapped her out of her stupor. A block later, she reached the bank at the corner of Sherman Street. Stepping through the door, she hovered inside the entrance long enough to catch her breath and let her eyes adjust to the relative dimness in contrast to the bright summer sunlight outdoors.

Through his open office door, she saw Hubert Murphy, the bank manager, working at his desk. Amelia shifted from one foot to the other and finally caught his eye.

He raised his hand in greeting. "Good morning, Miss Wagner."

Amelia nodded to the teller as she walked past him to Murphy's office and stepped through the doorway. "I wonder if I could have a minute of your time."

The bank manager spread his hands in welcome. "Of course. Come in and have a seat. Have you come to see me for a loan? Interested in purchasing some new equipment for the paper, perhaps?"

She smiled as she settled herself in the wooden visitor's chair. "No, Homer keeps that press of ours running along well enough to suit. I was just curious about something and hoped you could help me. What can you tell me about the McCaffrey foreclosure?"

Murphy raised his eyebrows and studied her closely. Looking down, he toyed with the inkwell on his desk for a moment, then appeared to make up his mind. "I hope you know I wouldn't discuss a foreclosure while it's in process, but since it's now public record, I suppose there's no harm in talking about it.

"That property had been in Bart McCaffrey's family for twenty years, but he hadn't done a thing to improve it. He received an offer on the place, which he turned down. Shortly after that, he took a notion to dam up part of the property and build a reservoir."

Amelia sat forward on her chair. "A reservoir? What on earth gave him the idea to do that?"

Murphy lifted both shoulders. "He said he wanted to be able to supply the farmers downstream with water during a dry spell. Figured he could make a tidy sum that way. He came in and borrowed money for the labor and equipment he needed to get things moving, with the land as collateral. But once the project was completed, he found himself unable to pay off the loan." His face took on a look of genuine sorrow. "We gave him as much time as we could, but he wound up defaulting, and the bank had to take it over."

"So he was doing this to help the local farmers and make a profit for himself." Amelia shook her head. Her story lead had apparently been nothing more than a wild-goose chase. "In that case, the bank owns the property now?"

"Not any longer." Murphy moved the inkwell to the corner of his desk. "Great Western made an offer on it shortly after the foreclosure was final." He looked at Amelia and spread his hands again. "That's really all I can tell you."

She nodded and rose. "Thank you very much. I appreciate your time." Exiting the bank, she turned down Sherman Street, lost in thought. Why would Bart McCaffrey decide to build a reservoir? Did he have some arrangement with the farmers he hoped to supply, or had it been—as one of the matrons had said—merely a bad business move?

Great Western certainly hadn't wasted any time in snapping up the property. What could that mean? She made a mental note to ask Ben about it.

Reaching First Street, she turned the corner in front of the Granite Springs Hotel. As she walked on, a man stepped away from the building and took up a stance in the middle of the boardwalk.

Amelia stopped short and looked up into Thaddeus Grayson's smiling face. Her hand flew to her throat. She moved to sidestep him, but he shifted slightly, blocking her way.

"Good day, daughter. I hope you're feeling better."

The endearment made her skin crawl, but she wasn't about to let him think he intimidated her. Resisting the urge to flee, she stood her ground and hiked up her chin. "Don't call me that."

"Why not? You *are* my daughter—by marriage, at least." His eyes traveled down the front of her bodice. "I'll be wrapping up my business here soon. Dare I hope you've started making arrangements to free yourself from the newspaper so you can accompany me back to Denver?"

Amelia swallowed back the words she longed to say. "Perhaps I didn't make myself clear. I will not be accompanying you to Denver . . . or anywhere else. I have no intention of leaving Granite Springs. This is my home now, and I'm staying here."

"But what about your mother?" Grayson stroked his salt-and-pepper mustache with his index finger. "She misses you terribly. She wants you to come make your home with us. We both do."

Bile scorched Amelia's throat. "Don't delude yourself. Even if I did move back to Denver—which is not going to happen—I wouldn't dream of spending one night under the same roof with you."

A glint of anger flashed in his eyes, quickly replaced by an amused glimmer. "You seem very sure of yourself, my dear. But—"

"I didn't expect to see you out and about at this time of day."

Amelia spun around at the sound of the familiar voice. Relief flooded her when she saw Clara and Martin Gilbreth approaching.

"Clara! What a pleasant surprise!" The rawboned woman and her square-faced brother had never looked more wonderful. "I was hoping we'd have a chance to visit before long. It's been a while since you stopped by the newspaper office."

"We've both been busy. Martin hired on a new crew, and I've had my hands full taking care of things up there." Clara's gaze shifted away from Amelia to a point over her shoulder.

Behind herself, Amelia heard Grayson clear his throat. "Good day. I don't believe we've met before. I'm Thaddeus Grayson, Amelia's stepfather."

Martin stepped forward and enveloped Grayson's fingers in

a work-hardened hand. "Martin Gilbreth. I own the sawmill here. And this is my sister, Clara."

After acknowledging the introduction, Clara turned back to Amelia. "I didn't realize you had family visiting. We were just on our way to the café for a bit of lunch, so we'll be heading along now. Didn't mean to interrupt."

"We had just finished talking." Amelia glared at Grayson, daring him to contradict her. "I was on my way back to the paper. Since you're heading that direction, I'll walk with the two of you." She linked her arm in Clara's and tugged the older woman along before she could say anything else.

Clara shot her an odd look. As soon as they were out of earshot, she said, "That fellow may be kin, but I get the feeling there's no love lost between the two of you. You couldn't get away from him fast enough. Are you all right?"

Amelia cast a quick glance over her shoulder. To her relief, Grayson stood where they had left him, with his hands in his pockets and a thoughtful expression on his face. "Let's just say he isn't my favorite person and leave it at that."

She squeezed Clara's arm. "Thank you for rescuing me. You came along just in time. You're a good friend." She smiled, looking up to include Martin in her thanks. "You both are."

CHAPTER 18

"How was your dinner last night with Miss Wagner and her stepfather?"

Ben looked up to see Owen Merrick standing beside his desk. He pushed aside the report he'd been writing on a parcel of land north of town and looked up at his boss. "I'm afraid it didn't go as well as I'd hoped. Miss Wagner became indisposed partway through the meal, and the evening ended early."

Merrick nodded slowly. Looking around at the other desks, he leaned nearer and lowered his voice. "How is our little project coming along?"

Ben bristled at the condescending tone. "I don't think of Miss Wagner as a project. She's a person I'm beginning to admire and look upon as a friend."

"And she's feeling the same way about you?" Merrick's eyes gleamed. "That's fine work, my boy. Has she said anything more about her opinion of Great Western?"

Besides asking me to find out what the company is up to? Ben shook his head. "Not in so many words, but I believe she still has some reservations." When he saw the other man tense, he added, "But as you know, the *Gazette* hasn't printed any more

184

negative stories about the company. In fact, the other day she implied she might be open to the possibility of a retraction."

"Really?" Merrick's face lit up, and he clapped Ben on the shoulder. "Well done, my boy. There's a lesson to be learned from the fable of the tortoise and the hare. People need to realize that much can be lost by trying to storm the gates and speed ahead. I believe this is a situation where slow and steady will win the race.

"In fact . . ." He looked out the window. "There's the fair Miss Wagner now. Why don't you go out and strike up a conversation while the opportunity presents itself?"

Ben glanced down at his report. "I'll need a little more time to finish this up."

"No, that can wait." Merrick swept his arm out in an expansive gesture. "Strike while the iron is hot, my boy. This is far more important."

Ben didn't need any more coaxing. Pulling his jacket from the back of his chair, he slipped it on and adjusted his tie before strolling out into the sunlit street. He spotted Amelia walking with Martin Gilbreth and his sister and angled across the street to intercept them.

Amelia looked like she was feeling better, he noted with relief. He was glad she seemed to have recovered from her unexpected meeting with her stepfather the night before. Not for the first time, he mused about the strange coincidence of Grayson's connection to both Amelia and Great Western.

According to Thaddeus Grayson, he and Amelia's mother had been childhood sweethearts. But that still didn't explain their haste to marry so quickly after Amelia's father died.

A thought struck him, and his steps faltered. A comment

Amelia made earlier implied that Grayson had been carrying on a dalliance with Amelia's mother while her father was still alive. Had Andrew Wagner known about it? If that were the case . . .

Ben stopped in his tracks, feeling like the pieces of the puzzle were finally beginning to fall into place. Could that knowledge—assuming Andrew Wagner also knew about Grayson's ownership of Great Western—have been the catalyst that prompted the hostile articles he'd written about the company?

He felt a sting of disloyalty to Amelia for entertaining such a thought, but it made sense. He knew how much she admired her father, but wasn't she the one who insisted on finding the truth? The possibility, unsavory as it was, had to be taken into consideration.

Ben picked up his pace and tipped his hat to the trio when they drew near. "Good afternoon."

The Gilbreths' greetings faded in the light of Amelia's smile. Her pleasure at seeing him warmed him even more than the summer sunshine.

"I was hoping we could talk for a bit," he told her. "But if you're busy . . . ?"

"Not at all." She turned to Clara Gilbreth, "Thank you again for coming along when you did. If you'll excuse me . . ."

He saw the older woman dig her elbow into Amelia's ribs and heard her mutter something under her breath. When he offered his arm, Amelia tucked her hand in his elbow, and they crossed back to the other side of the street.

"Was there something particular you wanted to talk to me about?" she asked when he helped her step up onto the boardwalk.

He grinned, appreciating the way she offered him an opening. "The concert at the Odd Fellows Hall is just a few days away. I was wondering if you'd be interested in attending with me."

Her face brightened even more. "I'd be happy to. I planned to go anyway, to cover the story for the paper, but I'd enjoy it much more in your company."

Ben wanted to let out a whoop, but he held himself in. He glanced down at her, feeling suddenly awkward. "That's a relief. I thought I heard Miss Gilbreth say something about my making you uncomfortable."

Her cheeks turned the scarlet of an Arizona sunset. "Not at all. What she said was, it didn't look like *you* made me feel uncomfortable." When he looked at her quizzically, the crimson color deepened. "She was referring to my stepfather. He caught me when I was coming down the street, and they rescued me."

Ben stumbled to a halt. "Rescued you?"

"Maybe not in a literal sense. I mean they helped extricate me from a disagreeable encounter." Her blue eyes flashed when she looked up at him. "You said you met my stepfather a number of years ago. How much do you know about the kind of man he is?"

"It was at a social function I attended with my parents. Our host introduced him to us, and we chatted for a time. Other than that brief meeting, I never saw him again until he arrived here yesterday. I never dreamed he was associated with Great Western, and I certainly didn't know about his relationship to your family."

Amelia took a moment to digest the information, then she nodded. "I'm glad to hear that."

Sensing she was ready to move on again, Ben resumed their walk toward the newspaper office. "What is it I should know? You hinted at something last night, but—" He broke off when he felt a shiver ripple through her frame.

She stared up at him, her eyes pleading. "I don't want to go into detail, but please believe me when I say he's a cad of the worst sort. Despite his polished appearance, he has no more scruples than a snake. He would be willing to do anything if he thought he could get away with it, in business or . . . or . . ." In a voice so low he almost missed hearing it, she added, ". . . anything else." She lifted her shoulders. "Let's just say he isn't someone I would ever want to be alone with."

A fierce protectiveness surged up within him. "Has he done anything to hurt you?"

"Not physically, no. But that's why I had to get out of the restaurant last night. Seeing him caught me completely off guard. I'm sorry I cut our dinner short. I had been looking forward to our time together."

Ben covered her fingers with his free hand. "I'm the one who owes you an apology. I never should have allowed him to spring such a surprise on you. I had no idea it would upset you so."

Amelia smiled her forgiveness. "How could you? You had no way of knowing." Her smiled faded, and she glanced down. "I'm not sure how to say this, but his involvement with the company makes me even more concerned about Great Western's integrity."

When they reached the *Gazette* building, she stopped at the door and faced him once more. "Can you come inside for a moment? I'd like to tell you what I learned this morning and see if you can make anything of it."

She unlocked the door, and he held it open for her. Once inside, she outlined her foray to the bank in a few brief sentences. "One of my father's notes seemed to indicate a concern about the methods Great Western has used to acquire so many properties in such a short time. Do you think there is more to their methods than appears on the surface?"

Ben sputtered. "Acquiring properties is part of my job. I can assure you I haven't taken part in any underhanded activity."

Amelia tilted her head and stared up into his eyes. "I believe you." The look she gave him warmed him to the core of his being. "But you don't handle every transaction, do you?"

"No," he said slowly. "I don't."

She nodded, as if she'd expected that answer. "Can you tell me why Great Western would be so interested in Bart McCaffrey's reservoir? Providing water to the local farmers doesn't seem in line with the rest of the company plans."

Ben scrambled for an answer, trying to remember any snippets of conversation he might have heard around the office. "We'll need a substantial water supply for the hydraulic mining. Since a reservoir was already set up on the property, I would assume that's the reason we acquired it, but I can't tell you more than that."

When she drew her brows together, he added, "Why don't I go back to the office and look up the paperwork on that transaction. I'm sure I can find the answer there."

"Would you? I'd appreciate that so much." She stretched out her hand and grazed his arm with a touch as light as a butterfly's wing.

Ben swallowed, trying to dislodge the lump that suddenly

formed in his throat. He would do a lot more than dig through a few files to prove himself worthy of that trusting blue gaze.

※

Ben had to wait until his fellow employees left for the day before he felt comfortable going through the files. He spent the intervening time finishing his report and poring over maps of Yavapai County, looking for properties that might be of interest to the company. He found a couple of likely prospects and made a note to check into the specifics of who owned them on his next trip to file papers with the county recorder's office in Prescott.

At last the office quieted down and he was able to begin the research he'd promised Amelia. He walked over to the bank of cabinets and searched through the drawer labeled *M* until he located the papers he sought. Carrying the folder to his desk, he spread its contents on his desk.

It only took a moment to locate the information he was looking for. A quick survey showed him the story checked out with what Amelia told him. Bart McCaffrey, the former owner, had taken out a sizeable loan to construct a reservoir. Then he defaulted, leaving the property available for Great Western to purchase at a substantial discount.

Just as I thought. Acquiring McCaffrey's land had been a shrewd business move, nothing more.

He put the papers back in order, scanning each one so he could assure Amelia he'd taken a thorough look at the documents. He had almost finished when a few scribbled words in the margin of one page stayed his hand.

He held the memorandum closer and frowned. *What's this?*

As he read the document from start to finish, his frown deepened.

According to the note in his hand, Great Western had made an earlier offer to purchase McCaffrey's land at market value, but the offer had been refused.

So the company had been interested in the land, even before the foreclosure lowered the price to a tempting range. Ben tapped his finger on his desk, deep in thought. If not for catching sight of those quickly scrawled words, he wouldn't have looked closely enough to discover this information.

What else have I missed? With his curiosity thoroughly piqued, he went back through every paper one by one, laying them out in chronological order as he read. The resulting sequence showed a trail of events much different from the story Amelia had been given.

One memo, dated after McCaffrey turned down the offer from Great Western, read:

> *This property is ideal for providing a water supply. See if McC will build reservoir with the understanding that we can purchase from him.*

So McCaffrey built the reservoir at the company's request? Ben's confusion grew when he located McCaffrey's land on the county map. The majority of the land below it had been purchased by Great Western some time before. Evidently, the story about supplying farmers with much-needed water was a fabrication.

Ben flipped the paper over and discovered more writing on the back:

McC demanding advance payment. Informed him, per O. M.'s instructions, no longer interested in buying water from him.

Ben stared openmouthed, letting the words sink in. Leaning back in his chair, he pondered the details he had uncovered. Pieced together, they explained McCaffrey's reason for building the reservoir in the first place. He obviously expected water sales to repay the loan he'd taken from the bank, plus assure him of an ongoing income once the loan was paid off.

But Great Western had broken off their end of the deal, and McCaffrey defaulted on the loan as a result.

Bart McCaffrey obviously made a poor choice, borrowing money he couldn't repay. That was a sad enough story in itself, but if he'd made that choice due to the urging of Great Western—who then reneged on their agreement—that threw a whole new light on the situation.

And after McCaffrey lost his property, the company stepped in and bought the land—reservoir and all—directly from the bank. Great Western had the property it wanted in the first place, and at a greatly reduced price.

Ben let out a low whistle. None of the company's actions had been strictly illegal, but he wouldn't characterize them as open and aboveboard. He gathered the papers slowly and stacked them back in the order he had found them.

A multitude of thoughts chased through his mind while he replaced the file in the cabinet, but one question stood out from the rest. Who had been in charge of that sale? Before sliding the drawer closed, he glanced at the top right corner of the folder to find the initials penciled there, according to office policy: *E F.*

So Eddie Franklin, one of Merrick's closest associates, had been responsible for contacting McCaffrey and setting up plans for the reservoir, only to renege on the company's offer once McCaffrey found himself head over heels in debt. And according to the note he'd found, O. M.—Owen Merrick—had given the order to call off the arrangement.

Ben leaned against the closed drawer and tried to think. Was this an isolated incident? What other deals had Franklin worked on? Moving to the file cabinet farthest to his left, he pulled open the top drawer and began a systematic search, pulling out all the folders bearing Eddie Franklin's initials.

Two hours later, he finished going through the stack of files on his desk. Not all of Franklin's deals followed a similar pattern, but he found several that raised questions in his mind. He looked at the list of names he'd written down:

Ephraim Seaver
Gabe Rogers
Josiah Smith

Each one had initially refused to sell, but later changed his mind. And neither of the files for Rogers and Smith contained a bank draft number showing payment had been made.

Ben shook his head. That didn't make sense at all, unless both men had demanded a cash payment. He glanced toward the front window, noting how far the sun had dropped in the evening sky. It was getting late enough that his presence in the office might be noticed—and questioned. He would have to wait for another opportunity to see what he could find out about those payments.

Right now, he needed to put the files away before anyone discovered what he was doing. As he hurried to complete the task, a sick feeling grew in his stomach. Had Amelia's father been right after all? Was Great Western involved in some questionable activity?

He slid the last drawer closed with a thump. And if Wagner's suspicions had been correct, what did that mean for the future of the company . . . as well as his own?

CHAPTER 19

The strains of a Sousa march rang through the streets of Granite Springs. All around the vacant lot next to the Odd Fellows Hall, groups of smiling people kept time to the music. Some sat on blankets spread upon the ground, while others relaxed on the benches brought over from their usual spots along the boardwalk on First Street. Still more listeners lined the pews borrowed for the evening from the Granite Springs Community Church next door.

Amelia had taken up her post with those who didn't care to sit, as they stood in clusters behind the pews. From her vantage point at the rear of the crowd, she had a clear view of everything going on. She held her pencil and notebook at the ready, wanting to capture all the color and life of the much-anticipated outdoor concert.

Ben, standing on her left, leaned closer. His breath tickled her ear when he murmured, "A wonderful turnout, wouldn't you say?"

She nodded. From the looks of it, nearly the entire community had shown up for the event. An air of excitement crackled through the crowd. The sun glinted off the band's brass instruments, its heat diminishing as it neared the horizon. Altogether, it added up to a perfect summer evening.

Amelia looked up at Ben and smiled, thinking how much their relationship had changed in such a short time. Unlike the time he'd invited her to the poetry reading, she had been thrilled at the thought of him acting as her escort on this occasion.

One of her escorts, she amended, remembering Homer, who stood on her right, his watchful eye keeping tabs on the two of them. Amelia smothered a chuckle at his vigilant attention. Homer was as protective as a mother hen with her only chick. In other circumstances, his hovering might have stirred her impatience, but knowing the love and concern behind it, she found it rather comforting.

Without glancing directly at him, she looked at him out of the corner of her eye, taking in his spindly profile. *Such a dear man!* For the thousandth time, she wondered whether Ben had been right about some wicked person dropping that brick on Homer deliberately. Could anyone really have wanted to hurt him? The longer the time stretched on without any sign of a further attack, the less likely it seemed. But Ben had made a convincing argument about the supposed accident being intentional.

She scanned the crowd, glad for the opportunity to observe the faces there without calling attention to herself. Struck by a sudden thought, her throat went dry. With so many people there, if anyone had intended to hurt Homer, there was a very good possibility that person was in attendance tonight. The realization dampened some of the pleasure she had felt up until that moment.

Bandmaster Achille LaGuardia raised his baton, and the musicians struck up the first lines of "Sweet Genevieve." The crowd joined in, singing along in chorus. Turning her attention back to the task at hand, Amelia jotted notes, describing in a few words the uniforms worn by the members of the Eleventh Infantry band.

When the number concluded, Pastor Edmonds stepped up to the front and beamed at the assembly. "I know we're all having a lovely evening, and I'm sure we'd like to express our appreciation for this fine music."

An enthusiastic round of applause greeted his statement. The bandmaster smiled his thanks and swept his arm to one side to include the members of the band, who rose and bowed as one.

"And now," the pastor continued, "while our musicians take a brief intermission, Miss Thelma Vickers and her Sunday school class have a special treat for us."

The Sunday school teacher stood and beckoned with her hand. A group of children made their way forward under her no-nonsense gaze.

Amelia's lips twitched as she watched them jockey into position. Her smile deepened when she caught sight of Jimmy Brandt in the center of the back row. The newsboy's usually grubby face fairly gleamed, showing signs of recent contact with soap and water. His hair was slicked back, and a starched collar encircled his neck.

Jimmy cast a furtive glance around the audience. When his eyes stopped on Amelia, she waggled her fingers at him and gave an encouraging nod. The boy's face turned beet red, and he quickly averted his gaze.

When they had taken their places, Thelma Vickers gave a satisfied nod and favored the audience with a bright smile. "Good evening, ladies and gentlemen. Our junior Sunday school class has been hard at work over the past few months, and we would like to share some of what we've learned with you."

Ben leaned over again. "I barely recognized Jimmy up there, all scrubbed and fresh."

"I know." Amelia couldn't hold back a gurgle of laughter. "He looks utterly miserable, doesn't he."

Ben's face split into a wide grin. "He does, at that. I know how much I would have hated standing up and performing in public like that when I was his age."

The children quoted John 3:16 in unison, then sang all four verses of "Onward, Christian Soldiers." When they finished, Miss Vickers turned to the audience again. "I am proud to tell you that our class has just finished memorizing the names of all sixty-six books of the Bible, in their proper order."

"*Ooooh.*" The sound rippled through the audience. Amelia easily identified the children's mothers, hitching themselves up straighter with identical looks of pride. The girls in the group fairly quivered with excitement, while Jimmy's comrades in the back row looked every bit as mortified as he did.

Thelma Vickers clapped her hands. "You may begin, children."

Three little girls in the center of the front row stepped out and chanted, "Genesis, Exodus, Leviticus, Numbers!" in high, clear voices.

When they stepped back smartly to their places, those on the ends of both rows moved out to the side. "Deuteronomy, Joshua, Judges, Ruth!"

The boys in the rear, including Jimmy, droned the next set of names: "First and Second Samuel, First and Second Kings, First and Second Chronicles." Their volume was audible, but their delivery lacked the fervor of the first two groups.

The process repeated itself as the class progressed through the remaining books, with the boys becoming more animated with each turn, and finished off in grand style with a rousing shout of "Jude and Revelation!"

The crowd erupted in wild applause and a scattering of whistles. Beside her, Amelia could feel Ben shake with laughter. When he glanced her way, she had to press her hands to her lips to keep from bursting into gales of mirth. She dug her elbow into his ribs, knowing she needed to compose herself before Jimmy looked over and saw her.

Flushed with triumph, Miss Vickers waved the children back to their seats. The bandmaster picked up his baton, and the musicians struck up a lively number and moved on through a list of well-known melodies before wrapping up the program with John Philip Sousa's "Washington Post March."

Before the final notes died away, the audience rose to their feet and cheered. Walt Ingram, representing the Odd Fellows, raised his hands to silence the crowd. "Thank you, folks, for coming out tonight. Didn't our Fort Whipple musicians do a fine job?" He paused while another round of applause rang out. "Don't forget, we want to invite you all to stop by the Hall for refreshments before you call it an evening."

The audience starting milling about, some going up to talk with the band members while others filtered into the Odd Fellows Hall.

Homer nudged Amelia's right arm and spoke in an undertone. "I promised Pastor Edmonds I'd help carry these pews back inside. Will you be okay without me for a bit?"

"Of course. And take some time to enjoy yourself when you're finished with the pews. Ben will see me home."

Homer aimed an appraising glance Ben's way, then he grunted and turned to pick up one end of the nearest pew.

Ben glanced at the men carrying the benches and pews back to their places. "I'd offer to help, but it looks like they have everything covered. Would you care for some refreshments?" He offered his arm and led her inside the hall, where a variety of baked goods had been laid out on plank tables.

The room was so tightly packed, they moved to a sheltered spot along one wall, waiting for the crowd to thin out a bit.

Amelia fanned herself and bobbed her head, still hearing the final march play over in her mind. "What a lovely way to spend an evening!"

"That band is one of the best I've heard," Ben agreed. "The kids were great, too. Remind me to tell Jimmy what a dashing figure he cut in that starched collar."

Amelia sputtered with laughter and gave his arm a playful swat. "Don't you dare! He's mortified enough already. He'd never forgive you."

Ben clutched at his arm in mock agony, then laughed along with her. "Don't worry, I won't tease him. I wouldn't want to do anything to spoil such a lovely evening." His eyes glowed as he looked down at her. "I enjoyed sharing it with you."

"The music was wonderful, but I'm sure it wasn't on a par with what must have been available to you in Washington."

Ben chuckled. "You may be right about that, but I'd still much rather be here."

Amelia's breath quickened. "Don't you miss your family?"

Ben's face darkened, and the light in his eyes dimmed. "Of course I do. I never thought I'd live such a long way from them.

We've always been close, but sometimes things just don't work out the way we expect them to."

He looked around the room. "Things seem to be opening up a bit over at the tables. Would you like me to bring you some punch?" At her nod, he smiled. "I'll be back as quickly as I can."

Her eyes followed him as he walked over to take his place in line near the punch bowl. Ben didn't talk much about his background. She wondered what he had been like as a little boy. Had he been every bit as rambunctious as young Jimmy? The thought brought a smile to her lips.

"Did you enjoy the concert, Miss Wagner?"

Amelia turned to see the pastor's wife standing beside her. "Very much. What a wonderful idea to bring the band up here and draw the whole community together!"

"I couldn't agree more." Mrs. Edmonds's face glowed. "I do hope we'll have more opportunities like this as the summer wears on."

"I'm sure you will," said a deep voice just behind Amelia. "Granite Springs is turning into quite the up-and-coming community."

Amelia whipped her head around and caught her breath when she saw Thaddeus Grayson at her elbow, a shade too close for comfort. She edged a step to her right to put some distance between them.

Grayson said nothing, but she caught the trace of amusement in his eyes.

Mrs. Edmonds's gaze darted between the two of them and settled on Grayson. "Good evening. I am Isabel Edmonds. My husband is pastor of the community church. And I believe you are Amelia's stepfather, is that correct?"

Amelia felt the muscles tighten at the back of her neck.

"That's right." Grayson squeezed the woman's outstretched hand. "Her mother and I only married recently, but I couldn't be fonder of Amelia if she were my own."

Amelia folded her arms across her chest and pressed her lips together.

"I know it's going to be hard for her to say good-bye to the people she cares about here, but her mother and I look forward to her return to Denver so the three of us can be together."

The pastor's wife's eyes widened, then she turned to Amelia with a gracious smile. "I didn't realize you were planning to leave us, dear. I'm sure your mother will be happy to have you at her side again, but we'll be sorry to see you go."

Before Amelia could set the record straight, Mrs. Edmonds's attention was caught by a stir at one of the tables across the room. "We seem to be running short of refreshments over there. Please excuse me while I fetch another platter."

As Mrs. Edmonds walked away, Amelia whirled on her unwelcome companion. "Whatever possessed you to say that? I thought I made it quite clear that I have no intention of leaving Granite Springs."

Grayson closed the narrow gap between them in one easy stride. Amelia took a quick step back, which brought her up short against the wall.

The gleam in her stepfather's eyes made her stomach roil. He leaned close and spoke as if he hadn't heard. "I can't tell you how much I look forward to the times we'll have together . . . as a family." He braced one arm on the wall, mere inches from her shoulder.

Amelia felt the familiar feeling of helplessness that encompassed her whenever Thaddeus Grayson came around. Nothing would have given her more pleasure than to slap the insolent smirk off his face. But such action would only make a scene, and any explanation would be her word against his. She knew all too well how easy it would be for him to explain it all away.

Across the room, Ben stood with his back to her, patiently waiting to be served at the punch table. Throughout the hall, people milled about, talking and laughing. A few glanced her way and smiled, but no one seemed to realize her plight.

Just the way it happened in Denver. How many times had he done this over the past year, maneuvering her into an intimate conversation in a crowded room? So far, his intrusion had been nothing more than suggestive words, but she knew it would only be a matter of time before he pressed the issue further.

She took a step to the side, feeling the wall's rough plaster scrape her shoulder blades through the fabric of her dress. "You and I both know you are the reason I won't return to Denver. My father left the *Gazette* to me, and I intend to make a go of it. I won't be dependent on my mother's money . . . or yours."

The amusement faded from Grayson's eyes, and his lips thinned. "You can't really be thinking of spending the rest of your life in this backwater town when Denver has so much more to offer you. You'd be throwing yourself away here. And that would be a terrible waste." His eyes raked the front of her dress with a slow, lingering look.

He opened his mouth as if to say more, when a hand clamped on his shoulder, turning him away from her. Amelia choked back a sob of relief when she saw Ben standing there.

"Good evening, Mr. Grayson. I didn't know you were in attendance." Ben's mild tone contrasted markedly with the stony look on his face. Without taking his eyes off the other man, he extended his arm toward Amelia. "Here's your punch, Miss Wagner. I'm sorry it took me so long."

She moved next to him, feeling like a storm-tossed ship coming in sight of a safe haven. Taking the cup in her left hand, she curled her right around his arm and clung tight.

Grayson eyed Ben with a measuring gaze, and his eyes narrowed slightly. "We were just discussing what needs to be done for Amelia to put her affairs in order so she can accompany me back to Denver."

A brief nod was Ben's only response. "If you'll excuse us, sir, we need to be moving along."

Amelia felt Ben's muscles bunch under her fingertips as he turned to lead her out of the hall. She set her punch glass down on a table as they exited and gripped his arm with both hands.

The sun had gone down behind the hills, and gas lamps flickered along the street. They moved from one pool of light to another without speaking. Near Walt Ingram's hardware store, Ben stopped in a pocket of shadow and studied her closely. "Are you all right?"

"I am now." She had to force the words out past the lump in her throat. "Thank you for stepping in when you did."

Ben's lips parted in a slow smile. "Always happy to rescue a damsel in distress."

Amelia drew a shuddering breath and tried to calm her racing heart. "How did you know I needed rescuing?" The words came out on a shaky laugh. "No one else in the room did."

"Maybe I was the only one who really saw you. Something about the look on your face told me you felt uncomfortable."

His voice hardened. "And I didn't like the way Grayson was crowding you."

Amelia could feel her pulse pounding in her throat. Right now, Ben was standing even closer than her stepfather had—but his nearness didn't bother her at all.

A troubled expression crossed his face. "You aren't really planning to leave, are you?"

She shook her head, dislodging a curl near her temple. "That's a total fabrication. I'm not going anywhere, and certainly not with him."

"What about your mother? Does she need you there?"

Amelia caught her bottom lip between her teeth at the reminder of her ongoing dilemma. "I care about her, and I try to honor her as God would have me do. At the same time, she and I are very different. My mother makes her own choices, and she has chosen to link her lot with Thaddeus Grayson. I can't change that . . . but I can't support her in it, either."

"I'm glad you're staying." Ben's voice took on a husky tone. "It wouldn't be the same here without you." Lifting his hands, he cupped her face between his palms and leaned forward.

Amelia fastened her eyes on his, then let her gaze trail down his face to focus on his lips, so tantalizingly close. In another breath, they would meet hers. A tiny sigh escaped her lips, and her eyelids fluttered closed.

Footsteps clattered down the boardwalk, accompanied by a boyish shout. "Miss Amelia! Mr. Stone! Did you hear me tonight?"

Amelia and Ben sprang apart as Jimmy Brandt raced toward them. His hair had returned to its usual disarray, and a collar stud had slipped its moorings, leaving one end of his collar sticking out to one side. There was no trace of his earlier embarrassment in the broad grin he bestowed on them.

Amelia caught her breath, hoping she didn't look as flustered as she felt. She shot a quick glance at Ben, then reached out to ruffle the boy's hair. "We certainly did. You did a fine job. I'm sure your parents are very proud of you."

Jimmy puffed out his chest and beamed even more. "I'd be glad to give you the inside scoop when you write up the story."

"Hey, Jimmy!" called a child's voice from across the street. "Want to play tag with us before it gets too late?"

With a whoop, Jimmy ran off to join his friends. Amelia turned back to Ben, feeling suddenly shy.

"Amelia." His voice breathed her name as he linked his fingers through hers and stepped close again. A tingle ran upward from her fingertips to her shoulders.

Farther up the street, the door of the Odd Fellows Hall burst open, and people began spilling out into the night.

Amelia gazed up at Ben, wondering if he felt as bereft as she did. With every fiber of her being, she longed to reach up and trace his lips with her fingers, feel his strong arms encircle her. But their private moment had come to an end.

She squeezed his fingers between hers, hoping the gesture conveyed some of the feelings she longed to express. Without speaking a word, Ben tucked her hand into his arm and they continued on their way toward the newspaper office.

But the look in his eyes promised there would be another time.

CHAPTER 20

During the interlude, a recitation by Miss Thelma Vickers's
Sunday school class met with rousing success. The second
half of the concert . . .

The bell over the front door jingled. Amelia looked up
from setting the type for her story on the previous
night's festivities. *Won't Jimmy feel proud when he sees his*
name in print! She felt her spirits lift when she saw Ben step
inside and close the door behind him.

She shot a glance toward Homer, who was busy locking
the week's ads into the chase. Seeing a smile of welcome on
her old friend's face, she brightened even more. When she
recounted the incident with her stepfather the night before,
she knew Homer regretted not being there to protect her, but
his gratitude for Ben's intervention had been genuine. Homer
seemed to be accepting his presence more with each passing day.

Ben walked past the counter with a nod for each of them.
Moving closer to Amelia, he said, "I know you have to get the
paper out tomorrow, but do you have a few minutes? I'd like
to speak with you in private, if you don't mind."

"Of course." Amelia set down the composing stick without

hesitation and led him back to the office. The weekly deadline was fast approaching, but her story on the concert was nearly finished. Another article, on the expansion in progress at Martin Gilbreth's sawmill, still needed to be fleshed out, but she could find time to do that. That still left her with a fair amount of space on the front page, though. Unless she uncovered something substantial to report about Great Western, she wasn't sure what she would use to fill that.

Ben leaned against the office desk, his eyes troubled. "It's about that research I agreed to do the other day."

She reached out and laid her hand on his sleeve, her fingers tightening on his arm. "You were able to go over the papers on the purchase of Bart McCaffrey's land?"

A crease deepened between his eyebrows when he nodded. "It wasn't as straightforward as I expected. As you know, McCaffrey turned down an offer on the sale of his property. What neither one of us knew, though, was that the offer came from Great Western."

Amelia released his arm and took a step back. "They wanted to buy his land in the first place? But—"

"Putting in the reservoir was their idea. The company made an agreement to buy water from him."

Amelia felt her heart begin to pound with strong, steady beats. "Then there never was any intention of supplying water to the farmers nearby. But that explains why he took out the loan."

"Right, but then they retracted the offer . . . after the reservoir was completed."

"So that's why he wasn't able to pay off the loan, which resulted in the foreclosure, meaning . . ." Her eyes widened.

The muscles along Ben's jawline tightened. "Great Western got the land after all, *plus* the reservoir. And at the lowest price imaginable."

At last! Maybe she would be able to run an account of Great Western's shady dealings as tomorrow's front-page story, after all. Amelia's sense of exultation was tempered somewhat by Ben's obvious distress.

"I'm sorry," she said, already composing the opening paragraphs in her mind. "I know that had to come as a shock to you."

"That isn't all."

Amelia's mental composition ground to a sudden halt. "What do you mean?"

Ben crossed his arms. "Seeing the way they dealt with Mc-Caffrey made me wonder if anything like that had happened to other people, so I looked through the rest of the files."

Reaching into his inside jacket pocket, he drew out a sheaf of folded papers. "I found three instances—all handled by Eddie Franklin."

Barely able to contain her excitement, Amelia leaned over as he spread the pages out on the desk. Her lips moved as she read each document in turn. "Ephraim Seaver, Gabe . . . Wait a minute!"

Spinning around, she hastened to the file cabinet and opened the drawer containing her father's notes on Great Western. Retrieving the slip of paper she wanted, she carried it back to the desk and held it out to Ben.

"Look at this: Ephraim Seaver, Gabe Rogers, Josiah Smith. The names on those papers are the same ones my father noted down. He must have learned something that pointed him to the same thing you discovered. I wanted to talk to the three of them, but they have all left town." She looked up at Ben. "You say the same thing happened to them as to Bart McCaffrey?"

"Not exactly the same, but there were similarities. All three refused an initial offer from the company, but each apparently changed his mind later on. None of them went through foreclosure, though." He shook his head. "Maybe I'm only imagining a connection."

"No, not when these names are the very ones that appeared in my father's notes." Amelia's thoughts raced. "Maybe this is linked to whatever was troubling him so much at the end."

She leaned over the papers again, and Ben bent beside her. She felt the warmth of his arm through the sleeve of his broadcloth jacket, and her breath quickened.

Pulling her attention back to the task at hand, she read through every word on the Seaver agreement, then went over the papers for the Rogers and Smith sales with equal care. Her brow puckered, and she picked up the Smith and Rogers contracts to study them more closely.

"Ben?" Her voice came out on a thin note. "Look at this."

"Did you find something?"

"I'm not sure. Take a look at the sellers' signatures on these agreements."

He studied the scrawls at the bottom of both pages, then took them from her hands and peered at them closely.

Amelia's heart hammered. "Do you see the same thing I do?"

His face hardened into a taut mask. "Both those signatures look like they've been written by the same hand."

"That's what I thought." She turned, closing the distance between them to mere inches as she looked up into his face.

"But why would anyone need to forge these papers? What does it mean?"

✗

"I'm not sure," Ben admitted. He looked down at those clear blue eyes staring so trustingly into his. The lips he had come so near to kissing the night before were only a few inches from his own. All he had to do was lean forward and . . .

A scuffing sound from the printing office caught his attention, and he looked over the top of Amelia's head to see Homer watching them through the open door. His watchful gaze cooled Ben's ardor as effectively as if he'd been doused with a pail of cold water.

He cleared this throat and turned his attention back to the paper in his hand. "It would have to mean there was something fraudulent about the way they acquired these properties, but why go to such lengths?"

He took a step back, letting his thoughts run free. "It would make sense to snap up the McCaffrey property, since they wanted the reservoir. But I can't make a connection with these others.

"The Seaver place is near the reservoir, but Gabe Rogers owned a square mile of nothing but forest, and the property Josiah Smith owned is a ways southwest of here." He shook his head. "They don't have anything in common, as far as I can see."

"There has to be a reason for all this," Amelia insisted. She planted her hands on her hips, and her eyes flashed. "Those forged names didn't get there on their own, and you know I don't trust Owen Merrick or Thaddeus Grayson one bit."

"I know, but let's not be hasty. I don't want to leap to unfounded conclusions. Your father's commitment to printing
nothing but the truth is one worth honoring. Merrick has
been in and out of my family's home all my life, and I know
how highly my father thinks of him. Besides, Eddie Franklin
is the one who did the paperwork on all of these transactions.
Let me find out more before we make accusations based on
nothing more than dislike."

He could see the struggle of emotions that played across
her face before she finally drew a deep breath and nodded.
"You're right. This paper is about the truth. I don't want to
settle for anything less. Go ahead and see what you can find
out, but rest assured, I'll be looking, too."

A smile tugged at his lips. "I have no doubt about that."
Mindful of Homer's watchful eye, he shifted to block the older
man's view from the doorway and lifted his hand to graze her
cheek with his fingers. "I'd better get going. I'll need to find
a way to slip these papers back into their files before anyone
notices they're gone."

With a quick good-bye to Homer, he strode out the door
and started back toward the Great Western building. With any
luck, he could find some excuse to stay late again that evening
to replace the documents and look through the financial records on the Rogers and Smith sales, as well.

The discovery that both those agreements had probably
been forged had shaken him more than he wanted to let on to
Amelia. Something was definitely amiss at Great Western. His
mood darkened. He had never liked Eddie Franklin, and he
wouldn't put it past the man to be part of any sort of chicanery.
If he could prove the man's guilt and take that proof to Mer-

rick, it would only remain for Merrick to deal with Franklin and put the whole ugly episode behind them.

When all was said and done, his boss might even thank Amelia for persisting in her quest for the truth. The thought brought a smile to his lips at the reminder of her fiery gaze and determination to move forward, whatever the cost.

So much tenacity in such a small package! He laughed aloud, drawing a curious glance from a passerby. He could still feel the warm pressure of her hand on his arm and picture her lips so close to his. How he longed to gather her into his arms and hold her close!

That day would come, he promised himself. And it couldn't come quickly enough to suit him.

CHAPTER 21

The rhythmic clank of the Washington press measured out a steady beat in the background as Amelia hunched over her desk, her head resting on the heels of her hands. Looking down at the mound of papers that littered the desk, she let out a low moan. She had spent every waking moment since Ben's visit the afternoon before going through every scrap of information she could pull from the files that had anything to do with Great Western.

The discovery of the forged documents had galvanized her into action, hoping that revelation would prove to be the catalyst they needed to make the last pieces of the puzzle fall into place. But it hadn't worked out that way.

There had to be some connecting thread tying the forgeries to her father's concerns, but it remained just beyond her reach. As obvious as it appeared that Great Western had acquired those properties by fraudulent means, she had no way of proving that without the documents Ben had returned to the company's files. Anything she might report about their underhanded activity would be a baseless accusation. The headache she'd been fighting since midmorning assaulted her temples with renewed strength, and she kneaded the sides of her head with her fingertips.

She had asked Homer to finish setting her story on the concert and told him to leave some space on the front page in case the big story she hoped for materialized in time to go to print. Instead, here she was again, pushing right up to the deadline with no solid information.

The printing press clanked on, adding to her guilt. Seeing how intent she was upon her quest, Homer had taken all her chores upon himself in addition to his own . . . again.

The rhythmic sound of the press ceased, and she heard Homer cross the floor to the office door. Looking up, she saw him knock on the doorframe with a somewhat gun-shy expression on his face. She couldn't blame him, after the way she'd snapped at him earlier that morning when all he wanted was to know where she wanted to place Walt Ingram's new ad for the hardware store.

She made a conscious effort to keep the impatience from her voice when she spoke. "What is it, Homer?"

Instead of entering the office as he usually did, he remained in the doorway. "I just finished the inside pages. I'll need to get the front page locked up soon if we plan to get the paper out on time. I've saved some space, the way you asked me to. Is the story ready yet?"

"No." Hearing the disgust in her tone, Amelia forced herself to speak calmly. "I don't have a story. I thought I was close, but I just haven't pulled it all together yet. And I shouldn't have spoken to you the way I did before. My head has been throbbing most of the day, but that's no excuse, and I apologize."

Worry twisted Homer's face as he stepped to her desk.

"What are we going to put in its place? We need something to fill that hole."

Seeing his distress only increased her self-reproach. They might not meet their deadline. And if the *Gazette* was late for the first time in its history, it would be all her fault. "I don't suppose we have anything on reserve that we could use instead? Have you heard anything more about that missing railroad man?"

"Not a thing. As far as I know, they're still looking, but they haven't turned anything up yet."

"What about that story on the sawmill? I've already made some notes." Hope flickered, then died away. "But there isn't enough copy to fill the space."

Homer shook his head. "Not unless . . ." His voice trailed off, and he clamped his lips shut.

"Unless what?" Her irritation resurfaced.

He drew his brows together. "I got a tip this morning, but I wasn't going to mention it."

Her interest quickened. "A tip? When? I didn't hear anyone come in." She'd been so engrossed in her research, she must have missed hearing the bell.

"Not here. And not in person, it was just a note. Someone must have slipped it under my door during the night. I found it when I was getting ready for work."

Amelia's nose crinkled. Had she detected the faint tinge of alcohol when Homer spoke? She opened her mouth to question him, but snapped her lips shut when a flash of pain streaked across her head. She closed her eyes and clamped her hand against the ache, as if she could hold the stabbing torment at bay.

A moment later, she opened her eyes and blinked slowly,

relieved when the pain ebbed somewhat. She took a deep breath and turned her attention back to the issue at hand. Now was not the time to speak to Homer about his tippling. She would wait until she was in a better frame of mind and they weren't under deadline.

She forced herself to sit up straight. "Something about Great Western? Why didn't you tell me?"

He shook his head. "It was about the sawmill, but there was no name on it. We can't take an anonymous note as fact, so I didn't want to bother you with it."

"Something to do with the sawmill?" Amelia's thoughts whirled. "Then go see if you can find some verification. If you hurry, it might be enough to flesh out that story and make it work after all."

Homer glanced at the clock. Amelia felt as though she could read his thoughts. Going out in pursuit of news would eat up precious time he needed to prepare and print the first page if he hoped to get the paper out on schedule. By all rights, she should be the one out chasing down that story.

But she couldn't. Not when she had to learn the truth about Great Western before Merrick decided to divulge what he knew about her father.

"I guess I'd best get going." Homer's lips tightened in a parody of a smile. *"Tempus fugit."*

She nodded and forced a tiny smile of her own. "Thank you for being such a wonderful help. I'll make it up to you."

And she would, she vowed to herself as she heard the door close behind him. Once she'd cleared up this mystery, she would be able to turn her full attention on her duties at the *Gazette* again.

Ben had been puzzled by the locations of the various parcels they'd discussed the day before. Maybe it would help if she could see where they were in relation to one another. Pulling a sheet of paper and a pencil from the desk drawer, she drew a rough sketch showing the locations of the properties. As an afterthought, she added the parcel her father bought from Virgil Sparks.

Now what? She stared at the paper, trying to ignore the pain behind her eyes, willing herself to see some pattern that would bring everything into focus. The Seaver property was adjacent to her father's, not far from the reservoir Bart McCaffrey built. Or the land Martin Gilbreth recently sold.

She remembered her father taking her on picnics in that area when she was younger. He had pointed out a number of mining claims on the hillsides nearby. Her interest quickened. Minerals were abundant in that area. The need for a reservoir would make sense, with Great Western's plans to start a hydraulic mining operation.

But what about the other purchases they had made? She tapped her pencil against the paper. Ben was right—the Rogers property lay some distance away and consisted of nothing but acres of trees. As far as she could remember, no one had staked a mining claim anywhere nearby.

And then there was Josiah Smith's property, even farther away, out in an open stretch of country to the southwest.

She set the pencil aside and bent over the crude map. Every instinct told her she was on the right track. The answers lay in front of her, almost close enough to touch, if only she could think clearly enough to see it.

Pressing her fingertips against her temples, she massaged

her forehead lightly, wishing she could rub away the weight of responsibility that crushed her, along with the pain.

Maybe she wasn't cut out for running a newspaper, after all. There were simply too many things to try to balance all at once, and she seemed to be doing a dismal job of it. She'd saddled Homer with her responsibilities on top of his own while she sat glued to the desk, obsessed by a desire to ferret out the secrets of the Great Western Investment Company. But in the grand scheme of things, that was the more important issue. Wasn't it?

Her father wouldn't have entrusted the *Gazette* to her if he hadn't thought her capable. Then again, he only saw her during the summer months. And a brief spell as his assistant was far different from trying to run the paper on her own. Considering the amount of time they had been separated over the years, maybe he didn't know her as well as he thought he did.

The memory of Millie Brown's visit sprang to her mind, unbidden. *Maybe I didn't know him as well as I thought, either.*

What would she do if word of that woman's business partnership with her father got out? That possibility had disturbed much of her sleep over the past three nights. Many who knew Andrew Wagner would be aghast at the news, while others would leap on it gleefully.

And Owen Merrick would be one of them. His not-so-subtle reference to a dark secret convinced her he had somehow learned about Millie Brown and intended to hold that knowledge over her head like the sword of Damocles, ready to spread the news about her father far and wide if she dared interfere with his business.

But if his business threatened the happiness and well-being

of the people of Granite Springs, didn't the readers of the *Gazette* deserve to know the truth about what his company intended?

What about the truth as far as her father was concerned? The thought tugged at her and wouldn't leave her alone. Shouldn't she be just as willing to dig into the particulars of his association with Millie Brown? And if their relationship turned out to be just as Millie claimed, didn't she have a responsibility to print that truth?

The ache in her head increased, and she let out a low moan. Amelia sniffed and brushed a tear away. More than anything, she wanted to preserve the reputation her father had so carefully built up over the years. But if she was willing to compromise the truth in order to protect a loved one, that was further proof of her unsuitability as a newswoman.

Pressing the heels of her hands against her eyes, she drew in a shuddering breath, then forced herself to sit erect. Suitable or not, she was the editor of the *Gazette*—for now, at least. It was time to get back to the business at hand.

She pulled the drawing closer and studied it again. Maybe she'd been too focused on these few properties, in effect, keeping her from seeing the forest for the trees. Walking to the storeroom, she grabbed a blank sheet of newsprint and carried it back to the office.

Working from the original drawing, she quickly copied the sites she had already noted. Then she proceeded to expand the sketch, penciling in a rough layout of Granite Springs and Martin Gilbreth's sawmill, then the locations of as many mining claims as she could remember.

She tapped the end of the pencil against her teeth, pondering what to add next. She made note of several ranches in the outlying area, then sketched in the hills to the west of the town and shaded in large areas to represent the vast stands of Ponderosa pine trees.

Cutting along the eastern edge of her map, she drew a meandering line denoting the Peavine, the railroad running from Ash Fork to Prescott. Construction for a new line from Prescott to Phoenix would be underway soon, but she didn't know its exact location in reference to her drawing. After a moment's hesitation, she made a series of dashes near the bottom-left corner. That might not show the correct path, but it would serve as a reminder.

How she wished Ben could be there to help her. He spent his days going over maps of the county and would know even more than she did about what lay out there that Great Western might be interested in.

Her eyes blurred as a jab of pain shot through her head again. Amelia choked back a sob. If only she could lie down for a few moments, maybe the blinding headache would subside. But her responsibility was here, with the paper. She didn't have time to coddle herself.

Another onslaught of pain made the decision for her. She couldn't find the truth when she was hurting like this. Surrendering, she made her way upstairs and curled up on her bed, with her head resting against the soft pillow.

The sound of voices from below roused her, and she opened her eyes. She blinked slowly, realizing that the vise squeezing her head had released its grip. She pushed herself upright on the side of the bed.

A young boy's laugh floated upstairs. *Jimmy?* But if he was there, ready to help deliver the paper, how long had she been asleep? Had Homer managed to finish printing the paper on his own?

Amelia got to her feet, flinching at the reminder of how much her preoccupation with Great Western had cost her dear friend. Poor Homer had gone far more than the extra mile today.

Descending the stairs, she walked into the printing office and smiled at Homer and Jimmy. Spying a stack of unfolded papers, she headed toward it. "Let me take care of these. It's the least I can do."

When Homer turned to her, the look in his eyes held none of its usual warmth. "You needn't bother. Jimmy came in early and helped me finish the printing. The two of us have it covered." Before she could protest, he turned away and went back to work without another word.

Amelia stared, openmouthed. In all the years she had known him, Homer had never spoken to her in that tone of voice. But—her conscience smote her—in all that time, she had never treated him in the abrupt sort of manner she'd used today. No wonder he wanted nothing to do with her at the moment.

Berating herself for her self-focused actions, she pivoted on her heel and walked toward the front door. She needed to talk to Ben. Now seemed like a good time to look for him.

CHAPTER 22

An hour later, Amelia walked back into the *Gazette* building, less frustrated than when she hurried out, and thankfully pain free now. She had covered the length of First Street from one end to the other but hadn't seen any sign of Ben. Letting a breath of air out in an exasperated huff, she slumped against the counter.

Where could he be? She'd scanned every face along the boardwalk and looked inside the window of every business on the town's main street—including the Great Western office—but to no avail. Perhaps he was out looking at a piece of property outside the town limits.

A glance at the clock told her it was nearly time for most of the local businesses to close for the day. The knowledge cheered her a little. Wherever Ben had gone, he might be coming back soon to wind up his business for the afternoon. Maybe she could still find him so they could discuss the day's progress . . . or lack of it.

At least she had managed to accomplish one thing that afternoon. When her search for Ben proved fruitless, she had walked out past the north end of town to the grove of trees near the spring. The quiet spot had long been a favorite of those seeking a bit of solitude, and the secluded stand of trees provided the privacy she needed to pour out her confusion and frustration to the Lord.

There had been no audible voice, no miraculous vision in response to her fervent prayer, only a prompting to trust her heavenly Father.

I do trust you, Lord. It's just that it's hard sometimes to know the right direction to go.

Looking around at the chaos left behind in the wake of producing a new issue, she felt a glimmer of satisfaction. At least the paper had gone out on time, thanks to Homer.

Her satisfaction slipped away in a wave of self-reproach. She had let him carry the full burden of putting the paper together while she spent the day on a wild-goose chase . . . and snapped at him, to boot. None of the pressure weighing her down—or the pain of that blinding headache—was his fault. Far from it! While others would have walked out and left her stranded in similar circumstances, Homer played the role of hero, holding everything together in spite of her short temper. She owed him her deepest thanks—and an apology.

It usually took him and Jimmy a little over an hour to make their delivery rounds. That meant he ought to be making his way back to the *Gazette* at any moment.

But as offended as he seemed the last time she'd seen him, he might not come back to the newspaper at all. She couldn't blame him if he decided to take time for dinner at the Bon-Ton—or even go straight home for a quiet meal in order to avoid any more of her sharp-tongued comments.

In that case, she ought to go out and look for him. She couldn't let her apology go unspoken one minute longer than necessary. With that thought in mind, she returned to First Street. She would find Homer and ask his forgiveness. And maybe, just maybe, she might spot Ben, as well. Perhaps they could have dinner together and find a quiet spot to talk over her questions.

She ambled along at a leisurely pace, giving herself time to look down every street and alleyway in the hope of spotting Homer. All down the length of the boardwalk, she saw people poring over copies of the latest issue of the *Gazette*.

Amelia couldn't help but smile at the familiar sight. One of the favorite moments of her week was when she walked down the street on publication day, catching the smiles and approving nods from her readers.

But something seemed different today. True to form, people glanced up when she walked by, but instead of responding to her friendly greeting, every one of them let their gazes slide away without speaking.

Her steps slowed even more, and she came to a stop. What was wrong with everyone?

"Amelia!"

She whirled around when she heard a familiar voice call her name and spotted Clara on the opposite side of the street. A smile sprang to her lips. The sight of a friendly face was welcome right now.

Or maybe not so friendly. Instead of responding with a smile of her own, the other woman stepped down off the boardwalk and angled across the street, bearing down on her like a loco-motive . . . and an angry locomotive, at that.

Amelia stared, openmouthed. What could have put that grim look on her friend's face?

Puffing like a steam engine, Clara stepped up onto the board-walk and planted herself squarely in front of Amelia. "I can't believe this. You could have knocked me over with a feather!"

A chill of concern added itself to Amelia's confusion. "What's wrong? Has something happened to Martin?"

"Has something happened?" Clara's eyes widened, and her nostrils flared. When she raised her arm, Amelia saw a fresh copy of the *Gazette* crumpled in her fist.

"How can you stand there with that wide-eyed, innocent look and ask me such a thing?" Clara's voice rose louder with every syllable. "*You* happened!"

Amelia saw curious glances turned in their direction and felt a wave of heat engulf her neck. "I don't understand. What are you talking about?"

"You put this out for everyone to see, and you're telling me you don't understand?"

"Clara, you're shouting." Amelia raised her hands and patted the air in front of her, as if she could blot the angry woman's words away.

"You better believe I'm shouting!" She waved the wadded paper in front of Amelia's nose. "If you have the gall to put this garbage out in public, you have no right to cringe because I raise my voice a little."

By this time, the people along the street had ceased pretending not to listen. A few stepped out from doorways farther down the block, the better to observe the show. Amelia felt her cheeks blaze. Her discomfort heightened when she saw Thaddeus Grayson lounging against the front of the general store, watching the goings-on with a look of keen enjoyment.

Trying to ignore their eager audience, she turned back to

Clara. "Are you talking about the article on Martin expanding the sawmill? Why should that upset you? Publicity like that is good for his business, and for the community, too. Everyone is so proud of what he's doing, and it seemed like a wonderful idea for a story. I thought you'd be pleased."

"Pleased!" A deep red flush suffused Clara's face. "The only one pleased about this is you. But if this is the kind of thing you'll stoop to printing in order to boost your sales, then you're no friend of Martin's. Or mine, either." She flung the paper down on the boardwalk, ground it under her heel, and stalked off without another word.

Feeling as if she'd just been run over by a locomotive, Amelia stared around at the people gathered nearby, hoping one of the onlookers might step forward and make sense of what just happened. Instead, they all turned away and went about their business.

In a daze, she bent over to pick up the paper Clara had thrown down and smoothed the crumpled folds open. Homer had placed a piece on Martin's sawmill in the center of the front page. Her forehead puckered. The notes she'd made for the article talked about his expansion of the sawmill, the addition of new employees, and the way this move would bring new business to Granite Springs.

Amelia shook her head. That was the kind of forward-thinking progress every town needed in order to grow, the sort of thing that would help the community and portray Martin as someone to admire. What could Clara possibly have found to cause such offense?

Mystified, she began to read through the article. The first paragraphs were just as she had written them. She shook her head as her puzzlement grew. There was nothing there that could have elicited such a strong response from Clara.

The story continued as she had outlined it, describing the expansion, and singing Martin's praises for his contribution to Granite Springs. Near the end were several paragraphs she didn't recognize, obviously something Homer had added based on the tip he had received.

> The newly expanded sawmill has been awarded a contract to provide ties and trestle materials for the extension of the Peavine, which will allow that line to run all the way from Prescott to Phoenix. The Gazette spoke to Albert Campbell and Wes Harvey, owners of sawmills in the Prescott area, about their reactions to this new development.

Amelia nodded. If the tip Homer had been given named those men as sources of information, it would make sense for him to follow up on that and contact them. He must have sent telegrams to Prescott while he was out that afternoon. She spotted some quotations a few lines down and read on.

> Harvey insists Mr. Gilbreth had an unfair advantage in acquiring the contract, and Campbell agreed.
> "Why would the railroad award that contract without getting bids from other sawmills?" Wes Harvey wanted to know. "Sounds like shady doings to me."
> Campbell said much the same thing and added, "I wouldn't be surprised if Gilbreth greased a few palms in the process."

Amelia's eyes widened, and her breath caught in her throat. Her horror grew as she read through the hateful accusations again, going clear to the end of the article this time.

Each man was obviously disgruntled at not receiving the contract himself, and both were outspoken in their opinions that Martin must have gotten the contract through some form of collusion with the railroad.

The breath whooshed out of Amelia's lungs. *Greased palms. Shady doings.* No wonder Clara had been so upset. And it explained the odd reactions she'd gotten from people on the street, as well.

Martin Gilbreth was a good man—a decent man. Everyone in Granite Springs admired his hard work and his reputation for honesty. But people had a way of accepting anything they saw in print as fact. Would seeing something like this in the newspaper—*her* newspaper—plant a seed of doubt about his character?

"'The dignity of life is not impaired . . .'"

Hearing Homer's voice behind her, Amelia turned. Her earlier intention to throw herself on his mercy and ask forgiveness faded in the shock of what she had just read.

"' . . . by aught that innocently satisfies.'"

Her anxiety deepened when she noticed the glassy sheen in his eyes and detected a bit of a slur in his speech as he quoted the lines from Wordsworth. Stepping closer, she sniffed surreptitiously. Her nose crinkled at the telltale odor of alcohol on his breath.

"Homer!" She let every bit of the disappointment she felt show in her voice. "What were you thinking, putting those awful things about Martin in that article?"

Homer drew himself up, rocking slightly from side to side. "What was *I* thinking? You're the one who told me to follow up on that tip."

Tears sprang to her eyes, and she shook her head vehemently.

"I told you to check it out and see what could be verified, not to print unfounded allegations."

Fumbling in his jacket pocket, Homer drew forth some crumpled, yellow papers. "I did just what you said. The quotes from Campbell and Harvey are right here, exactly as I printed them. You wanted the space filled, so I filled it. You weren't around to ask, so I made the decision to run it—just like I had to do when your daddy was ailing."

"But I—"

Homer didn't wait to hear more. With as much dignity as he could muster, he turned and walked away.

Amelia started to rush after him, then stopped. What more could she say? Homer was right—he'd followed up on the anonymous tip and gotten quotes from the sources mentioned. And now . . .

Her throat tightened, and she choked back a sob. A quick glance around showed her the street had cleared. That was one consolation, at least. She had no audience to witness her second confrontation of the afternoon.

Except for the lone figure outside the general store.

Rage filled her at the sight of Thaddeus Grayson, still leaning against the front of the building with a broad smile on his face, as if enjoying the afternoon's entertainment. Catching her gaze, he pushed away from the wall and sauntered in her direction, showing no more haste than if he'd been out on a leisurely Sunday stroll.

Her first impulse was to spin on her heel and walk away, but she couldn't let him think he was intimidating her. Drawing strength from her mounting anger and frustration, she strode forth to meet him.

Grayson favored her with an easy smile. "You seem to be having a difficult time of it this afternoon, daughter."

Amelia jerked back as if he had slapped her. "Don't call me that."

A deep chuckle rumbled from his chest. "Are you having trouble running that little newspaper of yours? It isn't as easy being in charge as you thought, is it?"

He clicked his tongue in a show of sympathy. "I couldn't help but notice your friend seemed a bit upset. I would imagine a story like the one you printed today about an admired local figure might make you very unpopular."

He shook his head sorrowfully. "Amelia, dear, when are you going to see reason and decide to come home?" He stretched out his hand as if to caress her cheek.

Amelia stepped back and swatted his hand away. "I told you before, I am not going back to Denver. Granite Springs is my home, and the *Gazette* is my newspaper. I never expected it to be all smooth sailing. My father weathered his share of storms, and so will I."

"It's going to be rather difficult trying to do it all on your own." Grayson gestured in the direction Homer had taken. "Not only have you lost a friend, but you seem to have alienated your only employee, as well."

A thought flashed into Amelia's mind, and she narrowed her eyes. "Did you have something to do with that note Homer found?"

"Note? I have no idea what you're talking about." The words were innocent enough, but his knowing smirk confirmed her suspicions.

"Oh, I think you do. Leaving a note that sent Homer haring

off in search of a story without having the decency to sign it—it's just the kind of thing I would expect from you."

Her stepfather raised his eyebrows. "It sounds to me as if someone intended to do a public service by pointing out another side to the story. And isn't that what a good journalist wants? Instead of being angry at whoever left that note, you really ought to thank him."

Amelia clenched her hands so tightly, her fingernails dug into her palms. "Deny it all you want to—it won't do you any good. I know you had a part in this. What a foul thing to do!"

"Foul? How can you call it that when it only helped to present all the facts? Aren't you the one who is so persistent on bringing the truth to light?"

"Those may have been their honest opinions, but that doesn't mean every bit of dirt has to be slung around in public. Now that those opinions are in print, people will start to wonder if what they said is true. Not everyone, maybe, but enough that it can harm Martin's reputation." Her voice cracked. "They'll trust that it's true because it was in the *Gazette*."

Grayson gave her a measuring look. "Hasn't it occurred to you that's why Owen Merrick is so upset about the stories your father ran about Great Western? Once he got hold of an idea, he refused to let it go, no matter what it did to the public's perception of the company. Maybe this will help you see things from a new perspective."

With a wink and a tip of his hat, he strolled off, leaving Amelia speechless in the middle of the dusty boardwalk. Anger rose until she felt it would choke her. If she'd had a heavy object in her hand, she would have been sorely tempted to fling it straight at him.

And wouldn't it start tongues wagging if she did?

Drawing herself upright, she forced her hands to unclench. No point in giving the citizens of Granite Springs more to talk about. The best thing she could do was to get out of the public eye. Lifting her chin, she turned and stalked back toward the *Gazette* building.

CHAPTER 23

Ben stared at the papers laid neatly across his desk and rubbed his temples. Something was wrong. He had come to the office ahead of schedule that morning, early enough that he'd had a chance to access the company's financial records before anyone else arrived.

What he found created more questions than answers in his mind. There might be a perfectly innocent explanation, but without that, those ledger entries were enough to raise suspicion about Great Western's business practices.

He glanced at the clock and swept the papers back into their folders. He needed to replace them before anyone else arrived. It wouldn't do for anybody to discover he'd been rifling the files. Scooping up the folders, he carried them back to the file cabinet and knelt to return them to one of the lower drawers. He froze when he heard the click of the outer door behind him.

Owen Merrick strode across the floor toward his private office. He stopped short when he spotted Ben crouching in front of the file cabinet. His glance flitted from Ben to the folders in his hand to the open file drawer, and back to Ben again. One eyebrow arched upward. "Good morning. What brings you in so early?"

Ben's stomach knotted. As much as he wanted to appear at ease, it was hard to look nonchalant when kneeling on the floor before his boss. Trying to control his racing heart, he pushed himself to his feet, hoping he didn't look as guilty as he felt. He searched for words that would offer an innocent explanation for him going through the financial records. Then he shook himself. Why should he try to cover anything up? He needed answers, and this was a perfect opportunity to get the information he sought. He drew a deep breath and prepared to take the bull by the horns.

"I'm a little confused, and I wonder if you could explain some things to me." Without waiting for a response, he crossed to his desk with the folders still in his hand. Opening the top folder, he laid four sheets of paper on his desk.

Merrick shot a sharp look at him. "What's this?"

"I was going through the files on some of the purchases we've made over the past year, and I discovered something that has me concerned."

Merrick followed him and glanced down at the papers. His face hardened, and the muscles tightened along his jaw. He looked back at Ben. "What exactly is bothering you?"

"On the Seaver and Gilbreth papers, there's a notation to indicate the number of the bank draft used to pay the seller." Ben bent over the desk and pointed out the figures in question. "But the Rogers and Smith papers don't show any means of payment at all."

"Is that all?" Merrick's face smoothed back into its usual placid expression. "I'm sure it's only a minor oversight. Who handled these transactions? I'll have a word with him and remind him to be more careful about following procedure from now on."

"They were both handled by Eddie Franklin, but there's more to it than a couple of missing draft numbers." Ben drew a deep breath and braced himself. "When I tried to find those bank drafts listed in the ledger, there were no entries for them. It would appear the payment was never made. Moreover, it looks to me like the same hand signed both documents with the sellers' names.

"And here—" He opened a second folder and retrieved the papers at the top of the file. "It appears to be the same handwriting again, transferring ownership of those properties to something called Southwest Land Development." He looked up at his boss, awaiting an answer.

Owen Merrick stiffened. His face became a stony mask. "As I recall, I am paying you to do the work assigned to you. That includes your normal duties as well as this special assignment with Miss Wagner. It does not include snooping through company files that don't concern you."

Ben squared his shoulders and held his ground. "My assignment was to befriend Miss Wagner and convince her to look at Great Western in a positive light, and possibly print a retraction of what her father had written. In order to do that, I had to find a way to allay her suspicions. I decided the best means of doing that was to go back through her father's articles to find out what sparked his concerns. To get a better understanding of what was going on in the company at that time, I went through records of the purchases the company made, and that led me to these." He gestured toward the papers on his desk.

"If I'm going to set her mind at ease, I need to be able to explain discrepancies like these, and frankly, I'm at a loss as to how to do that."

He paused a moment, wondering if he really wanted to add more fuel to an already heated situation. *In for a penny, in for a pound.* Drawing a deep breath, he added, "There is also the matter of the McCaffrey reservoir. Why did we give Bart McCaffrey reason to believe we would purchase water from him, only to jerk the rug out from under him after the reservoir was built? That kind of action doesn't paint the company in a good light . . . especially since we bought the land outright after he was forced into foreclosure."

Merrick shrugged and folded his arms. "That can all be easily accounted for, but I don't have time to go into it right now. I have too many other pressing issues to attend to at the moment." He fixed Ben with a speculative gaze. "After all the years I've known you and your family, surely you can grant me the benefit of the doubt instead of making mountains out of molehills."

Ben looked at the man who had been his father's lifelong friend, feeling as though scales were dropping from his eyes and letting him see Owen Merrick clearly for the first time. "Are they molehills, sir? Mr. Wagner was a very persuasive writer. He obviously had serious misgivings about the way the company handled its business, and looking at these"—he gestured again at the papers without taking his gaze from the other man's face—"it's hard for me not to wonder if his allegations didn't contain as least a nugget of truth."

Merrick's visage darkened. "I hope you're not suggesting I would countenance anything underhanded while I'm in charge here. The two of us go back a long way. Your father has been like a brother to me, and that's the reason I took you under my wing. Why else would I have given an opportunity like this to someone as young and inexperienced as you are?"

He laid his hand on Ben's shoulder, and his voice lost some of its steel. "Up to now, you've done well and shown a lot of promise. You could have a bright career ahead of you. Don't jeopardize that future by making rash allegations."

Memories of the past rose up, reminding Ben of all the stories he had heard about his father owing his life to Owen Merrick. He wouldn't have been born if the man standing before him hadn't saved his father from a Rebel bullet.

But people could change, he reminded himself. Every choice a person made had the potential to lead him in a new direction. How well he knew that! And he couldn't dismiss the fact that Merrick worked hand in glove with Thaddeus Grayson, a man Amelia thoroughly distrusted.

Ben steadied himself. "You're right. I don't want to be guilty of misjudging anyone. That's why I'm asking for clarification on these issues."

"It's her, isn't it? That Miss Wagner." Merrick let his arm fall to his side, and his face grew cold. "What kind of nonsense has she filled your head with? I entrusted you with the responsibility of making her see reason. I never dreamed you would be so easily swayed by a pretty face. But let me tell you something—underneath that attractive exterior, the girl has a heart as dark as her father's. And she is just as narrow-minded as he was in her perceptions of a company doing its best to bring prosperity to this whole region."

"To the region? Or to yourself?" Ben watched Merrick's

face change as his words hit home. "That's the way it's beginning to look, anyway. As for Miss Wagner, the idea that there is anything dishonest about her couldn't be further from the truth. If she really is like her father, he must have been quite a man, and it makes me more inclined than ever to take a second look at what he wrote."

Merrick's eyes flashed. "It sounds to me like you've reached a crossroads, Ben. And only you can decide which path to take. Are you a company man, or not? Where do your loyalties lie?"

Ben lifted his chin. His employer was right—his choices were all too clear. He eyed his boss with a level gaze and made his decision. "With the truth, sir."

Merrick drew himself up, his dark eyes boring into Ben's. "I don't appreciate what you're implying. If that's the position you intend to take, there may not be a place for you here any longer."

"I agree. And since that's the case, I quit." Pivoting on his heel, Ben walked to the coatrack to retrieve his hat and jacket. Slipping his arms into the jacket sleeves and settling the hat atop his head, he strode out the front door and kept on walking.

The dazzling morning sun cast the buildings along First Street into sharp relief. Ben wished his thoughts could be as clear as the crisp lines of the storefronts. What had he just done, walking away from a well-paying job and alienating his father's lifelong friend?

He shook his head as he walked along. Maybe he should go straight to the *Gazette* and let Amelia know what had happened. But he wasn't sure he felt ready to face Amelia with this news yet, not until he had some idea of what he was going to do next.

What he really needed now was time alone with God. With that thought in mind, he turned his steps toward his boardinghouse. Once he had gone to his room and picked up his Bible, he hiked up a nearby hill to the point where the cedars gave way to pine trees. Settling under a spreading Ponderosa, he opened the book on his lap. Of their own accord, the pages fell open to the story of Jonah.

He smiled at the irony. God couldn't have found a better way of getting his attention. He read through the familiar story, once again seeing all too clearly the parallels between Jonah's life and his own: a call to service that had been ignored, followed by a flight to a far-off land. But while Jonah found passage on a ship headed to Tarshish, Ben had boarded a train bound for Arizona.

Unlike Jonah, he hadn't encountered a life-threatening storm or been swallowed by a big fish en route. He made it safely to his destination, all the while trying to convince himself he could do the Lord's will there as well as anywhere.

And there he had encountered Amelia Wagner, whose passion for truth had turned his life upside down. Now he sat two thousand miles from home, without a job or any prospects for the future. Maybe in his case the storm had come at the end of the trip, not the beginning.

Would the parallels with Jonah's story end there? Ben pondered the question while he searched the open pages again. God had directed that big fish to swim all the way to the shore before depositing Jonah at a point where he could continue his journey and get his life back on track. But in Ben's case, he saw no similar form of deliverance or direction. Despite the heat of the day, a chill crept up his spine.

Had he run so far that he could never go back?

☓

Owen Merrick listened to the murmur of voices filtering in through his closed office door. He had barely stirred since dropping into his chair after Ben walked out, but his mind had been frantic with activity.

He looked down at the documents on his desk and ground his teeth. *Why now?* Of all the times for this to happen. He had been so sure he'd covered his tracks, but Ben had somehow stumbled upon the very records that had the potential to bring his and Grayson's plans to ruin. Who would have dreamed anyone would have a reason to look at both the Rogers and Smith papers at the same time? The similarities in those signatures would never have been noticed if they hadn't been seen side by side. He should have had Franklin sign one of them, rather than signing both himself.

He squeezed his forehead between his palms, trying to ease the building pressure. It was always the little things that seemed to trip people up. And added to those signatures was the tiny detail of missing draft notations. Why hadn't Franklin had the foresight to jot some numbers down before he filed the documents?

Or perhaps he should have just written out actual drafts and entered their numbers in the ledger, even though they never would have been cashed. Dead men didn't need money, after all.

Maybe all wasn't lost, even if Ben did take this news to that nosy Wagner woman. Even though he suspected something was amiss, he hadn't figured everything out. All he'd done was ask questions, and it would take more than mere questions to bring down the plans he and Grayson had so carefully constructed.

He beat out a light rhythm on the desktop with his fingertips. Was Ben capable of pursuing matters far enough to cause them actual harm? Perhaps. The boy was clever enough, and his obvious feelings for the comely newspaper editor had gone so far as to shift his allegiance from Great Western to Amelia Wagner. How much could the two of them find out if they joined forces?

Pushing his chair back, he rose to his feet and began pacing his office. The boy wouldn't get far enough to uncover their carefully laid plans, not if he could block his efforts.

It was like a game of chess, he thought, where a man had to think several moves ahead. There had been a shift in the game's strategy, but that didn't mean the winner was assured, only that he had to adjust his tactics.

Their grand design could still succeed. He would make sure it did. All he needed to do was move things ahead more quickly. He considered a number of strategic moves, trying to foresee what the opposing parties' response might be.

If only it hadn't been for the *Gazette*! He pounded his fist against his palm. Andrew Wagner and his insistence on asking questions had been the start of all their problems. When the man conveniently took sick and died, he'd thought problems from that quarter were over. But no—his upstart daughter had to come along and kept the paper going. As long as she was in charge, the potential for damage remained.

"You look like a man with a lot on his mind."

Merrick spun around and saw Thaddeus Grayson standing

in the doorway. He hadn't even heard the door open—the man moved like a cat when he wanted to. With an effort, he composed his features and assumed an air of confidence. He and Grayson might be working toward the same ends, but that didn't mean he trusted the man.

Grayson closed the door with a soft click, then walked over to settle himself on the corner of Merrick's desk. From his affable demeanor, an outsider would guess them to be two old cronies ready to settle in for a chat.

"You seem distraught." Grayson's voice was smooth as silk. "Is there anything going on I should be aware of?"

"Not at all. I was just working out the plans for our next move." He wasn't about to let the other man know about Ben walking out on them.

Grayson studied him with a long, thoughtful look, as if uncertain whether to believe his assurances or not. Then he gave a slight shrug and seemed to dismiss his doubts. "I just wanted to let you know I'm on my way back to Denver."

Merrick felt his eyebrows shoot up. "With your stepdaughter, I hope?" He saw a flicker of annoyance in the other man's eyes and felt a spark of pleasure at seeing his jab find its mark.

"Not yet." Grayson made a show of adjusting his jacket sleeve. "But I'm sure she'll be joining her mother and me shortly."

Merrick permitted himself a small smile at the other man's discomfiture. "I tried to tell you pushing her so hard wouldn't work. Remember, slow and steady wins the race."

"Are you referring to your plan of having your young protégé worm his way into her heart?" Grayson scoffed. "I thought it was a bad idea when you first told me of it, and I haven't changed my mind. That's why I have taken it upon myself to set my own plans in motion."

Merrick's body grew rigid. "What are you talking about?"

"Some of our investors back east are not happy with the progress you've made—or should I say the lack of it?"

Merrick balled his hands into fists. "What is that supposed to mean? You've been talking to them behind my back?"

"They're anxious to see a return on their investment, and your overly cautious attitude is holding up the whole operation. Their patience is nearing an end. We need to move ahead quickly, and so I've decided more persuasive methods are in order. To that end, I've called in some help, people who can't be tied to either one of us."

"Are you talking about shoulder-strikers?" Merrick took a step forward. "You can't bring rowdies into this town. You've spent too much time in the East. Out here, you can't mistreat a woman. A lynch mob would string you up as soon as they caught you."

Grayson chuckled. "I didn't realize you were so sensitive. Don't worry, I'm not going to harm the girl. I just want to discourage her enough to make her realize there's nothing here for her."

Merrick's head swung slowly from side to side. "People in this town already know there's bad feelings between me and the newspaper. If anything should happen to Miss Wagner, I'll be the first one they look at."

"In that case, I suggest you establish your whereabouts at all times so you'll have an unimpeachable alibi." A feline smile curved Grayson's lips. "That's exactly the reason I'm leaving today. I don't want my name to be tied to this, either."

He pulled out his pocket watch to check the time and stood, brushing a fleck of dust from the sleeve of his immaculate gray suit. "The train will be pulling in shortly, so I'd best be on my way." Striding to the door, he paused for a moment and turned back to Merrick.

"Our investors need to see some decisive action if they're going to ride this out with us. They won't hesitate to pull their money out if they think this may go badly. My intervention has given us a second chance. Don't ruin it."

CHAPTER 24

Amelia threaded her way through the Friday shoppers who bustled to and fro along the boardwalk, feeling as though she existed in some sort of bubble. The people around her seemed absorbed in their own activity, and she made no effort to connect with any of them. Not after seeing those hateful quotes about Martin Gilbreth that had been printed in the previous day's issue of the *Gazette*.

From the very beginning, this day hadn't gone well. She'd come down the stairs first thing in the morning, prepared to make amends to Homer. The discovery that he'd been drinking again had upset her, but further reflection made her wonder how much responsibility could be laid at her door. Had her sharp comments, coupled with the pressure of getting the newspaper out singlehandedly, been the catalyst that pushed him over the edge?

Her good intentions were thwarted when she'd found a note propped up on the press:

Need some time to myself. Be back this afternoon.

Thaddeus Grayson's taunting words came back to haunt her. She knew she had hurt Homer, but had she alienated him to the point he no longer wanted to spend time at the *Gazette*—or around her—on a regular basis?

She'd spent the morning cleaning up around the printing office, then fixed herself a quick lunch before venturing out to see what news she might gather. It was high time she resumed her role as the *Gazette*'s chief reporter. But except for her visit to the general store, she might as well have stayed at the newspaper. No one seemed to want to talk to her today. Even the usually genial Emmett Kingston seemed distant.

And once again, Ben was nowhere to be seen. She'd almost summoned up enough nerve to ask for him at the Great Western office, but she simply couldn't bring herself to do it. How she missed his company! She hadn't seen him since he brought those suspected forgeries to the paper.

Where had he been for the past two days? Had he discovered anything more? She longed to talk to him. Perhaps together they could find the elusive answers to the questions that plagued her. *Be honest,* she chided herself. *You'd be happy to talk to him about anything.*

And it was true. Ben Stone had become an important part of the fabric of her life. The image of his slow smile and the way his green eyes seemed to look into her soul filled her thoughts more and more with each passing day. And that near kiss the night of the concert . . . Amelia caught her breath at the memory of his lips, so tantalizingly close to hers. If only they hadn't been interrupted!

She brought herself back to the moment with a start, realizing her daydream had pulled her to a dead stop in the middle of the boardwalk. Feeling her cheeks burn, she quickened her pace and hastened back to the paper. Surely Homer would be back by now.

When she reached the *Gazette*, she pushed open the door, hoping he would be receptive to her apology. She stepped inside the doorway, then stumbled to a halt at the sight that met her eyes. Instead of the neatly organized printing office she left behind, a scene of complete disarray greeted her. The type cabinets lay on their sides, with bits of type scattered all across the room. Sheets of paper were strewn everywhere, and a puddle of ink glistened in the middle of the floor, with footprints tracking through it. Worst of all, the Peerless press had been toppled over.

And Homer was nowhere to be seen.

"Homer!" Amelia shrieked his name as she picked her way through the debris. She went first to her office, feeling her heart clench when she saw the contents of the file cabinets dumped onto the floor.

Whirling around, she raced to the kitchen and then the storeroom. In contrast to what she'd seen in the rest of the building, neither room seemed to have been touched. And there was still no sign of Homer.

The memory of the brick falling on Homer's head filled her with panic. *Where could he be?* She bolted up the stairs and checked each room, but it didn't appear anyone had set foot up there since she came down the stairs that morning.

Relief flooded her. Apparently, Homer hadn't been around when the destruction took place. Returning to the ground floor, she took another look at the devastation. Just putting all the type back into place would be a daunting job. And she couldn't begin to right the printing press on her own.

She had to find Homer. He'd weathered plenty of rough times with her father over the years. She needed him to stand beside her now.

If he had come back earlier that afternoon, only to find her gone, he might have decided to take the rest of the day off. Goodness knew, the man deserved a break. In that case, perhaps she could find him at his cabin.

She rushed out the alley door and hurried to the little cabin he called home. When she knocked on the door, it swung open to reveal Homer sprawled across the bed, looking like a rag doll thrown down by a careless child.

Fear leapt into her throat. So the intruders had been here, too! What had they done to him?

She sprang toward the bed, praying he was still alive. The moment she crossed the threshold, the reason for his ungainly position became clear. The cabin smelled like a distillery.

"Oh, Homer!" Amelia stood over him, anger warring with despair. "Not now."

Maybe he wasn't too far gone to help her. She nudged one arm and called his name. A low moan was his only response.

Gripping his shoulders, she gave him a hard shake. "Homer, wake up!"

His eyelids flickered open, and he lifted his head slightly to stare at her with an unseeing gaze. Then his eyes rolled back, and his head flopped to one side.

Amelia loosened her grip and looked down at him. Choking back angry tears, she stepped away. Her foot collided with an empty whiskey bottle and sent it rolling across the floor.

A thought struck her. Homer had been upset at her, no doubt about it. He had obviously spent much of the day trying to drown his feelings with alcohol. Just how angry had he been? Angry enough to create the wreckage in the printing office? The thought stabbed at her heart.

Stepping out of the cabin, she closed the door behind her, making sure it latched. She had plenty of questions for Homer, but she wouldn't be getting answers anytime soon. She might as well let him sleep it off. There was nothing more she could do right then, except begin the arduous task of putting the printing office to rights.

Trudging back to the scene of destruction, she circled around the pool of ink and stood near the overturned press to appraise the damage. Now that her initial panic over Homer had subsided, it was even worse than she remembered. Standing forms holding advertisements already set up for the week ahead had been knocked apart. Every one of them would have to be reset.

But that meant putting all the type back in order. She walked over to the overturned cabinet nearest to her. Bending her knees, she took hold of the top and heaved. She managed to raise it all of an inch before it slipped from her grasp and thudded to the floor.

Amelia stepped back and studied the sturdy cabinets. She would never be able to lift them without help. It would have taken strong arms to shove them over and tip the press on its side. How could Homer have managed that on his own?

Before she could begin sorting the type, she had to clear the loose papers out of the way so she could find the scattered pieces. Pulling her apron from its hook and tying it around her waist, she began picking up one armful of ink-stained newsprint after another and stuffing them into the wastebin.

With the papers cleared away, she turned her attention to the type. Thousands of pieces lay strewn helter-skelter across the floor, the different fonts and sizes mingled in a chaotic jumble. And every one of them would have to be put back into its proper place.

But first, she would need to clean up the spilled ink. She fetched a rag from the storeroom, soaked it in coal oil, and set to work soaking up the mess. As she stepped around the edge of the spill, she took another look at the footprints. More than one person had been there. At least two different sizes of shoes had marched through the ink. And neither of them looked like they belonged to Homer. It looked like she had been wrong in leaping to the conclusion that he had created this havoc. Thank goodness he didn't know of her suspicions.

A new thought struck her like a blow. Then that meant some outsiders had come in with malice in their hearts and wrecked the printing office deliberately. Her hands flew to her mouth. *What if I had been here when they came?*

She darted a glance at the unlocked front door. Whoever had done this might return, and she was in no mood to make herself a target. She strode past the counter to set the lock in place.

Without warning, the door flew open and banged against the wall. Amelia let out a terrified squeal and looked around for something she could use to defend herself.

Clara stepped inside with a bewildered expression on her face. "What on earth is going on here? I just happened to glance in the window as I was walking past. Looks like a tornado went through."

Amelia sniffled and swiped one hand across her nose. "I don't know what happened. I was away most of the afternoon, and when I came back, I found it like this."

Clara tilted her head. "You aren't hurt, then?"

"No." Amelia sniffed again. "Just a little rattled. I can't

imagine who would do something like this. Clara, I'm glad you stopped by. I need to talk to you about that story in yesterday's—"

"Where's Homer?"

Amelia flinched. Apparently, Clara was in no mood for an apology. She tried to answer with a steady voice, but it cracked as the reminder of Homer's condition smote her afresh. "He's in his cabin, out cold."

Clara's eyes widened. "Someone knocked him out again?"

Amelia shook her head. "He's been dipping into a bottle. Maybe more than one bottle, from the looks of it."

"So you're all on your own, then." Without another word, Clara shook her head and stepped outside again, closing the door behind her.

Amelia stared, unbelieving. She knew that article had wounded Clara deeply, but she'd hoped her former friend would have seen fit to offer a word or two of comfort. But now Clara had walked away again. Homer was of no use to her at the moment, and Ben was nowhere to be found. She had never felt so forsaken in her life.

Leaning back, she slumped against the counter and slid down to the floor. Wrapping her arms around her shoulders, she rocked back and forth while her whole body shook with sobs.

"I tried, Papa," she whispered. "I really did, but I can't do this. I wanted so much to carry on your work and make you proud of me, but I've failed. I didn't get the story you were after, and now I feel so alone. I can't do this on my own, and I'm sorry, Papa. So very sorry."

In the silence that followed, she felt an urging to shift her focus. Her earthly father now lay beyond her reach, but her heavenly Father was always with her, ready to listen. "Lord, I'm trying to trust you, but I don't know where to turn next. Something is wrong at Great Western—I feel sure of it. But I can't prove a thing. Every time I try to push a door open, it slams in my face."

She mopped at her cheeks with the back of her hand and tilted her face upward. "And maybe that's the problem, trying to do this my own way instead of yours. I've been focused on looking for the truth more to vindicate my father than to honor you, and I want to change that right now. Please give me the strength to keep on and the wisdom to know the direction you want me to take."

Little by little, she felt courage begin to seep back into her spirit. "Thank you, Lord. I know the battle is yours, and it isn't over yet. Please help me keep on fighting."

Pushing herself up, she scrambled to her feet and looked around. Where to begin? As Clara said, it looked like a tornado had created a swath of destruction. Not a tornado, she reminded herself. This chaos had been created by human hands.

By someone at Great Western? She froze when the thought struck her. It would make sense, but why now? Owen Merrick made no secret of his animosity toward the newspaper, but up to this point his hostility had been expressed verbally, never in a physical way.

She puzzled over the question while she picked up the composing sticks and laid them on the counter. She couldn't imagine Merrick doing this sort of thing on his own. But he might well have sent someone to perform the deed in his stead.

What if they came back? Her heart skittered in her chest,

remembering she had been in the act of locking the door when Clara burst in earlier. Stepping past the counter, she hastened to complete the task.

Scooping up a handful of type pieces, she spread them on the counter and began the arduous sorting process. The doorknob rattled, then a fist hammered the door. Looking up, she could see several shadows on the boardwalk. Her knees gave way, and she clutched at the counter for support.

CHAPTER 25

The doorknob rattled again, followed by a shout. "Open up, Amelia!"

Amelia could have wept with relief when she recognized Clara's voice. She hurried to unlock the door and swung it open. Clara stood outside with Martin behind her. The two of them were flanked by Jimmy and a couple of his pals.

"What are you all doing here?"

Clara shrugged. "It looked like you needed help, so I brought some. Martin can do whatever heavy lifting you need, and I figured these three might come in handy." She indicated the boys with a jerk of her head. "So I brought 'em along. Just put us to work wherever you need us."

While she spoke, the others streamed inside. Amelia stared at her unlikely crew of rescuers.

"Wow!" Jimmy turned in a circle, his eyes as round as saucers. "This place is a mess!"

"But not for long," Amelia said, feeling a glimmer of hope for the first time since she discovered the shambles. "With all of us working, we should be able to deal with it in short order."

Securing the lock, she turned back to her helpers and spoke

to Clara and Martin. "Before we get started, I want to tell you how sorry I am about the story that ran yesterday. Please believe me when I say I never intended to cause you grief. Homer got an anonymous tip and followed up on it. That's where those quotes came from. If I'd been thinking straight, I would have insisted on looking into matters further before we printed comments like that."

Looking at her friends, she felt her throat swell. "After all I put you through, I can't believe you're here to help me now."

Clara reached out and patted her on the shoulder. "The way I was feeling yesterday, I would have been surprised myself if you had told me I'd be lending a hand here tonight. Martin's the one who helped straighten me out." She aimed a crooked smile at her brother. "You can thank him for us bein' here."

The burly man shifted from one foot to another. "I know those fellows in Prescott, and what they're saying is just sour grapes. They had as much chance as me to get that contract."

"But what if someone believes the things they said? I feel terrible about putting thoughts like that in people's minds."

Martin lifted one shoulder in a dismissive shrug. "If those two are spreading rumors like that, folks were bound to hear about it anyway. Like I told Clara, people will believe what they want to, and most of 'em seem happy to believe the worst. We know what the truth is, so we'll just hold our heads up and keep on going."

Amelia squeezed one of his beefy hands in both of hers. "Thank you so much. I don't deserve such forgiveness, but I appreciate it more than I can say."

Behind her, Clara chuckled. "Honey, that's what the good Lord calls grace. None of us deserve it, but I'm sure thankful for it. Now, where do you want us to start?"

"That's a good question." Amelia looked around and ran her fingers through her curls. Her gaze lit on the type spread out across the counter. Turning to Jimmy and his friends, she said, "You boys all know your letters, don't you?"

The taller of Jimmy's buddies scoffed. "What do you take us for, a bunch of babies? Of course we do."

Smothering a smile, Amelia scooped up a handful of type from the floor and spread it on the counter near the rest. "I need you to sort these—and the others that are all over the floor. See how each has a letter on the bottom? You'll have to read them backwards to find out what they are. There are a lot of different styles of each letter, and different sizes, as well. You'll need to separate them into different piles."

She nodded toward the cases lying on the floor. "Once we set the type cabinets upright again, you can put each pile back into the section of the case where it belongs."

The boys nodded with an air of determination and set to work.

"What about Martin and me?" Clara asked.

"You mentioned heavy lifting." Amelia pointed to the printing press. "Martin, do you think the three of us can get the Peerless back on its feet?"

"Let's give it a try." Positioning himself in the center, he gestured to Clara and Amelia to take their places on either side of him. "On the count of three, everybody lift. One . . . two . . . three!"

Working together, they strained upward and managed to tip the unwieldy press back into place. "Oh, no!" Amelia's elation turned to dismay when she saw that one of the gears had been knocked out of alignment in the fall.

Clara waved her hand as though the damage was of no consequence. "Don't you worry about that. My brother's a good hand at mechanical things. I'll bet he can take care of whatever's wrong and have it ready to run again in no time. What do you think, Martin?"

The taciturn man eyed the machinery. "Looks like a simple enough thing. I'll tend to that while the rest of you go on about cleaning up."

Amelia looked at her friends, marveling once again at the wonder of unmerited grace. Then, seeing Clara struggling to lift one of the overturned type cabinets, she grabbed hold of the other corner. Together, they heaved it upright and shoved it back into place.

While Martin busied himself with the press and the boys continued with their appointed task, she and Clara went about raising the other type cabinet. They had just moved it back against the wall when the doorknob rattled again. Glancing toward the front window, Amelia saw Ben's face peering through the glass. With a surge of joy, she hurried to let him in.

When she opened the door, he stared at the hum of activity inside. "What's going on?"

His faced hardened while he listened to her explanation of what she found on her return to the newspaper that afternoon. "Do you think it was someone from . . ." Glancing around at the others in the room, he let his voice trail off, but the question lingered in his eyes.

Amelia dipped her head in a tiny nod and lowered her voice to a whisper. "I wouldn't be a bit surprised. We can talk about it later."

Ben slipped his arm around her shoulders. "Thank heaven

you're all right. That's the important thing. I'm sorry I wasn't here earlier."

She leaned into his embrace, heedless of others' presence and the openmouthed curiosity from Jimmy and his friends. "I'm just glad you're here now." As the words left her lips, she realized how true they were. The printing office still bore evidence of the earlier destruction, and plenty of work lay ahead of them to put it all back in order. But with Ben beside her, all seemed right again with her world.

A puzzled frown creased Ben's forehead. "Where's Homer?"

Amelia squeezed her eyes shut, then looked up at him. "Passed out in his cabin, with an empty whiskey bottle on the floor."

His lips tightened. "How long ago did you find him like that?"

She looked over at the clock. "It's been an hour or more."

Ben gave a brief nod. "It looks like you all have everything under control here. Let me go see what I can do with Homer. I'll be sure to lock the back door when I leave."

After checking the boys' progress, Amelia approached Clara. "It's going to be a slow process sorting the type. If you don't mind, I could use some help picking up all the files that were dumped out in my office while they're working."

"All right, let's get to it." When they stepped into the office, Clara's jaw sagged. "Have mercy. And I thought it was a disaster out front."

"Don't worry about putting the papers in order. Let's just scoop them up and set them on the desk so I'll have room to move around. I can sort through the files and reorganize them later."

With Clara's help, it took less time than Amelia expected to have the floor cleared of loose papers. They walked back to the printing office, where Jimmy and his friends met them with expressions of dismay.

"I don't know if this is going to work, Miss Amelia." Jimmy spoke in a defeated tone. "It's going to take nigh onto forever to get all these pieces sorted out."

Amelia looked at the array of type spread before them on the counter, then back at the multitude of pieces still strewn across the floor. "I see what you mean." She took a breath and squared her shoulders. "Do as much as you can tonight, boys. Homer and I will keep on sorting it out, and we'll see how much can be salvaged. In the long run, the easiest solution will be to contact the type foundry in St. Louis and order a new set, but for now we'll use whatever we can put together to set next week's paper. It's a hindrance, and the print might not be perfect, but we won't let it shut us down."

Martin stepped away from the press and cleared his throat. "I think I've got it fixed. Why don't you try it out?"

Amelia put her foot on the treadle and pumped it several times, then pushed the flywheel forward with her left hand to keep the momentum going. A broad grin broke out on her face. "That's perfect, Martin! Homer couldn't have done a better job himself. I can't tell you how much I appreciate your help." She turned a smile upon the rest of the group to include them in her gratitude.

Martin grinned and nodded. Clara stepped forward and wrapped Amelia in a quick hug. "We were glad to help. We'd best be on our way now. It's time these boys were getting home."

Amelia walked them to the door and locked it behind them.

"Thank you, Lord," she whispered. "You sent encouragement just when I needed it . . . and healed a friendship at the same time. What a gift!"

X

She made her way back to her office to tackle the stacks of papers. Working her way through each pile, she sorted them back into the appropriate folders and replaced them in the file cabinets.

As she slid a file drawer shut, she heard the alley door open and footsteps approaching down the hallway.

A frown puckered her brow. She and Homer were the only ones who had a key. Had he recovered so quickly? She stepped out into the hallway and saw Ben walking toward her, nudging Homer ahead of him.

When Ben met her eyes, he shook his head. "He was just starting to come around when I got there. It took a while before he was able to make it over here. I had to give him time to clean up, and then I poured nearly a whole pot of coffee down him."

Homer looked pale and appeared rather shaken. He kept his gaze from meeting hers directly, and when he spoke, his tone was so low she had to strain to hear him. "Ben told me what happened." Looking around the room, he added, "Looks like you managed to get it all put back together without me."

"I had help. The Gilbreths stopped by and brought Jimmy and a couple of his friends. We'll have to order more type, but apart from that, we're in good shape."

"I should have been here. Maybe I could have stopped it from happening." His shoulders drooped, and he hung his head. "I'm sorry."

Amelia's anger ebbed away in the face of her old friend's misery. Homer was like family—as dear to her as if he were an actual relative. Yes, she had been hurt by his drinking, but she had hurt him first, maybe even driven him to it by her attitude.

Tears welled in her eyes. "I'm the one who needs to apologize. You did everything I asked you to, even when I snapped at you. It was wrong of me to heap all that responsibility on you. And I'm truly sorry for the way I spoke to you. You did nothing to deserve that."

Homer shuffled his feet and stared at a point across the room. "It isn't only what I did yesterday. It's the . . . condition I was in this afternoon."

He lowered his head for a moment. When he raised it again, she could see a trace of moisture pooling in his eyes. "When I met your dad, I was sunk about as low as a man can go. Seems like I was always hiding in a bottle. But he looked past all that and treated me like a friend. That was when he told me about the Lord."

A gentle smile curved his lips. "He showed me passages in his Bible, and the more I watched the kind of life he led, the more I wanted to have that for myself. And it worked—for the most part."

Ben stepped up beside him and laid his hand on the older man's shoulder. "That's what the gospel can do. It makes us hungry for the Lord."

Homer hung his head again. "You know I've made a few slips from time to time over the years, but nothing like what I was doing back then." His Adam's apple bobbed up and down, and his voice grew husky. "I don't know why it's gotten so much worse since your dad has been gone. Maybe you've noticed?"

Amelia nodded. "I have . . . and I've been concerned for you."

"This isn't something I want to do," he continued. "I've tried to stop and told myself to just walk away from it. But then things get busy around here, and the pressure starts building up, and there I go again. I can't seem to stop, no matter how hard I try."

Amelia saw the pain in his eyes, and her throat constricted.

He pulled a handkerchief from his back pocket and swiped at his eyes. "Your father was one of the godliest men I've ever known, and I don't want to dishonor his memory this way. I know he'd be ashamed if he could see the way I've been acting."

Amelia wrapped her arms around him and hugged him tight. "My father considered you his dearest friend. It would grieve him to know how you're struggling."

Ben cleared his throat. "Mr. Crenshaw, I may be speaking out of turn, but it sounds to me like you may have been trusting Mr. Wagner to keep you on the straight and narrow instead of the Lord."

Homer spun around and glared at him, then his jaw went slack and his eyes widened. He leaned back against the wall, as if seeking support. "Andrew used to tell me a man can't get into heaven riding on another man's coattails. I trusted the Lord for my salvation, but I never thought I might be using Andrew as my conscience."

Ben's eyes shone with compassion as he gripped the other man's shoulder. "We need each other, no doubt about that. The Bible makes it clear that we're supposed to encourage one another, but no person can keep you from giving in to temptation. God is the only one who can do that."

Homer nodded, slowly at first, then with more conviction. "You're right, and I'm going to have to take some time to straighten things out with Him." He drew a long, shaky sigh and ran his fingers through his wispy hair. "I just wish I'd never taken that first drink in the beginning. I wouldn't be in this position now if I hadn't given in back then."

He swallowed hard, and his eyes misted over again as he turned back to Ben. "I don't suppose you know what it's like to make one wrong choice that changes your whole life."

To Amelia's surprise, Ben's face clouded, and his green eyes took on a wistful expression. "Actually, I do," he said. He paused and looked from Homer to Amelia and back again, as if deciding whether to go on.

Finally, he cleared his throat. "Back when I was in college, God placed a call on my life. Some men would have been thrilled, but I was scared to death. When I looked around at the pastors I knew, all I saw were stodgy men leading lifeless congregations. I couldn't stand the thought of spending my life that way and becoming like them. So I ran."

Amelia's lips formed an O. Homer tucked his thumbs in his waistband and leaned forward, listening intently.

"I didn't share God's call with anyone. I didn't want anybody forcing me into something I didn't want to do. After I graduated, I tried a few jobs, but none of them truly satisfied me." He gave a short laugh. "And to be honest, I wasn't particularly good at any of them. I had no idea which way to turn next . . . until Owen Merrick visited my father and offered me a job with Great Western.

"It seemed like a grand opportunity to be a part of building the West. I saw it as a way to do good and convinced myself I could minister that way as well as I could from behind a pulpit. So I jumped at the chance and came out here to Arizona."

The muscles along his jaw worked as he turned to face Homer. "I didn't crawl into a bottle, but turning my back on God's plan like that was just as bad. And it certainly didn't work out the way I'd hoped. I haven't had a moment of real peace since I ran away."

Fighting back tears of her own, Amelia stepped beside him and took his hand in hers. "But there's always a way back, Ben. For all of us." Her throat tightened. Hadn't she just been given a second chance by Clara and Martin . . . and Homer, too?

Ben gave her a grateful smile. He tightened his fingers around hers and didn't let go.

Homer used his handkerchief to swipe his face again and shoved it back in his pocket. "Thank you both. You've given me a lot to think about—and a lot to hope for." He squared his shoulders, looking more like his usual self. "If you don't mind, I think I'll go out for a while. Some of that fresh evening air ought to be just the thing to help clear up this old head of mine. And I might just stop by the church and see if Pastor Edmonds is around. He and I have a lot to talk about."

As he walked out the front door, Jimmy darted past him and charged inside. He pounded across the floor, his face alight with excitement. "Miss Amelia, I think I'm onto a story."

"Not now, Jimmy." Amelia pressed her free hand to her forehead. This day had already given her too much to think about. She simply didn't have the energy to deal with Jimmy's boundless enthusiasm right now.

Seeing the boy's crestfallen look, she had a change of heart. Hadn't she already hurt enough people over the past couple of days? She couldn't bear to add Jimmy to that list. With a sigh, she walked over to her young newsboy and bent down to put herself on his eye level. "All right, tell me about it."

His recovery was immediate. A wide grin split his face, and he bounced up and down like an eager puppy. "There's some strangers in town."

Amelia's lips twitched. "That's hardly a major story, Jimmy. Granite Springs is growing, and new people come to town all the time. That's why I check by the depot every week to see who has arrived."

"Yeah, I know." Jimmy continued bouncing, undaunted by her statement. "But not people like these. They look like bad guys, really mean."

Amelia stood and leaned back against the counter. She winked at Ben, remembering some of Jimmy's "story leads" from the past. "Mean like Freddie Thompson the time he gave Pete Roland a bloody nose on the schoolyard, or mean like Mr. Olsen when he chased you and some of your buddies out of his hayloft?"

Jimmy shook his head with an impatient frown. "No, these look like a bunch of toughs. And they're not kids, Miss Amelia, they're grown-ups. Come on and look." He grabbed her hand and tugged her across the floor to the front window, then pointed across the street in the direction of the corner cigar store.

Amelia followed his pointing finger. Her stomach clenched when she saw three men, all strangers to her, loitering in front of the shop. None of them had the look of typical Westerners. They reminded her of men she had seen in Denver, hanging around the train yards. One was heavyset, with broad shoulders. The second had a crooked nose that skewed off in an odd direction. The third was smaller than the others, with a narrow face that reminded her of a weasel's. She felt a sense of relief when Ben joined them at the window.

Trying to stifle the flutter of panic their appearance raised within her, she turned to Jimmy with what she hoped would look like a calm smile. "They are strangers, I'll grant you that. And they do look a little rough. But I'm not sure there's a story in it." She kept her voice light and confident, trying to convince herself as much as the boy.

Jimmy was not so easily persuaded. "But what are they doing, just hanging around the corner like that? They aren't doing anything, they aren't talking to anybody, and they keep looking over this way. See?" He jabbed his finger toward the window again. "One of them is looking over here right now."

Amelia stepped back with an involuntary gasp when the heavyset man looked straight toward the *Gazette* building. She let out a shaky laugh when she realized the sun's reflection on the glass would keep him from seeing her. She was as bad as Jimmy, letting her imagination run away with her.

Or was she? She glanced over her shoulder at the printing office and took a step closer to Ben. Someone had been in her building earlier, someone strong enough and malicious enough to turn the place upside down. These men looked like they would fit that bill quite nicely.

But why would total strangers target her paper? She could think of no reason . . . unless they had been sent by someone at Great Western. She gripped Ben's arm. "Do you recognize them?"

When she met his green gaze, his worried expression told her his thoughts had been traveling along similar lines. "I've never seen them before. From the way they're just hanging about, it almost seems like they're waiting for someone to come out and confront them."

He started to pull away, his lips set in a firm line. "Maybe I should accommodate them. I'd like to find out what they're doing here."

"Don't even think about it!" Amelia clutched his arm with both hands and held on tight. A flurry of thoughts whirled through her mind. There were three of the men, and only one of Ben. If that trio was responsible for the damage to the printing office, she didn't want to think what they could do to one lone man. "That may be the very reason they're out there now, waiting for you or Homer to come out and take them on. If there's an altercation, they could always claim you provoked a fight."

When he hesitated, her breath caught in her throat, and she tightened her grip. "Please don't do it, Ben. There has to be another way." She felt his arm tense under her fingers, and then he settled back and nodded.

"The best idea would be to let the law take care of it . . . if we had any to call upon in town."

Amelia nodded, her frustration mounting. Like many frontier communities, Granite Springs depended on the county sheriff rather than a town marshal to enforce the laws. But the sheriff's office was in Prescott, some twelve miles away.

Ben glanced at the clock. "The telegraph office is closed for the evening. I could go roust out the operator, but the sheriff isn't going to send anyone riding out this way tonight. It would be dark long before they got here."

He looked at the men across the street again. "Unless they rode in on horses—which isn't likely, from the looks of them—they won't be able to leave town before the train pulls out tomorrow. I'll send a wire first thing in the morning."

Amelia studied his face. "If you think that's the best thing, I guess it will have to do."

A furrow creased his forehead. "I don't like the idea of you being here all alone. Maybe Homer could sleep in the storeroom tonight. It would ease my mind considerably."

"Mine too," she admitted.

Jimmy turned away from the window, his face a mask of disappointment. "You mean you're not going to do anything about them?"

"Not tonight." Amelia stepped away from Ben and stooped down in front of the boy. "But we will tomorrow, I promise."

His lower lip jutted out. "I thought a reporter was always supposed to follow a story."

"That's right. But a good reporter has to decide the best time to go after it. It's important to know when to take action and when to wait."

Jimmy cocked his head to one side while he absorbed her words. Then he broke out in a grin. "So you're saying there really is a story here?"

"I think there may be." Amelia straightened and ruffled his hair. "You did a fine job, letting us know about this. Now you'd better go home. It's going to be getting dark soon, and I don't want your mother to worry." When the youngster started for the front door, she caught hold of his sleeve. "I think you'd better go out the back way this evening."

When Jimmy screwed up his face and seemed ready to

protest, Ben stepped in. "She's right. If these fellows are up to something, we don't want to let them know we're on to them, right?"

The boy's eyes lit up, and he nodded. "Okay, I get it. I'll slip out quiet as a mouse."

The three of them walked back to the alley door. After unlocking it, Amelia peered outside before she let Jimmy go past. "It looks like everything is clear," she told him. "You head straight home, now. Don't even think about going out where those men are." She exchanged a quick glance with Ben and added, "And don't spread this around among your friends, all right? This is something we have to keep quiet."

Jimmy puffed out his chest. "Sure thing, Miss Amelia. You can count on me."

CHAPTER 26

Amelia watched Jimmy scamper down the alley. Not until she saw him turn safely onto Second Street did she close and lock the door. When she turned around, Ben stood before her with a warmth in his eyes that sent a flush creeping up her neck. Her heart began to beat more quickly.

"I'm glad you came back," she said. "I've been wanting to talk to you." His slow smile sent her heart into an even more rapid pace. She glanced away a moment so she could refocus. "I looked for you yesterday, but I didn't see you anywhere around town. Or today, either, when I was out trying to gather news."

"I was gone yesterday, trying to track down some information. As for today, I went in early this morning to compare some things I've found with other items in the files."

Amelia looked at him more closely, noticing for the first time the weariness etched around the corners of his eyes. As much as she wanted to go over her questions with him right now, the kinder thing to do would be to wait until tomorrow. She forced a smile to mask her disappointment. "Maybe you'd better be getting home, yourself. Like we told Jimmy, it's getting late, and you have to be at work again in the morning."

Ben shook his head. "You're not getting rid of me that easy. For one thing, I'm not planning to leave until Homer gets back and I know you have someone with you. In the second place, I won't be going to the office in the morning. Or any other time, for that matter." When he saw her startled glance, his lips twisted in a wry smile. "I quit my job today."

"Quit!" Amelia echoed. She clasped her hands together and squeezed until her knuckles turned white. "Why? Was it because of those papers you brought to show me?" Even as she asked, she felt sure of the answer. Not only had she treated Homer abominably the day before, but her obsession with investigating Great Western had nearly cost her Clara's friendship . . . and now Ben's job.

He pursed his lips. "Let's just say that when I asked Merrick about some of the things I found, I wasn't satisfied with his answers."

She caught his sleeve in her hand. "Why? What did he say?"

"It was more a matter of what he *didn't* say. He was evasive, tried to fob me off until a more convenient time. I am more convinced than ever that we're on to something here. I'm just not sure what's behind it."

He ran his hand across the top of his head and gave her an apologetic look. "Maybe I shouldn't have walked out like that. Now I won't have access to the company files, and I'm sure there's a lot more we don't know yet."

Amelia's lips trembled as the significance of what he had done struck home. "I'm sorry. I never intended for you to lose your job—your income." What had she done? And would that mean he was going to leave? A deep emptiness filled her heart at the thought.

"Right now, that's the least of my worries. I haven't had a lot of expenses here aside from paying for my room and board, so I have enough saved up to carry me over for a while. Actually, it may work in our favor." His eyes lit up with a gleam that set her heart racing again. "Without any work responsibilities, I'm free to help you investigate. That is, if you still want me to."

Hope flickered within her. If Ben was offering his services, he couldn't be planning to go back east anytime soon. "Why don't you take a look at what I worked on yesterday. Maybe you'll see something I didn't. I have to admit I'm stumped." She led him to the office and picked up a stack of papers from the corner of her desk. Then she hesitated and turned back to face him. "But first, I need to talk to you about something else. You and Homer both shared some painful things a few moments ago. Now it's my turn."

Ben shot her a questioning look but remained silent.

Walking to the farthest file cabinet, she opened the bottom drawer and pulled out the folded document that had shattered her perception of her father. Its weight lay heavy in her hand, and she wavered for a moment, trying to decide if she really wanted to reveal the ugly secret. As much as she needed a listening ear to which she could pour out her heart about Millie's visit, she hadn't been able to bring herself to place that burden upon Homer. His admiration for her father knew no bounds. She couldn't believe he knew anything about this sordid partnership, and she couldn't bear to put him through the same turmoil she felt.

She studied Ben's face, trying to gauge what his reaction might be. She'd asked him to trust her enough to look into the possibility of wrongdoing by the company he worked for.

Was she bold enough to give him her trust when it came to her father's reputation?

The steady green gaze decided her. Breathing a quick prayer, she laid the document in his hand. "Up until a few days ago, I didn't even know this existed. It was brought to my attention by—" she swallowed once and lifted her chin—"a woman named Millie Brown."

Ben's eyebrows soared toward his hairline, but all he said was, "I've heard of her."

"Go ahead and read it." Amelia clenched her hands and tried to keep her voice from cracking. "It's easier than me trying to explain."

Ben unfolded the paper and began to read. Seconds later, his mouth dropped open and his eyes grew wide. "But this is—"

Amelia nodded, fighting back the misery that threatened to overwhelm her. "She told me she and my father had been in partnership for some time. Now that he's gone, she wants to buy out *my* share." The last two words came out in a bitter laugh. "Just a little while ago, Homer said my father was the godliest man he'd ever known. Before I saw this, I would have agreed with him wholeheartedly. But now . . ."

Her throat tightened, and she struggled to choke out the rest of what needed to be said before she broke down completely. "What am I supposed to think? My father gave me the principles I live by, and those ideals of truth and integrity have been ingrained in me since I was old enough to understand what they mean. If my father wasn't the man I thought he was, how can I trust anyone?

"It's impossible for me to accept that he could be involved in something like this, but there it is, in black and white, with his signature at the bottom." She reached over and tapped the document. "And even worse . . ." She looked into Ben's eyes, trying to bring his features into focus through the tears that clouded her vision. "I think Owen Merrick knows."

"Merrick!" Ben's tone sharpened. "What does he have to do with this?"

"I don't know. I have no idea how he learned about it, but he's made two comments to me lately that don't make sense otherwise. One was about not digging into other people's business, because I might not like what I turned up. Another time, he warned me that people who live in glass houses shouldn't throw stones." She fought back a sob as she gestured toward the paper. "I have no dark secrets, other than this. What else could he mean?"

Ben pondered a moment, then said, "I'd like to take a closer look, if you don't mind. Let's light a lamp so I can see it clearly." He bent over the desk in the pool of lamplight and studied the document again. When he straightened, a taut smile stretched his lips. "When was the last time you looked at this?"

Amelia tilted her head and thought back. "I only read it one time, the day Millie told me where to find it in the file. After I realized what it was, I shoved it back in the drawer and left it there. I had no desire to see it again."

To her astonishment, Ben's smile grew wider. "She told you where to find it?"

She nodded. "Why?"

Ben held the deed out to her. "Take another look—a close look, this time. Tell me what you see."

Mystified, Amelia held the paper under the lamp and read through the words that had turned her life upside down. Once again, she felt the bitter taste of bile rise in her throat. When she finished, she stared up at Ben. "What am I supposed to see here? Obviously, nothing has changed since the first time I read it."

He moved nearer and tapped the sheet. "How about the handwriting? Have you ever seen it before?"

She studied the looping cursive without comprehending his meaning, then recognition blazed. She swung around to face him. "It can't be."

Ben gave a grim nod. "I can't be sure without comparing the documents side by side, but it certainly looks to me like the same handwriting we found on the purchase papers for the Rogers and Smith properties."

"The ones that were forged." She stared at him and frowned. "But my father's signature is on there. How do you explain that?"

"Do you have something else here that bears his signature— one you know is genuine?"

"Of course." Going to one of the file cabinets, she pulled out a folder and extracted a paper. "Here's the record of sale when he purchased some land from Virgil Sparks." She handed it to Ben, who laid it alongside the first document.

"Here." He pointed to the signature at the bottom of the brothel deed. "See the way the W in Wagner is formed?"

Amelia nodded slowly. "Yes, the points at the bottom of the letter aren't really points at all. They're rounded, with a bit of a loop to them." A faint flutter of hope began to stir within her. "When my father signed his name, I used to tease him about how precisely he formed every letter. The points at the bottom of his W's were so sharp they looked like pitchfork tines."

She bent over the papers again, feeling her excitement rise. "You're right. Now that I know what to watch for, there are other differences, as well. Like the *A* in Andrew and the *J* he used for his middle initial. The differences are small, but they're obvious when you examine them closely." She straightened and rubbed the muscles in the small of her back. "I was so stunned when that woman came here and made those dreadful accusations, the idea of forgery never entered my mind. Once I saw that the signature appeared to be his, I never gave it a second glance."

"I'm sure she was counting on that. Not only would you be too shaken to examine it thoroughly, you wouldn't be likely to take something like that anywhere to have it checked for authenticity, even if you did suspect."

"But she offered to pay me two thousand dollars." Doubt reared its ugly head again. "She even showed me the cash, Ben. Why would she do that, unless there's some truth to this? It doesn't make a bit of sense."

"It does, if someone put her up to doing it." When she stared at him with a blank expression, he went on. "Think about it. The handwriting on this so-called deed is the same as those other documents that were in the files at Great Western. And you said Merrick seemed to know about your father's supposed alliance with Millie Brown."

Amelia gasped. "You mean he's behind the whole thing?"

"It certainly appears that way to me." Ben strode across the office floor, then back again, warming to his subject. "If he was trying to keep you from going further in your investigation and discovering whatever Great Western is up to, what better way to distract you than with something so repugnant it would turn

277

your focus away from the company and its dealings? If that didn't work, those veiled threats of his were designed to keep you in line. And if you'd accepted that money from Millie, he would have been able to hold that over your head forever."

"You're right." Amelia's chest felt so tight, she could hardly breathe. Ben's explanation might only be speculation, but it had the ring of truth. "That would explain so many things. And if they're trying so hard to cover things up, there *has* to be something they don't want us to find."

The confirmation of her suspicions galvanized her into action. Folding the deed, she shoved it into its drawer and turned back to the folders on the desk. Opening the one on top of the stack, she laid the contents out for Ben to see. "See if you can make any connections here. I even made a sketch of the area, showing all the properties I could think of." She pulled her handmade map from the desk drawer and spread it out before them.

Leaning over the desk, she indicated a number of properties she'd marked. "I thought at first it had to be something related to the mining claims, but that doesn't explain Great Western's purchases over in these other areas. Why would they be interested in those properties? I thought of the railroad, too. Several of the parcels are near the established line, but there doesn't seem to be any connection between those and the rest. Then"— she gestured at an area toward the top of her drawing—"there are these others out in the middle of the forest."

Stepping back, she folded her arms and shook her head. "I can't make any sense of what Great Western could be up to. Try as I might, I can't find anything these parcels all have in common."

While she spoke, Ben shuffled through the papers, sorting them into quick piles and arranging them along the perimeter of the map. A look of amazement crossed his face, and he let out a low whistle. "You're right—they aren't just interested in the mining. When I see it all laid out like this, it looks to me like their plans are far bigger than that."

Amelia stepped closer, her breath quickening. "What do you mean?"

"They've set their sights a lot higher than the ore they can take out of the ground. Ownership of these areas would give them control of so much more: vast tracts of timber and key locations along the proposed railroad route to Phoenix. This isn't just about mining, Amelia. They're positioning themselves to become the land barons of Arizona."

Amelia let out her breath on a shaky sob, and his brow furrowed. He reached out to steady her with his hand. "Are you all right?"

She hesitated, then gave a brief nod. "It's just the idea of Thaddeus Grayson wielding that much power. I can't bear to imagine what that might mean for the people in this area." She rallied enough to give Ben a reassuring smile. "But it certainly explains why Merrick has been so dead-set against those articles my father printed. Neither of them wanted the public to figure out what was going on."

To her surprise, Ben shook his head. "It would definitely have repercussions for the people living here, but there's nothing illegal about any of that, at least as far as what we can see. And that is what concerns me—Merrick had no reason to react the way he did unless there's something more at stake."

Amelia nodded, catching his drift. "Legitimate businessmen

don't send thugs around to intimidate people. And then there's that whole business with Millie Brown."

"That's right. And it would also explain why Merrick was so bent on assigning me to spend time with you." Ben snapped his fingers. "I haven't told you yet what else I found while I was going through the financial records. It seems a company called Southwest—"

Amelia raised her hand to cut him off. "Wait a minute. Merrick *sent* you to get acquainted with me?"

Ben looked startled at her sharp tone, then he gave a small shrug and chuckled. "He had a plan for me to strike up a friendship with you to try to sway your opinion of the company and convince you to print a retraction of those articles your father wrote. If he had any idea you had access to all this and we might join forces to piece it together, a retraction would have been the least of his worries."

He went on speaking, but Amelia seemed locked in a moment where time stood still. She could hear Ben's voice going on, but a loud buzz filled her head, and she couldn't make out the words.

She fought to fill her lungs with air. The deep breath cleared her head, and she turned on him, her eyes blazing. "Are you telling me the reason you started paying attention to me was because you were following Owen Merrick's orders?"

Cut off in midsentence, Ben snapped his mouth shut and stared at her. "That was his plan to begin with, but—"

Her chest heaved, and her hands tightened into fists. "The invitation to the poetry reading the first time you approached me—was that your idea, or his?"

His hunted expression was answer enough. Remembering

Homer's suspicions, she advanced on him and jabbed a finger at his chest. "Did you do something to disable that buggy so you'd be able to come along and be my valiant knight? So you could worm your way into my good graces?"

Without waiting for him to respond, she turned on her heel and marched out into the printing office. He caught up with her near the Peerless press. Catching her arm, he turned her to face him. "Everything I already told you about what happened that evening was the truth. I saw you driving out of town and thought if I could catch up to you, it would give us a good opportunity to talk and get acquainted. But I had nothing to do with that buggy wheel coming off."

Amelia squeezed her eyes shut and felt a tear trickle down her right cheek. She dashed it away with an angry swipe of her hand. "So that's all I was to you—a project? An *assignment*?"

He placed his hands on her shoulders and gave them a gentle shake. "I'll admit, our first encounter stemmed from my following orders. But once I got to know you—"

She pushed his hands aside and backed away from him. "I stuck up for you with Homer and told him you were a man we could trust. I even thought—" Her mouth twisted as the memory of their near kiss played through her mind. She choked back a sob. "I think you'd better leave."

He spread his hands wide. "But, Amelia, I—"

"Not now, Ben. Please, just go."

CHAPTER 27

Ben handed the money for his fare to Thomas Rafferty, who slid a pasteboard ticket across the depot counter in return.

"You won't have long to wait," the station agent told him. "The train's due in just a few minutes."

Ben nodded his thanks and carried his satchel across to the lone bench on the platform, where he sank down onto the wooden seat. Just a few minutes, Rafferty had said. He glanced down the length of First Street. If he hurried, he could make a quick dash to the *Gazette* and tell Amelia good-bye.

He got to his feet, hefted his satchel in his right hand, and trotted down the platform steps to the streets. It was unlikely she would welcome a visit from him after the way things had ended the night before. Still, he had to try.

He strode along briskly past the false-fronted buildings that lined First Street. What had possessed him to drop that comment about Merrick's assignment to him in such a casual manner? That slip of the tongue was almost as stupid as taking the duty on in the first place. But if he hadn't done it, he might never have gotten to know Amelia.

He had long ago discarded Merrick's order as his reason for continuing to seek out her company, but Amelia had no way of knowing that. And considering the way he'd blurted out the information, he couldn't blame her for the way she had reacted.

As he passed the Great Western building, a blaze of anger rose within him. Owen Merrick had gotten him into this situation. By ordering Ben to finagle his way into Amelia's good graces, the man had undermined any possibility of his relationship with Amelia beginning on a completely open footing.

Be honest, Ben. He turned his anger toward its rightful target—himself. He could have said no to Merrick's ill-advised scheme right from the start. It would have been the honorable thing to do. But he'd been too excited at the prospect of being hand-picked for an assignment that seemed sure to win Merrick's favor and help him move forward in the company.

A long sigh escaped his lips, and he shook his head. Merrick had played him for a fool, just as he'd tried to do with Amelia over the spurious agreement between her father and the local brothel owner.

What an idiot he'd been! His thoughts returned to Amelia and the confusion he had created in her mind. How could she possibly know his feelings about her when he had never managed to put them into words?

He had to make that right. There must be some way to win her trust again. The trip he planned to make might prove to be a start. Thoughts of Southwest Land Development had preyed on his mind all through the previous night. Merrick had shut down when he'd questioned him about it. If he could uncover information on that company, it might prove to give them the final piece they needed to solve this puzzle.

"Hey, Mr. Stone!"

Ben looked up to see Jimmy Brandt clattering toward him along the boardwalk.

The boy fell into step with him. "Did you send that telegram about those toughs I spotted yesterday? I've been looking around today, but I haven't seen them anywhere."

It took Ben a moment to refocus his thoughts and remember the men the lad had spotted the evening before. "Let's hope they've already left town." He aimed a stern look at the boy. "But just in case they haven't, remember what Miss Wagner and I told you? You are not to go anywhere near them. Do you understand?"

Jimmy's face scrunched into a scowl. Then he glanced up and caught Ben's unwavering stare. "Oh, all right. But I can still keep my eyes and ears open."

A piercing whistle sounded from the direction of the depot. Ben came to an abrupt stop. He cast a glance toward the *Gazette*, only a few buildings away. If he took time to see Amelia, he would miss the train. With a muffled groan, he spun on his heel. "I need to get back to the station, Jimmy."

The boy's eyes widened as he took in Ben's satchel. "Are you goin' somewhere?"

Ben gave a brief nod. "I have to take care of some business." He reached out to ruffle the boy's hair. "Take care of yourself, Jimmy, and be sure to stay out of trouble." With a last look in the direction of the *Gazette* building, he turned and sprinted toward the depot.

CHAPTER 28

The sudden clatter of the telegraph key seemed loud in the small office. Ben looked up from the bench where he'd been waiting and focused on the telegraph operator. The bespectacled man glanced up long enough to give him a quick nod before turning his attention back to the incoming message.

Ben strode to the counter, where the operator handed him a sheet of yellow paper. "I think this is what you've been waiting for, Mr. Stone."

Ben skimmed the message, and his lips drew tight. "It looks like I'll be staying around Prescott awhile longer. Can you recommend a good hotel?"

"You might try the Hotel Burke. It's right across from the courthouse plaza, on Montezuma."

Ben nodded his thanks. "I'm expecting another wire. When it comes in, that's where you'll find me." He took his time reading over the telegram once more as he walked down Cortez Street to the town square.

*WILL ASK SOME OF MY FRIENDS HERE STOP
WILL GET BACK TO YOU AS SOON AS I HAVE
INFORMATION STOP*

DAD

Ben sighed. His visit to the county recorder had yielded some, but not nearly enough, of the information he sought. The records for Southwest Land Development didn't include any names, only an address in Washington, D.C. His father was the one person he could think of who might be able to access more details in a hurry. But apparently it was going to take some time for his father to collect the information he needed.

He glanced at the last line of the message again and winced. He felt guilty about urging his father to ask questions without spelling out his suspicions about Owen Merrick, but there was no way he could explain his doubts about his father's trusted friend in a brief telegram. Regardless of how things worked out, he would have to follow up his request with a long letter, detailing recent events and what he had uncovered. He didn't relish the prospect. His father would be heartbroken at the news.

Once he located the hotel recommended by the telegraph operator and checked into a room, he found himself at loose ends, having no idea how long it would take for his father to reply or what he should do with himself in the meantime. He opened the satchel to unpack the single change of clothes he'd brought with him, and his fingers brushed against his Bible.

A smile touched his lips. He couldn't think of a better way to pass the time than communing with the Lord. Pulling the upholstered chair over to the window, he sat down with the Bible in his lap and settled in for a long wait.

❊

"Are we running Walt Ingram's ad in the same place next week?"

Amelia glanced up and met Homer's questioning look. "I'm not sure. Let me see if there's a better spot for it." She set down the half-filled composing stick she'd been working on, relieved to have an excuse to leave off setting the type for Hyacinth Parmenter's latest offering. She glanced down at the local poetess's most recent work:

> . . . O rapturous bliss of love's young dream
> that in one's eye ignites a gleam . . .

She scrunched up her nose. The cloying sentiment rankled, even when read backwards in the type she'd just set. The last thing she needed today was a reminder of young love. Walking around to the other side of the Washington press, she joined Homer, who looked as tense as she felt. Trying to piece the newspaper together with the type they had been able to salvage put him under even more time pressure than usual—it would take them days to set next week's paper. She could only hope it wouldn't be too long before the order arrived from the foundry in St. Louis so they could have their normal assortment of type available again.

He pointed out the ad in question, ready to place in the chase. "I can find room for it on the next page, if you'd rather." When she hesitated, he lifted a bushy white eyebrow and added, "Or I can make the call on it myself, if your mind is elsewhere."

Amelia felt a knot form in the pit of her stomach. She should have known her brooding wouldn't have gone unnoticed. The night before last, Homer had returned to the newspaper shortly after Ben left, with his spirits much improved after a long conversation with Pastor Edmonds. He'd found her in tears at her desk and spent the next thirty minutes coaxing out the story of her quarrel with Ben and the way she'd ordered him to leave.

She swallowed now as she tried to focus on the ad in question. "Ben didn't come around at all yesterday. I've been hoping he would stop by sometime this morning, but . . ." She broke off and looked at Homer.

Instead of the encouraging response she hoped for, he pressed his lips together and shook his head. "A man has his pride. After you threw him out like that, it's probably going to take him a while to cool off and sort things out in his own mind." He reached over and patted her on the shoulder. "I know your feelings were hurt, and I don't fault you for that, but I can't help thinking about what you told me back when I was having my own doubts about him."

Amelia sniffled and reached for her handkerchief. "What do you mean?"

Turning back to the press, Homer carefully moved the hardware ad to a new position. "You told me then to look at his actions and judge the man by what he was doing, not by my own preconceived notions. I'll agree that accepting an assignment like the one Merrick gave him looks bad, but that happened before he got to know you. Seems to me a lot has changed since then."

Amelia bit her lip and went back to finish setting the syrupy verse. Had she judged Ben too quickly, too harshly? He had openly admitted his first overtures to her were in accordance with Merrick's order. But what about the times they spent together after that?

One scene after another flashed through her mind like one of the magic lantern shows she'd seen in Denver. There was the day they first met, when he'd rescued her and the buggy, the way Ben had come to Homer's aid when he'd been injured—and again last night, when he spoke to Homer with compassion about deepening his relationship with the Lord.

He had even made the effort to go through the company files. And what he found not only caused him to come around to her way of thinking, but he'd quit his job because he wouldn't align himself with underhanded business methods.

Were those the actions of an untrustworthy man? *Hardly.*

Hot tears stung her eyes as other images sprang to mind— the times when Ben's nearness had made it hard for her to concentrate on anything else. And that moment after leaving the Odd Fellows Hall on the night of the concert, when she'd been sure he was about to kiss her.

She blinked rapidly to chase the tears away. "I guess I've been a bit on edge lately."

Homer's snort was soft but carried a wealth of meaning.

"All right, more than a little on edge." Her preoccupation with finding out what was happening at Great Western had clouded her judgment. If she could only resolve the questions that plagued her like a swarm of persistent gnats, surely life would settle back into some kind of order.

She had felt close to finding the answers when Ben agreed to look at the map she'd been working on. A soft smile tugged at her lips at the memory of the way his face lit up when he pored over the drawing on her desk, and her breath quickened when she remembered the warmth of his arm pressing against hers while they bent over the desk together.

Then a few brief words—and her reaction to them—had shattered that lovely moment. She went over the painful scene again in her mind. Ben had mentioned another company—Southwest something or another—when she'd interrupted him. What had he been about to say? He might have given her information that would have provided the key to unlocking the mystery right then, if only she had given him a chance. Instead, she had seized on his comment about Merrick, letting it drive every other thought from her mind.

She sucked in her breath, calling herself every kind of fool. Setting the composing stick aside, she buried her face in her hands. Regaining control of her emotions, she swiped at her cheeks with her fingers and turned back to Homer. "I'll be back later. I need to go find Ben."

His eyes lit up, and he gave her an approving nod. "Take all the time you need. I'll be praying for you both."

She hung her apron on its hook and spent a few moments tidying her appearance before she set out. Once on First Street, she considered where she should start looking. *His boarding-house*, she decided. If he wasn't there, maybe his landlady could give her some idea of where she might find him.

She had taken only a few steps before Jimmy jumped out of a doorway and ran up to her. "Where are you going, Miss Amelia? Are you after those thugs? Want me to come along and help?"

Amelia stopped in her tracks and tried to sort through the onslaught of questions. She hadn't seen any more of the ruffians Jimmy had spotted, and she assumed they had slipped out of town. With her concerns about the damage she'd done to her relationship with Ben, it had proven to be a case of "out of sight, out of mind."

She looked down at the boy. "Thank you, Jimmy, but I don't need any help at the moment. I'm just on my way to see Mr. Stone." When she started to move away, he fell into step beside her.

"You aren't going to find him."

Once again, she halted and turned to face the boy. "Why not?"

"'Cause he isn't here. He left on the train yesterday morning."

"What?" Amelia's jaw sagged. "Are you sure?"

Jimmy nodded vigorously. "I was talkin' to him when the whistle blew, and he took off running for the depot like something was after him. I watched him get on the train just before it started off."

Her knees threatened to buckle, and she grabbed at a nearby awning pole to hold herself upright. "Where was he going?"

Jimmy shrugged. "He didn't say."

Amelia's chest constricted, like a band was tightening around it, driving the air from her lungs. "When is he coming back?"

"I dunno. He just told me to stay out of trouble and take care of myself."

He's gone. Amelia clung to the awning pole while she let the truth sink in. And he'd left without saying good-bye. She had driven him away, and she would never have the chance to complete that interrupted kiss and tell him how much she cared for him.

Pushing away from the post, she tottered over to a nearby bench and sank down on the seat.

"Are you all right, Miss Amelia?" Jimmy stood before her, his face crinkled into an anxious expression. "Want me to get you a cup of water or some of them smelling salts?"

She raised her hand to wave away his offer. "I'll be all right. Just give me a few minutes." Even as she spoke, she called herself a liar. She had destroyed her budding relationship with Ben and broken her own heart in the process. After all the ways he'd come to her aid, after he had believed in her, supported her . . . How could she have treated him like that?

Pulling a handkerchief from her reticule, she dabbed at her eyes. Then she shook herself mentally. She wasn't some languishing heroine, the kind Hyacinth Parmenter might feature in one of her poems. She had failed Ben as a friend, but she was still a reporter.

Her eyes strayed to the opposite side of First Street, and her lips hardened when her gaze lit on the Great Western building. She might not know how everything linked together, or what schemes the company had in mind, but she felt sure of one thing: Owen Merrick was behind it all. He held the answers she needed.

And he no longer had any hold over her, not since she and Ben discovered the "deed" to Millie Brown's business had been forged.

At that moment, the object of her musings appeared at the opening to the alleyway behind the Great Western building. Amelia sat up as if an electric current had just run through her. What if she confronted Merrick right now and faced him with her knowledge of that forgery—the one tangible piece of proof she did possess? She might not know the whole story, but if she could make him believe she did, maybe he would be startled into giving away valuable information. She pushed herself to her feet. There was no guarantee her plan would work, but it was worth a try.

Jimmy bounced on his toes, looking ready for action. "Where are you off to now? Can I come, too?"

Amelia shook her head and smiled at the eager boy. "I have to take care of something. You remember what Mr. Stone said and stay out of trouble, all right?"

Turning back toward her objective, she paused for a moment. Was she crazy to think of facing the lion right outside his den? But Merrick was now a toothless lion, she reminded herself. Her discovery of the forgery had pulled his fangs, and there was nothing more he could threaten her with. Before she could change her mind, she marched across the dusty street.

CHAPTER 29

O wen Merrick turned to smile at Amelia as she stepped up on the boardwalk. "To what do I owe the pleasure of this visit, Miss Wagner? Have you decided you're ready to sell the *Gazette*?"

"You might as well stop asking that question. I'm here on a totally different matter. I don't want to waste your time, so I'll come straight to the point." She lifted her chin, wishing she could steady the racing beat of her heart. "My father suspected your company was involved in more than just land speculation. As you well know, he voiced his concerns in his articles, but he refused to put any specific accusations into print until he could present all the facts to his readers. Unfortunately, his investigation was cut short when he died."

Merrick nodded but otherwise didn't respond.

"You managed to cover your tracks quite well for a time," she went on. "But unsavory schemes can't be hidden forever. The truth will always come out in the end. And it has come out now."

She studied him closely, praying her impulsive idea would play out the way she hoped. If she could shock Merrick into spilling more information, he might just give her the key she sought.

He folded his arms, and one corner of his lips curled upward. "May I remind you of what I told you earlier? It isn't wise to go digging into other people's lives when you have unsavory secrets of your own."

"You mean that so-called partnership between my father and Millie Brown?" She had the satisfaction of seeing his body tense. "That ploy won't work anymore. I happen to know that document was forged. There never was any partnership, Mr. Merrick. It was just an unscrupulous way of trying to ensure my silence."

Anger flashed in Merrick's eyes, but he kept his tone smooth as velvet. "I have no idea what you're—"

"I don't know how you managed to slip that paper into my father's files . . . unless you sent one of your minions in there to do it for you when Homer and I were out of the building. But the fact that Millie Brown knew exactly where it was located should have alerted me right from the start. That woman never spent time in my father's office. Somebody would have seen her there, and the whole story would have come out long before now."

Merrick's glance darted back and forth at the people walking nearby. "I'd rather not discuss this out in public. Why don't we step back into the alley, where we can talk more privately."

Amelia followed him, moving only a few steps past the corner of the building, where their conversation would be screened from prying eyes. Continuing from where she left off, she said, "But sending people to do your dirty work isn't anything new for you, is it? Like those thugs you sent to wreck the *Gazette*. Was that supposed to make me want to give up and quit? If that was your intention, let me inform you that going to such lengths to intimidate me had quite the opposite effect. I'm more determined than ever to see this through."

To her surprise, Merrick seemed genuinely startled by her claim. He stared openmouthed and blinked a few times before recovering his poise. Then a smile creased his face, and he turned to move toward a door at the back of the building. "I had nothing to do with that incident," he said over his shoulder. "If you want to find the person responsible, I suggest you look closer to home."

It was Amelia's turn to blink. "What are you talking about?"

"Your stepfather. Before he left town, he told me he had something planned that was sure to convince you to give up that newspaper and go back to Denver." A smirk twisted Merrick's lips. "For all his boasting, he obviously doesn't know you as well as he thinks he does."

The statement hit Amelia like a blow. Merrick's words carried the conviction of truth. And the cowardice involved in that sneaky act was just the kind of thing she would expect of Thaddeus Grayson. But that didn't put Merrick in the clear, not by a long shot.

When he put his hand upon the doorknob as if getting ready to go inside, she hurried to close the gap between them. "My stepfather wasn't in town when you first warned me about the dangers of digging up information, back when you were laying the groundwork for springing your big news about that supposed agreement. He couldn't have been involved, so that places the scheme to make me question my father's character right at your doorstep."

Merrick's jaw clenched, but his voice was calm when he

spoke. "Miss Wagner, you're deluding yourself. I'm just a businessman, trying to promote opportunities for my investors and serve the people of this community . . . not unlike your father. What could possibly give you the idea that I'm responsible for a document you claim is a forgery?"

It was time to lay down her trump card. Unable to keep a note of triumph from her voice, she leaned forward and enunciated clearly: "Because I am aware you have additional forged documents in your company files, showing transactions that never took place."

A slight tightening of the skin around his eyes convinced her she was on the right track, and she pressed on. "Do you happen to know where Gabe Rogers and Josiah Smith are now? If you'll recall, you once reminded me that a good journalist wants to know more than one side to a story. I'd like to hear what they have to say about the property you supposedly bought from them."

Merrick's face went ashen. He clamped his lips together, and the doorknob turned under his hand.

Before he could disappear, Amelia stepped up close and pointed her finger straight at him. "Just be aware, this is not over. I'm not going to stop until—"

"Just a moment." Merrick held up his hand and let out a long sigh. "You leave me no choice. If you'll step in here for a moment, I have some documents you need to see." He opened the door and ushered her inside.

Thrilled by the thought she had just beaten the man at his own game, Amelia stepped into a narrow passageway. Merrick joined her and indicated a door to the right. "My office is through there."

He led the way, and Amelia followed, hope bubbling up inside her. Had she broken the arrogant man down so easily? Merrick pushed the door open, and Amelia took in a large, well-appointed office. She stepped toward the desk and fumbled in her reticule for her pencil and notebook.

"Just a moment." Merrick opened a door on the opposite side of the room and called, "Eddie, could you come in here a moment?"

He stepped back to allow a tall, wiry man with sandy hair to enter the room. "A situation has come up, and I need your help."

The newcomer eyed Amelia with a look of appreciation. "Where did you come from? I didn't see you walk through the office."

"I met Miss Wagner outside and brought her in through the back door." Merrick took up a stance in front of the desk and turned to Amelia with an air of renewed confidence. "Miss Wagner, let me introduce Eddie Franklin, my most trusted employee. In addition to land purchases, Eddie takes care of some of the more . . . delicate issues that arise in our business dealings."

Franklin hooked his thumbs in his waistband and nodded. "Pleased to make your acquaintance." He ran his eyes up and down her figure with a look that reminded her of Thaddeus Grayson, and she shivered.

Keeping her eye on Franklin, she spoke to Merrick. "What's all this about? I thought you had some papers to show me."

Merrick smiled. "Since you seem to be so interested in the way we conduct business here, I thought you might like to meet the man who finalized our arrangements on those land purchases. Unfortunately, you won't be able to contact Josiah

Smith or Gabe Rogers in person. I'm afraid they have departed this mortal coil."

The breath *whoosh*ed out of Amelia's lungs. "They're dead? Both of them?"

A silence settled over the room, and she darted a glance back and forth between the two men. Of all the shady dealings she thought Merrick might be involved in, murder had never entered her mind . . . until now.

She had to get away from these men. Thank heaven the back door was only a few steps away. She edged toward it, focusing on Owen Merrick. "You killed them?"

Merrick smiled. "I'm afraid I can't take credit for that." He nodded toward his taller companion. "Eddie is a man of many talents."

Amelia swung her head around in time to see Eddie Franklin grin as if accepting a compliment. "But why?"

Merrick shrugged. "They wouldn't agree to sell, and we needed those properties. We have plans in motion, Miss Wagner—bigger plans than you could imagine—and those two were in our way." His eyes grew cold. "Just like you are."

A roaring sound filled Amelia's ears. Whirling around, she bolted for the door. With the speed of a striking snake, Eddie Franklin blocked her way and reached out to cover her mouth with his right hand while his left arm wrapped around her waist, pinning her arms to her side.

Amelia struggled against his confining grip, but it was like being held in an iron vise. She tried to scream but could only force a muffled gurgle from her throat.

Still holding her tight, her captor turned to face his employer. "What now, boss?"

Amelia kicked backward as hard as she could. She had the satisfaction of feeling her heels connect with his shins, but it didn't seem to affect him any more than if she had been a struggling kitten.

"We can't let her go now. She knows too much. But we can't take her back outside, not in broad daylight, in full view of everyone on the street." Merrick tilted his head to one side. "Do you think we can find a place for our guest in the storeroom?"

Franklin let out a curse as Amelia ground her heel into his instep. "As long as we make sure no one hears her."

"I'm certain we can take care of that." Merrick's manner became brisk as he approached them and pulled a large hand-kerchief from his pocket. Stretching the fabric from corner to corner, he held it at the ready. The instant Franklin slipped his hand from Amelia's mouth, Merrick rammed the improvised gag between her lips and pulled it taut while he tied the ends behind her head.

He checked to make sure it wouldn't loosen and nodded as if satisfied. "Bring her back here."

The tight fabric bit into the corners of Amelia's lips, and the sharp tang of bay rum cologne filled her mouth. Tears sprang to her eyes, and her breath came in quick gasps as an overwhelming fear enveloped her.

Eddie Franklin held her upper arms in a cruel grip while they followed Merrick through the open door and back along the passageway to a small storage space at the other end.

Merrick stood before a set of shelves, unrolling a coil of heavy twine. He measured out a length and sliced it off with his pocketknife, then held it out to Franklin. "Would you do the honors?"

Sliding his grip down her arms, Franklin yanked Amelia's hands behind her back and wrapped the twine around her wrists several times before knotting it tight.

Freed of his constricting arms around her body, Amelia managed to jerk away. Pivoting quickly, she aimed a forward kick straight at his knee.

Franklin evaded the move with a quick sidestep and swung his arm in a backhanded arc that struck her squarely on the side of the head. She staggered backward and crashed against the opposite wall.

Franklin stepped forward with his mouth set in a hard line and spun her around again. "I'll need another piece for her feet."

A soft whimper gurgled from Amelia's throat as he shoved her down to the floor. While Franklin bound her ankles fast, she cast a pleading look up at Owen Merrick. She had considered him capable of all sorts of skullduggery and fraud, but she never suspected the depth of evil that lurked behind that self-satisfied demeanor.

Rather than softening, he seemed devilishly amused as he leaned against the shelves, watching Franklin work. "I once reminded Thaddeus that women are held in high regard out here in the West. I have always tried to abide by that, but as you can see, Eddie doesn't share my finer feelings."

Franklin jerked the last knot tight, then stood, panting slightly. "What do we do next?"

"I haven't decided yet." Merrick straightened and consulted his pocket watch. "I have a meeting with a client soon, but the rest of the afternoon is free. That should give me plenty of time to consider our options."

Eddie Franklin dusted his hands. "There's that old mineshaft up near the reservoir. The ore played out in that vein long ago, so there's no reason for anyone to poke around in there."

Owen Merrick pursed his lips as if pondering nothing more serious than what he would like for dinner. "That might work. As I recall, it's quite a drop to the bottom of that tunnel. We own the property, so it won't raise any questions if we close that mine permanently." He nodded and smiled at his companion. "Good thinking, Eddie. That should work out fine."

Franklin stepped over Amelia as though she were nothing more than a pile of rags and walked out of the room. Merrick paused at the door and looked down at her. "Thanks to your meddling, it looks like we have a full afternoon ahead of us."

She scraped her cheek against the wall, trying to force the gag from her mouth. There had to be some vestige of decency left in the man. If only she could reason with him!

"None of that, now." Reaching down, Merrick gripped the rope around her ankles and dragged her away from the wall. "And if you have any notion about making a racket to summon help, put that out of your mind right now. If I hear any noise coming from this room, I'll have Eddie make sure it's the last sound you ever make."

With that, he closed the door, leaving her in darkness.

⅄

"That's one loose end we won't have to worry about anymore." Eddie Franklin beamed as they walked down the passageway. "Once she's taken care of, that means no more newspaper, no more stories."

Merrick studied Franklin, taking in the glint of anticipation in his eyes. The man didn't seem at all put off by what they had just done . . . or what they were now committed to doing. He wished he could feel as confident he had done the right thing. He cast a glance over his shoulder at the closed door to the storeroom. Right or wrong, the choice had been made. There was no turning back now.

Once in the office, Franklin loitered by the desk. "Do you need anything else from me?"

Merrick sank into his chair and shook his head. "You might as well go about your normal routine. I don't want to let on that anything unusual has happened. I won't need you until later, when . . ." He jerked his head in the direction of the door to the passageway.

Franklin nodded. "When do you want to take care of our little problem?"

"We'd better wait until after dark. I don't want any prying eyes to see us."

Franklin frowned and shook his head. "The last stretch on that road to the reservoir is mighty rough. You don't want to try that in the dark."

Merrick drummed his fingers on the desk for a moment. "All right. Bring the buckboard around later this afternoon . . . say about four o'clock. We'll just have to find a way to get her out of the building without anyone noticing."

Franklin's mouth quirked up on one corner. "I'll figure something out, boss. You leave it to me. It'll all work out." With a wink, he strolled into the outer office with a jaunty step.

"That's what you said about dropping that brick on Crenshaw," Merrick muttered. He stared at the door long after Eddie Franklin closed it behind himself. No doubt about it, the man enjoyed the violent part of his job. Perhaps too much. Merrick hadn't gotten where he was without knowing when to cut a liability. Once everything was in place and money started rolling in, he wouldn't need Eddie anymore.

He pulled his attention back to the moment. Right now, he had a more pressing matter on his mind. Leaning back against the rich leather upholstery, he closed his eyes, the better to consider his options.

His earlier conversation with Grayson played through his mind again. He had been the one to upbraid Thaddeus about the very notion of harming a woman, yet now *he* had crossed that line. What had he gotten himself into?

Rage boiled up inside him at the thought of how his well-laid plans had been altered in only a few moments. *Stupid, nosy woman!* If only she had minded her own business.

He had checked every issue of the *Gazette* that had come out since she took over. Every week, he'd been relieved to see no further mention of the company or accusations against it. He had allowed himself to believe that the diversion provided by Ben, coupled with his own subtle warnings, would keep her from probing further.

But young Ben turned out to be a Judas rather than a loyal follower. Merrick's teeth clenched so tight his jaw ached. Somehow, that confounded female had managed to sway Ben's thinking, instead of the other way around. Why else would he have been snooping through the company files and turning up those falsified sales documents? He had to be the source of the Wagner woman's information about the Smith and Rogers properties.

Merrick took a deep breath to calm himself. At least Ben

had only found those two documents. Apparently, the rest of Eddie's handiwork still lay undiscovered—but that was small consolation under the circumstances. What those two snoops already found was enough to bring his and Grayson's bright dreams for the future crashing down around their ears.

He pushed himself upright and listened for any sound from the storeroom. When he heard nothing, he breathed a sigh of relief. Just a few more hours, that was all. Then Amelia Wagner would no longer be around to cause any further worry. With her out of the way, he could turn his attention to young Ben.

He chuckled at the memory of Thaddeus Grayson's disdain for his supposed lack of action. For all Grayson's blustering and his "grand idea" to call in those thugs from out of town, the man's puny efforts had done nothing. *So much for all your bragging, Thaddeus. When it comes right down to it,* I'm *the one who is getting things done.*

He rolled his neck from side to side, trying to ease the tension in his taut muscles. He found the idea of killing a woman distasteful in the extreme. But she had brought it on herself, threatening their success when the endgame was so close and the stakes were so high.

As he had told Grayson, harming a woman would be the equivalent of signing his own death warrant. But that would apply only if he were caught—and he would make sure that didn't happen. No one would ever stumble across Amelia Wagner's remains . . . or Ben Stone's, either.

CHAPTER 30

Ben swallowed the last bite of a late lunch and pushed the plate away. Settling back in his chair in the Hotel Burke's dining room, he sipped at his coffee, trying to keep his impatience under control. He had hoped to have an answer from his father that morning, but nothing had arrived as yet. Now it was nearly the middle of the afternoon.

A young boy who looked to be a little older than Jimmy Brandt walked into the room and glanced around. When he saw Ben, his face lit up, and he walked over to him with an air of self-importance. "The desk clerk told me I'd find you here. I'm supposed to deliver this to you." He held out a yellow envelope.

Ben sprang to his feet and took the envelope from the boy, handing him a coin as a tip. Breathing a quick prayer, he slit open the envelope and pulled out its contents. His eyes widened when he saw the brief message:

SOUTHWEST LAND DEVELOPMENT OWNERS
OWEN MERRICK AND THADDEUS GRAYSON

*STOP CURIOUS TO KNOW WHAT'S GOING ON
STOP*

So he'd been right. Ben lowered himself back into the chair and leaned back, pondering his next course of action. The sheriff's office was located in the basement of the courthouse in the center of the tree-lined plaza across the street. Tossing down his last swallow of coffee, he scooped up the telegram, picked up his satchel, and headed toward the town square.

It didn't take him long to trot down the stairs leading to the basement of the redbrick building and find the office he sought. The rugged man behind the battered desk looked up when Ben approached. "Something I can do for you?"

"I certainly hope so." Ben introduced himself.

"I'm Sheriff James Lowry." The other man stood and took Ben's hand in a firm grip, sizing him up with a brief, no-nonsense glance. "Sit down and tell me what's on your mind."

Taking a seat on the wooden chair, Ben leaned forward. "I've come across some information that may be of interest to you." In a few well-chosen words, he outlined his work at Great Western and his investigation on Amelia's behalf. Then he laid out the telegram he'd just received. "My father made some inquiries for me, and this is what he found. It's obvious Grayson and Merrick are planning something big."

The sheriff glanced at the telegram, then settled back in his chair and eyed Ben. "I'd have to agree with you that they're big operators, but that doesn't make it anything I can—or would—act upon. Acquiring a lot of land isn't illegal."

"But I believe some of their methods are." Ben pulled out his notes about the spurious contracts. "I have a list of names here, people who supposedly sold their land to Great Western recently. I have reason to believe the signatures on at least two of those contracts were forged."

Lowry sat up, his interest sharpening. "You have some proof of that?"

"Not with me. Those documents are still in the files at the office."

The lawman blew out a puff of air and settled back in his chair again. "Without any evidence, you're not giving me much to go on. What about those former owners? Why haven't they made any complaint?"

"After I confronted my boss about the contracts in question, I tried to locate the land owners. They seem to have disappeared." Ben spread his hands wide. "I know that doesn't give you anything tangible to go on, but Owen Merrick is up to something, I'd stake everything I own on that."

"Owen Merrick," the sheriff said slowly. His eyes took on a far-away look.

Ben's interest quickened. "Does that name mean something to you?"

"It might." Lowry fished through a disorderly stack of papers on his desk and pulled out a sheet of handwritten notes. He scanned them a moment, then looked back up at Ben. "I've been looking into the disappearance of Arthur Copeland, a board member of the Peavine Railroad. He vanished under rather peculiar circumstances, and we haven't been able to find a trace of him."

When he saw Ben's confusion, he added, "Owen Merrick has been appointed to fill the opening on the board created by Copeland's absence."

Ben's thoughts raced. "That would mean he could influence the route of the new line from Prescott to Phoenix."

Lowry grunted. "Disappearing landowners, disappearing board member . . . I'd say this idea of yours is worth looking into."

Ben stared at him. "Do you think Merrick had something to do with getting Arthur Copeland out of the way to create that opening on the board?"

"I plan to find out." Lowry rose and reached for his Stetson. "I'm going to round up some of my deputies and head up to Granite Springs this afternoon."

It took every ounce of self-control Ben possessed to hold back a shout of triumph. "I'm catching the train back. I'll see you when you arrive."

Lowry checked his pocket watch and pursed his lips. "Seeing as how the train leaves in thirty minutes, I think we'll load our horses on one of the stock cars and ride up with you. We'll get there faster that way, and the horses will be fresh."

Ben picked up his satchel and grinned. "In that case, I'll meet you at the station."

※

The bristly hemp twine bit into Amelia's wrists as she stared into the darkness. How long had it been since the door had closed behind Owen Merrick, confining her to this dismal room? It seemed like an eternity, although reason told her it couldn't have been more than a couple of hours.

She scooted across the plank floor for what seemed like the thousandth time, in search of anything she could use to free herself from her bonds. She had explored the items on the bottom shelf and along the floor as well as she could with her hands anchored behind her back, but her fingers encountered nothing sharp enough to cut or even wear through the cord Eddie Franklin had secured around her wrists and ankles.

Working her way to the wall, she managed to push herself into a sitting position, hoping the maneuver would help her breathe more easily. She leaned her head back against the rough wall, trying to ignore the sting of the raw skin on her wrists as she took stock of her situation.

Is this the end, Lord? Tears welled up in her eyes and trickled down her cheeks. *I had such dreams, so many hopes and plans for my life. Does this mean I'll never have a family of my own?* The image of Ben's face swam into her mind. What would have happened between them if she had given in to her heart's yearning instead of letting her obsession with this story get in the way?

Would she never again walk into the newspaper office to see Homer's dear face light up with a smile or hear Jimmy's latest idea for an earth-shaking story?

Sobs racked her body. What a fool she'd been! Why had she ever let herself believe she could beard a lion in his den without being torn to pieces? Owen Merrick wasn't just a crooked businessman. He was a murderer, and he intended to add her to his list of victims—this very day, from the sound of the plans he was making with Eddie Franklin.

She had no time to waste. There *had* to be something in this tiny room that could help her get free. Maybe she could find something on one of the higher shelves, if she could only reach them. Digging her heels into the floorboards, she pressed against the wall and inched her way upward until she stood upright. Taking a moment to steady her balance, she made one tentative hop, then another, into the blackness in the direction of the shelves. On the third hop, the hem of her skirt tangled in her feet. With a muffled cry, she toppled over onto her knees, then fell forward.

Lying with her face against the wooden floor, she felt despair well up within her. How much longer would it be until Merrick and his odious henchman returned to carry out their plan to throw her down a mineshaft near Bart McCaffrey's reservoir?

A sound from beyond the door jolted her fully alert. With her heart pounding in her chest, Amelia rolled across the plank floor and pressed her ear to the wall that adjoined the passageway. Voices. Footsteps.

They were coming.

A moment later, the door swung open, and Amelia blinked against the light.

"Kinda dusty, isn't she?" Eddie Franklin chuckled and prodded her shoulder with the toe of his boot. "What have you been doing—worming around and trying to get loose?"

"Enough of that." Owen Merrick's voice sounded taut and strained. "We have a job to do. Let's get on with it."

Amelia peered up at the men silhouetted in the doorway. Merrick stood just outside the door watching Franklin, who held an oversized burlap bag in his hands.

With a flip of his hand, Franklin tossed the bag to Merrick, then bent down over Amelia. She caught her breath as he seized her arms in a rough grip and hauled her to her feet. Pain shot through her strained muscles, and she uttered a low cry. Ignoring her misery, Franklin wrapped his arms around her from behind and lifted her off her feet.

Merrick frowned. "What are you doing?"

"Open the bag and slip it up over her feet," Franklin grunted. He held her dangling in the air while Merrick worked the bag up over her body, then he dropped her back onto her feet.

Amelia tottered but tried to pull away from his grasp. Holding her steady with one hand, Franklin lifted his other arm. "Settle down. Remember what happened last time?"

She flinched away from his upraised hand. *How could this be happening?* And yet it was. She felt as if she had stepped into a nightmare and couldn't wake up. Her vision dimmed, and her knees gave way.

Franklin released his grasp and let her sink to the floor. Pulling the open end of the bag up over her head, he made quick work of tying it shut.

Amelia tipped her head back and struggled to breathe. If the air in the storeroom had seemed stifling, this was far worse.

"There you go," Franklin said. "Tied up as neat as a Christmas package. If you'll give me a hand, boss, we'll pick her up so we can carry her out." Hands took hold of her through the rough burlap, raising her up and balancing her on her bound feet again.

"I don't know about this." Merrick sounded skeptical. "She may be hidden by that bag, but if she wriggles around, it will still attract notice. That's why I wanted to wait until after dark."

Inside her dark cocoon, Amelia felt a glimmer of renewed hope. She might not be able to see out of her burlap prison, but others could see the bag—and any movement from within it. If she could manage to create enough of a stir to alert passersby, there might still be a chance for rescue. She braced herself to take advantage of what might be her last opportunity for escape.

Behind her, Eddie Franklin snickered. "That won't be a problem. I told you I'd figure something out."

The next moment, something crashed against the back of Amelia's head, and the world went black.

CHAPTER 31

Ben eyed the platform, hoping for a glimpse of Amelia as the train pulled into the Granite Springs station. She often met the train to see if anyone newsworthy had arrived in town, but apparently not this day. He swallowed his disappointment and turned to Sheriff Lowry. "I appreciate you hearing me out and acting on the information I brought you. If you need me, I'll either be at my boardinghouse or the *Gazette*."

The lawman nodded and led his deputies back toward the stock car to unload their horses. Ben headed down First Street toward the *Gazette* building. As he walked, he wondered what kind of reception he would receive. Would Amelia welcome him with a smile and a sparkle in her blue eyes? Or would she feel more inclined to throw a composing stick at him?

He rubbed the back of his neck. Surely two days would have given her time to calm down . . . he hoped. But even if she wasn't happy to see him, she would want to hear the news he brought. When he reached the newspaper office, he shifted his satchel to his left hand and pushed the door open.

Homer looked up when he stepped inside, and a wide grin split his face. "It's about time the two of you showed up. I was beginning to wonder how long it was going to take for you to mend your differences." He leaned to one side and peered past Ben.

Ben frowned. "I'm not sure what you mean. I just got back from Prescott. Do you know where Amelia is?"

The grin slid from Homer's face. "I thought she was with you. She went out to look for you quite a while ago." He glanced at the clock, and his brow furrowed. "Going on three hours."

He turned back to Ben. "She probably just got on the trail of some story, but it makes me uneasy, not hearing from her for that long." Pulling off his printer's apron, he tossed it onto the counter. "Maybe we ought to go look for her. I'll feel better if I know where she is."

Catching Homer's concern, Ben set his satchel down inside the door. "I'll check at the general store. Maybe you could try the livery."

Homer shot a startled glance at him, then ducked his head in a grim nod. "I hope you're wrong, but it wouldn't be the first time she's taken a notion to go haring off after a story on her own . . . although I hope she'd have better sense than to do something like that right now, after all the peculiar doings we've had going on around here lately."

They parted ways on the boardwalk. Ben set a rapid pace, finally breaking into a trot as he neared Emmett Kingston's store. Inside, a quick glance showed Emmett setting cans of fruit in a neat row on the shelves near the back of the store. Ben hurried over to him. "I'm looking for Amelia. Have you seen her?"

Emmett paused with a can of peaches in each hand. "Not today. You look worried. Is anything wrong?"

"I hope not. If you see her, let her know Homer and I are trying to find her, will you?"

"Sure thing." Emmett gave a nod, then resumed stocking the shelves.

As Ben turned to leave, Clara Gilbreth stepped into the aisle ahead of him. "I couldn't help but overhear. Is there a problem?"

Ben hesitated. He didn't want to create needless panic, but he couldn't shake the worry that had taken root and refused to let go. Besides, Clara was Amelia's closest friend. "I'm not sure. Homer hasn't seen her for a while, and I want to be certain she's all right. I just got back from Prescott with a piece of news she'll be interested in hearing."

Clara regarded him with a sharp-eyed gaze that seemed to pick up on his unstated concern. Thankfully, she didn't waste time asking questions. "I'll be glad to help. Where have you looked so far?"

"She wasn't at the station or the newspaper." Ben ticked the locations off on his fingers as he spoke. "This is the first place I've checked besides those. Homer went to talk to Carl Olsen at the livery."

Clara started for the door. "I'll head over to Second Street and ask if anyone's seen her at the hardware store or the bank."

Ben nodded his thanks and set off down the boardwalk. *What next?* Amelia could be anywhere, doing any number of normal, everyday activities. But he couldn't push away the increasing feeling that something was wrong.

He decided to try the café next. She might have stopped in for a cup of tea or a bite to eat. As he neared the Bon-Ton, he spotted a familiar figure farther along the block. Cupping his hands around his mouth, he shouted, "Jimmy!"

The boy wheeled around. His face lit up when he recognized Ben, and he trotted over. "When did you get back?"

"I just came in on the train. Have you seen Miss Wagner?"

"Yep. I talked to her earlier. She was out looking for you. I told her you'd left town, though. She wanted to know where you'd gone, but I didn't know that . . . or when you'd be back, either."

Ben stifled a groan, wondering how she would have taken that news. "Where is she now?"

The boy shrugged. "Last time I saw her, she was headed for your office."

Ben stiffened. "You mean the Great Western building?"

"Sure. Your boss was standing in front of the building, and it looked like she was going to talk to him. But that was a long time ago. Right after I finished lunch."

Questions whirled through Ben's mind. Focusing his gaze on Jimmy, he tried to keep his voice level. "Did you see her later?"

Jimmy shook his head. "I had to run some errands for my ma. I didn't see her after that."

Ben turned and eyed the building where he had worked for the past few months. "Thanks, Jimmy. I think I'll go talk to Mr. Merrick and see what he can tell me."

"You can't. Talk to Mr. Merrick, I mean. He went some-where with that other man who works there—the really tall one. I saw them loading a sack of potatoes into the back of a buckboard, and then they headed out of town."

Ben stared at the boy. The only man at Great Western who fit that description was Eddie Franklin. He tried to imagine any reason those two would be handling a sack of vegetables—or doing anything resembling manual labor. His sense of urgency heightened, and he knelt down in front of Jimmy. "Potatoes? You're sure?"

"That's what it looked like. It was a big burlap bag, about this size." Jimmy stretched his arms out to their full width, then indicated a point above his head. He looked back at Ben and wrinkled his nose. "What else could it have been?"

Ben struggled to force air into his lungs. He wasn't about to tell the boy the possibility that had entered his mind. "How long ago did you see them? Which way did they go?"

Jimmy screwed his face up, as if deep in thought. "Not more than a half hour, maybe not even that long. They took off that way." He pointed toward Jefferson Road. "On the road that goes out toward the sawmill."

Dread seized Ben by the throat. He twisted around to view the street behind him, but there was no sign of Sheriff Lowry. He turned back to Jimmy. "Listen carefully. I need you to go find Mr. Crenshaw and tell him I think Merrick may have taken Miss Wagner. The sheriff and some of his deputies came to town on the train with me. They might still be at the station, unloading their horses or maybe they're on their way to the livery. I want you and Mr. Crenshaw to find them and let them know what's going on. Tell them I've gone after Merrick, and they need to follow as quickly as they can."

Jimmy's eyes rounded, and his eyes lit up. "Sure thing, Mr. Stone. You can count on me."

Springing to his feet, Ben took a step in the direction of his boardinghouse, then jolted to a stop. He didn't have time to fetch and saddle his horse. Spying a strong, sorrel gelding tied to the hitching rail on the other side of the street, he raced over to it. Untying the reins, he leaped into the saddle and spun the horse around. As he galloped past Jimmy, he called, "And if whoever owns this horse wants to know where it's gone, tell him I'll bring it back later."

Digging his heels into the gelding's flanks, he turned onto Jefferson Road. When he bent low over the sorrel's neck, urging him to greater speed, he noticed the stock of a Winchester rifle sticking out of a scabbard. *Good.* He had a feeling a gun might come in handy.

For the second time, he found himself following wheel tracks out of town in search of Amelia. He stared along the length of road ahead of him, although he knew he couldn't expect to see any sign of Merrick and Franklin yet. They had too big a head start.

Galloping around a curve in the road, he recognized the spot where he'd come upon Amelia's wrecked buggy. His throat tightened at the memory. He had been concerned for her safety that evening, but that was nothing compared to the fear that gripped him now.

He slowed a bit when he reached the side road that branched off toward the sawmill. There was no fresh sign of any vehicle turning that way, but one clear set of wagon tracks marked the dust in the road ahead.

Ben kicked the sorrel back into a gallop and rode on.

҉

Amelia winced when another blow landed on her head, and she tried to move away. Who was hitting her, and why wouldn't he stop?

She tried to raise her arm to protect herself, but her hands remained fixed behind her back. A flash of memory jolted her back to awareness of her plight. Eddie Franklin had tied her hands and feet. He was the one who was striking her. Another blow smote her, and pain blazed through her head again.

A rocking motion threw her from side to side as she blinked against the pounding ache, and she realized she was lying on her back. *What's going on? Where am I?* She heard the sound of horses' hooves and the grate of a wheel on rock. Feeling through the burlap with her hands, she touched a hard surface beneath her. She must be in the back of a wagon, which meant they were already on the move.

The knowledge chilled her. Merrick or Franklin—or both of them—were making good their threats. They were on their way to the reservoir . . . and the mineshaft nearby.

The wagon bounced again. Amelia cried out as her throbbing head took another blow. Gathering her wits, she rolled onto her side. Every muscle in her body protested, but the maneuver afforded the wound on her head some protection.

The jouncing slowed, then it stopped altogether. Up ahead, a horse nickered and stomped its foot. She heard a creak as the driver set the brake. Then the wagon rocked again, followed by what sounded like two sets of boots hitting the ground.

Everything inside her seemed to turn to ice. They must have reached their destination. Fear overwhelmed her as she pondered what would happen next.

Would they leave her bound and gagged inside this horrid sack while they tossed her down the shaft? *Please, God, no!* Bound or not, the end result would be the same, but she couldn't bear the thought of plunging to her death in this awful darkness.

Please, if I have to die, at least let me have one last glimpse of the world around me.

Chains rattled, and the tailgate dropped open. A hand closed around her ankle. Amelia let out a muffled shriek and jerked away.

She heard Eddie Franklin's grating laugh. "Looks like she's awake, boss." The unseen hands grabbed the sides of the sack and dragged her over the edge of the tailgate. She landed on the ground in a heap.

"That's good," Merrick replied. "That way we don't have to carry her up that hill. She can walk there on her own."

The end of the sack above her head rustled against her hair, then Franklin stretched the opening wide and let it settle around her shoulders. He pulled her to her feet with a rough grip, and she felt the burlap slide to her ankles.

She blinked to let her eyes adjust to the afternoon sunlight. The three of them stood on a level area at the foot of a steep hill. Through the trees, she saw the sunlight glitter on the placid waters of what she assumed was Bart McCaffrey's reservoir. A light breeze soughed through the pines and stirred the curls at her temples.

Amelia shuddered. To have such a peaceful scene be the place where she would meet her death!

Owen Merrick steadied her while Franklin pulled out a pocketknife and slashed the twine that bound her ankles. "You might as well take that gag off, too," Merrick said. When Franklin raised an eyebrow, he added, "There's nobody around for miles. She can scream all she likes, but no one will hear her."

When Franklin pulled the sodden fabric away from her mouth, Amelia gasped in the first full breath she'd taken since the gag had been forced between her lips. She worked her jaws to restore feeling to her cheeks, then turned on Merrick. "You can't possibly think you'll get away with this."

Franklin lifted the gag. "Are you sure you want to take that out? I don't want to listen to her yapping all the way up the hill."

Merrick waved the objection away. "It won't last long. You can leave her hands tied until we get up there, but be sure you bring the twine back with you. I don't want to risk leaving anything behind that could link us to Miss Wagner's unfortunate demise."

Eddie Franklin scoffed. "Why worry about that? You said we were going to close the opening to that mine later. No one is ever going to find her there."

Merrick turned a steely gaze on his minion. "You said no one would ever realize those documents were forgeries, either. This time, I don't plan to leave anything to chance."

Franklin only grunted before he swiveled Amelia around, pointing her toward the footpath that led up the hill. Reaching under his jacket, he produced a heavy pistol and prodded her shoulder with it. "That way."

Amelia dug in her heels and refused to budge. Walk to her death like a lamb to the slaughter? Not likely!

Cold steel pressed against the nape of her neck. "Carrying your lifeless body up that hill would be easier than putting up with your nonsense. We can end this right now, if that's the way you want to do it."

A low groan rose in Amelia's throat, and she staggered forward. Moving ahead might only extend her life by a few brief moments, but those moments were now precious in her sight. Her mind raced while she stumbled along the rough trail. Was there anything she could do to elude the men and get away?

Her heart sank as she took stock of her situation. There was no place to run—assuming her weary limbs cooperated—and nowhere to go for help. Even if she managed to slip away, they would be able to catch her before she'd gone a dozen steps. She clenched her teeth to choke back her sobs.

The narrow trail followed the slope uphill through scattered pines and clumps of manzanita, and she could hear the steady footsteps of the men as they trudged behind her. Taking her eyes from the rough path, she cast a glance up to the top of the hill. Through a stand of pines, she could make out the wooden A-frame of the hoist used to haul ore out of the mineshaft. Her lips trembled, and she felt tears course down her cheeks. With all her heart she wished she could turn around and flee to the safety of the newspaper office.

"Keep movin'." Franklin punctuated his order with a sharp jab of his pistol between her shoulder blades.

Amelia focused on the trail again and trudged ahead.

CHAPTER 32

Ben slowed the horse, chafing at the need to reduce his pace as the road wound upward. For the past couple of miles, he had been traveling on Great Western land. Merrick seldom made personal visits to the property, and Ben could think of no good reason for him being out there today.

The road leveled out at the top of a rise. Up ahead, he spotted the buckboard stopped on the edge of the road. Even at this distance, he could see the bed was empty and no one was in sight.

Reining his borrowed mount off the road, he tied the gelding in a clump of scrub oak and pulled the rifle from its scabbard. He slid the action open far enough to assure himself the gun was loaded and snapped the action back in place. He hadn't used a firearm since coming to Arizona, but he'd hunted deer with his own Winchester back east. He had plenty of experience being quiet in the woods and sneaking up on game.

Tucking the rifle under his arm, he crept his way up to the abandoned wagon and peered around to make sure no one was watching before he approached the buckboard. As he drew near, he spotted a pile of burlap on the ground. His lips tightened at the sight of the "potato" sack Jimmy spoke of. But like the wagon, it was empty now. Stepping closer, he noticed a length of twine and a twisted piece of cloth.

Ben's stomach knotted. Exactly what a captor would use to bind and gag a prisoner. That confirmed his suspicions— Merrick and Franklin had someone with them. He bent to examine the scuffle of footprints near the wagon's tailgate and nodded when he saw two sets of men's prints, apparently belonging to Franklin and Merrick. His mouth went dry and he caught his breath when he spotted a set of smaller prints made by a woman's shoe. Those had to belong to Amelia.

The tracks led away from the wagon. Ben forced himself to breathe again. She was alive, or at least she had been at that point. But Merrick wouldn't have brought her out there under such rough conditions only to let her go again. Ben set his lips in a grim line. He had to find her before it was too late.

Stepping lightly, he followed the tracks up the hill, stopping every few paces to scan the trail ahead. He didn't spot anyone, and he couldn't decide whether that boded ill or not. There were no buildings for miles around. Where could they be going? The trees thickened, blocking his view of the path. He moved off the trail and ducked into the brush along the side. It wouldn't do to have one of the men he was following turn around and spot him.

He made his way over the rough terrain as quietly as he could. Near the top of the hill, he stopped in the shelter of a towering Ponderosa to catch his breath and leaned out from behind the broad trunk to study the hillside. A flash of movement higher up caught his eye, and Ben's heart began to race when he made out three figures.

Whatever Merrick planned, it would surely take place soon. He didn't have a moment to waste. With a surge of renewed energy, Ben raced toward the hilltop, keeping the trees between him and his objective as he closed in.

※

Amelia staggered into a clearing at the top of the hill. Her knees locked when she saw the gaping hole at the foot of the A-frame hoist, bringing her to an abrupt stop. Franklin crashed into her from behind. Letting out an oath, he grabbed her right arm and shoved her ahead of him toward the frame. He jerked her to a halt a few feet short of the yawning abyss.

Looking back over his shoulder, he called out to Merrick. "How do you want to do this?"

"Take that rope off her hands and then finish the job."

Amelia twisted around to face Merrick. "You really can't get away with this. Even if no one on earth ever finds out what happened to me, God knows."

Merrick let out a bark of a laugh. "That's a lovely sentiment, but what am I supposed to do? Do you expect me to take you back to town and turn you loose so you can tell everyone what you know? I'm afraid it's gone too far for that."

Franklin took a step back and holstered his gun. Keeping a close watch on Amelia, he dug in his pocket for the knife.

"At least give me a chance to pray. You may not fear God, but I want to be ready to meet Him face-to-face."

Merrick's face darkened. "You've had all afternoon to pray." He nodded to Franklin, who moved behind her. "Let's get this over with."

Amelia drew in a shuddering breath when she felt him slip

the sharp blade between her wrists. She swept her gaze over
the hillside, wanting to take in every detail of her last sight
of life on this earth. Out of the corner of her eye, she caught
a flicker of motion in a stand of pines. Trying not to draw
Merrick's attention, she darted a glance in that direction and
held back a cry when she saw Ben edging toward them with
a rifle in his hands.

Some fleeting expression must have given her away, for Merrick whirled around just as Ben stepped forward with the gun
leveled at the two men. "Put your hands in the air, both of you!"

Instead of complying, Merrick made a sideways leap, putting Amelia between himself and Ben's rifle. Franklin threw
the knife to the ground and stepped away from her. His hand
reached under his jacket.

"Look out, Ben!" she screamed. "He has a gun!" Summoning
all her strength, she lunged at Franklin, knocking him off balance. The move toppled her, as well, and she skidded into the
dirt. Amelia rolled to one side, away from the opening. She lay
with her face in the dust, her breath coming in ragged gasps.

Franklin staggered in a wide arc, trying to regain his balance. His lurching steps brought him up to the edge of the
hole. Franklin's eyes widened when he saw the chasm at his
feet, and he scrambled backwards, his boots skidding on bits
of shattered rock left over from the mining operation. He let
out a hoarse cry, and his arms flailed wildly. But his efforts to
regain his footing failed, and he tumbled over the edge. His
scream echoed from the depths, then stopped abruptly.

Ben was the first to move. With his rifle trained on Merrick,
he rushed over to Amelia and reached down with one hand to
help her sit up. He motioned to Merrick with the tip of the

rifle barrel. "Step away from that hole, but don't get any ideas about taking off. I've got my eye on you."

Keeping his gaze focused on Merrick, he scooped up the knife Franklin dropped. With a quick glance down, he slipped the blade under the twine that held Amelia's wrists together and severed it with a quick jerk.

Amelia's arms dropped to her sides. With a sob of relief, she pulled her hands into her lap and cradled her burning wrists while she stared in horror at the place where Eddie Franklin had stood only moments before. "Is he . . . ?"

Ben dropped the knife and used both hands to hold the rifle steady. "Don't worry about him. He's beyond any help we could give him. Right now, we have a more pressing issue to deal with."

His face hardened as he jabbed the tip of the rifle in Merrick's direction. "I am sorely tempted to send you down there to join Franklin."

Merrick backed away and patted the air with his hands. "Don't be hasty, Ben. I'm sure we can come to some agreement. What would it take to put all this behind us?"

Ben's features contorted, and Amelia could see the muscles tighten along his jawline. "You're deluded if you think any amount of money could wipe away what you've done. When I think about the regard my family has held for you all these years! What happened to the man my father admired so much, the hero who risked his own life to save my father's all those years ago?"

Merrick's lips twisted. Then his voice took on a persuasive tone. "Your father has been most generous in introducing me to influential people in his circle of friends. The connections

I've made there have helped me immeasurably . . . and I can do the same thing for you, Ben. I'm on the verge of making millions, and part of that can be yours. All you have to do is forget this ever happened."

Ben set his jaw and cast a longing look toward the hole where Franklin fell.

"Don't do it." Amelia pushed herself to her feet and stepped over to join him. "You're not the same kind of person he is. We'll let the law take care of this."

He let out a slow breath and nodded. Looking at Merrick, he said, "The best thing for you is to keep quiet and head back to the wagon before I change my mind." Tucking the stock of his rifle under his right elbow, he slipped his left arm around Amelia's waist. She leaned into him, grateful for his support as they made their way down the hill behind Merrick.

He looked down at her with a worried expression. "Will you be able to make it?"

"I'll manage." She nodded and pressed closer against him. "I'm just happy to be coming back at all."

His Adam's apple bobbed up and down. "I wasn't sure I'd get to you in time."

"But you did."

He tightened his arm around her waist, and they continued down the trail.

As they neared a curve in the trail, they heard crackling in the brush ahead. Ben pulled his arm away from Amelia's waist and used it to steady his rifle. "Hold up, Merrick."

A moment later, four men came into view. Amelia shrank back until she saw the badges pinned to their vests. Ben nodded to the man in the lead. "I'm glad to see you here."

He let the tip of his rifle drop and turned to Amelia. "This is Sheriff Lowry. He came to check into some of the things we've turned up about Merrick . . . and your stepfather." Looking back at the lawman, he said, "Sheriff, this is Amelia Wagner, the woman I was telling you about. She's the editor of the *Granite Springs Gazette.*"

The sheriff tipped his Stetson to Amelia. "Pleased to meet you, miss." Taking in her disheveled appearance at a glance, he added, "It appears Stone showed up in the nick of time."

Amelia rubbed her tender wrists and tried to keep her voice steady. "If he'd gotten here a minute later, it would have been too late. They were planning to kill me."

The sheriff's eyes narrowed. "Is this Merrick?" When Ben nodded, the lawman frowned. "They told me in town you had gone after two men."

Ben pointed back along the path. "The other one fell down the mineshaft at the top of the hill. The same shaft they were planning to throw Miss Wagner into."

Lowry's eyes flared wide. "Is that so?"

When he advanced on the prisoner, Merrick spread his hands. "Sheriff, I'm afraid this is all a dreadful misunderstanding. I don't know what you've been told, but I'm certain I can explain everything to your satisfaction."

"It's going to be hard to explain away something like attempted murder, especially when the intended victim is still around to testify against you." Lowry jerked his head toward Amelia. "Those marks on her wrists are proof enough of your mistreatment."

Ben stepped forward. "And while you're trying to explain those away, I'm sure the sheriff would like to hear what you have to say about those forged documents."

"Not to mention whatever light you can shed on the where-abouts of Arthur Copeland." Lowry's face looked as if it had been chiseled from granite.

Merrick's jaw sagged, and he seemed to shrink within himself.

Lowry gestured to one of the other men. "Bill, you and Jack go on up and check that mineshaft." While the pair headed up the trail, he looked at the remaining deputy. "Keep your gun on him, Wilbur. I want the pleasure of cuffing him myself." Pulling a pair of handcuffs from his gun belt, he approached Merrick and snapped the metal rings around his wrists.

Amelia's anxiety began to melt away when she heard the sound of the shackles clicking into place. At last, her ordeal was truly over.

When they reached the buckboard, the sheriff looked at the four horses tethered nearby and turned to Ben. "We spotted a sorrel gelding tied to some scrub oak a ways down the road. Is that your horse?"

Ben's lips curved up in a crooked grin. "I rode him up here, but he isn't mine. He just happened to be available when I needed him." His smile widened. "I'm hoping I can count on you to vouch for me that the horse was borrowed, not stolen."

The sheriff chuckled in response. "Why don't we put Merrick on the sorrel and let you drive the young lady back to town in the buckboard." Looking at Amelia, he added, "I'd like to make the trip back home as easy for you as possible, after all you've been through."

While the deputy trotted down the road to retrieve the bor-rowed gelding, Ben turned to Amelia. Placing his hands lightly on her shoulders, he drew her toward him and looked deep into her eyes. "Thank God you're alive! Are you really all right?"

She swallowed hard. "There isn't a part of me that doesn't hurt right now, but I'll get over that. I'm alive, and that's what counts." Looking up, she searched his face. "Have I thanked you for saving me yet?"

A faint smile played across Ben's lips. "That works both ways. If you hadn't thrown yourself at Franklin and knocked him off balance, this might have ended very differently for both of us."

She nodded and leaned her forehead against his shirt, wondering if she would ever forget the sight and sounds of Eddie Franklin's fall.

The deputy returned leading the sorrel and helped shove Merrick up into the saddle. The businessman sat with his head drooping low, his former confidence depleted.

While Sheriff Lowry checked the gelding's cinch, the other two deputies scrambled back down the path.

"We found him," the taller one said. "But there's no way to get him back up right now."

His companion nodded. "We can use that A-frame to raise him, but we'll need to bring a couple of hundred feet of rope back from town. No need to rush, though. He isn't going anywhere."

Lowry hooked his thumbs in his gun belt and regarded the two men. "You're sure he's dead?"

The taller deputy nodded. "Not a flicker of movement. He's splayed out like a rag doll." He caught Amelia staring at him, and his face reddened. Clearing his throat, he added, "I don't see how anyone could survive a fall like that."

That was supposed to be me. Amelia's legs began to tremble, and her knees gave way. Ben scooped her up and set her gently on the buckboard seat, then climbed up beside her. She collapsed against his arm, drawing strength from his presence.

The lawmen stepped into their saddles, and Wilbur took up the sorrel's reins. With a tip of his hat to Ben and Amelia, the sheriff took the lead, and the small procession set off down the road toward town.

CHAPTER 33

Amelia clung to the wagon seat while Ben guided the horses over the rough, rutted road. In the distance, she caught the glitter of light on the reservoir. *I never thought I'd see that again.* With tears stinging her eyes, she lifted her face to the sky. *Thank you for delivering me. For getting Ben there in time. For a second chance at life.*

The road smoothed out when they reached the lower level, and the constant rocking finally ceased. Sheriff Lowry rode back to come alongside the buckboard. "I wanted to make sure you got over that rough patch without any problem. Will you be all right now if the rest of us ride on ahead? I want to get back to town in time to send two of my deputies along to Prescott with Merrick and make sure that sorry excuse for a human being is locked away. I'll stay here with Wilbur and pack up every file in that office. I want to make sure we don't miss a thing."

Ben shot a questioning gaze at Amelia, then nodded at the lawman. "We'll be fine."

Amelia watched them ride away. Then she let out a long sigh and looked up at Ben. "Jimmy told me you left on the train. I didn't know if I'd see you again."

Ben shifted the reins to his left hand and slid his right arm around her shoulders. "I only went to Prescott. I needed to check on a few things there, and it took longer than I expected."

Amelia straightened on the seat and studied his face. "Prescott? What were you looking for there?"

"When I saw the way you laid everything out in that map you sketched, it all started falling into place. Acquiring all those different properties didn't make sense until I started looking at it as part of one grand scheme. The mining profits would set the stage for the company to clear-cut miles and miles of forest—millions of dollars' worth of lumber."

Amelia gasped. "I hadn't thought of the connection, but when you piece it together that way, it begins to add up."

"That isn't all, though. Remember the land out near the railroad line? Merrick managed to get himself appointed as a director of the Peavine. Grayson already has influence with the Denver & Rio Grande. Once they had those railroads in their pocket, there would be no limit to the control they could exert over this part of the country."

Amelia frowned. "But if you were able to work all that out based on the sketch I made, why did you have to go to Prescott?"

A quick smile crossed Ben's face. "I had a feeling there was something even more to all this, and I was right. Southwest Land Development—remember, I started to tell you about them when . . ." His gaze shifted to the side, and his voice trailed off.

"When I blew up at you and threw you out of the office," Amelia finished, regretting for the hundredth time her loss of temper that night.

He looked back at her with an expression that made her heart skip a beat, then begin to race. "Let's put all that behind us. The important thing is what I learned about the company. I told you I had an altercation with Merrick the morning I quit my job, but I didn't tell you I discovered more than those forgeries. I also came across documents showing ownership of those properties had been transferred from Great Western to a company called Southwest Land Development."

Amelia wrinkled her nose. "I've never heard of them."

"Neither had I. That's why I wanted to visit the county recorder's office. I had a feeling it might be helpful to find out what else Southwest owns and who is in charge of it. As it turns out, Southwest Land Development owns several other properties in the area, all transferred to the company by Great Western, and all done without any money changing hands."

Amelia's jaw dropped. "But that doesn't make sense at all. Who are the people behind the company?"

"That's what I wanted to know, but the recorder's office didn't have any names listed, only an address in Washington, D.C. I sent a wire to my father and asked if he could check into the company for me." He looked down at her and traced her jawline with his thumb.

His touch made it hard for her to concentrate on what he was saying, but she didn't want him to stop. "And he was able to get the information you needed?"

Ben nodded. "It took him until this afternoon to get back to me—which is pretty quick work, considering. Still, it seemed like the longest wait of my life. All I could do was sit there in the hotel, drinking coffee and reading my Bible."

Amelia closed her eyes and laid her head against his shoulder. "I'm glad you had it with you."

His chin ruffled her curls when he nodded. "Like I told you

and Homer, I had a lot to get straightened out between me and the Lord. I'm glad I had the time to do it, even though it was hard waiting to hear back from my father."

She stirred enough to raise her head so she could watch his face. "What did he tell you?"

Ben pulled the team to a halt and wrapped the reins around the brake handle. When he turned to face her, excitement sparked in his eyes. "You and your father were right all along about Great Western—even if you didn't know just what you were looking for."

A current of electricity seemed to shoot through her at his words. "What are you saying?"

"Your instinct about something shady going on was right on the money. Do you have any idea who the owners of Southwest Land Development are?"

She shook her head, mystified. "How could I know anything about the ownership of a company based in Washington? Who are they?"

Excitement glimmered in Ben's eyes as he leaned toward her. "None other than Owen Merrick and Thaddeus Grayson. Do you see what that means? They used Great Western as a cover to acquire those properties, then transferred the ownership to themselves. The two of them stood to gain millions through the scheme. When the sheriff heard about Merrick picking up those properties from men who had already left the area, using forged documents—"

Amelia caught her breath and held up her hand to stop him. "It's more than that, Ben. Those men didn't just move away. Merrick killed them—or had Eddie Franklin do it for him. Merrick told me so himself."

Ben gaped at her, then stared off into the distance. "He never dreamed a confession like that would ever be made public. That should give Lowry more than enough to make sure Merrick never sees the light of day again."

After a long moment, he turned to her again and spoke in a solemn tone. "You need to prepare yourself for the possibility that your stepfather will be held responsible for those murders, along with all the other crimes Merrick committed."

She nodded slowly, trying to grasp the implications. "He's an evil man. I've known that for a long time. I can't say I'm sorry at the prospect of him having to pay for what he's done, but it's going to be a terrible blow for my mother."

Letting out a long sigh, she pulled her thoughts back to the moment. "With so much at stake, it's no wonder Merrick was willing to go to the lengths he did to protect himself." Her throat tightened. "Ben, if you hadn't come when you did . . ."

He touched his finger to her lips. "Don't think about that. It's over now, and it belongs to the past. From this point on, we can look ahead to the future." A smile curved his lips. "This never would have come to light without your passion for the truth. Your father started the ball rolling, but you're the one who took hold of what little information you had and wouldn't let go."

His eyes darkened, and she stared up at him as he cupped her face with his hands. He lowered his head toward hers, and she felt his breath fan her cheek when he whispered her name. A tremulous sigh escaped her lips, and she raised her face to meet his kiss.

"Hallooo!"

Ben jerked his head back at the loud cry and stared down the road. Following his gaze, Amelia looked up to see a group of five riders approaching. As they drew nearer, she recognized

Homer, Emmett Kingston, Carl Olsen, and Martin Gilbreth . . . with Clara in the lead.

Within moments, the group reached the buckboard. Homer swung down from his horse and hurried over to her, his face lined with worry. "Can you forgive me for not coming out to look for you right away? I should have known something was wrong when you were gone so long."

She reached down to give him a hug and clasped his hands. "I should have let you know where I was going. It would have saved us all a lot of grief." She looked around at the circle of friends that surrounded them. "What are you all doing here?"

Clara nudged her horse closer, looking far more comfortable in the saddle than did Emmett Kingston. "Ben said he was worried about you, so I started trying to track you down. I was coming out of the bank when I ran into Homer. He'd just finished talking to the sheriff. When he told me what was going on, I decided we all needed to pitch in. Between the two of us, we rounded up the rest and put this posse together."

Carl Olsen shook his head and laughed. "I never saddled a bunch of horses so fast in all my life. Martin, that sister of yours can be one persuasive woman."

"Don't I know it!" Martin replied with a grin.

"That's for sure." To Amelia's astonishment, Homer gazed up at Clara with an expression of pure admiration . . . and maybe something more. "She took charge of everything and got us organized without a hitch."

Clara's cheeks turned a dusky red as she shrugged off the compliment. "We didn't know how much help Ben might need, and we wanted to make sure that skunk Merrick was brought to justice."

Amelia wrapped her arms across her chest. "He's already in custody. The sheriff says he'll be on his way to the Prescott jail this evening."

Martin nodded. "We met Lowry and his deputies on the road. We knew they had that part under control, but we had to come along and see for ourselves that you were safe."

Tears stung Amelia's eyes. "I am," she whispered. "Thanks to Ben."

"And we're going to make sure you stay that way." Clara turned her mount around. "We're not going to let you out of our sight until we see you safely home."

"That's for sure." Homer swung back into his saddle. "I'm not taking my eyes off you until I know that scoundrel is behind bars."

Ben shifted on the wagon seat and cleared his throat. "Say, Homer, what's that quote about mice and men?"

Homer frowned a moment, then his face cleared. "That's from Robert Burns—'The best laid schemes o' mice an' men gang aft agley.'" He pursed his lips. "It means our plans can go awry, no matter how well we think we have things worked out."

Emmett Kingston pulled up beside Homer and nodded. "I'll have to remember that one. It pretty well sums up what happened to Merrick's plans."

Ben smiled agreement, then murmured low enough that only Amelia could hear, "Merrick isn't the only one who just had his plans foiled."

She smothered a laugh as he unwound the reins and released the brake. Then the little band of rescuers surrounded the wagon and escorted them back to town.

CHAPTER 34

Amelia sat behind her desk, trying to concentrate on putting her story on paper while her mind insisted on drifting off to the events of the past few days. After the rescue party delivered them back to town, she and Ben met Sheriff Lowry at the Great Western building, where she gave a detailed statement of what had happened to her and showed him the storeroom where she'd been held prisoner.

Lowry's stony expression spoke his disgust more eloquently than any words could. "Franklin got off easy," he growled. "Hanging's too good for the likes of him and Merrick."

The lawman asked Ben to help him pack up the office files while his deputy rounded up Ben's former co-workers for questioning. Ben got to work, giving her a regretful glance that told her he was as sorry as she was about their second interrupted kiss.

Homer led her back to the *Gazette*, where she started for her office, intent on writing up her experiences while the details were still fresh in her mind. But Homer blocked her way, insisting the only place she ought to be going was straight up to bed for a good night's sleep.

Apparently, he recognized the signs of exhaustion better than she did, for as soon as she laid her head on the pillow, she fell into a dreamless slumber that lasted all that night and through most of the following day. Ben, according to Homer, had stopped by earlier to check on her before taking the train back to Prescott to help the sheriff go through the files and talk to the county attorney. How she wished she had been awake when he'd come! His absence left her with a lingering ache.

True to his word, Homer kept her in sight while he puttered around the printing office. As far as Amelia knew, he hadn't left the building since the night of her rescue from Merrick.

She turned back to the sheet of paper she'd been working on, perusing the possibilities she had scribbled down as headlines for the biggest story in the *Gazette*'s history. Which would be better—*Murder and Mayhem*? *Murder in Our Midst*? Or *Local Businessman Arrested: Great Western's Evil Plot Exposed*?

She lingered over the last entry. Word of Merrick's arrest had already made its way to Denver. Homer had shown her the telegram that arrived that morning from Clayton Sloan at the *Denver Journal*, who informed them local law enforcement was looking into Thaddeus Grayson's activities, as well.

Tired as she was, she couldn't summon up the energy to worry over what that would mean for her mother. All she wanted to do was finish the story and focus her mind on more pleasant things.

Like being with Ben. How much more time would she be able to spend with him? When he talked about getting things straightened out with the Lord during his earlier stay in Prescott, she'd been too caught up in the aftermath of her abduction and rescue to give it much thought. Now she wondered what it might mean for the future. He had talked about feeling like Jonah, running away from God's call in the East. A lump thickened her throat, and she swallowed hard. Would Ben feel compelled to go back east and pick up where he'd left off?

As if her thoughts had summoned him, the street door swung open, and Ben walked into the printing office. Amelia shoved her chair back and hurried to greet him. He wrapped his arms around her and held her close . . . until he noticed Homer's presence and took a step back.

Homer cleared his throat. "We may need a bit more for the back page. I think I'll mosey along and see what news I can scare up." He gave Ben a wink and a nod of his head as he ambled out the door.

Amelia laughed and stepped back into the circle of Ben's arms. "That was a surprise."

"And a welcome one." He held her at arm's length for a moment and peered into her face. "Are you feeling better today?"

"Still a little stiff and sore, but nothing more permanent. Thank God. What about you? Were you and the sheriff able to find more evidence against Merrick?"

He nodded, seeming a bit distracted. "Even more than I expected." Taking her hands, he led her over to a stool beside one of the type cabinets. "I need to tell you something. Just before I left the sheriff's office, word came in from Denver. Grayson has been arrested."

Amelia sagged onto the stool. After hearing from Clayton Sloan, she thought she'd been braced for the possibility, but hearing the news still came as a shock. "My mother is going to be devastated."

Ben pressed her hands in his and eyed her closely. "Are you thinking of going back to Denver to be with her?"

She paused for a moment. "I'll offer to go back and spend a week or so with her, but I'm not sure she'll want me there. My presence would only remind her of the reason she's facing this kind of disgrace in the first place. I'll suggest she join me here, although I don't expect her to take me up on that, either." She searched Ben's face. "What about you? You told me you spent a lot of time praying. Did God give you direction on what you're supposed to be doing?"

He nodded, his expression somber.

Amelia knotted her hands into fists under the folds of her skirt. "Does that mean you'll be going back east?"

To her surprise, he broke into a smile. "That's exactly what I thought would happen. I fully expected to be led back to pastor one of those stuffy churches I was so set against. But as it turns out, it seems He has a job for me to do right here."

Her heart started beating double time. "Here? You mean, helping Pastor Edmonds?"

Ben chuckled and shook his head. "I was apparently a little presumptuous about the direction my calling would take. While I waited to hear from my father, I had plenty of time to dig into God's Word, and I was amazed at what I discovered in the stories of the people who served Him best. They were shepherds, fishermen, tentmakers, doctors—the list goes on and on." Excitement shone in his eyes. "God's call on a man's life doesn't always mean that man is called to stand behind a pulpit. God wants us to be ambassadors for Him in whatever circumstance He places us."

Tears sprang to Amelia's eyes, and she gave a shaky laugh.

"So what circumstance does He have for you here in Granite Springs?"

Cupping her chin in one hand, he ran his thumb across her cheek. "In recent days, I've been greatly influenced by a person who was willing to stand for the truth, no matter what the cost. I've been giving some serious thought to getting involved in the newspaper business. Do you happen to know if any openings are available?"

Her breath caught in her throat, and her heart seemed to stop abruptly. Then it picked up its pace again, pounding in her ears. "I believe a position might be open . . . for the right man."

Ben raised his other hand to push a wayward curl back from her face. A quiver shook Amelia from head to toe as she gazed into his eyes, feeling as though their souls connected. Her breath quickened when he raised her to her feet and slipped his hands behind her shoulders.

She pressed her hands against his shirtfront and felt his heart beating against her outstretched fingers. Once again, he breathed her name and leaned toward her.

The door crashed open, followed by a shrill cry of, "Hey, Miss Amel—"

Amelia froze, then turned to see Jimmy framed in the doorway, with Clara and Homer close behind him. She felt her face flame when she saw their startled expressions, and she didn't dare look at Ben.

Clara planted her hands on her hips. "Homer said you were up and around again." A grin stretched her mouth wide. "Appears to me you're feeling pretty spry."

Homer only chuckled, while Jimmy remained rooted to the spot, his eyes and mouth open wide.

Amelia floundered for something to say. "We . . . we were just . . ."

"No need to explain." Clara's lips spread in a wide grin. "It's pretty clear what was going on . . . and I must say, it's about time." She stepped closer to Homer and tucked her hand into the crook of his arm.

Ben blinked and turned to Amelia. "Did I miss something while I was in Prescott?" he murmured.

Laughter gurgled from Amelia's throat, and she spoke just loudly enough for him to hear. "It looks to me like God has been working in more lives than just yours and mine. After being a confirmed bachelor for so many years, it's a miracle Homer isn't running for the door."

Ben's chuckle vibrated beneath her fingertips, still pressed against his chest. "I'm beginning to think it'll take a miracle for us to finally get that kiss without someone interrupting."

Amelia stared up into his face, only a breath away. "Or maybe we just need to step out and take matters into our own hands." She slid her arms around his neck and pressed her lips to his. After an instant's hesitation, Ben tightened his arms around her and returned the kiss with gusto.

Several delicious moments later, they drew apart, and he stared down at her with laughter in his eyes. "So does that mean you can find a place for me at the *Gazette*?"

Amelia nodded and raised her lips to his again. Just before they met, she whispered, "It does indeed. And to tell the truth, right at this moment, I don't care who's watching."

Acknowledgments

I owe a tremendous debt of gratitude to Sky Shipley, owner of Skyline Type Foundry, who patiently walked me through the operations of a 19th-century newspaper. The insights and information he shared enriched the story immensely and kept me from committing some whopping errors. Any mistakes I've managed to make in spite of his guidance are strictly of my own doing.

And special thanks to Mary Rigby, Micki Davis, and the staff and patrons of the Ash Fork Public Library. I appreciate your encouragement and support more than I can say!

Author's Note

Dear Reader:

Like the towns of Pickford, the setting for *Love in Disguise*, and Cedar Ridge, where *Trouble in Store* takes place, you won't find Granite Springs on any Arizona map. But all three of these fictional places are firmly rooted in real locations. In the case of Granite Springs, that would be the area around Camp Wood, an abandoned town site about twelve miles northwest of Prescott. With its rich history of logging and mining, and the wide array of scenery—ranging from flat ranch land to hills dotted with dense stands of cedars to pine-covered slopes—it made a perfect place for Amelia and the *Granite Springs Gazette* to call home.

While the settings for these Arizona stories only exist in my imagination, I've taken pleasure in sprinkling some actual sites and people in amongst the fictional. The Hotel Burke, where Ben stays during his visit to Prescott, was the original name of the present-day Hotel St. Michael, which stands on the corner of Gurley and Montezuma, directly across the street from the

Courthouse Plaza. My first meeting with Karen Schurrer, my wonderful editor, took place in the hotel's dining room, where we enjoyed the same view of the plaza Ben did while he waited for a reply to his telegram.

The Eleventh Infantry Band from nearby Fort Whipple really was directed by Achille LaGuardia. And if the name LaGuardia strikes a chord in your memory, you might be thinking of Achille's son, Fiorello, who spent part of his childhood at Fort Whipple before growing up to become the mayor of New York City.

In writing a story about a frontier newspaper, I needed to fill the gaps in my knowledge about 19th-century journalism and printing processes. I was able to find information from books and online sources, but not nearly enough to capture the essence of producing a small-town weekly. Fortunately, a solution was closer to hand than I dreamed. A phone call to Prescott's Sharlot Hall Museum led me to Sky Shipley, owner-operator of Skyline Type Foundry, one of only three type foundries left in the United States.

Sky graciously allowed me to visit his foundry in Prescott and showed me his extensive collection of antique printing presses. Further teaching took place at the print shop in Sharlot Hall Museum, where Sky took me step-by-step through the process of setting up and printing a newspaper on a Washington Press, just like the one in this story. My appreciation for his help—and my admiration for his passion to keep letterpress printing alive—knows no bounds.

Sky offered an especially valuable insight in letting me know that newspapers during the late 19th century were often funded by special interest groups intent on furthering their own agendas. Therefore, the passion Amelia's father had for digging up and printing the truth, and nothing but the truth, would have been something of an anomaly at the time. It's that very contrast with the typical newspaper editor of that day that would have made Andrew Wagner stand out and have a story worth recounting, and it was a joy to let his character and love for truth shine forth.

Thank you for taking the time to follow Amelia's adventures in *Truth Be Told*. May God continually reveal His truth to you as you walk in His light!

Carol
Philippians 4:4

꒰

Author of thirty novels and novellas, **Carol Cox** has an abiding love for history and romance, especially when it's set in her native Southwest. As a third-generation Arizonan, she takes a keen interest in the Old West and hopes to make it live again in the hearts of her readers. A pastor's wife, Carol lives with her husband and daughter in northern Arizona, where the deer and the antelope really do play—within view of the family's front porch.

To learn more about Carol, please visit her at:

Her website: www.AuthorCarolCox.com
Her blog: www.AuthorCarolCox.com/journal
Facebook: www.facebook.com/carol.cox
Twitter: www.twitter.com/authorcarolcox

If you enjoyed *Truth Be Told*, you may also like...

Melanie Ross and Caleb Nelson both claim to have inherited the mercantile. Even as they contest ownership, the two are forced to band together to protect their livelihood against external threats. And when a body shows up on their doorstep, there's deeper trouble in store...

Trouble in Store by Carol Cox
authorcarolcox.com

When undercover Pinkerton agent Ellie Moore's assignment turns downright dangerous—for her safety *and* her heart—what's this damsel in disguise to do?

Love in Disguise by Carol Cox
authorcarolcox.com

Answering a plea for help from a retired actress—and an old flame—Drew and Madeline, now his fiancée, dive into investigating the murder of the lead actor in a stage production of *The Mikado*. But they discover more going on behind the scenes of this theater than they could ever have imagined.

Murder at the Mikado by Julianna Deering
A DREW FARTHERING MYSTERY
juliannadeering.com

More Fiction
You May Enjoy